DRUID'S BANE

A DRUIDVERSE URBAN FANTASY NOVEL

M.D. MASSEY

SAMHSA NATIONAL HELPLINE

The Substance Abuse and Mental Health Services Administration operates a free, confidential, 24/7, 365-day-a-year treatment referral and information service for individuals and families facing mental and/or substance use disorders.

Call 1-800-662-HELP (4357) for assistance.

FOREWORD

Readers are advised that they shouldn't read too much into this book. There are no hidden messages or political statements here, except perhaps that people shouldn't allow outside forces to divide them. However, that's my personal opinion, and it bears no impact on the story or characters you'll find within.

Remember that it's just fiction, people.

~M.D. Massey

Foreword

CHAPTER
ONE

I stood in the midst of an airy, open country landscape with the bright noonday sun overhead, at the edge of a field that had been plowed into neat furrows months prior. I'd left this timeline during the height of summer. Now, I found myself enjoying a relatively mild Texas winter, and wondering what I'd missed while I was away.

Click had gone silent, lost in reverie while staring off into space—or perhaps across the sands of time, for all I knew. After a barely perceptible shake of my head, I swung my gaze beyond the two-lane strip of cracked, pitted blacktop before me, focusing on the deceivingly plain building on the other side.

It wasn't much to look at, just a matchbox-shaped thing with gray asphalt siding, a rusted, corrugated metal roof, and a concrete stoop with stairs that led to an old-fashioned, four-panel wooden entry door. The door was unadorned as well, unless you counted the multiple layers of paint that covered it, chipped and worn to reveal every last stratum but the original wood underneath.

There were no windows on the exterior walls and no "OPEN" sign, but on the front of the building a faded, neatly hand-painted tin placard was on display. Roughly two feet by six, it was framed in sun-bleached wood that had weathered to match the siding. The sign had once been white, but it too had fallen prey to time, dulling to a chalky eggshell color. Rust showed through in a faint patina that a collector would pay dearly for, the off-white and red-orange expanse broken by letters blanched so pale they were difficult to make out.

JOHN'S ICEHOUSE

'John's,' not 'Rube's,' and certainly not 'Rübezahl's.' Nobody used that name, at least not within hearing distance of the gnome king. Not if they wanted to remain in his good graces—and it was wise to stay on his good side.

The last time I was here, I could've sworn the building had been white clapboard—or was it red brick, worn and cracked with time? Had the sign been above the door as well? Or had it been nailed to a post in the sparse, weed-infested lawn, next to the gravel parking lot entrance?

For all I knew, the building's appearance might be entirely attributable to the look-away, go-away glamour that hung heavy on the structure and its surrounds. That was the thing about ancient fae places; they were always shifting and constantly changing in subtle ways. Once these places gained a mind of their own, well—those changes were something even a powerful glamour couldn't hide.

The building's cosmetic schizophrenia revealed that an old power resided here—deep magic, indeed. The knowledge made me wary to approach the place, much less enter, but Click swore the only way to find Fallyn was through Rübezahl's realm. That being the case, there was no question about whether I'd enter the lonely, unassuming building.

Anything for Fallyn. She'd do it for me in a heartbeat.

Besides, I'd been here twice before, having parlayed with the proprietor both times and lived. Then again, I'd never gone past the front stoop on those previous occasions. Word was, no human had ever entered The Mountain King's realm and returned. Good thing I wasn't completely human.

Eventually, the pressure inside my head became too great, as the "look away" effect of the spell on the building grew to a migraine inducing crescendo. I swung my gaze to my right, noting for the first time a large white billboard down the street that said, "DISCORD IS PEACE" in stark black letters. It was peculiar and incongruous, out here in the middle of nowhere.

Then again, so was I, currently. I might have been a druid, but a country boy I was not. Dismissing the sign as an anomaly, I glanced left, allowing my gaze to rest on Click's handsome, boyish features.

"You sure this is where we need to go?"

"Huh? Who's there?"

The James Dean lookalike startled at the sound of my voice. Which version of the wizard formerly known as Gwydion that I might get at any moment was a crap shoot at best. His immortality-induced madness made him skittish at times, but I'd take a little jumpiness over his batshit crazy moments, any day of the week.

Waving my hands back and forth to get his attention, I let out a low whistle. "It's me, Colin. Remember? We were traveling from the Hellpocalypse and back to our own timeline to save Fallyn, but we got sidetracked by Claus. I helped him, and now we're back home again."

For the moment, at least, I reflected with an internal sigh.

"Claus? Where is he?" Click scowled as he raised his dukes, shuffling his feet in a fair imitation of a young Ali. "I'll wring his pudgy pink neck, that scoundrel. Show me to 'im!"

In truth, Saint Nick had handed Click's ass to him, but I wasn't about to remind the quasi-god of that. Despite my erstwhile mentor's considerable power, he'd proven to be no match for the Fat Man in his own realm. While I'd studied under him, I'd learned that Click had an ego to match his magical might. Thus, I'd decided it would be best to avoid bringing up that recent humiliation.

"Settle down, he's gone," I said as I raised my hands in a placating gesture. "We're back in our timeline, where Claus doesn't exist."

"Where he carked it, ya' mean."

"Huh? You know what, I don't even want to know. Listen, I need you to focus and answer a question. Do we really need to enter Rube's to find Fallyn?"

He relaxed, his usual Cheshire grin settling over his features once more. "Aye, lad," he replied with a dismissive wave. "The only way forward, 'tis through."

Adjusting Dyrnwyn's strap over my shoulder, I nodded. "Then let's get this show on the road."

My feet kicked up puffs of dry earth as I made my way through a bone-dry ditch that comprised the bulk of the road's shoulder. Oddly, winter hadn't brought precipitation to central Texas. I wondered if the dry conditions were some sort of omen, a sign of things to come.

But I don't believe in omens, or fate. Only bad luck. Speaking of which...

The hair on the back of my neck stood up, just as soon as the sole of my left combat boot hit the blacktop. Somebody was spooling up an elemental spell nearby—lightning, if my druid senses were correct. It seemed it wasn't drought I'd be facing, but a storm.

Figures.

"Colin McCool!" a deep, cultured voice shouted from across the road. "A word, if you would."

Glancing in that direction, I was pleased to see a familiar face. Although, it belonged to someone who was only marginally cordial to me in this timeline.

Crowley.

Still, he *was* an ally, and I'd be needing help soon. A smile began to tease at the corners of my mouth due to my anticipation of this reunion. When I noticed the shadow wizard's cloudy expression, I let that smile fade.

He looks pissed. Huh.

Having spent considerable time with his counterpart in another timeline, I'd recently grown rather fond of the taciturn wizard. That Crowley did save my life, after all, but he was an entirely different person. I reminded myself again that this Crowley could barely be considered a friendly acquaintance, despite all we'd been through together.

Not my fault that Bells chose me over him. Or that we led Fuamnach to his farmhouse. Or that she leveled it. Hmm... okay, maybe that was my fault.

"Crowley, I should warn you that the last time I saw Fuamnach, she asked where—"

He crossed the street in a flash, using some sort of weird wizard magic to move almost faster than the eye could see. Next thing I knew, his fist connected with my jaw.

Crack!

What the hell?

"Where's Cressida?" he seethed with madness in his eyes, one hand wrapped in the lapel of my jacket, the other clenched into a cocked fist. "What did you do with her?"

I'd already stealth-shifted ahead of my meeting with Rübezahl, and while my skin was human, the rest of me was now made of much hardier stuff. The punch hadn't phased me, but the unexpected aggression was unsettling. Pausing to assess the situation, I rubbed my jaw as I sized him up.

Crowley had changed since I last saw him—*this* timeline him, that was. There was less of an air of evil about him, or more of an air of purity, if that made any sense. He also now wore a short sword at his hip, which was weird because he'd always been the type to prefer magic to brawn. Moreover, the sword had been hidden by a pretty decent glamour, and for good reason—it crackled with energy, indicating it was a powerful artifact.

As for the man's mental and emotional state, he was angry, sure. Yet, something in his eyes told me his fury came more from worry than contempt. Besides, I had no idea what he was talking about, and hell if I was going to fight the guy over something I didn't do.

"Wait a minute," I said, raising my hands peacefully for the second time in as many minutes. "Who's Cressida?"

"She said you'd deny your involvement," the wizard hissed as he narrowed his eyes. "Don't try to hide it. I know you sold her to one of the fae, likely as part of one of your many schemes to save the world, or at least your own small part of it. Tell me, or this will not go well for you."

I honestly did not want to antagonize him, but the barest chuckle escaped my lips, despite myself. "Oh-kay. Why don't we back up a second, Crowster..."

"Enough games," he said, cutting me off as he palmed me in the chest.

The force of the blow was impressive for someone with mere human strength, as he'd planted his weight and rotated his hips for maximum effect. If it had been a merely physical blow, I'd have absorbed it and stood my ground. Instead, he released a lightning spell at point-blank range, right into my chest.

The force blew me off my feet, over the shoulder and ditch and onto my ass in the tilled soil behind me. I slid a good five feet, scuffing my brand-new jeans and boots in the process. As I skidded to a stop, only one thought came to mind.

I do not have time for this shit.

TO ADD INSULT TO INJURY, the salty bastard knew how to channel a lightning bolt at that distance without suffering any blowback—an impressive display of magical skill. Honestly, the fact that his hand wasn't a charred, bloody stump pissed me off more than being sucker-punched twice. Glancing down at the smoking hole in my fresh, new t-shirt, I shook my head as I fixed him with a rueful gaze.

"I really wish you hadn't done that."

Crowley was no slouch when it came to magic, and that was a fact. In my estimation, he was at least the match of any fae mage or sorceress of average years. That was saying something when you considered that a five-hundred-year-old faery would barely be considered middle-aged.

But I was back in my timeline, sitting on good, solid earth. We were out in the country where concrete was scarce, and where vegetation and wildlife were common. I was a master druid in my element, and he was just an interloper passing through.

Ya' done messed up, Ay-Ay-ron.

I called on my Oak's magic, connecting to it through our mental connection. In the same instant, I rooted myself to the earth. With a thought, I instructed the plants that grew along the roadside to sprout and grow at a tremendous pace, causing a literal hedgerow of thick vegetation to sprout between me and the wizard.

Instantly, tendrils of creeping Charlie, nutsedge, henbit, and clover snapped through the air and slithered across the ground at Crowley, like a quiver of cobras chasing after easy prey. My druid senses allowed me to watch the action through the eyes of a crow perched on a power line nearby. Thus, I didn't need to see through the hedgerow to know he was backpedaling while snapping off rapid-fire elemental spells to fry the rapidly advancing plants.

And straight into my trap.

Unbeknownst to Crowley, I'd tapped into the plants on the other side of the road as well—the side directly in front of Rube's. I had five thick vines ready and waiting to entrap him as soon as he got close. Just as I ordered them to strike, a translucent, shimmering wall of energy snapped down from the sky, right at the road's edge.

Not only did the ward lop off those five vines before they could reach Crowley, it cut off my connection to the vegetation that resided on Rube's patchy front lawn. The giant plant life I'd conjured receded, just as the shadow wizard bounced off the magical barrier that sprang into existence behind him.

"Oh no, you don't," a gravelly male voice echoed from somewhere nearby. He spoke with a Texas twang, marred by a German accent so slight most would miss it. "You'll conclude your mages' quarrel on land other than that occupied by my demesne."

Now that the fighting had started, Click was nowhere to be seen, else I'd have allowed him to smooth things over. He might have been crazy, but he knew how to placate gods and ancient fae when necessary. Failing Click's intervention, common courtesy dictated that I acknowledge the slight, even if it wasn't intentional. Remaining behind my protective hedgerow on the far side of the road, I pushed myself to my feet, brushing the dirt off my backside.

"Understood, Herr Johann," I said to no one in particular. "It won't happen again."

My "crow-sight" allowed me to see Crowley's reaction. He remained in a defensive crouch in the middle of the road, keeping one eye on the plant life that swayed and threatened to his right, and the other on the magical barrier to his left. When he saw that I'd stopped my attack to address Rube, he relaxed slightly, bowing his head in the direction of the tavern.

"Likewise, I had no intention of trespassing on your land, *Sehr geehrter Herr*," Crowley said. He glanced in my direction. "If the druid is so inclined, we will remove this quarrel from your front step."

"Agreed," I replied. I backed away to the center of the field, then I lowered my hedgerow. Locking eyes with Crowley, I spread my arms wide. "There's plenty of space over here."

He sneered. "Fine, I will give you the advantage. Considering your meager magical pedigree and talent, you shall need it."

I held a hand up and tapped my fingers to my thumb several times. "All I hear is yapping. Feel free to come out here and back that smack talk up."

"My pleasure," Crowley said as he drew himself up to his full height.

He turned slightly, hiding his left hand as he adjusted

the sword that hung at his hip. Then he sauntered across the road and through the ditch, taking his time as if he hadn't a care in the world. His nonchalance was infuriating, but I did take some small pleasure in the fact that he chose to walk around my now rapidly withering hedge of weeds.

I'd already queued up numerous spells, having spent the last many seconds connecting more fully to the plant and animal life in the field on which I stood. By this time, I'd expected to see Crowley doing evil wizard or necromancer stuff, maybe sprouting some shadow tentacles or summoning a pack of zombified roadkill. Instead, he simply took up a bladed stance at the edge of the field, his left hand resting on his hip and his right extended, palm-up.

He made a come-hither gesture with his fingers, like an action movie star during the final showdown scene with the bad guy. "Let us see what that old, decrepit druid taught you before he died, boy. Then I'll pry your secrets from your cold, dead corpse."

"MAN, THAT GOT DARK QUICK," I muttered. "And who you calling 'boy'?"

"Didn't it tho'?" Click's disembodied voice said from somewhere behind me and to my right. I wasn't surprised in the slightest by his sudden reappearance, as I was used to it by now. "By the way, ya' have an audience. If ya' want ta' maintain yer' reputation amongst the fae, ye'd best handle this tosser quick-like."

I glanced past the shadow wizard, where a small but growing crowd had gathered in Rube's parking lot. It consisted of a motley bunch of fae, most glamoured to hide their true nature. There were *erdhennen* and *feldgeister*, *Weiße Frauen* and alps, kobolds and *näcken*, plus a few other varieties that I didn't recognize. All were looking our way with great interest, and I saw gold and silver coins change hands more than once.

Keeping an eye on Crowley, I spoke over my shoulder. "Not taking bets? That hardly seems in keeping with your character, Click."

"Oh, please. I set up a pool amongst The Mountain King's patrons whilst ya' were fartin' around with them plants. How d'ya think they knew ta' come out an' watch?"

"Hope you bet on me." When Click responded with silence, I snuck a glance at him. "You *did* bet on me, right?"

"'Course I did, lad, 'course I did," he finally replied as his voice trailed away. "Eyes up, an' go get 'im!"

I turned my gaze back to my opponent, just in time to see a fireball coming at my face. There was no time to raise an earth barrier or call on a gust of wind to divert it. Instead, I ducked, rolling to my right at the same time and coming up in a four-point crouch.

The smell of burned hair assailed my nostrils. I reached up with my left hand, only to realize that all the

M.D. MASSEY

hair was missing from the left side of my head. A look through the crow's eyes confirmed that I was now the proud owner of half a mohawk. Oh, and half my left eyebrow was gone as well.

Why you dirty little...

There was no time to finish that sentence, as Crowley was on the move and tossing elemental spells like candy from a firetruck at a Fourth of July parade. I took off at a brisk run, which was roughly thirty miles an hour in my stealth-shifted form. Dodging and weaving across the field, I zigged and zagged in a pattern that would quickly bring me within range of the choleric conjurer.

Meanwhile, the wizard backpedaled with exceptional grace and speed for a human—perhaps too much, in fact. In the past, he'd relied on his shadow limbs to protect him and to propel him out of danger, as he lacked the superhuman reflexes that were common to the other, non-human races. But today I saw not a single sign of any dark magic, yet he was moving more like a fae creature than a mortal man.

Magic, of course. But what kind, and how?

I didn't know of any spells that would allow a mortal to move like a supernatural creature. Only transformed humans could pull that off—werewolves, vampires, and the like—and that was because normal human anatomy and physiology simply wouldn't allow for it. Even if a normal human *could* run over seventy miles an hour, they'd break a leg or tear an ACL doing it.

Or, they'd suffer an aneurysm or heart attack with the effort.

Whatever he was doing, it was damned impressive, as I wasn't closing the distance with him. I *could* pour on more speed, but Crowley's new talents intrigued me, and I couldn't resist the urge to tease out a further display of his newfound skills. Grinning in spite of myself, I batted aside an ice spike as I commanded thick vines to sprout from the ground behind and around him.

The vines did their best to obey my commands, attempting to wrap around Crowley's ankles and trip him up as he ran backwards away from me. But somehow he managed to skip past, sidestep around, and even backflip over every attempt I made to capture him with the vegetation. At first, it was impressive, but then it just grew monotonous.

So, I tried a different tack. Instead of trying to capture him with a vine, I collapsed the ground behind him, forming a trench across the field that was thirty-feet wide and just as deep.

Dodge that, motherfucker.

Moving that much earth at once caused a tremendous amount of noise and vibration, so there was no hope that Crowley wouldn't notice. And notice he did, but with a wall of six-inch thick vines and brambles chasing him, he had little alternative but to attempt to leap the chasm. A broad smile split my face as I watched him turn and face the massive ditch.

"You're stuck, Crowley," I taunted. "You may as well give up."

No way he makes it across that gap.

Indeed, I was right. Instead of jumping across, he dropped off the ledge, disappearing from sight.

TWO

I stood near the ledge, leaning forward in tiny increments to peek over the side of the crevasse, hoping to see where the wizard went. He was nowhere in sight, even though I could see nearly the entire chasm floor below. All except for the area directly below me, of course, and I wasn't about to lean that far forward and give away my position.

Click shimmered into view beside me, a lit cigarette hanging from his lower lip. He leaned to look over the side, hands on his knees, staring over the edge without a care in the world. The trickster clucked his tongue before taking a drag from his coffin nail, exhaling and blowing smoke through his nostrils like a dragon taking a nap.

"Halloooo!" he yelled, cupping his hands around his mouth. *Hallloooo!* his echo replied. Click nodded knowingly. "Aye, no doubt 'bout it. Someone's definitely down there."

Although I knew he was in no danger, I still found myself waiting for Click to get zapped by a lightning bolt from below. Of course, it never happened. Even if a powerful wizard like Crowley wanted to see him, they'd never manage it. Not if Click didn't want to be seen, that was. How Claus had been able to detect his presence was anyone's guess, but it was certainly a testament to the Fat Man's power.

"Well, $#!&," I said. "I guess I'd better go after him."

The quasi-god and trickster glanced my direction as he did a double-take. "What in the bloody balls of Balor whazzat?"

"Huh?"

"That thing ya' jest' did, lad. The bubble and the glyphs."

"I have no idea what you're talking about," I replied as I took a step back to assess the situation. "Obviously, that crafty little &^#!@$% is waiting down there—"

"There it is again!" Click exclaimed, pointing at me and jumping up and down.

"What the %^$& are you talking about?"

"That," he said, pointing next to my head. "Say something naughty."

I raised an eyebrow at him. "Click, this is hardly the time, and besides, you're really not my type."

"Gah," he hissed. "I meant, say a curse word or two."

UID'S BANE

"Oh-kay..." I said the first words that came to mind. "&$$ $#!+."

"Oh, that is peculiar," he remarked, his eyes widening as he looked at a spot directly next to my head. "Quite the nefarious curse, 'tis, if harmless."

"What?" I asked, truly perplexed.

"You can't see it, cuz' 'tis over yer' head. Hang on."

He stuck his hand out as if to reach for something that wasn't there. Half his arm vanished, and it appeared as if he was rummaging around inside a bag or box of some sort. When he pulled his arm back, he held a hand mirror. Click thrust it in front of my face, roughly two feet away.

"Say somethin' yer' mam would slap ya' fer."

"Um, %$&+!@#?"

Instantly, I saw what Click was talking about. Although I couldn't pick it up in my peripheral vision, when I said that curse word, a white cartoon speech bubble appeared above and next to my head. That bubble contained characters that were sometimes used to represent cussing in print.

"What the #^@&?"

"Egg-zactly," Click said with a nod.

"What the heck kind of messed up trick is this?"

He shook his head ruefully. "The Claus kind. Now ya' know why I hate that fat ol' jolly bastard."

"But, I don't get it? Why would he do something like this?"

"Because he's a self-righteous prick. An' ya' probably did somethin' dumb 'round him or one o' his servants, like promisin' ta' stop cussin' up a storm all the time."

"I don't recall promising anything, only apologizing," I groused.

"Same thing ta' the likes o' that tub o' lard."

"Not anymore," I said as I rubbed a hand down my face. "He went keto."

Click's eyes narrowed. "He would. None are more self-righteous than some fecker who gives up bread an' sweets fer' the sake o' vanity."

"Or to avoid developing diabetes," I remarked absently before throwing my hands in the air. "Man, cussing was like my superpower. What am I going to do now to intimidate my enemies?"

"Speaking o' which..." Click tilted his head sideways, toward the chasm. "Forgettin' somethin' are we?"

"Oh, right." I resisted the urge to cuss as I cupped my hands around my mouth. "Crowley, you can come out now. I don't want to fight you anymore."

"This ought ta' be good," Click muttered.

He answered by tossing a fireball at me, which I narrowly avoided by leaning away. "Well, that was rude."

"Best go down an' sort him out then, eh lad?"

I side-eyed the trickster. "Why do I feel as though you're egging this fight on?"

"Pshaw, ma' boy," he said as he thumbed an imaginary pair of suspenders. "Why would I have any interest in seein' how ya' fare 'gainst Fuamnach's hound? Why would any god, trickster, or fae, fer' that matter?"

"Uh-huh," I replied with a sideways smirk. "I bet you knew he'd be here. $#!+, you probably tipped him off, just to set up the fight."

He grimaced as he raised a crooked finger, pointing next to my head. "Hate ta' be the one ta' tell ya', but that's startin' ta' get jest a wee bit creepy."

"Ah, #&^$ it," I said. "Be right back."

I backed up twenty feet or so, then I sprinted forward and leapt off the edge of the cliff.

As soon as I dropped into the chasm, a shimmering, iridescent barrier snapped shut above, locking me in. When my feet hit the ground, I rolled and came up in a crouch, glancing to my left and right for some sign of Crowley.

"I know you're here," I said aloud. "Obviously," I added under my breath.

I waited for him to respond, but got no answer. Waiting any longer was inviting disaster, as the wizard was one sneaky son of a gun. Muttering softly to myself, I prepared a druidic spell that would flush him out.

"Think you can hide from me—I'll just conjure up a mess of vines from the earth, and we'll have you flushed out in no time."

I rubbed my hands together in anticipation of wrapping up this task, and set to work on my spell. Initially, I had no issues connecting to my Oak. However, when I attempted to channel its energy to cast the spell, the effort fizzled out immediately.

"What the—"

At that moment, Crowley stepped out of a shadowy niche in the wall of the chasm some twenty feet in front of me, sword in hand. "Don't bother. I've cast an anti-magic field across the entirety of this great, gaping hole you created in the earth. Combined with the ward that I placed above us, you have no chance of escaping. Now, I shall have the answers I seek."

"So dramatic," I remarked, rolling my eyes. "But well played."

"Indeed. Draw steel or suffer, druid. Your choice."

I had no intentions of actually fighting Crowley, no matter how pissed off he was, or how violently he attacked me. People might think that Crowley was an evil person, but I knew better. Sure, he was a first-rate prick, but I didn't think he was evil. He'd even helped me in the past, which meant that I owed him a solid— or several, in that regard.

Besides, the way he attacked me was strange as hell, even for him. I had a feeling he was acting under the influence of a spell of some sort. Short of saving my life, there was no way I was going to hurt him—at least, not seriously.

"Now, Crowley," I said, backing up as I raised my

hands in a nonthreatening gesture. "We don't have to do this—"

The look on his face was one of stark determination, combined with just a hint of reticence. "Perhaps we don't, but I don't have time to trifle about. Likewise, I don't trust you enough to place my faith in your sense of altruism. So, either draw that sword that you carry over your shoulder, or taste my blade. This is my last warning."

What Crowley likely did not know was that I could avoid him all day. I tried my hardest not to let others see how much of my Fomorian powers I could utilize while still appearing human. It had always been a sort of ace in the hole for me, since nobody expected a human to move like a vampire or a werewolf.

Yet, if he didn't already know my secret, I certainly didn't want to reveal it to him unnecessarily. The trick here would be to move just quickly enough to avoid him without tipping my hand. If I really needed to, I could move at full speed to prevent getting skewered.

Crowley wasted no time in coming at me with carefully measured malice. Rather than attacking with a series of slashes, he advanced with an intricate combination of feints and thrusts. That threw me off quite a bit, but I still managed to dodge, slip, and skip out of the way.

However, the last of those attacks came dangerously close to stabbing me through the throat. I misjudged the timing and barely managed to lean sideways as the tip of his sword snagged on my jacket, poking a hole through the collar. Surprised as I was that he'd nearly scored a hit, I reacted by batting the flat of the blade away and stomping at his knee.

The kick barely glanced off the wizard's leg, but it was enough to stagger him and give me some breathing room. When we disengaged, I detected the barest limp as he retreated.

So, he has fae reflexes, but not fae durability. Good to know.

I danced several feet away from him, feeling the damage in my leather and kevlar bomber by poking my finger through the hole.

"Dammit, Crowley," I said with a grimace. "Did you really have to ruin my brand-new jacket?"

"Holes in your jacket will be the least of your concerns, momentarily," he replied as he flourished his sword.

"Speaking of which, that's a hell of an interesting weapon. Where *did* you get that thing?"

He shrugged and came at me again, thrusting and feinting alternately at my face, body, and legs. I was forced to move even faster as I evaded the flurry, matching his enhanced speed with my own.

Time to end this before he sees what I can really do in this form.

I waited until he overextended a thrust—which was bound to happen, eventually—then I pivoted past his sword to come up next to him, shoulder to shoulder. As

I did, I grabbed his wrists with both of my hands, my left arm over his to control his left wrist, and my right hand controlling his right. My left leg was behind his right, and I had full control of his weapon hands.

Crowley hissed his displeasure at me. Unfortunately, I couldn't disarm him from this position, not without letting go and potentially getting slashed on a disengagement. Thus, I did the next best thing—I threw him backwards over my leg by slamming his chest with my left arm as I kicked my left leg forward.

I might've used a bit more force than necessary, but I wanted to end the fight quickly. If I dropped Crowley hard on his back, the impact could very well knock him unconscious. However, in an insane display of acrobatics, Crowley did not, in fact, end up on the ground. Instead, he did a one-handed back-hand-spring, flipping head over heels in the air to land lightly on the balls of his feet some ten feet away from me.

"As you can see, I've acquired a few new skills since last we met," he said with a smirk. "You'll not defeat me with such simple tricks."

"Between the sword and whatever spell work you're using to move like a fae, I am *very* curious about what you've been up to lately," I quipped as I spun and circled away from him. "As much as I'd like to stick around and find out, my schedule does not include farting around with you at the bottom of this pit."

His expression darkened considerably. "While you

might find the current situation to be laughable, I do not share the sentiment."

"Yeah, I'm starting to get that impression," I said, shaking my head ruefully as I bladed my body to hide my left side. "I'd rather not do this, but you leave me no choice. Just remember, I gave you every opportunity to talk this out."

Almost quicker than the eye could see, I reached behind my back with my left hand to push Dyrnwyn's scabbard up and slightly over my shoulder. That small movement was enough to facilitate a single-handed, over-the-shoulder draw with my right hand. As I drew the blade, I leapt forward at Crowley with a near super-human speed, slashing down at his weapon.

According to Celtic myth and legend, Dyrnwyn was a unique, semi-intelligent weapon designed to ferret out and destroy malevolent persons and creatures. In the presence of evil, the blade would light on fire, burning with a white-hot flame that cut through nearly anything it touched. If I faced a foe that it deemed other than evil—for example, a wild animal that lacked the intelligence to make moral and ethical decisions—the sword would remain as cold and lifeless as any normal blade.

Strangely, instead of bursting into flame, an odd blue-white energy flickered up and down its length. In the past, the sword either lit up or it didn't. In all the time I'd owned it, and in all the battles I'd fought, not once had it reacted in such an ambiguous manner.

Before I could consider the sword's peculiar behavior, I was in midair and delivering a downward, two-handed stroke in an attempt to knock Crowley's sword from his hands. He was no fool, and no stranger to a sword fight, either. Rather than being caught off guard, he was able to raise his sword up in an awkward, hand-and-a-half grip, blocking with a reverse roof block that met my blade cleanly before I could finish the attack.

When Dyrnwyn met his blade, a loud *ping* rang out, followed by a brilliant flash of blue and silver light. There was a thunderclap combined with an explosion that threw me across the chasm, bouncing me off the ward above us with enough force to knock me silly. As I connected with it, the magic barrier released about 100,000 volts of electricity into my body.

Damn, I should've expected that.

I landed on the chasm floor, stunned and smoking from the spot on my shoulder where the electricity had entered my body. My skin and clothing were charred, and I had a very nasty electricity burn that would take some time to heal. However, my Fomorian innards had held up well, and I was none the worse for the wear.

As I pushed myself to my feet, I dusted my pants off, momentarily regretting how quickly my new duds had been ruined. You didn't enter this business expecting to maintain a pristine wardrobe, that was for sure. Of course, the question that statement evoked was the exact nature of "this business," a question I'd found myself asking more and more of late.

It wasn't like I chose this life—it chose me. As much as I'd like to deny the existence of fate or destiny or whatever bullshit excuse people generally gave for fucking up their lives, I couldn't argue against it. Some outside force always seemed to be moving the pieces on the game board, and it sure in the hell wasn't me. If I ever ran into the fucker running the game, they'd definitely get a piece of my mind.

As I reflected on the existential nature of being a punching bag for the gods, Crowley was moaning and groaning his way back to reality. I was a bit scraped up from the magical detonation that had occurred when our weapons clashed, but having Fomorian internals had saved me from serious injury. He wasn't as lucky. Though he'd been trying to kill me moments before, I was still concerned he might be seriously hurt.

"Yo, Crowley," I yelled from a safe distance, magic at the ready. "You alright over there?"

He moaned again and twitched a finger. It might've been a ruse, but the anti-magic field he'd cast had gone kaput—a sure sign he was out cold. His pulse was thready and his breathing shallow, which caused me to suspect internal injuries.

"Well, $^#."

There was a time when I was not exactly the best druid in the history of druidkind. Meaning, I was a shitty student when Finnegas was alive, something I would regret until my dying day. Thankfully, I'd been able to rectify some of my past mistakes by studying the library the old man had left to me, and by getting alt-timeline Lugh to help me out.

Not to mention the *Teinm Laida*.

Chanting that massively powerful spell had been my first step toward achieving druid mastery. The *Teinm Laida* had been a sort of gift Finnegas left me after his death. He'd hidden it within the pages of a grimoire he'd cleverly concealed, so only I would discover it. Casting the enchantment had allowed me to progress decades in the druidic arts almost instantaneously, while suffering few if any side effects.

Yet, knowing wasn't the same as doing, as I'd since discovered. The problem with all that unearned knowledge was that I lacked experience, the kind that could only come through years of practice. Although I understood the theories of druid mastery, I was learning to apply them on the fly.

I only hoped I could do so in time to save Crowley's life.

A quick scan of his body using my druid senses revealed a ruptured liver, a few broken ribs, and a concussion. He must've hit the earthen wall of the chasm just as hard as I did to sustain those injuries. That impact would've killed most humans, and I could only speculate at the magic he'd used to prevent his untimely demise.

Shadows and chattering voices drew my gaze skyward, where several of Rube's patrons were watching me work. The wizard's pulse was getting weaker, so I ignored the growing crowd that had gathered at the edge of the chasm above. While it wasn't prudent to leave myself vulnerable in the presence of entities unknown, I'd have to rely on Click to watch my back while I worked.

It took all of two seconds to drop into a proper druidic trance, at which point I set myself to the task of healing the worst of Crowley's injuries. Druid magic relied on working with nature's energies, not violating them, and the healing magic we used was no different. My job was to bolster his natural healing abilities by speeding those processes up. The main challenge in doing so was providing his body with the energy and resources to perform three months worth of healing in three minutes. That meant I had to feed his system nutrients in massive amounts, and rapidly.

There were more than just weeds lying dormant in the soil, as this field had yielded all manner of crops over the past many decades. It took only a small amount of the Oak's power to coax the soil into producing corn, beans, potatoes, and strawberries from the surrounding earth. From those plants I drew the stuff I needed to help the wizard's body heal—glucose, electrolytes, proteins, and fats. These I combined into a sort of intravenous solution that I pumped into his veins using tubules grown from the plant life itself.

I formed a makeshift I.V. line from a vine, the end of which was tipped by a tiny, hollow thorn. The "needle" slipped into a vein in the crease of his elbow nicely, and soon I was pumping him full of nutrients, just as fast as his body and my magic could use it to heal him.

After about a minute, his pulse strengthened and his breathing became less labored and shallow. Unfortunately, as soon as he began to regain consciousness, he reached for the intravenous line in an attempt to remove it. That wouldn't do, so I asked the Grove to help me manufacture a bit of morphine to add to the I.V. fluid. My druid grove was basically one huge, extra-dimensional biochemistry lab, so in short order Crowley was snoozing like a baby as his body healed.

Once Crowley was stable, I opened my eyes. Above us, a few dozen fae stood at the chasm's edge. All eyes were on me, and all stood silent as I returned their gaze. Finally, a grizzled old man in dirt-stained coveralls and work boots caught my attention. He had piercing green eyes and skin like old leather, and he carried himself with a regality that belied his humble appearance. Instinctively, I knew he was ancient—maybe older than the surrounding hills.

The old man gave me a nod. He stuck his thumbs in the straps of his coveralls, then without a word, he turned and walked away. One by one, the other fae followed him, until the only one left was Click himself.

I shifted my attention back to Crowley, checking on his progress by using my druid senses. He'd healed nicely, although he'd have a headache for a day or two. It wouldn't be prudent to leave him under the influence, so I had the Grove help me whip up some makeshift

Narcan and a bit of adrenaline. Easing it into him drop by drop, I gradually woke him from the healing coma in which I'd placed him moments before.

"What was that all about?" I asked Click as he appeared at my side. "The fae, I mean. They looked, I don't know—concerned, or something."

Click distracted himself by rolling a gold coin across his knuckles as he replied. "'Tis been an age since any o' them have seen a druid master at work. An' ta' see ya' heal the wizard so handily, well..." He gave half a shrug. "I s'pose it makes 'em a bit nervous, is all."

"What about the dude in the overalls?"

"A woodwose. Probably a good thing he approved. Things could've gotten nasty if he hadn't."

"The old man always said that the fae didn't like the idea of druids coming back into power. I guess they prefer us humans to be nice and weak."

"Ripe fer' the pickin', so ta' speak." Click chuckled. "S'why they made it so hard fer' me ta' ascend. I've been payin' fer' it ever since."

"Ascend? What do you mean—?"

"Oh, looky there—yer' patient awakens."

I stole a glance at Crowley, and when I looked back, Click was gone. "Dag-nabit."

Crowley opened his eyes as he slowly pushed himself upright. The wizard looked at the makeshift intravenous line in his arm, then at the plant life all around, and finally at me. Frowning deeply, he harrumphed and rubbed his head.

"I take it I attacked you?"

"Yup."

"And that it didn't go well for me?"

"You were doing alright at first," I said as I scratched my nose with a knuckle. "Tossing spells right and left, and moving like a fae assassin. Consider me impressed. If it hadn't been for our swords clashing—"

He raised a hand in protest. "Stop right there. I attacked you with a sword? Where is it?"

"Don't worry, I hid it for you. Too many prying eyes around here." I twitched a finger, causing the vegetation next to him to part and reveal the magical short sword he'd been carrying. "Darned powerful, that. Where'd you get it?"

He plucked it from the bed of leaves and vines on which it sat, sheathing it at his side before concealing it with a spell. Then he closed his eyes and placed his index fingers on his temples. After several seconds, he opened them again and rose to his feet.

"Did I just witness you using healing magic?" I asked.

"Nothing so mundane," he said as he pulled the I.V. line from his arm. "I simply instructed my brain to ignore the residual pain left over from my head injury."

"Right. So, why'd you attack me?"

"Fuamnach, perhaps? She must've implanted a suggestion in my mind, something that had been subtly growing over the past many weeks until it became a compulsion. It wouldn't be the first time, although I shall take steps to ensure that it shall be the last."

"Ah." I looked around, avoiding eye contact. It was an awkward moment. He did just try to kill me, after all.

Crowley brushed off his slacks. "Well, I suppose I'll be off."

"Er, sure. But—"

He cocked his head at an angle as he fixed me with a weary look. "Who is Cressida?"

"Right."

Crowley exhaled heavily. "My sister."

"You have a sister?" I said as I scratched my head. "Since when?"

"She is my twin. I thought she'd died when we were children, but according to Fuamnach, she yet lives."

"And you trust her? Fuamnach, that is."

"You know as well as I do that her kind cannot lie. For insurance, I secured her word on the matter, and her promise of assistance."

Something here wasn't adding up. A fae's word was inviolable, and that of a goddess more so. If she really had agreed to help him, then why would Fuamnach glamour him and cause him to attack me?

Curiouser and curiouser.

I made a fist and coughed in my hand. "Wow. You'll have to tell me how you did that sometime. I take it you're trying to find her? Cressida, I mean."

He nodded. "The search—or rather, Fuamnach's suggestions—led me here."

"To Lord John's Icehouse. Where you can't enter."

"Just so."

I chuckled. "It so happens that I'm going in there."

Crowley's eyebrow nearly hit his hairline. "Really?"

"Fallyn's in some sort of trouble. Click says it's the only way to find her."

"Ah," he said knowingly.

"So, you want me to ask about your sister while I'm in there?"

Crowley demurred. "Oh, I couldn't—"

"It's no trouble, really. I mean, you'd do the same for me, right?"

"No," he said without hesitation, meaning it. "But I shall owe you, should you do so."

I gave an involuntary, disbelieving laugh. "I guess it's pretty much the same thing. Sheesh, Crowley, don't ever change."

He stared at me, blank-faced. "I hadn't planned on it."

For someone who was so slick and stylish, he could be such a socially awkward dweeb at times. I decided to give him the benefit of a doubt and blame it on the head injury. That said, it took a concerted effort to keep a straight face as I continued.

"Um, how do I get in touch if I learn anything?"

"Oh yes, of course. Just call Belladonna, she'll get the message to me."

An obvious dig, but I'll allow it.

"Will do." I turned to go, using druid magic to form

a staircase in the chasm wall ahead of me. "And Crowley?"

"Yes, druid?"

"Stay on the straight and narrow, yeah?"

"Always."

Somehow, I doubt that.

CHAPTER
THREE

As I walked across the road toward the entrance to Rube's, I considered how the two swords had reacted on first contact. The only theory I could come up with was that the blades somehow cancelled each other out, creating a repellent force similar to magnetic repulsion—magical feedback, so to speak. Whether that was by design or chance, I couldn't say.

What I did know was that Crowley now carried a weapon that was at least as powerful as Dyrnwyn. He also appeared to have given up or lost his ability to cast shadow magic. And, he'd somehow survived an encounter with Fuamnach.

Was I concerned? Absolutely. However, I had bigger fish to fry at the moment. Besides, if Crowley was now dating Bells—and I suspected he was—I trusted that she'd keep him in line.

Turning my attention to the task at hand, I stared at the plain metal door that marked the entrance to Rübezahl's demesne. It would be no small matter to enter. Not only because of the dangers involved, but also because by entering and returning I'd be announcing to the entire supernatural community that I was not entirely human after all.

I'd sure in the hell like to ask Click for further clarification before I went in there. First, I'd like to know what kind of peril Fallyn was in; second, why we needed to go through Rube's to find her; and third, if this really was the only path to take.

Of course, he'd disappeared, along with Rube and all the Mountain King's patrons who'd been watching the fight minutes earlier. Presumably, they'd all gone inside, Click included. On previous visits, the old gnome had met me outside the building, fairly warning me off from entering without ever saying so directly.

Either Rube has decided I'm a big boy and capable of making my own decisions, or he's inviting me into his demesne.

"Here's another fine mess you've gotten us into," I muttered under my breath as I reached for the weathered wooden door handle.

When my fingers touched the sun-bleached handle, time was momentarily suspended. Next, I had the distinct sensation I was being examined by an entity both enormous and timeless. I felt myself being thoroughly searched by a gaze that saw through my thin human skin, right down to my dense Fomorian bones.

I sensed hesitation there, and uncertainty. For a moment, it seemed as though I teetered on a precipice, my fate hinging on the entity's decision. As quickly as the sensation arose it passed, and I sensed the overwhelming, ancient visage settling back into its natural state—eternal, watchful repose.

I'd been frozen by magic while I was being examined—rude—and a wave of vertigo hit me as the spell released. Soon it passed, and I recovered, catching myself in time to avoid falling through the door as it swung inward. Leaning sideways, I held myself up by placing one hand on its worn, smooth surface, just below a chipped and faded decal that said "PUSH" in silver lettering.

Strange. I could swear there was a pull handle on the door a moment ago. Yet another reminder that nothing is as it seems when dealing with fae places.

I scanned the scene before me. All eyes turned to me, the entire crowd of fae who sat along the bar to my left, and also in shadowed booths that lined the wall to my right and around the back wall of the tavern. The interior of the place was rather underwhelming, and I experienced a bit of unexpected regret at how mundane it all appeared.

The floor consisted of faded wooden planks, the grain worn shiny and smooth in the most heavily trafficked places, but nearly blackened by dirt and time in far corners and along the walls where shod feet rarely stepped. The bar itself had been fashioned from reclaimed barn wood and mesquite logs, with a long, thick cypress slab top covered in glassy acrylic, rubbed down nearly to the grain in places by elbows and beer mugs. The barstools had rough-cut lacquered cedar frames, their red cushioned vinyl seats torn and discolored by many years of use.

Dim pendant lamps lit the booths, their light directed by conical metal shades that seemed to avoid illuminating the patrons' faces, no matter how close to the tables they sat. Sawdust and peanut shells covered the floor in a scattered, scant layer that looked as though it had been there since the cornerstone had been laid. I took it all in as I stood in the open doorway, casting a lengthy shadow while daylight played across the honky-tonk floor.

You could hear a pin drop when I stepped fully into the room, at least until the door slammed shut behind me. As soon as it closed, the patrons returned to whatever had occupied them before I entered. Immediately, a low drone of conversation, clashing billiard balls, and tinkling glasses rushed in to fill the uncomfortable silence.

A visual sweep of the room revealed no sign of Click. Likewise, Rube was nowhere to be seen, either. I was just about to ask the bartender where I might find Rübezahl, when I felt someone clap a rather large hand on my shoulder from behind.

"Hey, fella'—your kind ain't welcome in here," someone said in a thick Chicago accent.

First I glanced at the hand, which was thick, hairy, and calloused in the manner of someone who worked at manual labor all day. It was attached to an equally thick and hairy wrist belonging to a towering specimen of a humanoid who easily stood eight feet tall. He was generally misshapen in the way many giants, ogres, and trolls were, sort of lumpy in odd places and lacking any real symmetry of form.

Yet, that wasn't the oddest thing about this giant's appearance. Atop his very broad, muscular shoulders sat three heads. The right-most head had red hair, and it was the most normal-looking of the bunch, almost handsome save for a few warts and a mouthful of crooked, yellow teeth.

The one on the left still looked human, but it was much uglier, with a bulbous nose that sat in the center of a round, ruddy face that suffered from the worst case of rosacea I'd ever seen. Add to that the shock of snow-white hair that stuck straight up atop its skull, and you had a face only a giant's mother could love.

Yet, it was the centermost head that drew my attention. That one was small in comparison to the others, almost shrunken, really. As well, it was misshapen in the extreme, with one drooping eye, a conical, nearly bald skull, a flat, crooked nose, and a mouth that was so lopsided as to mostly be located on the left side of its face.

I slowly turned around, gingerly removing the hand from my shoulder as I did so. Having seen some ugly creatures before—and being no cover model myself when I fully transformed into my alter-ego—I managed to maintain a neutral expression. The problem wasn't my reaction, but the fact that I had no idea which head had addressed me. So, I kept glancing back and forth between them.

After witnessing my inability to choose, the center head sighed in a put-upon fashion. "Eyes here, human. I dunno' how you got in here, but rules are rules. If you ain't fae, you gotta' pay."

"What, like a cover charge?" Purposely acting dense, I reached for my wallet.

The shrunken head smirked. "You wish. Naw, the price is servitude."

"You mean, washing dishes or something?"

The center head frowned, the left head chuckled, and the right glared. "Now you're just being stupid on purpose-like." The giant smacked a fist into his other palm. "But if ya' want a clobberin', then I'm more'n happy to give it to yooze."

Time to gamble.

"I got in, didn't I?"

"Sure, but—"

"Then that must mean I made the grade. Have you

seen any other humans come in here by themselves lately?"

He scratched his rightmost head as he blew smoke from its nostrils. Meanwhile, the leftmost head yawned toward the ceiling, exhaling a cloud of vapor that coated the metal tiles in frost. This was obviously no ordinary giant. If he attacked, I'd need to make sure I didn't get fried or frozen by his breath weapons.

"No, but that don't mean I hafta' let yooze in, either." He clapped his big, meaty hand on my left shoulder. "Let's go, bub—"

Before he could begin to giant-handle me, I reached over, grabbing his pinky and third finger with my right hand. Moving with supernatural speed, I pivoted clock-wise, folding his wrist as I rotated his arm elbow side up. I turned and tucked his arm under my armpit, yanking his hand up as I cranked his shoulder and elbow in a standing arm-bar.

Then, I dropped to the floor on top of him, savoring the satisfying crunch his shoulder made as I pinned him face down on the floorboards. This had the effect of driving the nearest head—the right one—into the ground forcefully, knocking it out cold. That marked one down, two to go.

The center head yowled in pain, a completely reasonable response when someone forcefully dislo-cated your shoulder. His other head turned toward me, opening its jaws wide so he could take a nice, deep inhalation. I'd expected as much, and had planned accordingly.

That was the main drawback to breath weapons, that they required preparation to use. If I had wanted to be mean, I'd have forced him to inhale water and frozen his lung. Yet, I was only trying to make a point, not kill the giant, so instead I superheated the air going in his mouth.

Once the giant had filled his lungs, he exhaled forcefully, blowing at me with all his might. All this managed to do was raise a slightly cool breeze, one that ruffled my hair but did nothing to harm me in the least. The center head's brow creased with dismay, and the leftmost head inhaled again. Again I pulled the same, simple trick using druid magic, cancelling out his freezing breath.

"Care to try a third time?" I asked while keeping him pinned in place. "Or are you going to admit I'm not entirely human and let me in?"

"Any magician could pull that off," he grumbled.

"While keeping a giant pinned to the floor?"

The center head frowned while the left hung defeated. "Alright, you win."

I released him and stood, offering the giant a hand. He took mine in his left, and I pulled him to his feet. "No hard feelings?"

"Naw, comes with the territory. Just don't cause no trouble, alright?"

I shook his hand and released it, and he walked off,

exiting through a doorway behind the bar. It was only after he passed through that he began rubbing his shoulder, presumably after he felt he was out of sight of the other patrons. The door swung shut behind him, then there was a *boom* and a *crack* that made the walls shake, followed by a muffled yelp.

Ew, he must've tried to put it back into socket himself. Somebody should've told him, that Lethal Weapon bullshit never works in real life.

That was when I spotted Rube behind the bar, a white towel draped over his shoulder as he poured beer from the tap for his patrons, laughing and joking with them all the while. He definitely hadn't been there when I walked in, so I could only assume that either the ruckus had drawn his attention, or he'd remained hidden to see how I'd fare against his bouncer. One thing was certain, he was a wily old coot.

Since he hadn't acknowledged me yet, I sauntered over to an empty barstool that offered a two-seat gap on both sides. Rube continued filling mugs, glancing my way only passingly as he finished serving his customers. He rubbed the bar down with his cloth, tossing it on the counter as he gave a wink and a nod to a taciturn, whip-thin male bartender wearing a leather eye patch and a wicked facial scar. Why I hadn't noticed the second server before, I couldn't say, but he took over for Rube without missing a beat.

The proprietor took his time making his way down the bar to me, stopping to clear away glasses and retrieve tips as he went. By the time he reached me he had a fistful of gold and silver coins in one hand and a bouquet of beer mugs in the other. He dropped the change in a glass pitcher that had been long ago adorned with a taped and frayed handwritten sign that said "TIPS".

As for the mugs, he carefully dunked them in a soap and water-filled sink to my left, at which point he began washing them with a bottle brush he pulled from beneath the suds. I watched as he rinsed the mugs, one at a time, setting them upside down on a clean, folded bar cloth behind the counter.

"Greetings Lord John, Prince of Gnomes," I said as I gave him a protracted, deferential nod of my head.

"You'll hafta' forgive the greetin' you received from Bal," he said without looking up. As usual, he spoke with a slight Texas drawl, with just a hint of that Germanic accent mixed in beneath it.

"No need, he was just doing his job."

"Just so. Know thou art welcomed here, Cailean MacCumhaill, son of Colm," Rube continued in a formal, regal, and decidedly European tone of voice. When he spoke next, his drawl returned in full force. "Here to retrieve what you left when last we met?"

"Is she well?"

"Why'd she not be?" he asked as he thoroughly dried the mugs he'd just washed. "You left her in my care, didn't you?"

I realized I'd offended him, and raised a hand in

apology. "I didn't mean to imply that I doubt the quality of your hospitality. I was only asking if she'd recovered from her ordeal."

He frowned, thrusting out his lower lip with a nod. "As well as can be expected. The Sorceress was not so kind to her, not in body, not in mind. She was changed by Fuamnach as well, altered in ways that nature never intended. Some might never recover from such an experience."

"And her? Will she recover, do you think?"

He tilted his head slightly. "Who can say? Resiliency is the domain of humanity, is it not? Else the fae would have overrun the earth and wiped their kind from existence long ago." He fixed me with his steely gaze, those pale blue eyes momentarily piercing my soul. Then he smiled, not unkindly, and the sensation passed. "You are proof enough of that, eh, *Halbblüter*?"

"I suppose. Although in truth, I doubt I'd have made it this far if it weren't for being different."

He chuckled as he finished drying the last mug. "Probably true. But you didn't come here to discuss your unique parentage, did you? You require passage, and information as well, yes?"

"So I'm told."

He tossed the towel on the counter behind the bar. "Come then. We can check in on my guest while we discuss terms."

◞

RUBE WALKED to the end of the bar, moving a transom door out of the way and replacing it as he came from behind the counter. I de-assed from the barstool and followed him through a swinging door next to the bar. We entered into a sort of kitchen-slash-pantry area, down a hall and through another door that said "MAN-AGEMENT" on an engraved plastic plaque at eye level.

The old gnome stopped with his hand on the knob, turning to me as he tipped his straw cowboy hat back. He winked and placed a finger on his lips.

"Quiet now. I want to surprise her. She hasn't had many visitors."

"Wait—people know she's here?"

"Some. Not many. The folks who've come by did so at my request. And they're the kind to keep secrets." His expression grew somber. "Now, hush. If she hears your voice, she'll know it's you."

He opened the door, revealing a lush garden beyond, filled with all manner of flowering plants, ferns, and fruit-bearing trees. The undergrowth was a mixture of soft grass and moss-covered soil in those places where the sun did not reach. Bright blue sky stretched from horizon to horizon, meeting mountain peaks in every visible direction.

It looked like a cross between Eden and a scene from *The Sound of Music*. I didn't need my druid senses to know that the place teemed with life, not just of the green variety, but also insects, mammals, reptiles, and birds. As proof, birdsong played a soft counterpoint to the sound of frogs croaking, crickets chirping, and a brook bubbling over stones nearby.

Rübezahl stepped through the doorway, pausing again to gesture me to silence before beckoning me through the opening. He strode on, completely at ease in his demesne. As for me, I'll admit I looked over my shoulder more than once to make certain the doorway was still there. It was, and its presence reassured me enough to continue on.

I followed roughly ten feet behind the Mountain King, startling only momentarily as I felt a powerful concealment spell settle over me. He led the way down a white gravel path that took us into a copse of trees and through a natural archway formed by tall, lush conifers grown thick and close together. Some fifty feet beyond, the wooded area gave way to a grassy knoll that sloped down to a gently flowing, crystal clear stream.

At the water's edge, a willowy, blonde-haired maiden sat side-saddle in the grass with a lacy white dress pulled up to her knees. Her toes barely touched the water as she held court for a motley collection of animals that had gathered around her. I counted two squirrels, three rabbits, a robin, a triplet of brown field mice, a mole, and one very grumpy looking wolf. For fear of revealing my presence, I resisted the urge to use my druid senses to see how she was controlling the animals.

Siobhán sang softly to her audience, trilling away in the language of the fae. It was a song of longing and regret, mournful and yet hopeful all at once. I couldn't understand the words, but that much I gathered from the tone and her expression.

Rube stood by, stern-faced, eyes glued to Siobhán as she completed her fairy tale performance. Finally, the last note rang out across the meadow and the animals began to disperse. Only then did The Mountain King clear his throat and approach.

"In rare form today, as ever *meine Zaubermaus*," he said, smiling warmly. "Even Meister Wolf is calmed by your presence."

"Although I fear he'll return to his natural ways presently, once the spell fades," she replied, batting her bright green eyes as she rose to greet her host.

Siobhán gave a formal curtsey, holding it until Lord John returned a shallow bow. She'd yet to sense my presence, so I took the opportunity to note how much she'd changed since I left her in Rübezahl's care. Her complexion had gone from sallow and pale to a healthy, almost ruddy glow, with just a hint of an olive tan beneath. Her figure had filled out as well, and while she still maintained the trim, willowy figure of a runway model, she no longer looked malnourished and weak.

Yet, the most significant change was evident in how she carried herself. While she bowed her head when she greeted the Mountain King, afterwards she met his gaze with a carefree confidence that spoke volumes about her emotional state of being. The half-crazed, trauma-tized girl was gone, replaced by a confident, lively young woman. Young in the manner of the fae, that is, as she was likely many times as old as I.

All-in-all, she seemed to be at peace, and that made me happy. It was all I could do to hold my tongue, but I managed, as I didn't care to spoil John's surprise. As it so happened, I didn't have to wait long at all. I'd barely completed my brief assessment of her when the fae girl's eyes narrowed.

"You've brought a visitor with you, John," she whispered, her cheery smile fading into a taut line of resignation. "You may as well show yourself. I know you're there."

Rübezahl harrumphed. "Can't get anything past you, can I? You might have at least pretended to be surprised, to allow an old gnome a bit of fun."

He snapped his fingers, and the spell of concealment broke. The magic dispersed, and Siobhán's jade eyes widened as they settled in my direction. It was then that Rube realized the wrinkle he'd failed to anticipate, his eyes darting back and forth between me and his guest.

"*Ach*, I should've told you he was here," the gnome king hastily added. "Never fear, little mouse-bear. The druid has promised he's not here to take you away."

Siobhán's expression softened at that. "Hello, Colin," she said shyly.

"Hello, Siobhán," I replied, flashing my warmest grin. "You look well."

She returned the smile, reservedly. "You've been at

battle, and you're kitted for war. Are you certain you're not here to take me back?"

I felt the Mountain King's hard, piercing stare settle on me again. "No, not unless you want me to. I came for a different reason, but I couldn't resist the opportunity to check in on you as well."

An atmospheric tension that I hadn't noticed earlier diminished, and if I didn't know better, I'd have said that Rübezahl sighed with relief. I honestly didn't know if the shine he'd taken to her was good or bad, as it was obvious she was completely safe from harm while under his care. Yet, it did make me wonder what might happen when Siobhán decided she was ready to face the world again. Until such time, at least she was in good hands.

As for the girl, I couldn't blame her for being fearful. I'd seen what her former captor could do, the lengths she'd go to for revenge. Being hunted by a goddess, even a minor one like Fuamnach, was no small matter. The gods and ancient fae like Rübezahl could be relentless when they wanted something, and they were endlessly patient in attaining their goals.

"That's good to hear," she said. "Not that I'm *not* pleased to see you—you are the reason I'm here and not wasting away in some dungeon in Underhill, after all."

"Shush, *Mäuschen*," Rube said. "You should not talk of such matters."

Siobhán addressed the Mountain King directly. "You

know as well as I that without Colin's intervention, I would be as good as dead right now."

She was right, but her concession to that fact made me uncomfortable. "Oh, c'mon. I'm sure you'd have found a way to evade that old bitty."

Rube turned his formidable gaze on me, crossing his wiry, sun-browned forearms over his chest. "You know as well as anyone what it is like to be the focus of a god's displeasure. And while fair Siobhán is far from defenseless, she lacks such gifts as you've been granted."

I gave a halfhearted shrug as I glanced away. "I've survived through sheer luck, that's all."

They shared a look between them. Rube smiled knowingly, while Siobhán gave a rueful shake of her head.

"Everyone knows that isn't true," she said. "You've survived because you are strong, brave, noble, and kind. When combined, these are qualities the gods will always and ever underestimate—someday, perhaps to their ruin."

"*Ja*, and that is why they fear you, druid," Rübezahl remarked drily. "You would do well to spend several decades consolidating your power, instead of chasing after that mad magician who fancies himself their equal."

"I don't really have a choice," I replied, flashing him a resigned frown. "Click says Fallyn is in danger. When my friends need me, I don't hesitate to help."

When I swung my gaze back to Siobhán, she was

right next to me. Before I knew it, she'd leaned in to plant a kiss on my cheek. Her emerald eyes twinkled with admiration, and perhaps a little regret, as she quickly retreated to arm's length.

"Some might call it weakness, but that's your strength. It's also why your friends love you," she said, glancing down and away, then back again. "'Though one may be overpowered, two can defend themselves, and a cord of three strands is not easily broken.' Remember that when next you find yourself in dire straits."

I recognized the quote, but I couldn't remember from where. Based on John's disapproving harrumph, I assumed it to be of human provenance. Rather than refuse good council, I smiled and inclined my head.

"I will, Siobhán."

My response seemed to please her, or at least I assumed it did, considering how her eyes lit up. An instant later her tinkling, playful laugh echoed across the meadow, and before I knew it, she'd intertwined her hand in mine.

"Come on—there's so much I want to show you!"

The lithe fae girl dragged me away with surprising strength, to where I hadn't a clue. I spared Rube an apologetic glance. While his mouth curled in a disapproving frown, the warm gaze he directed at Siobhán told a different tale. Yet, I sensed hesitation there, as well.

Go on, he mouthed, shooing me away. *I will wait.*

CHAPTER
FOUR

Time passed differently in the fae lands, and The Mountain King's demesne was no different. Over the years I'd become accustomed to such strangeness, having taken full advantage of it many times to rest and heal in my Grove. Thus, I didn't worry about the time as Siobhán took me on a rather lengthy tour of Rube's gardens and grounds.

To say she was enthusiastic was an understatement. Obviously, this was a side of Siobhán I'd never previously seen. When I'd first met her, she'd ostensibly been in the employ of the queen, and back then she'd been as aloof and cold as Maeve herself. Little had I known she was a spy placed in Maeve's court by Fuamnach, with little reason to show me any warmth or friendship.

How the sorceress had managed it was anyone's guess, although she'd once claimed to have infiltrated Maeve's home personally. Even though the Celtic gods and fae couldn't tell an outright lie, they could twist the truth like anyone's business, so it was hard to know what to believe. Maybe Fuamnach *had* taken on Siobhán's form a time or two—who knew?

Maeve had as much as said that she knew Siobhán was a doppelgänger, but she'd never admit to being infiltrated by Fuamnach herself. The queen was hellaciously hard to fool, however. For that reason, I thought it more likely that Fuamnach had captured the girl and brainwashed her to do her bidding.

Regardless of how it had gone down, Siobhán had gaps in her memory where the sorceress had mind-wiped her. In doing so, Fuamnach would've replaced those missing pieces with memories fabricated by mind magic. Unfortunately, such false memories had a tendency to fray over time. If the changes were extensive, temporary or even permanent psychosis might result.

Thus, the trauma caused by Siobhán's experience had left scars that would take time to heal. The good news was that she appeared to have been healing just fine while under Rübezahl's care, and I wasn't about to take her from this place before she was ready. She seemed so happy here. How cruel would I have to be to deny her that happiness?

It might have been minutes or hours later when Siobhán finally led me back to the meadow where we'd last seen Lord John. The Mountain King awaited us there, sitting on a large boulder, whittling a stick into a whistle. He seemed completely at ease, as a king should be in his domain. However, I noticed a tightness around his eyes as we approached, and I couldn't help but note of the surreptitious glance he flashed when Siobhán gave me a parting hug.

"Let's discuss this arrangement you mentioned," I said as we both watched Siobhán trot off toward her cottage, merrily whistling a tune as she went.

"I hope you realize what she is, and what she's come to mean to me," the old gnome said as he continued to whittle on his stick. "She is both more and less than she once was, and that makes her special and precious. I would ask you to consider carefully before taking her away from this place prematurely."

It's not that I thought John was threatening me, but rather that there was a threat inherent in what he said. Even I wasn't foolish enough to challenge an ancient Fae creature in his demesne, but I also wasn't dumb enough to appear weak to such a being, either. Still, I wanted to get some clarification before I made my position known.

"You don't have anything to worry about," I said, smiling jovially. "She seems happy enough where she is, and besides, I don't own her. I brought her here to save her from slavery, and I don't intend to make her mine."

John nodded, carving a few more shavings from his stick before lifting it to his lips. He blew a single shrill note before folding the knife and placing it and the stick in the front pocket of his Western shirt.

"Bah," he scowled. "Never was good at making things with my hands. Rumpelstiltskin was the gnome for that sort of thing, if ever you needed it. Damned shame what happened to him, getting mixed up with the Tuath Dé."

"I hadn't heard that story," I replied in a neutral tone.

"Hmph. He decided to get between one of the gods and the mortal woman that God loved. Rumpelstiltskin thought he was owed something, but in fact, he had no right to the claim." Lord John fixed me with a hard stare. "You'd do well to remember that."

Ah, so now we get to the heart of the matter.

It appeared that Rübezahl had more than taken a shine to Siobhán, and now he wanted to lay his claim. In truth, he was the one who had no right. Mountain King or no, it was best to nip the situation in the bud—tactfully, of course.

I pursed my lips as I considered his words, pausing for effect. "Let me be clear. What I said about rescuing her from slavery? I meant it. If anyone ever decided to imprison her like Fuamnach did, they'd answer to me for it."

The old gnome narrowed his eyes as he sized me up for several seconds. Unexpectedly, he tsked and marched off at a brisk pace, back the way we'd come. Having no other choice, I followed him. The heck if I was going to get lost or stuck in some crazy Fae realm with no one to guide me out again.

"At least now we understand each other," John said over his shoulder as he trod up the hill at a rapid pace. "About that arrangement... you'll soon need to get somewhere, and the only way you're going to get there is through my realms. Though you don't know it, you'll also need information on the person you'll be following."

"You mean Fallyn?"

Rube shook his head. "No, the one you're *really* after. Getting your woman back will involve dealing with that party, eventually."

I let out a low whistle. "I suggest you don't ever let Fallyn hear you referring to her as 'my woman.'"

He chuckled. "I sometimes forget how much things have changed in the human world over the last century. These modern women with their liberation and self-determination and what-not. But never you fear. Chances are good, she and I will never meet, so there's little danger of my insulting her unintentionally."

He was awful chatty all of a sudden, and that had me worried. It likely meant he was about to con me, or he'd try to, anyway. I didn't like being conned, especially not by the fae—even if I did somewhat like the guy.

"It's clear you want something," I replied. "Just tell me what it is, and I'll decide if it's worth the bargain."

His pace slowed for half a step, and thunder rumbled long and low across the mountains in the distance. Yeah, I was treading on thin ice, but I was tired of the games that ancient fae and gods played. For once, I just wished one of them would come right out and say how they were screwing me.

It'd never happen, of course, because it wasn't in their nature. Still, I could dream. And I could force a dodgy old codger like Rube to cut to the chase, even if I did risk pissing him off.

"First, you need to know what you're getting in return," he said as we approached the doorway that led back to his tavern. "I'll show you, then I'll tell you of my price for passage. Come."

He stepped through, and from my perspective it appeared as if he'd walked back into the hall that led to the bar. But when I crossed that barrier, the scene shifted in the most jarring way possible. One second I thought I was stepping through a portal into the icehouse, and the next I was standing on a high, narrow stone walkway that wound away into a hazy ether of nothingness.

The sky above was painted in vibrant, pastel hues of pink, violet, and orange, reminiscent of a desert sunset, or maybe the sunrise after a storm. Except, there was no sun visible on the horizon, and no apparent source of light, either. Why the fae never tried to imitate the sun was anyone's guess, but I'd never seen a facsimile of that great yellow ball of burning gas in any of the *sídhe* lands I'd visited.

The path beneath our feet looked to be made of granite, gray and worn by many thousands of footsteps and the ravages of time immeasurable. No more than five or six feet across, the smooth, shallow furrow that ran down the center indicated those who traversed it tended to avoid the edge. Out of curiosity, I stepped as close to the side as I dared to peek down.

Nothing but pink fog and a long fall into forever.

I shivered involuntarily at the thought of falling off, then I carefully inched my way back to the center path. Rube chuckled to himself as he began walking away from me.

"Why are we here?" I said as I glanced over my shoulder to ensure the doorway was still there.

The rectangular, three by seven foot opening was indeed where I'd left it, although now all I could see through it was a dense, gray mist. On looking back again, I received the answer to my question.

When we'd first stepped through the doorway into this area of John's realm, only a single path lay before us. Now, the pathway branched off into a seemingly infinite number of extensions, each leading to another, identical doorway. Most disturbingly, every last one displayed nothing on the far side but the same feature-less ashen fog seen through the doorway behind us.

Shee-it. There must be thousands of doors here, and no way to choose the right one.

"You'd never find your way back—not without me to guide you," Rübezahl said with a knowing grin.

"Oh, so you read minds now?"

He shook his head. "No, but I've seen that expression thousands of times. I know what folks are thinking when they see this place."

"Makes sense. You say Fallyn's abductor took her through here?"

"The one you seek has been where these doorways lead, yes."

I took a good look around, finally settling my gaze on the old gnome's face. He was being evasive, but that was to be expected when dealing with the fae. His eyes twinkled with mischief, or maybe it was just anticipation for the one-sided bargain he was about to make.

Same thing, come to think of it.

"I don't get it. Based on what Click told me, whoever took Fallyn is a force to be reckoned with. Heck, they'd have to be to overpower her and cart her off to who knows where. Why would someone with that kind of power come through here, instead of just portaling themselves to their destination?"

The old gnome produced a filterless cigarette from thin air, already lit. He puffed on it and blew smoke from his nostrils. Immortals loved smoking, probably because it was one more way to rub their immortality in our faces.

"Anonymity," he said, stabbing the cherry end of the cigarette at me. "I control these ways, so they're untraceable."

"Except by you, of course."

"Of course."

I crossed my arms, glowering at him beneath

hooded eyes. "I imagine there's a price to be paid for keeping secrets. Which means you must want something very badly to break that trust."

"You just let me worry about that," he said, looking away as he flicked ash over the side of the path. "Old John keeps his word, sure enough."

Thunder sounded again, this time from an indeterminate direction. I decided I'd best let that topic be. "Okay, so what is it you want me to do?"

He flashed a sly grin. "I need you to deal with a god."

"You want me to kill a god?"

"No, nothing like that," Rube said as he spat a fleck of tobacco into empty space. "I want you to *apprehend* him. To capture him, and to bring him back here if you can, so I can deal with him."

I hung my head, rubbing my temples as I processed his request. "Do I look like the pantheon police to you? I mean, I can barely keep up with staying one step ahead of the gods who already want to kill me. And you're asking to make enemies with another one?"

Rube frowned. "What difference does one more immortal enemy make?"

"And just who is this god in question?" I asked, finding myself struck by a morbid curiosity all of a sudden.

Rübezahl stared into the distance, flicking his fingers as if shooing a fly. "Just a minor god from the Slavic pantheon. You've dealt with worse."

"I've—say what?"

He took a drag off his cigarette and flicked it over the edge. "Allegedly, of course. But word does get around. Immortals talk, you know... 'God-Killer.'"

He bit off that last phrase like he was taking the choicest mouthful of a particularly juicy steak. I feigned nonchalance. It wasn't as if I hadn't been called that before.

However, it seemed John had acquired information regarding my recent adventures, and he wasn't above using an implied threat for leverage. I'd lately been responsible for the demise of more than one powerful deity. If I had my way, I'd like to keep that information on the down-low—permanently.

"Just because it's been said, it doesn't make it true." I scratched my nose with a knuckle, stalling for time while I collected my thoughts. "I'm curious, what did this minor Slavic god do to you?"

"He broke the rules. Came into my place, stirring up trouble and picking fights. My tavern is neutral territory, and that's how I like it. I can't have some *schweinehund* breaking the rules and getting away with it." Rube's gaze shifted up and to the left. "Plus, he took something of mine. Nothing major, mind— just my lucky churchkey. But I'll need you to get it back."

"Your lucky bottle opener. Seriously?" Rube nodded. "And you want me to get it back?" Another nod. "I guess I should ask, which is more important to retrieve, the kitchen utensil or the third-rate deity?"

He stroked his beard. "Eh, the churchkey. But if you can make 'im pay while you're at it, so much the better."

This was all smelling fishier than a tuna cannery in a power outage. However, that didn't mean it wasn't necessary. Despite my reservations, I decided to press on. I exhaled sharply, scratching my head as I looked at Rube askance.

"Don't you have bouncers who could handle this—folks like Bal? For that matter, aren't you sovereign in your demesne? Seems like you could have taken care of this dude on the spot when it happened."

"I was *indisposed* at the time. This pissant broke the peace and ran before I caught wind of it."

Yep, fishier than Jonah after a beach vacation. Click, this had better be worth it.

"Okay, so let me get this straight. I track this bad actor down and get your lucky what-zit back. Then I either subdue him and bring him back to your place, or I make him pay on the spot for what he did. Then I get what? Passage to wherever Fallyn's abductor went?"

"If you wish," John said, tipping his hat back.

"Uh-uh, not good enough. I want intel on the entity I'm chasing, and I want to know their end destination."

He pursed his lips, shaking his head emphatically. "I can't do that. For one, I don't have the info. After they leave my realm, I don't track passers-through. Bad for business. But I can identify the 'entity,' if you request of me to do so, on completion of the assigned task."

I tugged on my nose, hiding my lips as I mouthed

several nasty words. "It'll have to do. Since you can't get me intel on Fallyn's captor, then I want five round trips through your lands, free of charge."

"Two."

"Three. And that's my final offer."

"Gah!" Rube squinted as he drew his mouth in a taut line. "I—yes, I s'pose I can do that."

"Can, or will?"

He scowled. "Yes, I'll provide it."

"And no time limit on using them. Plus, I can come through here as often as I like while I'm still working this churchkey job."

"Of course, as long as you hold up your end of the bargain."

I smiled wickedly, even though my stomach was doing flips. "Give me a name, a disguise, and a lead, and I'll bring back your errant godlet."

FIVE

Rübezahl informed me that the god's name was Poor-Something-Or-Other, assuring me he was just a no-account third-tier deity I could handle with both hands tied behind my back. Any god named Poor Whatever had to be a loser, but I resolved to look him up before I took off after him, just in case. Rübezahl was almost a trickster god in his own right— no way was I about to trust him at his word when it came to a work-for-hire bargain like this one.

Rube and I agreed I'd be given as much time as was needed to fulfill my end of the contract. Personally, I didn't care to waste any time at all, as Fallyn was in danger. In fact, I had even tried to convince Rube to allow me passage now, promising to return later to complete the bounty hunting job, but he wouldn't hear of it.

"No one receives passage through my realm except

by way of earning it," he replied, crossing his arms. "Either get to work or get packing."

As I was leaving Rube's by way of the front entrance, I remembered Crowley's request. The old gnome had decided to escort me out, for fear that one of his patrons might decide to jack with me out of spite for past transgressions. It wasn't as though I was loved by the fae, after all, no matter how I might have impressed the woodwose earlier.

I pulled up at the doorway, turning to address Rübezahl. "By the way, a friend of mine is looking for someone. He heard she might have passed through your demesne. Does the name 'Cressida' ring a bell?"

He responded in a suspiciously abrupt tone. "Can't say I know of anyone who goes by that name."

"Uh-huh. Then do you know of anyone who might've used that name in the past?"

"Don't you have a job to do, and a maiden to save?" he asked as he scowled at me. "Now, off with you."

The next moment, I was standing on his front stoop. When I turned to try the door again, it was gone. Not locked, but simply not there.

Great. Yeah, she's definitely been through there.

I realized that I should've bargained for info on Crowley's sister as part of the deal I'd made for passage. Capturing a god, even a minor one, was no small feat. Surely, it'd be worth a bit of additional intel. But, the deal was done. I'd just have to find out about her whereabouts some other way, after I returned with Rube's bounty.

Before I could apprehend my quarry and rescue Fallyn, I needed to rest and regroup. Between surviving the Hellpocalypse, fighting river goddesses, burning down Fuamnach's castle, and helping Claus save Christmas, I was beat. It took visiting Rube's demesne to remind me I had my own pocket dimension to rest in, right here in this timeline. The time differential was so great between earth and my Grove, I could go there, catch up on sleep, prep myself magically, and devise a plan, all while only losing a few minutes of time Earthside.

I called on the Oak, willing it to transport me to my Grove. No sooner did I land in the pocket dimension than I felt the entity hammer me with mental images of greeting, absence, and concern. Despite having been the master of my Grove and Oak for well over a year, the intelligence, perception, and growing autonomy they each displayed never ceased to amaze me.

I'm fine. Just got sidetracked in another timeline, is all.

The Grove returned an image of a fish on dry land, then of a waterlogged eagle struggling to launch itself out of a lake and into the sky. I took that to mean that the Grove thought I'd been to places I didn't belong. It understood well what it meant to travel to other timelines and dimensions. The Dagda had crafted it to be capable of teleporting from place to place, even between planes of existence like Earth and Underhill. It knew I'd endangered myself by traveling the Twisted Paths.

They need me there, too. I can't help but help them. You know that.

The Grove responded with images of the animals and plants it cared for here inside its own pocket dimension. Meaning, it understood responsibility to others. What I didn't tell it was that its counterpart in that other timeline had been in dire straits before I brought it under my control. I didn't think it could comprehend that other versions of it existed in other timelines, and I would rather not confuse or upset it, any more than it already was.

As for the Grove itself, physically it seemed to change every time I returned to it after an absence. The parts I'd shaped and formed remained the same, but beyond the original boundaries, it was always adding onto itself. Where it got the raw materials, I couldn't say.

If I had to guess, it was probably from some dead planet or asteroid that lacked an atmosphere and therefore couldn't sustain life. My knowledge of organic chemistry was limited compared to the Grove's, and since I wasn't completely certain as to what would be required to create arable soil, I had no idea if I was right. I wasn't about to ask, either; it seemed a bit intrusive to ask my Grove how exactly she'd been putting on weight.

As for the why, it was continually improving upon the ecosystem it had created in this pocket dimension.

Maintaining a balance of moisture, heat, light, precipitation, and so on took a delicate touch, especially in such a small area. The information I gleaned instinctively through our bond told me that the Grove was constantly using its magic to balance things out. By expanding its borders and adding useful subsystems, that job was made all the easier for it.

The last time, it had merely added more soil and rock, perhaps doubling the overall size of the place. This time, however, I noticed it had added wetlands into the mix. That was smart, as they provided biodiversity as well as a means of filtering groundwater of the biocontaminants that the growing population of animal life here created. One day, I fully expected to arrive from an absence to find mountains and deserts, or to discover that the Grove had expanded itself into a moon-sized planet. It seemed well on its way, already.

Once I'd sufficiently assuaged the Grove's fears and anxieties regarding my potential demise in alt-timelines, I headed to my Keebler cottage for a well-earned nap. While I could've directed the Grove to build me anything here—an adobe home, a concrete dome home, or even a hobbit house—I'd become attached to my little cottage in the hollowed out tree trunk. It was warm, cozy, and just large enough for me and my things, such as they were. Truth was, I didn't need much these days, and what I did need I usually carried on my back inside my Craneskin Bag.

As I was tugging off my combat boots, I surveyed

the interior of the cabin and its contents. A bed, a small table, two chairs, some shelves lined with wooden cups, dishes and tableware, and a roughly fashioned armoire containing some spare clothes. I'd made it all with druid magic, shaping and guiding the wood to grow into whatever I required. It was spare, clean, and utilitarian, and it suited me.

I nodded in self-satisfied approval and stretched out on the bunk, propping my head up with my hands as I stared at the tree rings on the ceiling. I could use some sleep, but what I needed even more was guidance about my next steps. All I ever seemed to do was react to events, which were typically caused by the gods. Like now, for instance. They took Fallyn, Click told me about it, and here I was, doing Rube's bidding to save my friend.

I needed to start planning ahead, to make moves that would put me in the driver's seat. How I wished that Finnegas were here to guide me, but that ship had sailed. I glanced over at the wall of the cottage, where a cache of grimoires and tomes remained hidden inside a secret compartment. Those books represented the legacy the old man had left me, the accumulated knowledge of the greatest druid the world had ever known.

"How am I ever going to fill your shoes, old man?"

Even though my eyelids were beginning to droop, I exhaled heavily and pushed myself upright. As I swung my feet to the floor, I asked the Grove to make me some coffee, then I strode across the room to my hidden library. The wall receded with a thought and a single sweep of my hand, revealing two shelves occupied by perhaps a dozen tomes of various manufacture.

Here lies the gathered wisdom of three-thousand years of druidry.

Some were properly bound in thick, worn leather, filled with high-quality vellum pages lined in neat script. Others appeared to have been written on papyrus or some other equally rustic material, rolled into scrolls that were tucked inside bark cylinders with carved wooden caps. Still others were nothing more than stacks of animal skin bound together with leather strips.

I grabbed a volume at random, just as the scent of hot, fresh, coffee hit my nostrils. A brief look around revealed that a wooden mug of liquid manna had appeared in a new alcove nearby. One sip of the java the Grove provided, and I felt revived—caffeine and magic were a powerful concoction, it seemed. I sat down on the bed, propping myself against the wall as I began to read one of Finnegas' more recent grimoires, opening the volume to a random page.

A note in the margins, written hastily in shaky script, caught my eye:

"Remember always, druidry follows nature's laws. A druid's bane is chaos."

I chuckled at the irony. My life was nothing *but* chaos. It made me wonder if he'd ever experienced as much craziness as I had. Who knew? It could be that was why he wrote the note.

While I flipped through the rough, musty pages, I thought about my place in The World Beneath. Rübezahl had been right when he called me "God-killer," even though I hadn't actually killed any gods on my lonesome. However, it was the reputation that mattered, not the deed, and it was hardly the sort of rep to get if you wanted to live a long, quiet life.

Did I really want to be that guy? The tragic figure from the epics who defies the gods, only to eventually be crushed under heel for his hubris? I hated them, honestly I did. These little gods were petty, cruel, and fickle, even more than the fae in most instances. Despite having nearly been forgotten by the majority of humankind, they still treated us like chattel, objects to be owned, used, and tossed away.

'Us'—that's a funny thought. Am I really even part of humanity anymore? Was I ever?

As far as my personal identity was concerned, I was, although by blood I was something else. Being half-Fomorian didn't even make me a demigod—I was more like a demi-titan, if you wanted to split hairs—and I sure as hell wasn't intending to throw my hat in with the gods because of that.

No, I was human, if not by blood, then by adoption and intent. That was why I saw it as my job to protect those who couldn't protect themselves. The real question was: How best to do that?

Due to my Fomorian DNA, my default setting was to tackle any problem head on and beat the shit out of it. Thinking about all that my temper had cost me, I could almost hear the old man's voice chiding me inside my head.

And how's that been working for you, eh, knucklehead?

Admittedly, it hadn't worked out very well. I'd gotten some good people killed, folks I loved and cared for deeply. I'd burned bridges, been hunted by the gods, and lost my mentor to boot.

Speaking of which, Finnegas survived for millennia in The World Beneath while dealing with the supernatural races and the gods both. It wasn't just because he was powerful, the old man was crafty as well. He knew when to raise a stink, and when it was time to keep his head down and avoid garnering the attention of the powers that be. He also knew you needed to do more than just get by—you had to plan for the future.

And man, am I tired of just getting by.

Even if I had survived a string of calamities, the cost had been steep. Despite what Siobhán had said about me, I didn't see myself as a crusader, and I sure as hell didn't see myself as a victor. To be honest, my track record thus far was break-even at best. And break-even wouldn't cut it if I was going to be the guardian of humanity.

That is what you intended, right, old man? You said it yourself, you were bound by oath never to create more than one apprentice. But if you could teach someone else how to bring the druids back, well...

Just as I formed that thought, something caught my eye in the old man's grimoire. It was a drawing of an oak tree, scratched out in deft lines of Celtic knot-work. On closer inspection, I noticed that the tree's branches and roots were interconnected, and each section terminated in a small, round object.

Fruit? No, don't be dense—those are acorns. Seeds.

And where did seeds come from? From pollinated plants. With that thought, wheels began turning in my mind. I thought about why the Dagda had made my Oak different, and why he'd given it to me in the first place.

Why was it two separate entities—both Oak and Grove?

I flipped back a few pages, and there I found it—another drawing, this time of an oak in a meadow. Yet, the meadow was surrounded by darkness and shadow.

A void. Shit, that's the Void.

Flipping back further, I found a drawing of a sapling, and before that, an acorn being planted in the ground. Every few pages the old man had left an illustration, all sequential, each one innocuous apart from the others. But when interpreted together, they told a story.

My heart beat ever faster as I flipped ahead to the end of the grimoire, a few pages past the first illustration that had caught my eye. When I saw it, I did a double-take. The implications were almost too much to imagine.

It's a grove of oaks. Sweet Caroline, these images are instructions.

It'd been staring me in the face the entire time. Heck, Finnegas, the Dagda, and Lugh had even hinted at it, but I'd failed to see it. The old man didn't want me to just carry on and find another apprentice.

Nope. The Oak and Grove were the key. Finnegas the Seer had foretold a future for druidkind. One where there were oaks, groves, and druids on every continent —perhaps even in other timelines.

The old man wanted me to rebuild the druids to their former glory, before the gods and Romans conspired to destroy us. That's why he'd worked to ensure that I would become a druid master, despite his untimely passing. I could see it all so clearly now. He chose me to be the future of the druids.

That's also the reason the Dagda had made my Oak two entities and not one. You had to have one, the Oak, representing male energy, and the Grove, representing female energy, to reproduce. Pollination, germination, fertilization.

Jiminy flippin' Christmas. I have to get the Oak and Grove to reproduce.

The more I thought about it, the more it seemed too much, too big, and way more responsibility than I felt capable of handling on my own. I needed to talk to someone about this, someone knowledgeable both about druidry and regarding the politics of the gods and supernatural races. And I knew just the person.

Lugh.

Not this timeline Lugh, but the other Lugh, the one who actually saw me as a brother more than a rival. He'd already proven himself an ally by helping me, and besides, it'd only require a slight detour to see him, considering where I was headed. If I was going to take down a god, deliver him to Rübezahl, and rescue Fallyn from whatever dark entity had managed to subdue her, I was going to need help.

First a nap, then I'd go get Fallyn, then it was back to the Hellpocalypse.

It was a good plan. After I thought it all through, I was a little too excited to fall asleep. To pass the time, I flipped through the pages of the tome some more, looking for clues or perhaps other hidden instructions that Finnegas might've left. After a while my eyes grew heavy, so I placed the book back where it belonged, then I drifted off with one, comforting thought on my mind.

I don't have to do this alone.

CHAPTER
SIX

I awoke an indeterminate amount of time later, perhaps hours in the Grove, but only minutes in the primary timeline. I arose energized and feeling refreshed, not just from getting adequate sleep, but also from the renewed optimism I felt at discovering the old man's instructions.

Funny how the old codger is still looking out for me, even after his passing.

It was in my nature to keep my chin up, but hope had been in short supply lately. Maybe it was all the time I'd spent in the Hellpocalypse, and the monumental tasks that lay before me there, but I hadn't exactly been feeling chipper recently. The old man's hidden message was just the ticket to help me refocus and get moving toward a meaningful goal.

But first, I have to find Fallyn.

After swinging out of bed, I made a cup of joe for the

sheer comfort the activity brought me. Then I bathed in my favorite swimming hole, I found some clean clothes, and I got kitted out for the coming trip. The first step was gathering supplies and sticking them where I could easily reach them inside my Craneskin Bag.

Food and water, check. Ammo and munitions, check, check. Firearms, of course. Clean clothes, spare footwear, and medical supplies, yup.

Spare weaponry always came in handy in the Hellpocalypse, both for trading and for equipping allies, so I packed some of that as well. That included the firearms I was bringing, as well as extra swords, maces, battle-axes, and the like. I liked coming prepared. Magic had failed me often enough to know that throwing tons of lead downrange would solve most problems, and blades never ran out of ammo or magic.

Once my preparations were complete, I shouldered the Bag, then Dyrnwyn, and I left my final instructions to the Oak and Grove.

Hide out until I return, following standard procedures. Stay on the move, and at the first sign of trouble retreat to the Void. I'll be back before you know it.

The Oak simply sent back an image of an old, gnarled oak tree. I guess that was its way of saying it'd be here when I returned. On the other hand, the Grove sent me an image of a bird's nest full of chicks crying to be fed. It actually made me chuckle. The more those two matured, the better they got at manipulating me.

Oh, stop trying to make me feel guilty. You two are more than capable of surviving on your own.

That was true. Yet, I couldn't help but think about what had happened in the alternate timeline after my counterpart's passing. There, the Hellpocalypse version of the Oak had turned into a vengeful killing machine, and I'd had a hell of a time bringing it to heel. That was because the Oak was impossible to track, and it had a mind of its own.

In the past, druid oaks were stationary and lacked the ability to teleport from place to place. Since each Oak was the doorway or entrance to a druid master's grove, that meant the Groves were stationary as well. Yet, the druids could still use them to travel great distances instantly, as they could teleport from oak to oak via portals created by each individual grove.

Limited as it was—especially in comparison to any ancient fae or deity's power to portal—this still proved too much of a tactical advantage for the gods to allow. That was why some of them decided to partner with the Roman Empire to burn the druid groves down. As potent as each Oak was, they were no match for the gods' power combined with Roman ingenuity. Eventually, every last grove and oak fell. That in turn weakened the druids, leaving them vulnerable. Eventually, none but Finnegas and the Dark Druid remained.

By giving my Oak the ability to teleport away from danger, the Dagda had seen to it that such a chain of events would never happen again. And by giving the

Oak and Grove the power to portal their master virtually anywhere in the contiguous timeline, the Dagda had done the same for me. That was what made my Oak and Grove so special, and so very dangerous to the gods and other races. It was also why I needed to keep them safe and protected.

Few people knew the truth about my Oak and Grove, although some outside my circle of friends suspected it. Maeve for one, and probably Macha and Fuamnach. Did any other gods suspect I had an oak and grove? Possibly, but in my experience, the gods rarely shared tactical information between each other. That was because they naturally distrusted one another, a weakness that worked in my favor.

But if it became common knowledge that I had mastered a grove—one with such unique capabilities, as well—I had no doubt they'd band together and come after me in force. If that happened, we'd have no choice but to run away and hide.

It's not as though we haven't done it before.

Putting those thoughts aside, I sent the Grove a few more words of encouragement, then I asked the Oak to take me to earth. Or, more specifically, to Hemi's garage apartment on the South side of town.

At this point, I didn't even need to touch the Oak anymore to portal. I just thought about it, and the Oak made it happen. The act was effortless—that was how well established the bond between us had become.

So, when we ended up at the junkyard a split-second later, I was more than a little confused. "We" meaning the Oak and me. It had portalled us both to somewhere in the back of the junkyard, close to the stacks. After I got my bearings, I realized we weren't far from where I'd kept it in those early days of chaos and mayhem, just after the Oak was born.

"Hey, what gives?" I asked in a friendly, chiding tone. "I said Hemi's place. You remember where that is, right?"

The Oak sent back a jumble of images, mostly different locations we'd portalled to before.

"Nope, none of those places." I sent back a clear, very specific image of Hemi's apartment, then I sent an image of where it was located on a map of Austin. "This is where I want to go. Right there."

I got mental silence back from the Oak for several seconds, then it sent back an image of a large, weathered mountain. In other words, it wasn't going anywhere. Instinct told me to pay closer attention to the message it was sending, and I examined the image further. Storm clouds were gathered around the mountain, and large, black birds circled the peak.

"Something has you spooked?" I asked as I patted the thick, rough surface of the Oak's trunk. "Whatever it is, I'm trusting that it must be bad. No worries. I can get there the old-fashioned way, until we figure out what's up."

The Oak sent back an image of a peaceful meadow, which was its way of saying it was relieved by my response. Something had really spooked it. What that was, I had no idea—but I intended to find out.

"Meanwhile, stay here," I commanded it. "At the first sign of trouble, I need you to bug out to the Void, alright?"

Bugging out had always been our "break glass in emergency" plan for the Oak and Grove. The Void was just that, a void. While some terrifying things dwelt there, it was nearly impossible for anyone or anything to find us in that vast emptiness. That's because it was inconceivably difficult to track us in the nothingness that was the Void. It was the very reason why I'd chosen to use it as bug out location numero uno.

The images the Oak sent in response were the same mountain, then the junkyard. When I examined the image of the junkyard it had sent, my wards were clearly glowing, all around the perimeter of the place. The Oak was more or less saying, 'No, fool—I'm staying right here behind these wards.'

I honestly didn't know what to make of that. The Oak and Grove were essentially tweens at this stage in their development, still children in the grand scheme of things. When threatened, it made sense they'd go to a place where they felt safe and comfortable. But if they felt that endangered, why not just split to the Void like we'd always done?

It was urgent that I gather my team, deal with Rube's third-rate deity problem, and then rescue Fallyn as soon as possible. The Oak and Grove were more than capable of protecting themselves, if not by fighting, then by teleporting away with a thought. Despite my misgivings, I'd have to figure out what was up when I got back from this mission.

After saying a few more soothing words to the Oak, I poked my head in the office, hoping to see Maureen there. If anyone knew what was going on, it was her. But, no luck.

It was weird to walk in the office during daytime hours and not see Maureen behind the counter. I figured she must've run out to do errands or something. In lieu of speaking to her, I spent a few minutes strengthening the wards around the junkyard, just to be safe. Then I headed to the garage, where an old friend awaited me.

MY DRUIDMOBILE WAS much as I'd left it, covered by a dusty tarp and protected and hidden by druid wards. Nobody who worked here would mess with it anyway, as it was an unspoken code among mechanics and enthusiasts that you didn't mess with another person's ride. Still, it was my baby, so of course I safeguarded it with magic when not in use.

Besides, the wards also kept it from succumbing to the ravages of time. Not permanently, mind, but druid magic could keep the battery charged, the brake fluid fresh, and the fuel system dry while it sat for weeks or months at a time. And it had been too long since I'd been behind the wheel of my beast.

The car was a vintage AMC Gremlin with a 304 cubic inch V-8 under the hood, souped up and modded out with a cam, headers, the works. I'd been looking to replace it with a 6.6 liter engine from a Randall 401-XR, which would really make the thing scream. But considering that less than a hundred had been made, I had a better chance of winning the lottery than locating that engine.

Of course, the alternative was to restomod it by dropping in a modern crate engine and transmission and calling it a day. I'd get better performance, more reliability, and fewer headaches to boot by going that route. But I just couldn't do it, not just because the car was a classic, but also because Finnegas had built it for me.

Yeah, that made me a bit sentimental about it, but that wasn't the only reason. When a two-thousand-year-old druid master builds you a street rod, you don't mess with what they built. I wasn't exactly sure of everything he did to the engine, but it was a heck of a lot more reliable than it should've been, and faster, too.

Every mechanic knows if it ain't broke, don't fix it. Besides adding extra protective wards to the paint— look away spells worked great for avoiding speeding tickets—I chose to leave it as he built it. The fact that it started on the first turn of the key and purred like an angry, overgrown kitten was a testament to the wisdom of that decision.

While pulling out of the garage and around to the front lot, I couldn't help but notice there was hardly any staff around. Moreover, it looked like work had piled up in my absence. A line of used cars sat in the yard, waiting for someone to declare them basket cases and thereby only worthy of parting out, or redeemable for rehab and resale.

It wasn't like Maureen to let stuff pile up like that, but I chalked it up to me being busy doing druid stuff. In reality, I hadn't been gone that long—but who knew what had happened in my absence? I made a mental note to offer Maureen my assistance with catching up around the yard, after I'd saved Fallyn and kicked the ass of whoever abducted her.

The ride to Hemi's was, to say the least, weird. For one, I passed at least three fender benders, and two of them had escalated to actual fist fights. I was tempted to stop and break one of them up because it looked like a major mismatch. However, I resisted the urge to get involved, reciting one of the old man's favorite mantras: "Not my clowns, not my circus."

Besides the roadside altercations, I noticed more of those weird black and white billboards along the way. The first one said, *"There is neither truth nor falsehood."* Odd, but I guess it made sense from a relativistic perspective.

A little further down the road, the next one read,

"Declare yourself what you wish." Then, a half-mile after that, *"Do what you like."* The next one said, *"There are no rules anywhere."*

Soon, I began to assume that some bored millionaire decided to spend a crap-ton of his kids' inheritance spreading his own personal philosophy of dopey anarchism. Whatever, people could waste their money however they liked. After a while, I started ignoring them, until I saw a message that gave me pause.

It said, *"The goddess prevails."*

Huh.

I pulled over for that one. Not necessarily because it required contemplation, but because I wanted to read the fine print underneath the big black letters on the massive white billboard. Underneath the quote in the bottom righthand corner of the sign, it read, "Brought to you by the Enlightened Society of Discord."

There were a couple of things that bothered me about those signs. For starters, I couldn't remember ever having seen them before I left for the Hellpocalypse. Besides that, they were stupid as fuck. It was like some goofball had created a cult based on post-structuralism combined with an ass-backwards interpretation of Taoism.

That would be some peak stupidity, right there.

What really tweaked my nipples was the mention of a goddess. The old man had once told me there were two factions of the gods. One faction was fine with the fact that humans had more or less forgotten about them. They were happy enough living in other dimensions and planes of existence, only occasionally coming here to screw with humans.

And the other faction? They wanted to return to their former glory, enjoying the widespread worship of mortals everywhere. That faction apparently included dickwads like Fuamnach, Badb, and Aengus. Or, at least, it had until my mom killed Aengus and I gave Badb a frontal lobotomy before casting her adrift in the Void.

Good times.

Of course, the signs had me wondering—had another player managed to get a foothold here by tricking a bunch of humans into starting a religion? It wasn't hard, apparently, as people would believe anything these days. Heck, my social media feeds were full of ads for hucksters selling courses on "manifesting" and "changing your vibration to harmonize with the universe."

Shit, if people only knew.

The fact the ads kept running indicated there were plenty of gullible people buying those silly courses. Who wasn't looking for something to give their lives meaning, whether it was a relationship, a career, a philosophy, or a religion? If mere mortals could take advantage of humanity's base desire for existential context, any deity could wreck some motherfuckers by exploiting the same tendencies.

I considered all these things during the remainder of the drive, setting them aside to focus on more pressing matters as I pulled up in front of Hemi's house. After parking along the curb to avoid pissing off his landlady, I walked up his driveway, past his beat-up Japanese tuner to his front door. Just as I was about to knock, the door opened, and Maki's face appeared in the opening.

"Aw, just the one I wanted to see," she declared. "They've been at it for days, Colin. Days. You have to help me, 'cuz they're driving me bonkers."

"Okay, back up a minute. Who are 'they' and why do you need my help with them?"

She blew a strand of strawberry-blonde hair from her face, crinkling her pale, pert fae nose as she did so. No matter how many times I spoke to Maki, I always found it peculiar how someone who was native to New Zealand could look so very, well—Irish. Hemi once said that all the *patupaiarehe* looked like her, which made me wonder if the entirety of the earthbound fae had originally come from the same place. Who could say?

Maki stepped back as she swung the door wide. "See for yourself."

FROM OUTSIDE THE FRONT ENTRANCE, the apartment looked much as it should, just a simple double garage the owners converted into an efficiency apartment. Bed on one side, couch and TV on the other, with a small bathroom and kitchenette in back. The moment I crossed the threshold, however, my perspective changed considerably, expanding to reveal a space much larger than it had any right to be.

That was Maki's doing, of course. When Hemi had refused to move, she'd somehow managed to expand the small domicile to suit her needs. Now the interior resembled a modest three bed, two bath ranch home on the interior. But that was not what drew my attention on entering.

No, what first caught my eye was the absolute carnage that had been made of the living area. Garbage, dirty plates, and half-eaten food lay everywhere— empty potato chip bags, candy and microwave burrito wrappers, beer and soda cans, not to mention crumbs and the odd piece of trampled popcorn. It was shocking, considering how neat their place had been since Maki moved in, forcing the former bachelor to change his slovenly single dude ways.

Still, that wasn't the most peculiar thing I noticed. I primarily focused my attention on the insane shouting match taking place in the center of all that trash and wreckage. One of the participants sat on the edge of the couch, the other sat cross-legged on the floor in front of the television.

The first was a massive Maori dude wearing a food-stained black t-shirt and equally dirty floral board shorts—that was Hemi, of course. The other was an elderly Native American man dressed in jeans, a white t-shirt, and a plaid flannel top. Everything the older gentleman wore was on backwards or inside out.

What the heck is he doing here?

Hemi jumped to his feet, shaking with rage as he bellowed at the old man. "No! I told you to use Dragon's Icy Breath, then Mortimer's Elastic Fireball."

"?do will one when spells two waste Why !Bah"

"Because, you backwards-talking muppet, the ice spell has a massive AOE effect, *and* it freezes all the mobs in place. Then the fireball copies the AOE range of the first spell, incinerating the low-level mobs and taking the leaders down to half-health."

".thing same the does effect time over damage The ? spell ice the using keep not why Then"

Hemi threw his hands up in the air, tossing potato chip and popcorn shrapnel everywhere as he did so. "Because it takes forever to finish them off, that's why! Do you want to be farming mobs all day, or do you wanna' level up, so we can hit some end-game dungeons?"

Heyókȟa shrugged. ".rush any in not am I .immortal I'm"

"Arrrrgh!" Hemi replied, throwing his controller onto the couch cushions. He ran his fingers through his greasy, unwashed hair, then he bent over to retrieve the controller, oblivious to my arrival. Maki cleared her throat, once, then again at a greater volume.

"Hemi," she said at a polite volume, just as he sat down on the couch once more, his thumbs furiously working buttons. "Hemi... HEMI!"

"Yeah, love?" he replied without taking his eyes off

the television screen, where his barbarian and Heyókȟa's wizard were laying waste to a large group of goblin-like creatures.

"company have You," Heyókȟa said.

"Aw, didja' pull more mobs when I wasn't looking? I told you to let me draw aggro," Hemi snapped. "Again, I'm the tank, so it's my job, mate."

Heyókȟa hit a button on his controller, pausing the game. ".here ,game in Not"

"Huh?" Hemi glanced around, blinking and blocking the sunlight as he looked in our direction.

The door remained open, as Maki was waving a small rug back and forth in an effort to get some fresh air in the place. Soon, Hemi's eyes adjusted to the light, and he blinked several times as he realized he had actual company in his home. He glanced down at his shirt, brushing away crumbs from his chest, before he ran a hand across the stubble that nearly obscured his *tā moko*.

"Oh, hey there, bro. We were just in the midst of a wicked MMO sesh. Gimme a sec." The demigod bent over, turning his attention to digging around in his couch cushions. He tossed out loose change and all manner of trash until he found another controller, which he held up like Excalibur. "Found it! Care to join in?"

The look Maki gave him could've made vinegar from grapes on the vine. I took the hint, shaking my head.

"Uh, no—I'm good. Thanks, though."

Maki set the doormat back in place, ever so carefully, then she moved directly in front of me. The fae sorceress placed her hands on my shoulders before leaning in to hiss in my ear. "Get him out of my house, please."

She may have said please, but it was clearly a directive, not a request. "Which one?"

Maki glanced over her shoulder, eyes narrowed. "Come to think of it, both of them."

"Er, right." I leaned to the side, so I could look around the flustered fae's face. "Um, Hemi? Could I have a word with you—outside?"

"Yeah, sure," he said distractedly as his gaze drifted back to the screen once more.

"gone you're while management storage some do just I'll ,worry Don't," Heyókȟa assured him without taking his eyes off the TV.

"Don't you dare enter that dungeon until I get back!" my oversized buddy replied, shaking his index finger at the Native American trickster god.

Heyókȟa waved his complaint off as he opened his inventory screen. I stepped outside, sparing Maki a sympathetic look as I passed. Hemi tossed the controllers on the couch before following along, keeping a wary eye on Heyókȟa as he walked out the door.

"I'm serious!" he yelled from his front stoop, before turning his attention my direction. "Noobs—what to do with 'em, eh?"

I scratched my brow with a knuckle. "Er, Hemi—

how the heck did you end up making friends with Heyókȟa?"

Hemi shrugged. "Dunno. He just showed up the other day, said he was waiting on you. I got bored with staring at him, so I fired up that MMO and asked him to play." He blinked a few times, blocking out the sunlight with his hands. "That was what—two, three days ago?"

"Try three weeks!" Maki yelled from the other side of the door, her voice strained.

My brow furrowed. "Three weeks and you're still not at end-game content?"

Hemi gave a frustrated sigh. "He does everything backwards, mate—everything! Sometimes, we'll end up at the final part of a dungeon or mission that we just started, with no idea how we got there. It's like he's clipping us through to the end or something. Can't tell you how many times I died because of him. Leroy Jenkins has nothin' on that munter, yeah?"

"Speaking of running headlong into impossible situations—do you have any plans for the next few days?"

"Yeah-nah, I got nuthin' goin' on. 'Sides, Maki's more than a little miffed at the moment. Probably a good idea to get out of here for a day or two. Lemme' clean up and see Bizarro out, and we'll be on our way."

CHAPTER
SEVEN

It might have seemed strange that Hemi would agree to come with me without first knowing where we were going or what the mission was, but that was Hemi. I figured part of it was his personality—being how he was just a heck of a good guy and all—and the other part was cultural. From what I'd seen, Kiwis tended to be really laid-back people, the Maori even more so.

And Hemi? That dude turned being mellow into an art form.

Come to think of it, it was weird that he and Maki were fighting. Sure, that whole scene I'd witnessed wasn't much of a fight when you compared it to some of the arguments I'd had with Bells and Jesse. But for Maki and Hemi, it was a major falling out.

In all the time I'd seen them together, I'd never known them to have a spat. The two were just far too agreeable for that. The reasons went far deeper than just their love for each other, back to Hemi's upbringing and his cultural roots.

To the Maori, *whānau*, family, was everything. Considering Hemi's background, he took the concept of *whānau* more seriously than most. To him, maintaining the peace in his household was mission-critical. Maki was his family, and he'd never jeopardize the bond they had over a petty little argument.

By the same token, the things that Hemi and I had gone through had bonded us more deeply than a common parentage ever could. In the Maori culture, kinship often extended beyond genetic and marital ties, and once you were adopted as family you may as well be blood. When he called, I came, and vice-versa—that was just how it was.

Never mind that Hemi wasn't afraid of anything. Spending part of your childhood in the underworld with a death goddess for a mother and a jealous volcano god for a stepfather would probably do that to you. After he'd survived that, any trouble I could cook up likely paled in comparison.

Although I did get him killed that one time. But we didn't talk about that.

Hemi was only gone briefly. When he emerged from the apartment minutes later, he wore a clean blue t-shirt under a Hawaiian floral shirt, board shorts, and brown leather jandals—his standard uniform. No matter how cold it was outside, I never saw him in long pants, ever.

I took one look at his bare legs and chuckled. "Dude, what are you going to do if I ever get married? I can't have my best man wearing shorts to my wedding."

"Hah! For one, you'll never get married. You're too much of a wildcard for that, bro. And second, I wouldn't wear shorts to your wedding. I'd wear a suit."

"Seriously? I might have to get married, just to see that happen." I glanced around. "And Heyókȟa? I thought you said you were kicking him out."

Hemi clucked his tongue. "Who knows? When I went back in, he was gone. I'm sure he'll walk out the door backwards after we leave, saying hello or some nonsense."

I harrumphed and nodded. "Trickster gods are weird."

"Tell me about it." He raised an eyebrow. "By the way, where's Fallyn?"

"That's why I came to ask your help. Click says some mysterious god-like being abducted her, so we're on a mission to get her back. The trail leads through Rübezahl's demesne. I have to do a favor for the gnome to earn passage." I paused, chewing my lip. "We, uh, have to apprehend a minor god who busted up his place a while back."

Hemi frowned slightly. "Huh. That's weird."

"I know, right? Why didn't Rube handle this himself? It's his demesne and all, so you'd figure he'd be sovereign there, even if this troublemaker was a minor god—"

Hemi cut me off. "Naw bro, not that. It's odd that Fallyn's gone missing. Maki just had brunch with her this morning."

"Yeah, but Click said..."

I paused mid-sentence as I realized just how fishy things had been since he'd found me in the Hellpoca-lypse version of my Grove. First, there was our little detour to Claus' reality on our way back from the alternate timeline. Sure, Click was easily confused, and he often forgot things—for example, forgetting that he left me in that other timeline for six months—but I'd never seen him screw-up time magic. I had chalked the whole thing up to the Fat Man's intervention, but now I wasn't so sure it was entirely his doing.

Second, there was Crowley's unprovoked, out of the blue attack, just as soon as I landed in this timeline. Did Crowley lean evil? Yeah, absolutely. But if anyone was ever *lawful* evil, it was that guy. It just wasn't in his nature to lose his cool and try to solve things with his fists. He was more of an "abduct you and torture you to get what he wanted" kind of guy.

The third strange occurrence was Hemi and Maki's spat. If it had been any other couple, I wouldn't give it a second thought. But those two? Uh-uh, something was up.

And of course there was the whole cartoon bubble, "I can't curse anymore" thing. Click might've blamed it on Claus, but now that I thought about it, vengeful curses simply weren't the Fat Man's style. This was the dude with the naughty or nice list, after all. If anyone believed in free will, it was that guy.

I swept my gaze in random directions, my brow knit in anger. "Click! You'd best show your face and tell me what the #$+& is going on."

Hemi raised an eyebrow as he pointed above my head. "You got bubbles, mate."

"Yeah, yeah—tell me something I don't know," I groused. "Click, get your tail out here and explain yourself!"

".here He's," Heyókȟa said from behind me, causing me to jump.

"Gah! What is it with you tricksters and your disappearing, reappearing act? Can't you just enter and exit a conversation like a normal being?"

".sometime it try shouldn't You .fun less is way This," the Native American personification of clownish behavior replied.

"He means it's fun, and you should try it," Hemi commented in an aside.

"Yeah, I got that," I replied, trying to avoid sounding snappish and failing. The big Maori shrugged as if to say, 'I tried.' Wincing at my slip in self-control, I turned to address the trickster. "I keep asking Click to share that trick with me, but apparently I'm not high enough in the club to learn the secret handshake."

".me beyond is it use don't you Why .so do to means the have You," he replied with a knowing nod.

"Aw, that cloak hates 'im, bruh." I gave Hemi a look of betrayal. "What? Truth hurts, eh?"

"Anyway," I said, stretching the word out to indicate a change of topic, "where the heck is Click?"

Heyókȟa laughed hysterically for several seconds, finally wiping tears from his eyes before he spoke. ".here I'm why not That's .way his on definitely is He"

"If he's laughing, it means he's serious," Hemi whispered to me behind his hand.

"Dude, for the last time, I get the whole 'backwards and reverse' thing."

The Maori frowned and raised his hands as if in surrender, saying nothing. That only made me feel worse, but I was feeling hellaciously irritated and damned confused about this whole mess. I'd apologize to Hemi later, after I'd figured out what was going on.

With a put upon sigh, I turned to address Heyókȟa once more. "Okay, so tell me this—has Click been captured?"

"Yes," he said, shaking his head in the affirmative.

I glanced at Hemi before he could comment. "So, no."

"Hey bro, I was just trying to be helpful."

I hid my face in my hand, rubbing my temples. "Sorry, it's just that I'm a little pissed at being tricked..."

That was when it hit me. Hemi and I shared a look, each of us nodding knowingly.

"Ya' thinking what I'm thinking?" the Maori warrior asked.

"Yup." I turned to Heyókȟa. "That's the entire point of this exercise, isn't it? Something or someone is #^$%ing with this timeline, and Click needs my help to fix it. Am I right?"

Heyókȟa shook his head in the negative. "No." Then he pointed above my head, frowning deeply. ".seen ever I've thing saddest the That's"

"Uh-huh, I'm aware. So, Click is off doing other stuff related to fixing said #$^%-ery with the timeline. Did he give you a message about where we're supposed to meet?"

".junkyard the not Definitely," Heyókȟa said as he swung his head in circles clockwise.

"Finally, we're getting somewhere," I muttered, turning to Hemi. "Jiminy Christmas, how'd you put up with that for the last three weeks?"

Hemi gave a halfhearted shrug. ".it to used get you, Eh"

HEMI OFFERED TO DRIVE, but with the way things were going, there was no way I was going cross-town in his hooptie. Not that I had anything against Japanese vehicles, but he was notoriously bad with a set of tools, and that car was mostly put together with JB Weld and duct tape. Whatever the curse was that was hanging over

Austin, I didn't want to risk getting stranded by riding in an unprotected vehicle. The Druidmobile was warded nine ways to Sunday, so the three of us hopped in, and off we went.

We were on the access road, heading onto IH-35, when I pointed at one of the ubiquitous billboards. "What's with those signs?"

Hemi's brow knit in confusion. "Whadya mean?"

"Like, when did they start showing up?"

"I dunno. They've always been there, haven't they?"

Heyókȟa sobbed a little in the back seat. ".probably, Years"

I glanced in the rearview mirror to gauge his expression, even as I checked my side-views to merge onto the deathtrap that was IH-35. "Ah, so it is a new thing. Even with all the time I spent, er, *elsewhere*, I can't have been gone but a few days, tops. There's no way those signs cropped up all over in that time, not without magical intervention. And what the heck is the Enlightened Society for Discord, anyway?"

"Ah, now that I can tell you," Hemi said as he reached for the stereo.

I smacked the back of his hand, warning him off from it. Best friend or no, if he didn't like Blind Lemon Jefferson, he could fuck off. Nope, that was the curse talking, probably. I managed to stop myself from saying it out loud, anyway. Yay, me.

"Anyway," Hemi continued, as if nothing had happened. "That outfit? Yeah, they're everywhere. Talk show circuit, morning news, fundraisers for politicians, busking on street corners—everywhere."

"Oh yeah?" I asked, turning only momentarily to address him. "So what are they, a cult or something—"

Hemi's eyes grew big as saucers as he gripped the dash hard enough to crack it. "Oi, look out!"

I'd only taken my eyes off the road for a moment, but we were trucking down IH-35 at highway speeds. Even with his warning, I slammed on the brakes just in time to screech to a halt, inches from the rear bumper of a late model Beemer. The Chad driving it stuck his head out the window, yelling obscenities at me as he flipped me the bird.

In response, I stuck my head out my window and yelled, "Aw, go back to California where you belong!"

"Classy," Hemi remarked.

Realizing what I'd just done, I took a deep breath to center myself, then I yelled again. "Sorry, it's just been a really cruddy day."

The guy stuck his head and shoulders out his window, turning to flip me the bird with both barrels in a feat that would challenge most circus contortionists. I waved cheerfully, painting a smile on my face, despite that I suddenly had the urge to rip his head off.

Up ahead, traffic was backed up for a good quarter mile. Cars were honking like crazy. As the congestion piled up behind us, every so often the sound of screeching tires, shattered glass, and crunching metal indicated other drivers hadn't been so lucky.

I happened to be in the far-right lane when traffic halted, so I inched my car around the ass end of Mr. Beemer and continued ahead on the shoulder. Rules didn't apply when you were trying to save the city, right? Anyway, I wanted to see what was holding us up.

As I passed cars on the shoulder, other drivers honked, cussed, and threw soda and coffee cups at us. "Get back on the road!" one driver yelled. "Think you're special? You're an idiot!" some Karen shouted in a shrill voice.

I ignored them all, barely keeping a lid on my anger as I neared the cause of the traffic jam. Farther down the highway, a wall of protestors had set up across the highway, stopping the flow of traffic by first draping a huge white flag from an overpass across all four lanes. The flag, or banner, or whatever it was, had a weird cross-shaped arrow symbol spray-painted in the center. No other words or messages could be seen on the flag, and apparently they assumed that onlookers would recognize the meaning of the symbol.

This had slowed the passing vehicles enough to allow roughly two dozen protestors to lock arms across the highway. Behind them, even more protestors backed them up, carrying signs that said, "DISCORD IS THE WAY" and "ORDER = LIES" along with the usual stuff about corporate greed and political corruption.

I was all for exposing greed and corruption. However, blocking traffic on the main north-south thoroughfare through town was a hell of a selfish way to bring attention to your cause. The more I thought about it, the angrier I got, until finally, I opened my door and hopped out.

"Be right back," I said, slamming the door behind me.

"Probably not a good idea," Hemi said as I walked away.

Of course, I ignored him, choosing instead to march up to the picket line. "Hey, you guys mind taking your little demonstration somewhere else?" I said to no one and everyone in particular.

"May the goddess put a twinkle in your eye," said a skinny dude in his early twenties. He'd styled his dishwater blonde hair in a man bun, and he was wearing a salmon pink designer V-neck, loose tan muslin pants, and Birkenstocks. The outfit looked both ridiculous and pretentious on him, all at once.

Here we go, a perfect example of the bougie-ass posers taking over Austin.

It was bad enough that this guy represented the new privileged class that had taken over the city, driving up rent and property values, which forced locals into the suburbs. Yet, it was the manner in which he spoke that really pissed me off. Although it sounded like a blessing of some sort, the way he said it indicated that the goddess could shit in my eye for all he cared. Not cool.

"I couldn't care less about your goddess, I just want to get—"

That was about all I managed to say before they started chanting to drown me out.

"Discord is life, no more strife! Discord is life, no more strife!"

"What? That doesn't make any sense," I responded. "Discord *is* strife, you morons!"

Instead of allowing me to speak, they simply chanted louder.

I got right up in Man Bun's face, so he could hear me. "You do realize that some of these people have to get to work, or pick up their kids from school or daycare, or whatever, right?"

Man Bun and his friends screeched even louder, drowning me out through sheer numbers and abject stupidity. I was about to clock him, then I came to my senses and realized I was in my stealth-shifted form. If I hit him, I'd probably kill the guy.

No bueno, Colin.

All this anger wasn't me. Something had to be pulling my strings, and I wanted to know what it was. I took a step back, hands held up in a gesture of peace. Even so, someone spat on me as I was turning to leave.

With a monumental display of self-control, I ignored the slight, marching back to the car stiff-backed as I counted to ten. Once I reached the Druidmobile, I leaned on the hood with both hands and dropped into a druid trance. Within seconds, I'd tapped into the wards I'd etched into the metal underneath the paint, reinforcing them with the Oak's magic. Then I expanded the ward barrier, pushing the anti-curse field out in a bubble that reached a few feet beyond the vehicle.

When the wards' effective range had expanded far enough to protect me and not just the vehicle, it was as if a dark cloud lifted. Instantly, I felt clearheaded for the first time since I'd left Rube's.

Earlier, I'd headed straight from Rube's to my Grove. It occurred to me that Rübezahl's lands were essentially in another dimension. It appeared that whatever this curse was, it couldn't affect me or my connection to the Oak while I was in Rube's demesne.

The Oak and Grove must've been elsewhere at that time, beyond the reach of this weird curse when I called them. It was only after I'd asked the Oak to take me to Hemi's that things got screwed up. We ended up at the junkyard instead because that was the closest safe place the Oak could take me.

Now that I was protected inside the Druidmobile's ward bubble, I had the wherewithal to use my mage sight. As soon as my vision shifted into the magical spectrum, I clearly saw what was causing my anger—and possibly the growing chaos across the city. Above us, three hideous creatures stood on the overpass, chanting curses in time with the humans below.

CHAPTER
EIGHT

That I hadn't noticed the trio before told me they were hidden behind a concealment glamour. I took a moment to analyze the magic they wove, emanating as it did from them in sickly, transparent red waves that spread out like ripples in a pond across the city. It took a lot to cast a curse like that, even as a linked coven, and it took more skill and power to do it without being found out by the local powers.

Meaning, these were no run-of-the-mill witches. Chances were good that they were ancient fae creatures, or perhaps even minor gods.

Great.

Regarding their appearances, they were lanky, hunchbacked, human-bird hybrids, repulsively ugly in a way that was almost hypnotizing. From the knees up they were more or less human, shaped like wizened old hags with sagging pale skin, pendulous breasts, bulging pot-bellies, and wrinkled, hook-nosed faces partially hidden by long, straggly gray hair. Dress them in Salvation Army clothes, and they'd be indistinguishable from any unfortunate, cart-pushing homeless person down on 7th and Neches.

It was their limbs that gave them away as being "other than" human. From the knees down they had the clawed, three-toed feet of raptors, covered in black scales that faded to pale yellow at the edges. Their arms were similarly avian, consisting of gangly, black-feathered wings that sprouted from their shoulder sockets. Each "wing" ended in a long, thin-fingered, nearly humanoid hand tipped with sharp black talons that gleamed in the afternoon sun.

In other words, they were harpies, which made me wonder what the hell a trio of human-vulture hybrids were doing in my city.

Typically, the supernatural creatures one found in a given area reflected the cultural roots of the local dominant populations. Celtic and Germanic fae we had in abundance, as well as a few creatures that originated from Central American folklore and legend, and some Afro-Caribbean beings as well. Yet, Austin wasn't known for its Greek population, and therefore we didn't have a lot of Greco-Roman species in the area.

Besides that, when it came to the fae everyone knew this was Maeve's city, and therefore dominated by her subjects. Thus, most of the supernatural species that settled around here originated from the British Isles and

Western Europe. Greco-Roman creatures generally didn't reside in Maeve's demesne, except in rare instances in which they'd received special dispensation.

And why was that? Because the fae were territorial as fuck, and they didn't like to share space with other creatures or races. It went without saying that the equilibrium the vamps, 'thropes, and fae had reached in Austin was an anomaly, one only achieved due to the foresight and leadership of Luther, Samson, and Maeve. Go to any other major city, and what you'd find is that one species or faction dominated the local area.

In New Orleans it was the vamps, same for Dallas, although the two covens couldn't be more different. San Antonio was also part of Maeve's territory, but south of that it started getting iffy, with hedge witches, lay sorcerers, and creatures of Mesoamerican origin dominating the landscape. And Houston? All we knew was that something deadly lived there, and it didn't allow *anything* else to encroach on its territory.

These three hags definitely did not belong, and the fact they were here causing trouble unopposed really pissed me off. Where the hell were Maeve, Luther, and the Austin Pack, never mind The Circle and Cerberus? Click would likely have those answers waiting for me back at the junkyard. For now, it would be up to me to deal with these interlopers.

Well, not completely on my lonesome, since I had Hemi to back me up. As for Heyókȟa? I was about as likely to get an assist from him as I was to get an invitation to The White House.

The gods disliked getting involved in territorial disputes, at least not directly. Which was how I ended up getting pulled into shit like this current mess. The immortal powers that be just loved to manipulate hapless, unsuspecting assholes like yours truly to do their dirty work. Maeve had done it to me for years until I screwed her over well and good, then Click sucked me into his schemes after the old man passed on.

So, it'd be me and Hemi against three powerful spell-casting demi-deities. Truth was, I liked those odds.

The big Maori warrior had already stepped out of the car, and while his ink wasn't glowing yet, I could tell he was gearing up for a scrape. Up ahead on the overpass, the harpies held their grotesque, feathered arms in the air as they continued to chant their spell of discord and confusion over the local populace. The fact they were casting it together made me wonder whether taking out one would break the spell. It was worth a shot.

"Those three the reason everyone's all bent out of shape?" Hemi asked, his voice almost casually neutral as he inclined his head toward the overpass.

"Looks that way," I replied. "FYI, once we leave this ward bubble, we'll likely be exposed to their curse again."

"Eh, I got protections for that, yeah?" he replied. "Once they're activated, I should be good. You?"

I stroked my chin as I considered the problem at hand. "The good news is that they're so focused on casting that spell, they haven't seen us yet."

"Or they think we're beneath their notice," Hemi said.

"Um, right. The bad news is that I'm worried they'll direct the full force of that spell at us after we attack. The vibes they're sending out were nearly enough to make me bash Man Bun's skull in over there. I'd hate to think of the carnage that might result if I did a full shift under the influence of the hate magic they're casting."

"So, what do we do?"

"Give me a sec, I'm thinking." The kernel of an idea began to form in the recesses of my mind. As it wriggled to the forefront of my consciousness, I snapped my fingers as a smile crept across my face. "The plan is, we play this like an MMO."

WATCHING Hemi and Heyókȟa playing earlier gave me the idea for how we might defeat these harpies. Hemi would be protected from the spell while the wards in his ink were active, so I only had to worry about avoiding the effects of the curse myself. That meant staying inside my little ward barrier, which naturally limited my ability to engage the enemy at close range.

However, I wasn't just a druid-trained hunter anymore—I was a druid master. A wet behind the ears druid master, but still, and I needed to start thinking like one. Back in the day, druids rarely engaged in hand-to-hand combat, instead opting to use ranged spells on the battlefield whilst the *fianna* handled the sword and spear work.

Which was precisely what we were about to do. A broad smile split Hemi's face as my plan dawned on him. "Tank," he said, pointing a thumb at his chest. Then he stabbed an index finger at me. "Ranged attack and AOE."

"You got it, my man," I said. "But first we need to get rid of the protesters and the traffic."

I looked up and down the freeway, trying to find a means of doing both. Before long, I found what I needed nearby, at a construction site along the IH-35 downtown corridor. For years, skyscrapers had been going up in the city just as fast as developers could bribe the council to approve them. For the most part, they ruined the skyline and increased property taxes in the area, as only millionaires could afford to live in the damned things.

As a consequence of their construction, there were always a handful of mega-cranes set up to lift heavy steel girders and concrete to the top floors of those buildings. One of them happened to be set up close enough to the highway to fall right next to the overpass. That is, with a little druidic assistance.

First, I reached out with my druid senses, connecting with a pigeon that had roosted atop the crane's massive arm. Looking through the bird's eyes, I checked to make certain no one was in the cab or below it along the path where I intended to drop it. Once I was certain no one would be hurt, I began calling a gale from the west, up from Ladybird Lake and through the buildings downtown, causing it to pick up speed as it reached the precariously positioned construction crane.

Soon, the thing started swaying in the hurricane force winds. I cupped my hands around my mouth, adding a bit of magic to my voice to be heard over the chants of the protesters. "Look out—that crane is about to fall over!"

The increasing winds had already caused the protesters to lose some steam, as they were getting pelted with sand, small pebbles, and other debris that was being blown from the shoulder of the freeway. It didn't take much to get their attention after that, and soon they were pointing, screaming, and then scattering away from the apparent fall zone of the teetering monstrosity.

Likewise, motorists who were stuck in the traffic jam either took the opportunity to drive through the banner that hung off the overpass, or they exited the freeway by driving over the shoulder into the grass. Soon the sign was shredded, and the area was clear. Unfortunately, all that commotion had garnered the attention of the harpies, who were now staring daggers at me from the overpass ahead.

"How dare you interfere with the work of the Neikieia?" the tallest of them shrieked. "We who serve the goddess in her divine mission?"

"Ugh," I grunted as I glanced over at Hemi. "Why do these @$$#^%$ always affect that fake formal language?"

Hemi squinted with one eye as he considered my question. "Inflated sense of self-importance?"

"How about we disabuse them of that?" I replied. "Coming in hot in three... two... one."

On cue, the westernmost support cables securing the crane snapped with a loud, metallic report and twanging noise. The crane arm tilted as the metal arms at the base groaned under the uneven load. Finally, one of the legs gave way, and the whole thing fell like a giant tree, right toward the overpass where the harpies stood.

"Tiiiimmmmm-berrrrrrr!" I shouted, just before the crane arm crashed into the bridge.

WHILE I THOUGHT the whole "crashing a crane into the overpass" thing was hilarious, the harpies did not find it so amusing. Although I'd hoped to crush at least one of them in the effort, luck was not on my side. The harpies, or "Neikieia," as the apparent leader had referred to themselves as, turned out to be incredibly agile.

Just before the crane hit the bridge, the trio scattered in all directions. The leader launched herself off the side, and with a mighty sweep of her wings she soared into the sky. The other two somersaulted in either direction, easily avoiding the falling length of structurally welded steel and cable.

"Huh," I said, scratching my head. "I guess having wings and hollow bones is as useful for harpies as it is for supervillains."

"Yup," Hemi remarked as his tattoos lit up with a light blue phosphorescence all over his body. Hemi pointed with a long, axe-shaped club, a weapon he'd magically produced while I was focused on the crane. "Incoming, mate."

The lead harpy hovered about thirty feet above us, and just as I tracked her position, she released a three-foot wide fireball in my direction. Hemi dove away, rolling and coming to his feet in one smooth motion as he sprinted after one of the other, still earthbound, harpies.

Meanwhile, I had the fireball to deal with. I could have left the Druidmobile's ward bubble to handle it. However, using the anti-fire magic I'd woven into the wards would weaken the overall protection they provided against the curse the witches had cast. Waves of angry red energy were still floating in the air all around, telling me the curse possessed some staying power. Since it appeared that I'd need my car's wards to protect my mind, I chose to handle the fireball directly.

The major drawback to druid magic was that, although it was perhaps the most powerful of all magical schools, it took time and preparation to use. But the cool thing about it was that a druid could rather easily draw on any existing energy source and turn it to their advantage. Obviously, birdbrain numero uno up there didn't realize she was dealing with a druid, else she wouldn't have sent that fireball my way.

With a thought and a gesture, I created an absorption barrier in front of my extended palm, collecting the spell's heat and energy before it could reach me and detonate. Once I had control of the witch's spell, I sent it right back at her in the form of a single, disorganized burst of flame.

Even as she dodged the blast, the harpy squawked in surprise at how quickly I'd reversed her spell. Unfortunately for her, she didn't move fast enough, and I managed to singe the feathers from under half of her left wing. With a screech, she began to lose altitude, spiraling to the earth some three-dozen feet below her.

Figuring she'd impact the asphalt with enough force to at least temporarily incapacitate her, I turned my attention to how Hemi was faring. Beneath the overpass and out of the line of sight of spectators, he was engaged in mortal combat with the other two harpies. Hemi spun his club like a baton twirler, stepping and pivoting to avoid claw swipes while snapping the club out in attacks that would easily shatter bone should they connect.

However, the harpies were more agile than he was, if not faster. Using their wings and ability to fly to their advantage, they each flipped and twisted away from Hemi's attacks, diving and spinning back in to swipe or kick at him with their deadly claws.

If the Maori was only dealing with one of them, he'd already have ended the fight. However, the avian-human hybrids had obviously fought together on many occasions, and they timed their attacks perfectly, so my friend was always defending high on one side and low on the other. This forced him to move in ways that prevented him from pressing his attacks.

"Enough of that shit," I muttered. "Magic artillery to the rescue!"

I had several decent spells at my disposal, including a few vicious druid battle spells that could absolutely wreck most supernatural creatures. However, I was dealing with extremely agile enemies who could probably dodge most standard attacks. Plus, Hemi was in close proximity to them, so I had to make sure I didn't hit him accidentally.

Fighting vampires for months on end in the Hellpocalypse had taught me how to deal with supernaturally quick and agile foes. My go-to attack for vamps was a sunlight spell that I could cast over an entire area, or in a single beam of intense light at one target. However, I could only store so much sunlight, and it usually ran out after the first or second use. But there was another elemental spell that I had almost unlimited access to, even under the stress of battle.

Lightning it is, then.

While most magic users formed lightning spells from sheer magical energy, druids used energy from nature. Thankfully, there was almost always an excess of static electricity in the atmosphere. And where there wasn't, a skilled druid could make their own.

I started by gathering electricity from the surrounding air, gathering it in between my hands, and then letting it go at the nearest harpy. Lightning moves at 270,000 miles an hour, so there was no way that bitch was going to dodge my lightning bolt.

KERBLAM!

The spell hit with a thunderclap, nailing the winged witch between the shoulder blades and sending her sprawling. She tumbled ass over teakettle, stopping fifteen feet away where she landed in a smoldering heap. While that one might have still been breathing, she sure as shit wasn't moving.

One down, two to go.

I was just about to put the whammy on the second one, when I got hit by a freight train from behind. The next thing I knew, I was outside my ward bubble with one-hundred-fifty pounds of screeching, clawing harpy in my face. A buck-fifty might not sound like much, but when it moves like a hellcat and can bench press a Buick, it's a handful. I'm about two-ten in my fully human form and close to four-hundred when I stealth-shift, and I was still having a hard time grappling that crazy half-human, half-vulture broad.

"Bee-yotch, get off me!" I growled as I grabbed her by the throat and pushed her at arm's length to keep those claws away from my eyes.

"We are children of the goddess, mortal," she screeched. "Who are you to interfere with our work?"

"Yeah, yeah," I said as I grabbed one of her weird wing arms by the wrist to prevent her from slashing my face. "Clod, god, shmod. To me, you're just another monster."

With that, I twisted and pulled on her arm, using her neck as my anchor point in an effort to rip her wing off. She had a hell of a wingspan, though, and she was clawing the shit out of me with her other hand. Seeing that I wasn't going to have enough space to yank her shoulder out of socket before she rearranged my face with her other hand, I decided to change tactics.

Letting go of her neck with my left hand, I jumped into a flying arm-bar. I leapt up and wrapped my legs around the backside of her left wing-arm thingy as I spun to get my ass close to her shoulder and my legs across her face and chest. Once I was in position, I clamped my knees together to keep the witch from twisting out. Then I arched my back and cranked on her elbow for all I was worth.

Snap-crack-pop! went her arm as I hyperextended her elbow while simultaneously snapping her radius and ulna. Despite the creature's strength, the arm gave surprisingly easily. Maybe it was the hollow bones or something, I wasn't certain. What I did know was that monsters with osteoporosis shouldn't get into grappling matches with half-Fomorian druids.

By this time, the witch was screaming bloody murder. She was clawing me with her other hand while chewing the shit out of my leg in between shouting curses in Greek. That just pissed me off. The latent effects of the spell she and her sisters had cast now worked against her, because my Fomorian side was coming out. And wouldn't you know it, my Hyde-side had come down with a case of the fuck-its.

"That's it," I growled as my voice grew deeper and my muscles started bulging in odd places.

The plan had been to avoid fully shifting into my *other*, other form, and I really did not want to complete my change. For starters, it hurt like hell to shift on the fly, what with the bones rearranging, the skin tearing, and the muscles stretching and growing all over again.

Moreover, I didn't know if I could control myself while in that form—not with these witches casting rage curses all over the place. What I really needed was to let off some steam. So, I did the only thing that seemed proper at the time.

I ripped that ugly hag's arm off.

Yeah, I know—that's messed up. But, that's not even the half of it. When I snapped her forearm, that became the weakest part of her wing. When I yanked and twisted on it, her wing-arm thingy tore, right there at the break.

I ended up with a taloned hand and one-third of a large vulture's wing in my hands, and she ended up with a bloody, spurting stump. Wow, but did she flip her stack at that.

I had to hand it to her, most sentient creatures would pass out, or go into shock, or just go limp after sustaining an injury like that. But this chick? She was definitely cut from sterner stuff. She took that bloody stump and punched me with it, right in the nuts.

Yeah, it was ugly. Getting stabbed in the jewels with jagged shards of bone was not my idea of a good time. I roared and kicked her across the freeway, and then I focused on shifting all the way.

By the time I finished shifting, the one I'd been tangling with was limping through a portal. Meanwhile, the third harpy was carrying the one I'd zapped and flying off toward the horizon. Since the third witch had to use her wing-arms to fly, she'd latched onto her sister by digging her taloned feet into her shoulders. It did not look very comfortable, but the one I'd zapped was still unconscious, so I guess she didn't mind.

On the downside, my sack was a bloody mess, and I was pissed as all hell. Of course, I rushed after the one who cold-cocked me in the nuts, but I was too slow. She made it through the portal, and it snapped shut before I could reach her. I was still holding on to the witch's wing, so I turned and pitched it at the other two—just in time for it to disappear into another portal that opened in the sky in front of them.

As the portal closed, Hemi strolled up, wiping blood from his club with a rag. "Maybe next time, I should be on ranged support, eh mate?"

CHAPTER
NINE

When we finally arrived at the junkyard, the gate was shut but unlocked. Someone had taped a sign that said, "Closed due to staff emergency" over the hours and contact info. I figured it was Maureen, and felt a bit of unexpected relief that she might be present.

After parking the Druidmobile behind the office and out of sight—look away spells worked on mortals, but they weren't foolproof against demi-human witches—I led our trio into the office. There I found Maureen and Fallyn sharing conversation over a cup of coffee.

"Well, look what the cat dragged in," my erstwhile nanny, personal assistant, proxy junkyard manager, and former swordsmanship trainer said. "An' from the looks of ya', it's been nuthin' but fun and games on this lovely day."

"Hi Maureen," I said by way of acknowledgement.

The half-kelpie's gaze flicked to Fallyn, so I took the hint and approached my girlfriend. I'd been gone from this timeline for six months, after all. Without saying a word, I approached her from the side, as she was still facing Maureen—ignoring me, natch—and I kissed her on the cheek.

"Sorry for taking so long to return," I whispered.

Her expression softened slightly, but the tightness around her eyes told me I had some work to do. "We can talk about it later, after you're caught up on what's been going on in your absence."

"Alright," I said, stepping back and taking in Hemi and Heyókȟa in a broad sweep of my arm. "Of course, you two know Hemi. The distinguished gentlemen accompanying us is Heyókȟa."

Of all the things I'd expect from that dodgy old trickster, the last was what he did next. As soon as I introduced him, he was across the room and on one knee in front of Maureen, holding her hand.

".me Marry," he said.

Maureen's eyes narrowed as she addressed me, but the barest smile played around her lips as she spoke. "Colin, what's this tosser about?"

Hemi cleared his throat. "The bloke does everything backwards and in reverse."

Maureen's crooked smile broadened, although her tone said she was as annoyed as she was amused. "Ah, so he's flirtin' then." She patted his hand before letting it go in the gentle manner of someone who's humoring an eccentric. "Charmed, I'm sure."

That seemed to mollify the clown god. He stood and walked backwards to the coffee station, where he poured three packets of sugar and two creams in his mouth, swallowing them before drinking hot coffee out of the pot.

Fallyn snickered as Maureen gave Heyókȟa the side-eye. Already having become accustomed to the trickster's antics, I hopped my ass up on the counter as I addressed the ladies.

"Hemi was filling me in on the way over, before we were interrupted by three spell-casting harpies and the most idiotic picket line I've ever seen. Anyone want to tell me what the hell has been going on since I left?"

Click's voice piped up behind me—of course, he'd been there all along. "Mayhaps I kin' address that question."

"Nice of you to join the party," I said as I glanced over my shoulder.

He wagged a finger at me in protest. "Now, now—if 'yer insinuatin' that I abandoned ya', I'll direct 'yer attention ta' the fact that I sent Heyókȟa along in my stead."

"I fail to see how that helped," I remarked drily. "He's about as useful in a fight as an umbrella stand in Dubai. All he does is sit there and look like that." I glanced over at Heyókȟa, who was now chewing up coffee beans and swallowing them. "No offense."

".me about things such say should you that incensed I'm," he replied around a mouthful of coffee beans. ".out helped I why that's, time difficult a having were you like looked You"

"Hey, I get it. Even a trickster god's hands can be tied by politics." I turned my gaze on Click. "So you sent help, and apparently weeks ago. Mind telling me what the ruse regarding Fallyn's kidnapping was all about?"

Click's expression soured. "As if there were any way I'd get 'ya ta' abandon that fool quest o' yer's, wit' out tellin' ya' a damsel were in danger."

Fallyn harrumphed and muttered something to the effect of, *'Wasn't enough to keep him from going.'* I ignored her, operating in the full knowledge that I'd have to work my way out of the doghouse.

"Fair enough," I said. "Answer me this, then: What's the deal with the Enlightened Society of Discord? Why are Maeve, Luther, and the Pack letting a trio of Greek demi-creatures cast a curse over the city? And, why is the junkyard closed on a weekday?"

"It's all related, lad," Maureen said. "Things changed when ya' left, although none o' us noticed due ta' the nature o' that change."

Sensing that the conversation was about to drift into the delicate topic of time travel, I coughed into my hand. Maureen frowned and dismissed my concern with a wave of her hand.

"Aw, relax. The magician's filled me in already, an' it's not like 'yer girl don't know about 'yer extracurricular activities." She pointed at Hemi. "If he doesn't know yet, he's likely already figured it out, and the clown god's volunteered ta' submit ta' a geas o' secrecy."

I scratched my head. "So everyone here knows I can time travel."

"If ya' kin call the blunderin' ye've been doin' time travel," Click muttered.

"Oh, please," I said as I sat a little straighter. "I performed every single jump under your close supervision. If I've made any mistakes, the fault's as much yours as it is mine."

Click crossed his arms and clammed up, but Fallyn rolled her eyes and sighed. "That's why he's so upset. Mister 'I am the greatest magician of all eternity who can see the future and time travel' couldn't see that you two got hoodwinked into jacking up this timeline. Now he's miffed that he has to admit he screwed up."

"Oh? Do tell," I commented as I turned my gaze on Click.

The quasi-god's boyish face reddened as Fallyn continued. "Apparently he let you get manipulated into leaving the timeline at a very inopportune juncture. You know how you ended up there six months longer than you were supposed to be gone? Yeah, the plan was for you to die there."

"Which Click warned me of, and which I dealt with before returning," I interjected.

Fallyn gave me the 'don't interrupt me while I'm

proving I was right' look. "Yeah, but you were still gone for six months. Click couldn't bring you back to the exact point of your departure, because of quantum physics or some shit. I guess once your future becomes your past, you can't change it. And while you were gone, one of their number went rogue and sent this timeline into disarray, big time."

"Meaning, one of the tricksters?" I asked.

"Righto, boyo," Maureen said. "An' she planned the whole thing, right under Gwydion's nose."

"B-but how were I ta' see what she'd planned?" Click sputtered. "The woman is chaos personified—there's no way ta' see down paths that ha'nt been created or e'en thought o' yet."

"Wait a minute—you guys are saying that Eris is behind all this?"

".genius a is boy The," Heyókȟa said as he dumped a fresh pot of coffee into the trash.

THEY SPENT the next five minutes filling me in on what happened since I left for the Hellpocalypse. While Fallyn was on assignment, her mother had returned to Switzerland. That left Samson as the de facto alpha over the Austin Pack until his daughter's return.

Meanwhile, Maeve had disappeared, and no one had heard from her or her court for months. With Leto and I gone, Maeve MIA, and no other gods or titans around to stop her, Eris saw a hell of an opportunity in that power vacuum. That's when the goddess of discord made her move.

Eris' influence had quietly, insidiously spread across the city, happening gradually, so nobody even noticed the change. True to form, she sowed discord everywhere she went, including between the factions. Petty little arguments eventually turned into major disagreements, and now the vampire and werewolf factions weren't even communicating with each other.

Because the whole thing involved time magic, and exposing Eris' plot would likely reveal I'd been using it, they'd refrained from telling anyone else what was happening. Although Eris obviously knew my secret, she wouldn't dare risk running afoul of the other tricksters by ratting one of her own out. According to Click, the Trickster's local wouldn't get involved until they convened and voted that Eris was in violation of their charter.

The question was, where was Maeve? Although it wasn't common knowledge, Maeve was the goddess Niamh, a daughter of Manannán mac Lir. No way would she let another goddess encroach on her turf. Unless, of course, Maeve had become indisposed. If so, that would leave us to deal with the mess ourselves.

After all the cards had been laid on the table, everyone but Click and I had left the office so we two could speak in private. When it came to time magic, there were some things that were for chronomancers' ears only. Click said that just knowing certain secrets could place my friends or the timeline in danger.

That seemed like pretty much the same thing in the latter case, but I didn't bother pointing that out to him. Although the magician was surprisingly lucid at the moment, he was in enough of a tizzy as it was. Getting outmaneuvered by Eris had really bruised his ego, and I saw no sense in upsetting him further.

"Let me get this straight," I said as I used druid magic to sanitize and clean the coffee pot, machine, and station. A little heat, some ionizing particles, and voilà —a clean coffee pot. "Eris got me out of the way just so she could start a cult?"

Click shook his head. "Nay, lad—she gotcha' out o' the way so she could sow discord. The worship is jest a side benefit."

"Okay. Call me slow—"

"You're slow," he interjected.

"Gee, thanks," I said, thinking that maybe I *should* rub in how Eris had gotten the better of him. "As I was saying—I thought you tricksters liked sowing chaos and stuff. Not that I approve of what she's doing, but why would you be opposed to her plan?"

"Because, chaos an' trickery must serve the greater good. 'Tis in the charter."

"Seriously? You mean to tell me that all the crap that Loki, Coyote, Veles, and all the rest of you pulled was for the greater good?"

"'Course not, don't be daft. We formed the locals in

latter years, ta' oppose those gods who thought they'd upset the natural evolution o' humanity by forcin' 'em back inta' worship an' slavery."

"Ah—so Eris is of that faction." I returned the coffee pot to the machine, replacing the filter with a new one, full of fresh grounds. After flipping the switch, I knuckled the pressure point between my eyes—it seemed I was getting a headache from lack of caffeine. "I still don't understand why she needed me out of the picture."

"Cuz' yer' pivotal ta' this timeline—this bein' the primary one. All others branch off o' this line, an' ye've become a sort o' fulcrum point fer' this main branch o' the Paths. That placed ya' in direct opposition ta' her plans, meanin' she'd hafta' face ya' in combat at some juncture. Getting' ya' out o' the way was apparently her preferred response."

"So she's a schemer, not a fighter."

"Egg-zactly," he replied. "An' she has cousins n' kiddos fer that—a ton o' them, each one nastier than the last."

"Three of which we met on the way over here." Click gave a curt nod. I stroked my chin as I thought through the preceding revelations. "And you can't predict anything she's planning?"

"Nay. She's pure chaos, flies by the seat o' her drawers. Makes her absolutely unpredictable." He tapped the side of his nose with his index finger before pointing at me. "Which is also why she fears ya' so much, an' likely why ya' find yerself in opposition ta' her."

"Oh?" I said as I poured myself a hot cup of java. "Do tell."

"Druids have always abided by natural laws. Order is sort o' yer' thing. As it happens, yer' choices have placed ya' in a position ta' champion law an' order. So, ye've unwittingly become her nemesis."

I'd just taken a sip of coffee, and nearly did a spit-take at that. "Uh-uh, nope. I mean, I'll happily kick her kin out of Austin and even send them across the Veil if necessary. But I'll be damned if I get roped into doing the gods' bidding one more time."

Click closed his eyes and shook his head slowly. "S'not that simple, Colin. Time an' fate have a way o' flowing a natural course, an' our choices dictate it as it happens. Yer' course is determined by the very nature o' yer' previous actions. Whether ya' like it or not, yer' a champion o' order in this timeline."

I set my coffee cup down on the counter, then I rubbed a hand over my face. "Isn't there some god or goddess of law and order out there who can do this instead? Like, someone who was Eris' natural enemy way back in the day?"

Click tsked. "Unfortunately, none who care ta' bother. That's the thing wit' gods in an age o' disbelief. Many o' the ones who should care have moved on an' lost interest in the mortal world. Others chose ta' fade away, across the Veil fer good. But the universe abhors a vacuum, an' someone always seems ta' step up ta' do what needs ta' be done."

"You keep telling me I volunteered," I sighed. "Why does it feel like I'm being voluntold?"

He clapped a hand on my shoulder. "I've been 'round a long time, lad, an' here's what I've come ta' believe. Forces greater than the gods are always an' ever movin' behind the scenes ta' keep things from flying apart at the seams."

"I have to admit, the idea that there's a benevolent force far greater than the gods is appealing. I suppose that's what keeps me attending mass."

Click looked like he'd just tasted sour milk. "Bleh. I doubt it's intelligent in the way you an' I think. Way I see it, 'tis more like a universal consciousness that keeps checks an' balances, despite what we ephemeral bein's get up ta' down here."

"A 'universal consciousness'? That sounds like B.S. to me."

"So do lots o' things, lad. An' yet, ya' recently met Santa Claus. Explain that one, why don'cha?"

"Good point." I held the coffee mug up to my nose, breathing deeply while seeking some calm in the pleasant and familiar. "Then tell me, what's the plan?"

"Like many deities, Eris' powers are limited by her province an' how she's invested them o'er the eons. Some o' the gods choose ta' consolidate their power inta' objects that allow them ta' focus their abilities. Lucky fer' us, she's jest such a deity."

"Seems like a tactical error waiting to happen," I said. "Lose your doohickey, and you lose a lot of your power."

Click snapped his fingers and pointed at me. "Precisely so. Many a deity has fallen from the heights fer' that very reason. An' as it happens, Eris invested a great deal o' her power inta' jest' such an object."

"Troy," I said, remembering one of the old man's mythology lessons. "She caused that whole thing."

"Zeus gave her the idea, but yes. An' while the legends say she tossed the Apple inta' their midst, that'd ne'er happen. 'Twas more like she brought it in the room, and its influence made the goddesses an' mortals do stupid things."

"An artifact like that is not something a goddess would just leave lying around. Not even a goddess of chaos would be that careless."

"Still, 'tis the key ta' her power. If we kin locate it an' abscond with same, we'd foil her in one fell swoop." He tapped a finger on his lips. "First tho', we need ta' stymie her local help. Since she's in hidin', there must be someone else pullin' the strings. First order o' business is findin' 'em and dealin' wit' 'em accordingly."

"So, we're looking for her lieutenant—or lieutenants, plural." I sighed. "Where do we start?"

"Fer' the sake o' secrecy, we may need ta' traverse Rübezahl's realm, so ya' may as well fulfill yer' deal with him. Start there, an' while yer' busy, I'll do some diggin' inta' where Eris' offspring are laid up when they're not castin' curses and stirring up the natives."

"In other words, I do the hard work while you get the cushy assignment."

Click clucked his tongue. "When ya' gain the ability ta' turn invisible an' snoop around undetected amongst gods an' men, ya' let me know. Til' then, yer' on shit patrol."

CHAPTER
TEN

"Hey Fallyn, you got a minute?"

She nodded rather noncommittally. That had me worried, but at least she followed me outside.

After Click and I finished our discussion, we all met up back in the warehouse. Maureen and I had gear and weapons hidden there, so everyone was kitting up for their individual assignments from our stash.

Hemi, Fallyn, and I were going after Rube's errant godlet to get back his whatzamathingy, Click and Heyókȟa would attempt to track down Eris through her children, and Maureen was going to keep an eye on things around the junkyard.

It seemed kind of a waste to leave Maureen behind, as she was hell on wheels with a blade. But she'd volunteered for the job, citing age and a general dislike of dealing with gods. I frequently forgot how old she was, as she still looked like a woman in her late twenties, if that. Anyway, she did more for me than any human ever had, so if she wanted to pull seniority to get her pick of assignments, she'd earned the right.

While Hemi helped Maureen set up various traps and hide weapons around the junkyard, I walked with Fallyn to the Oak. There was definitely an awkward silence between us, but she soon broke it by blurting out an obviously planned protest.

"I'm not going to just sneak away to the Grove with you and act like nothing happened. If that's what you're thinking, that is," she added as she pursed her lips and crossed her arms over her chest.

"I just want to talk. Honest."

Not that I wouldn't mind getting away for some alone time with her, but for me, it'd only been a few weeks since I left. For her, it'd been six months of not knowing when I was coming back. Honestly, I couldn't blame her for being pissed.

She must not have expected me to be so agreeable, but my experiences during my absence had given me plenty of perspective on life in general, and Fallyn in particular. Living in the Hellpocalypse would do that to a person. There was nothing like living with the sword of Damocles hanging over your head daily to make you sit up and appreciate the people who cared for you.

Fallyn cocked her head as she scrutinized me for a moment, then she glanced away as her scrutiny gave way to frustration. "It's difficult, you know, loving you. I used to criticize Belladonna for failing to give you the benefit of a doubt, but now I'm starting to see what she must've gone through with you."

"I get that," I said.

"Do you?" She turned on me suddenly, and I wasn't sure if she was going to hit me or hug me. "Did you know that wolves mate for life? No? Well, we do. Once we choose a partner, that's it until someone dies."

She'd mentioned something to that effect before, but I'd just thought she was being dramatic. Damn. Despite what I'd said when I was kidding around with Hemi, I wasn't sure I was completely ready for that kind of commitment. However, I also wasn't about to leave Fallyn, either.

"Then I guess it was hard for you, not knowing if or when I was coming back."

"You think? And I warned you not to go. Hell, I even split by taking an assignment from Mom, thinking you'd reconsider once you saw how pissed I was. But did you wait around, or follow me? Nope. You took off anyway, not just to another city or country, but to another freaking timeline."

I tongued a molar as I struggled to find the right words. It was then I realized that there were no right words at times like these. Sometimes, you just had to do the best you could with words that failed to convey all the conflicting emotions you felt inside.

"All I can say is that I'm sorry. I thought I'd be able

to leave and come back moments later, and you'd hardly know I was gone."

She chuckled humorlessly. "Did you? Honestly, Colin, do you ever expect any of your plans to work out exactly the way you hope they will?"

I suddenly found that my shoes were very, very interesting. "No, I guess I don't."

"That's what I thought," she replied.

Man, this is not going the way I thought it would.

"Fallyn, please look at me," I said as I attempted to attract her gaze. She glanced at me and looked away again, mouth set and arms crossed, so I trudged on. "What I'm about to say is not an excuse, so please don't take it that way."

"That's going to be tough," she snarked.

I resisted the urge to sigh, pressing on. "You're absolutely right, I typically don't expect things to go my way. After my dad died, I learned not to hope too much. Instead, I just started expecting things to go to shit, no matter how much I wanted them to go otherwise."

She grimaced. "This sounds suspiciously like excuse-making to me."

I hung my head as I exhaled heavily. "I'm just stating facts. My mom checked out on me after dad's passing, and until I met Jesse, I didn't have a friend in the world. Once the old man and Maureen started looking out for me, things got a little better.

"Well, things were still shit because the fae had a hard-on for killing me, but at least I knew of two people in the world who cared for me—three including Jesse. But still, I knew deep down that no matter how much I tried or how hard I wished, my life was always going to take a sharp left turn into misery, just as soon as things started going my way."

Fallyn's shoulders relaxed slightly. "That's—that's just sad."

"Meh. Lots of people suffer, and my suffering isn't anything special. You know the rest. Jesse died, and at my hands. Finnegas turned to the needle, fairly abandoning me because he couldn't admit how much he blamed me for her death. Maureen tried to fill the gap, but she was raised by the fae, and you know how good they are at being human."

"Colin—"

I held up a hand. "Wait, let me finish. I lost my will to live, then I attempted suicide, many times and in many different ways. The shitty thing was, my Hyde-side wouldn't let me die. So, I hid here behind six acres of rusting steel and druidic wards, and I learned to cope. But guess what? People came along to help me find my way. Ed and Sabine, primarily."

She was staring at me now with a look of shocked disbelief on her face. "I didn't even think about them—about what happened to them, I mean."

"It's okay. But I realized something in losing them, and that was how the people close to me would always be in danger. It's the Fomorian in me, you see. We attract death and mayhem—heck, we're magnets for it.

Plus, my Fomorian blood makes me an enemy of the fae by default. There's history there, genetic and otherwise, that simply cannot be denied."

She had a faraway look in her eyes as she replied. "As the daughter of a titan, I get that."

"I figured you would. Unfortunately, Dad didn't survive being a McCool who married a Fomorian. Likewise, Ed, Sabine, and Jesse weren't strong enough to survive being around me." I reached for her hand, slowly, like I was reaching out to a skittish, wild creature. "Belladonna had pushed me away, and I figured I was done with relationships. Then you came along."

"And?"

"I wasn't afraid of losing someone I loved anymore, for the first time in a long time. Sure, Belladonna's a fighter, but she couldn't accept me for who I am. You did, and from the moment we started dating I knew you were tough enough to hang with my crazy life. Tougher than me, even."

"Wow. Thanks, I guess?" At least she smiled when she said it.

"You know what's nuts? Even when Click had me believing that some crazy deity had kidnapped you, I wasn't worried. That's because I was thinking, 'Dang, they don't know who they're messing with. That's Samson's daughter, the baddest alpha I've ever known. She's Leto's daughter, a fricking titan who makes alphas come to heel. By the time I find her, she'll probably have kicked that stupid god's butt and have it crying like a little bee-yotch."

"Probably," she said with a genuine chuckle.

"So yeah, I figured you were strong enough to make this work." I gently lifted her chin, so she was looking me in the eyes. "But if that's not the case, it's okay—more than okay. I'll still love you even if you decide you have to bail. Because I don't want you to feel like you're stuck with me, ever. By the same token, don't expect me to change for you, because I can't."

"I know, and I already told you I wasn't going to try to change you."

"Yes, you did. But I'm saying I won't hold you to any past promises you made, because the things I'm about to attempt are going to make everything else look like child's play."

Fallyn looked at me through slitted eyes. "You mean going after Eris?"

"Naw. Not that I think she'll be a cakewalk, but she's just one goddess. No, I'm talking about carrying the druidic tradition forward. I think the old man had plans for me, stuff he couldn't do because his hands were tied. Me? I never made the deals he made with the gods, so I'm free to do my own thing."

"I'm not sure I'm liking where this is going," she said as her mouth twisted into a lopsided frown.

"To be honest, me neither. But the Dagda and Finnegas entrusted me with the future of druidry, and for the first time I'm starting to realize how important that is to humanity. Just look at what one piddly little goddess can do without checks and balances in place to stop her. She's disrupted an entire city, all because there's nothing and no one to keep her from doing what she pleases."

"And what? You're going to be the stop-gap between humans and the gods? C'mon, Colin. You and I both know that one person, even you, can't prevent them from doing what they want."

"You're right. One person can't."

Her eyes narrowed even further, and she bit her lip as she stared at me. "Shit, you're thinking of bringing them back. Colin, Mom told me what the gods did to the druids the last time they became a threat to the pantheons. You think they're going to sit around and let you train a bunch of druids up just so you can oppose their power?"

"Of course not. But I have a plan, or at least the beginnings of one. It'll require me to go places and do things that you might not like. I'm telling you this now because you didn't sign up for that, so I'm not holding you to your past commitments."

She hung her head, covering her eyes with one hand. When she looked up, incredulity was written across her face. "Did you not hear me when I said 'for life'? That wasn't a figure of speech. Hell, I don't even think it's something I can control."

"Let's say that's true. If you had the choice, would you stick around, knowing what I just told you?"

"Of course, you dipshit." She punched me in the chest, a bit too hard to be considered a 'playful' punch. "Just don't expect me to follow you around like a puppy dog. I have my own life and responsibilities, too."

"Fair enough. But if I have to go, and you can't follow, where does that leave us?"

She chewed her cheek as she considered my question. "I think we're both strong enough to allow the other to live their own life. Don't you agree?"

"I do."

She stepped in, clutching my jacket as she laid her head on my chest. "Then I'll always be here for you. That's the best I can promise."

"And I'll always come back to you," I said as I placed a light kiss on top of her head. She looked up at me, so I planted another on her lips.

"Next time, though, get it right. Six months is too long for a she-wolf to wait for her mate." She glanced around mischievously, just to make certain no one was listening in. "I changed my mind. Let's you and I steal a few hours inside the Grove. We have *lots* of catching up to do."

FALLYN and I spent only a few hours inside the Grove—minutes in the outside world, if that. After we'd sufficiently reacquainted ourselves, we took a dip, then we got dressed and headed, reluctantly, back to reality.

Click was already gone, Maureen and Hemi were busy fortifying the compound, and nobody had any idea what had happened to Heyókȟa.

With nothing better to do, Fallyn and I decided to find out what had happened to Maeve. Click had indicated that I'd need to fulfill my deal with Rube at some point, presumably to facilitate finding and dealing with Eris and her cronies. If I was going to be tied up on some errand, I'd feel better about it knowing Maeve was on the case as well.

One thing you could say about Maeve, she did not take shit from other gods and goddesses. That's why I thought it was really weird that no one had heard from her. When Fallyn and I pulled up to her manse in the Druidmobile, everything looked very normal and quiet behind those vine-covered garden walls.

"Does it even need saying that I have a bad feeling about this?" I asked, while keeping my eyes glued to Maeve's front gate.

"Nope," Fallyn replied. "And if I said something like, 'It's too damned quiet,' that would be a waste of breath, right?"

"Yep. C'mon, we may as well get this over with."

I exited the car and headed up the front walk to the ornate, wrought iron gate that marked the boundary between our world and Maeve's demesne. Or rather, the physical representation of her demesne. In truth, Maeve's territory reached north about two-thirds of the way to Dallas, east almost to the city limits of Houston, west halfway to El Paso, and south all the way to the border. While the interior of her home was essentially its own pocket dimension, the many branching and bifurcating corridors within reached to the farthest corners of her territory in this world.

The place wasn't infinitely vast, but it was close. That's why it was so terrifying to enter her home—if you became lost in there, you were well and truly screwed. Never mind the fact that the thing was sentient and, if not outright malevolent, hostile to intruders.

I stopped at the gate, my hand hovering over the latch. "Yo, Lothair! Anyone home?"

Lothair was Maeve's watch-gargoyle. She used to have a pair of them, and the one that was left never forgave me for what happened to the other. When I saw and heard nothing in response, I couldn't honestly say if it was a good or bad thing.

An inadvertent growl escaped my lips as I considered what came next. "I guess that means we need to investigate."

"Wait," Fallyn said as she grabbed my wrist to prevent me from opening the gate. "Something smells wrong."

I glanced at her, chuckling in spite of the situation. "You're cute when you crinkle your nose like that, you know?"

"I am always cute, and occasionally unbelievably sexy," she replied smugly. "Now, maybe you should get your mind back on the job and use your druid vision to see what's going on behind this gate?"

She was right, and I felt stupid that she'd had to suggest it. It had simply never occurred to me that I should examine Maeve's home and grounds in the magical spectrum. This was Maeve's place, after all, the queen of all Fae courts and a Celtic goddess to boot. Why would I even consider something being amiss on her property?

Because another goddess is involved, that's why.

Instantly, I was reminded of what had happened to this place in the other timeline. Now feeling doubly chastised, I shifted into the magical spectrum to see what I could see.

"Notice anything?"

"I'm looking, give me a sec." Nothing was amiss. "Hmm, all's clear so far."

"If the coast is clear, but her guard monster isn't coming to greet us, I'd be even more concerned."

"Agreed. Give me a moment." I sat down on the concrete and assumed the lotus position, then I slowed my breathing to facilitate a deep druid trance. A few breath cycles later, I extended my senses out beyond the gate and wall, searching for any living creature that might be residing there. If I could connect with something, even a creature as small as an ant, I might be able to get some perspective on what was amiss.

What I sensed on the other side was pure chaos. Where normally I'd have felt grass, trees, shrubbery, and presumably, a shit-ton of fae and deific magic, instead it was a jumble of energy flows, and none of it made sense. Nothing seemed to be where it should be—there was no order, rhyme, or reason to any of it.

The whole damned thing made me nauseous and uneasy in a way I couldn't easily describe. It was like someone put everything inside the walls in a blender, then they dumped it out again. Up was sideways, sunlight was prickly, and the flowers smelled like silence.

I snapped my eyes open, disconnecting and coming out of my trance. "Gah—that was unsettling. Yeah, something is definitely wrong in there."

"Should we go in?"

I stood, brushing off the seat of my jeans. "No, but is that going to stop us? This place is normally a magical fortress, impregnable for all intents and purposes. If someone managed to breach Maeve's defenses, I need to know about it, and I want to know what happened to her. Technically, I'm still the justiciar of this demesne, after all."

Fallyn shot me a playful eye roll. "Okay then, sheriff, I guess I'll back your call."

"Har, har," I replied, glancing up and down the street to see if anyone or anything was watching. "Listen, we could run into anything in there. You're tough, but of the two of us, I'm the only one equipped to deal with magic. If it gets hairy, I need to you to head for the exit, okay?"

Fallyn's frown could've curdled milk. "You did not just ask me to leave my mate's side in a crisis."

"Um, I was asking you to go get help." Her countenance darkened, if that were possible. "Okay, forget I said anything. But I should go first, considering I'm the magic user and all."

"I thought the tank always went first?" she asked in a mockingly serious tone.

"Not when the tank is with her overprotective boyfriend, even if she's a badass alpha werewolf." I placed my hand on the gate latch, levering it open with a metallic click. "Here goes."

THE GATE SWUNG open with the sound of a gong. Yet, I could taste the sound of it, and it was the color blue. We hadn't even set foot inside Maeve's yard, and already the weirdness was out of control.

"Did you catch that?" I asked.

"Uh-huh. Man, I thought my rave days were over. On second thought, we need a better plan. What say we tie a rope around your waist, and I stay out here so I can pull you out if you get in over your head?"

I considered the insanity of a sound that tasted like the color blue, and nodded. "That's an excellent idea."

After shuffling around in my Bag for a minute or so, I found a length of sturdy rope made from natural fibers that I could imbue with druid magic. We tied that around my waist, then I secured the knots with more of the same mystical energy.

"The magic should stabilize it, regardless of whatever weirdness is going on past the gate." I gave Fallyn a peck on the lips. "If I'm not back in five, pull me out."

"What if I pull and nothing happens?"

That possibility had already crossed my mind, but I preferred to avoid bringing it up. "Don't come in after me. Instead, get Maureen. She'll have contacts within the fae community who are better equipped to deal with this sort of thing."

I took a deep breath, then I did something I probably shouldn't have done out in the open—I encased myself in a chronourgic stasis field. That would prevent whatever was happening inside the walls from affecting me—I hoped. Once the field was in place, I stepped over the threshold and into a hellscape that looked like the love child of a Dalí painting and an Escher print.

It hurt my eyes to look at it, the place was so weird. Pieces of the ground were floating in the sky, and the surfaces tilted at odd angles. The plants and trees were every color but what nature intended, there were frogs the size of horses, birds the size of gnats, and Maeve's mansion looked like a Lego house that had been rearranged by a demented five-year old. Here was a section of roof, there a window where there should be a door, walls were canted at peculiar angles, and nothing was as it should be.

At least it's maintaining some semblance of congruency. That's a good sign.

Even more disturbing, the sidewalk dropped away into a lime green sky just a few feet in front of me. The distance from where I stood to the front entrance of the house—which happened to be upside-down and angled inward at a forty-five-degree angle—looked to be fifty feet or more. For all I knew, it could be two miles or two inches in this topsy-turvy world of chaos.

I saw no way to get from 'here' to 'there' but to leap. Yet, when I looked down into that infinite green sky, broken only by pink clouds and a purple sun that dripped paint down the sky toward the horizon, I couldn't help but hesitate.

Aw, fuck it. Nothing ventured, nothing gained.

Using every bit of my Fomorian strength, I took two quick steps and went for it.

"Fuuuuuuuuuccccccckkk!" I yelled as my feet left the small patch of intact pavement, although something like "$^@&!" is what likely came out.

It wasn't so much that I intended to yell for a long period of time, it was that it took a lot longer to cross that gap than I expected. Despite being inside a stasis bubble, time outside had been warped beyond belief. While my stasis bubble functioned to filter the reality-bending properties of the yard, it did nothing to normalize the space around the mansion.

Thus, it seemingly took several long minutes for me to sail across that space. That was, until I reached the halfway point, then time was compressed into the blink of an eye. The next thing I knew, I hit the front door of Maeve's mansion.

Stasis bubbles were weird things. Once you contacted something, it became caught in the bubble. To prevent that, you had to create a surface membrane of magic that repelled matter.

That was why, when I impacted the solid surface of the house, that I nearly bounced off into the oblivion of that chaotic green and pink sky. Gravity simply wasn't working properly here, so the physics allowed for me to pinball off the wall at speed. It was only by luck that I happened to snag a jagged, warped section of porch bannister, turning off the repelling function of the stasis barrier covering my hand to latch on.

There I hung, my body extended out at an odd angle over empty space. It was as if the house were turned on its side and suspended in the air above the ground, and I was hanging from it. It took a great deal more physical strength than it should have to pull my feet onto the small section of porch in front of the door. Once they touched, however, "gravity" took over, and I was able to stand upright in front of the entry.

With my feet firmly on what was definitely not terra firma, but the closest thing to it that I'd find here in this madhouse outside the madhouse, I knocked on the door.

"Hello? Anyone home?"

Yeah, that felt stupid.

Despite feeling foolish, I received no response, so I knocked again. "Yo, Maeve. It's me, Colin. Are you in there?"

Normally if Maeve were home, one of her flunkies would answer the door, or it would swing in of its own accord—then she'd be waiting in her parlor just on the other side. The parlor wasn't always there, as the halls and rooms inside constantly shifted and changed. Yet, as I understood it, the house more or less catered to her whims. If she wanted a parlor to receive guests, it'd be there.

This time, however, nothing happened. I wondered, was it wise to try the door? After glancing around to make sure I wasn't about to be ambushed by the harpies from hell, I reached for the knob, only to find it wasn't there.

However, a shiny brass mail slot had appeared in the door—one that I was certain had not been there before. Before I could comment on it or question its appearance, a letter slid out from the slot.

"My, how very Harry Potter of you," I remarked, whether to the house or to Maeve, I wasn't certain.

The envelope was in my hand before it hit the slatted floor of the small section of porch on which I stood. After checking my six again, I flipped it over to examine it in the strange, green light.

"Hmm—fine parchment, gold filigree, royal wax seal, and addressed to 'Foolish Child.' Yep, this is from Maeve."

I tore open the letter, breaking the seal and unfolding the sheet of parchment within. In flowing, handwritten script, it said:

Druid,

While any fool could see this was a trap, We are not displeased that you walked right into it. How you've escaped the madness field's effects is beyond Our ken, yet We shall not look a gift-púca in the mouth.

"Use of the royal 'we'? Yeah, that cinches it." I shook my head at the world-class display of pretension, then I continued reading.

Do not, under any circumstances, enter the manse. It is cursed and infected with the same madness as the garden and grounds. The spell caught Us unawares, and We lost half Our court before We were able to retreat to a safe location, deep within the bowels of Our demesne.

We are unable to escape at this time, as the source of the spell is beyond Our reach. If you can manage to free Us, We shall be happily inclined to remove any and all interlopers from Our demesne, with all due force and prejudice.

Find the source of the madness, and eradicate it. Know that it is not the trickster goddess who has cursed my manse with this chaos spell. Although she deals in same, this has a tinge of insanity to it that does not suit

her. Again, madness is the key. Deal with the source, and
We shall be in your debt.

    Regards,

    M

I dug around in my Bag until I found a pen, then I scribbled 'CONSIDER IT DONE' on the back of the letter. After folding it up and shoving it back through the slot, I turned to face the expanse between me and the gate. Just as I was about to jump, the rope went taut, and I was violently yanked off the porch and into empty space.

ELEVEN

"Fuuuuuu—" was what came out of my mouth when I got pulled off Maeve's porch.

"@@@@@%!" was what likely appeared over my head after I flew through the gate at fifty miles an hour, right into Fallyn.

We collided with each other, or rather I collided into her, bowling her over as we rolled ass over heels off the sidewalk and into the street in a tangle of rope and limbs.

And yeah, it hurt. Between my Fomorian mass and her dense werewolf bone structure and musculature, it was one hell of an impact.

I'd ended up on top of her, so I was the first to disentangle myself. "Are you alright?" I asked as I stood up and offered her a hand.

She wiped a bit of blood from her lip, which came

from a cut that was already healing. "Yes, I'm fine. Shit, I thought I'd never get you out of there."

"What do you meh—" I froze mid-sentence, realizing it was now well after nightfall. "Whoa. How long was I in there?"

"At least six hours, and I've been pulling on that stupid rope the whole time. Must've looked like an idiot to all the passing cars."

"Nah. The glamour on this place likely took care of that. Besides, in this town people would just think you were doing some new, weird form of Crossfit or something."

"Probably." She gave me a quizzical look. "So, was that word bubble over your head part of the spell, or—"

"You saw that. Dang it, and I was trying so hard to avoid cussing. It has something to do with the curse on the city, I think. Must be affecting me differently than everyone else for some reason."

"Why does that not surprise me?" Fallyn snickered, but her laugh turned into a sniff as she sampled the cool night air. "Ah, hell. We have company."

I cocked my head, listening for whatever had caught her attention. Yet, the scent tipped me off long before I heard the whisper quiet sound of their feet on the pavement and nearby rooftops.

Vamps.

I'd recognize that smell anywhere, the slight scent of decomposing flesh and coagulated blood, intermingled with graveyard dirt and whatever fancy-ass cologne or perfume was en vogue among Luther's coven these days.

They moved quickly, surrounding us even as I was coiling the rope and putting it back in my Bag. Luther wasn't with them, that much was clear, but when a patrol of a dozen vampires showed up out of the blue, they weren't there to sell Girl Scout cookies. I ignored them, taking my time with the rope as I let them know they were beneath my notice.

"Knew we smelled dog," one of them said, a skinny female in a tight leather miniskirt, a matching leather halter, and platforms that were probably worth more than the Druidmobile. How they managed to run and fight in those things was beyond me.

Fallyn stood feet apart, arms layered over her chest instead of crossed, in a stance that would allow her to spring into action without looking like she wanted to fight. I glanced at the female vamp with hooded eyes.

"I know you're not referring to my girlfriend, right?"

"This has nothing to do with you, Druid," a male vamp said. He wore a dark, tailored suit that was more Wall Street than Sixth Street. Combined with his pricey haircut, gold Rolex Oyster, and manicure, he likely worked finance at one of the firms downtown. Since most trading happened during daytime hours, I figured he was in management, or he owned the place.

Thing was, I didn't recognize any of these vamps. Most of the ones I dealt with were closest to Luther, folks who worked at his café or club. They put on a show like they were low-level, but in reality they were his heavy hitters—lieutenants, bodyguards, and the like.

Which meant that however wealthy this group appeared to be, they were flunkies at best. And I did not like being braced by flunkies. I closed the flap on my Bag, then I addressed the one in the Italian suit.

"I don't know any of you, and I don't care to know you, either. But what I do know is that Luther does not take kindly to coven members who cause trouble."

"Trouble?" the suit said, spreading his arms as he flashed a grin full of too-white teeth. "We're simply following orders. Luther said we're to keep the streets clear of 'thropes from Riverside north to Koenig, West to 360 and East to 183."

"Since when does Luther enforce curfews?" I asked.

The female spoke up this time. "Since we're at war with the Pack, that's when."

It was clear that the weird curse impacting the city was also affecting these vamps. Luther's people had never been the kind to hunt humans, to start fights, or to murder innocents. I didn't want to hurt any of them if I could avoid it. Yet, the tension in Fallyn's posture told me she was not only expecting a fight, but prepping for it. And a dozen vamps or no, between Fallyn and me they didn't stand a chance.

When dealing with predators, once their prey drive had kicked in, negotiation went out the window. Only a show of force would do in such instances. Knowing this,

I raised my fist above my head, slowly so as not to cause alarm. I let a bit of my sunlight spell burn from my palm, opening my fingers just a tad, so bright rays of light seeped from between.

"My suggestion," I hissed as I swept my gaze across the group, "is that you stand down, before someone gets a permanent sunburn."

The spell wasn't bright enough to burn flesh—yet—but it caused the weakest of the vamps to fall back, just the same. But wouldn't you know it, Heels and the suit stood their ground.

Huh. Must be older than I figured.

I guess Heels thought she had a shot. She shielded her eyes and zipped forward from my blind side, thinking I wasn't paying attention. Of course, I was, but I also knew that Fallyn had my back.

Before that Skinny Minnie could lay a fake nail on me, my girl had body slammed her on the pavement, facedown with an arm twisted behind her and a knee in her back. Vamps are strong, sure, but you need leverage to use that strength, and Fallyn had taken all but a fraction of hers away.

"Keep squirming, and I'll twist it off," the female werewolf growled.

The alpha's eyes had taken on a yellow sheen that fairly glowed in the soft, sodium light cast by the street lamps above. While the other vamps shied away, the suit turned to face Fallyn and Heels as his weight shifted ever so slightly to his toes. I let a little more sunlight escape my fingers, aiming a tight beam in his direction.

"Uh-uh, buster. Don't even think about it." I had the other vamps fully cowed, so I kept an eye on him as I addressed Heels. "Darlin', think you can be a good little fanger and behave if the alpha lets you go?"

"I'll fucking kill her—unnnngghh!" she said, her words turning into a grunting whine as Fallyn torqued on her shoulder socket.

I chuckled mirthlessly. "As I understand it, only older vamps can regrow limbs, and only after a shit-ton of feedings. Ain't that right, pretty boy?"

The dude in the suit shielded his eyes, keeping them downcast as he replied. "Let's go, Nadia. The druid and his bitch have won, for now."

"But Victor—" Nadia protested, until Fallyn cranked a little more.

"Best do as he says, cupcake," Fallyn hissed as she leaned to whisper in the vamp's ear. "I don't eat spoiled meat, but that doesn't mean I won't rip your arm off and feed it to my neighbor's doggos."

"I said, let's go," the suit named Victor ordered as he backed away. Once he'd made space enough to escape the sting of my sunlight spell, he fixed me with a hateful gaze. "This isn't over, druid. Once Luther hears of your interference, he'll come looking for you. I wouldn't want to be you when he does."

"Luther and I go way back—well, in human years,

anyway. He'll know I just did you a favor. Half of you would be dead right now if I hadn't intervened."

"Half?" Fallyn objected. "Only half?"

"Sorry, I felt like being generous," I said as I watched the rest of the vamps fade off into the darkness. "Let her up, else they'll hang around out there until dawn."

Fallyn rolled her eyes, then she twisted the vamp's arm until something popped. To Heels' credit, she didn't let out more than a soft *eep*. The werewolf leapt off her, taking a back-to-back position with me immediately.

As soon as his friend was free, the suit danced backwards, slipping into the shadows like a wraith. Almost as quickly, the female vamp skittered away after him, cradling her arm so it wouldn't flop around uselessly as she ran.

"Next time," the suit called from the darkness. I flipped him off in response.

"Did you have to dislocate her shoulder?" I asked.

"She was tensing to take a swipe at me, just as soon as I let her up. I had no choice."

I nodded slowly. "What do you think the odds are we're going to run into that crowd again?"

"Oh, I'd say one-hundred percent."

"Knew you'd say that. Let's just hope Luther stays out of it."

"You won't be able to back him down with the threat of a little sunlight, that's for sure." She snickered, punching me on the shoulder. "C'mon, tough guy. I'll drive, and you can tell me what happened behind those walls."

BACK AT THE JUNKYARD, we filled Maureen and Hemi in on what had happened at Maeve's place. As was typical for him, Hemi took it in stride. He gulped down a cup of instant ramen while we related the incident with the cursed house and the Coven patrol. On the other hand, the half-kelpie stroked her chin pensively as she considered the story we shared.

"Well, what do you think?" I asked, leaning forward from my perch on the counter.

Maureen pushed her thick red hair out of her face, tucking it behind her fine, elfin ear. "I think Maeve was givin' ya' hints without makin' it obvious. P'raps she has a mole, or she thought somethin' was watchin' ya' outside her house."

"You mean the part about how 'madness is the key'? That makes sense," I replied.

"Aye boyo. An' where'd madness dwell, if it had its way?"

Fallyn reclined in a chair by the front door, a steaming mug of cocoa in her hands. "You mean, where would something that caused madness go, if it had the choice?"

Maureen tapped the side of her nose as she winked at Fallyn. "'Zactly."

The alpha sipped her cocoa, eyes narrowed. "I'd say someplace where it could have easy access to crazy people."

"Uh, they don't say that anymore," I said. "'Mentally ill' would be the proper term, I think."

Fallyn frowned as she dismissed my protest with a wave. "Crazy is crazy, dude. And if you want to find crazy people, you go to the loony bin."

I winced, but it was useless arguing such matters with the alpha. Fallyn had grown up around a biker gang—a 'thrope biker gang, at that. One percenters weren't exactly known for being politic when it came to sensitive topics, nor were 'thropes, and she was no exception. Despite her occasional lack of tact, at least I could count on her to be straightforward with me.

Hemi sat in the corner, slurping the last of his ramen broth as he listened in on the conversation. "It's like she missed out on a decade of political correctness, eh?" he commented, not taking his eyes off his work.

"Well, I was raised by wolves," Fallyn replied.

"She was raised by Samson," I added. "That man has no fraks to give when it comes to hurt feelings, believe me."

Fallyn looked away, and I realized I'd hit a nerve. "Ah, sorry to bring up a sore subject, babe."

"I just hope we don't run into him," she said. "The last thing I want is to have to put the hurt on my dad."

"I'll take care of him for you. I did it before, right?" I

replied, realizing it was a mistake even as I finished the sentence.

Fallyn set her cup down forcefully on the desk, bristling as she sat straighter. "How would that look to the Pack? No, never mind that—what makes you think I even need saving?"

"Aw, here we go," Maureen muttered.

"I don't—I mean, didn't I mention that earlier?" Fallyn's eyes turned from hazel to yellow to gold as I stammered my way to doghouse status again. By the time I finished, she was out the door and storming off into the yard. I stood to go after her, but Maureen motioned for me to sit.

"Let 'er go, boyo, let 'er go. 'Tis not you she's mad at, 'tis the position she finds herself in. S'naught often that daddy's little girl has to consider the prospect o' kickin' his arse."

Hemi whistled softly. "I can't imagine going up against me mum."

"Right?" I said. "I don't even get along with my mom, and I wouldn't want to be at odds with her."

"Naw mate, I said I can't even imagine it. She'd squish me like a split grape."

Maureen chortled softly. "Somethin' tells me I'd get along just fine with that woman. Gettin' back ta' where ya' might find this madness causin' entity, I believe I recall just such a place."

"Do tell," I said, resisting the urge to drum my fingers on the counter's edge.

Maureen, being a few hundred years old, hated to be rushed. Showing any sign of impatience would only make her stall longer.

The fae woman who helped raise me pointed a finger at the ceiling. "If I were such a bein', an' if I were ta' choose such a place, I'd go ta' the ol' Texas State Lunatic Asylum."

"Um, Maureen—we don't have 'asylums' anymore."

"The building is still there," Hemi interjected. "Saw it on The Day Trippist. It's the admin building for the State Hospital now."

The State Hospital was where people were treated for mental illness, at least those who fell under the state's purview. The institution had been around since the 1800s, so it only made sense they'd have historic buildings on the campus.

"You really think this deity will be there?" I asked.

Maureen chuffed. "Does Manannán piss in the incomin' tide? Ta' gods an' elder fae, symbolism matters. Ya' bet yer' lily-white backside it'll be there. At least, that's where I'd look."

"You're not coming with us?"

She swiveled her chair around to face her work station. "An' who do ya' think'll take care o' the books and work stackin' up, whilst yer' off chasin' after spirits an' savin' the city? Not Colin McCool, that's fer sure. Mayhaps ya' should go an' apologize ta' that lovely young lass, then get your arses over ta' the hospital ta' stop that thing."

Maureen was already typing away before I could reply, so I looked at Hemi.

"Meet ya' out front," he said, as he tossed his empty ramen cup away. "After you two kiss and make up."

"The big oaf is smarter than he looks," Maureen muttered.

It was still night when we drove to the State Hospital. We had a few hours left until dawn, and it was certainly dark enough for vamps to be patrolling, making us wary. I doubted they could see the Druidmobile, spelled for stealth as it was, but a sharp, older vamp would notice something passing by.

That might be enough to draw attention. The last thing I needed was to fight a running battle with a bunch of Luther's coven members while driving through the streets of Austin. Thus, we remained alert while sticking to the main traffic arteries, as much as possible.

Speaking of which, the streets were in chaos. Folks were out everywhere, rioting in some places, merely gathering in protest in others. But protesting what, who could say?

People were angry and they didn't know why. We knew it was Eris' influence, or at least that of one of her many wicked relatives. That said, I frequently saw people holding signs that displayed slogans matching those on the billboards all over town.

"Instigators," Fallyn said as we passed a crowd that gathered in front of a burning restaurant.

"That's someone's life, going up in ashes," I replied. "And for what? Just because Eris is nuts, and she wants to see the world burn."

"Fan theory," Hemi interjected from the back. "Joker is a god of chaos."

"Heard that one," I answered as I made eye contact in the rearview. "I think he's more like a manifestation of it, the personification of madness."

"Lots of gods are," the big man replied. "Personifications, that is."

"True." A glance to my right revealed Fallyn knitting her brow with concern, so I turned the conversation back to more serious matters. "Getting back to what we're seeing here, this is messed up."

"It's sad," Fallyn agreed. "All these people losing their livelihoods, just because some asshole goddess got pissed off and decided to take it out on the world."

That was when it hit me. Although Fallyn felt empathy toward the folks whose lives were going up in smoke, she was also voicing concern for her Pack. I reached across the seat to lay a hand on her shoulder so I could give it a squeeze.

"Hey, don't worry—they'll be alright."

Just as I said it, she tensed under my touch. "Colin, look!"

Due to the people milling about everywhere, I eased off the accelerator as I swung my gaze in the direction she'd indicated. Down a side street off Lamar, two groups faced each other across an empty restaurant parking lot. At first, it appeared to be another riot, then several members of the group on the right began to shift.

"Aw $#!^," I said.

"You oughta' get that fixed," Hemi remarked, pointing at the word bubble over my head. "Kinda' getting annoying."

Fallyn ignored us both, her hand gripping the door handle hard enough to bend it. I reflected that my poor car's interior was going to be a mess after this whole thing was over.

"Pull in, pull in," she ordered. I complied. "Damn it, they're going to kill each other."

"Think you can talk them down?" I asked as I turned off the headlights and engine, shifting the car in neutral so we could coast into the parking lot unannounced.

"The Pack? Yeah, of course. But that won't keep the Coven from attacking." Her eyes were already taking on that golden hue, the one that told me things were about to get serious. "Anyone see Luther or Samson out there?"

"Nada," Hemi replied.

"Naw, I don't see either of them. We should break this up before one of them shows."

"Alright, I'll handle the Pack," Fallyn said. "Just keep the vamps away until I get my people out of here."

"Can do," I said, although I wondered if I could.

I counted at least three dozen Coven and as many Pack members on either side. A little conjured sunlight wasn't going to keep them corralled, that was for sure. This would call for more creative means of controlling a crowd.

Fallyn was already out the door and running toward the Pack as I turned to address the Maori warrior. "You have some dominion over the dead, right? Does that extend to undead species?"

He shrugged. "I got influence, eh? But if I use it, there's consequences."

"You're talking politics." He nodded. "Well, don't do anything that'll get you in trouble. Still, if it comes down to it, I may need you to back me up."

He pushed the front seat on the passenger side forward, making room to get his massive bulk out of the car. The big guy paused to look at me with one foot out the door.

"You want I should call Maki?"

I seriously considered it. She was a power in her own right, and that was a fact. Yet, I knew she just wanted to be left alone, and out of pantheon politics.

I shook my head in the negative. "I'd say that's our nuclear option. Let's not bother her with this crap."

He inclined his head slightly, letting me know he appreciated that I hadn't made the ask. The car righted itself as he exited, and by the time I'd followed his tattoos were already glowing, up and down his arms and across the lower half of his face.

"Whassa' plan?"

Fifty feet away, Fallyn stood in front of her Pack, motioning them to stop even as she used her influence to talk sense into them. Perhaps as much distance again remained between her back and the Coven, many of whom bounced on their toes in anticipation of the coming brawl. The bloodkin looked twitchy, which was not a good sign. This could become a bloodbath in short order if I didn't do something.

"I'll slow as many of them down as I can. Those that slip through will have to be dissuaded from attacking the 'thropes."

Hemi inclined his head, while keeping his eyes on the action. "Following your lead, mate."

That made me feel moderately better. I only hoped we three would be enough to prevent an incident that could have lasting repercussions between the factions.

CHAPTER
TWELVE

I cast a chameleon spell on us, not that it would fool the vamps for long. Both they and the 'thropes had senses far keener than even my Fomorian enhanced capabilities. However, it'd keep us hidden long enough to do what needed to be done.

"Oi, mate—one of the fangers is eyeing Fallyn's back."

"On it," I said, leaving the ward bubble the Druid-mobile provided, even as I braced for the effects of Eris' influence to wash over me.

While at the junkyard and inside the car, my wards had mostly protected us from the curse. Now, it was as if invisible fingers were prying inside my brain, poking and prodding all the places where I was most vulnerable to feelings of resentment and anger. It wasn't easy to resist, but I managed to keep my cool by dropping into a druid trance.

When I tuned into the swirling energies of nature around me, the harmony calmed my mind and soothed my soul. Nature had always been a balm for my frustration and rage, and now it could be my saving grace. Without it, I might've shifted and destroyed every last one of the vamps who threatened Fallyn.

Moving on after that close call with my homicidal Fomorian rage, I reached into the earth beneath the asphalt surface of the parking lot. I probed the layers of soil and rock, going all the way to the water table, no more than thirty feet underneath. Being careful to avoid disturbing things too much, I coaxed the water to the surface, pushing it into the earth just under the blacktop where the vamps stood.

After softening the soil into muddy quicksand, I melted the tar that held the blacktop together, destabilizing the surface until it crumbled under the Coven's feet. Instantly, two-thirds of their number sank to their armpits in the muck and mire. Like werewolves, vamps were very densely built creatures, so they went under quickly.

Once I'd caught as many as I could, I hardened the ground and the pavement all over again by drawing the moisture from the soil and the heat from the blacktop. Screams of surprise, frustration, and rage arose from the vampires, along with warnings regarding the source of their current situation. It wasn't perfect, but it'd hold them for a few minutes, at least.

"The druid is here," a familiar, commanding male voice shouted.

Ah, so the suit is part of this little gang. Go figure.

"I see him, Victor, over there."

That was Nadia. She, Victor, and nine other vamps had managed to avoid falling into my trap. All eyes turned toward me at once as the female vampire directed their collective gaze.

"Don't just stand there like idiots," Victor said. "Attack!"

The vampires milled about as they exchanged glances with each other. A dude in a black t-shirt, jeans, cowboy boots, and a black felt hat spoke up first.

"I heard he can burn ya' to a crisp with sunlight."

A tubbier, balding, middle-aged looking vampire in dad jeans, a Darth Vader t-shirt, and green Crocs nodded. "Nobody said anything about getting fried tonight, Vic. If I'd have known we were going to fight the druid, I'd have stayed in. You know he's one of Luther's pet humans."

Hemi snickered. "That's rich, aye?"

"Hey now," I warned. "I'm nobody's pet anything."

The vamps ignored my protest as a chorus of concerns arose from those vampires who'd avoided the quicksand trap. Nadia stood to the side, scowling. Victor raised his hands above his head, waving to get their attention as he whistled sharply.

"I don't give a shit what you losers think, he can't fry us all at once. When I say go, we're going to attack, and anyone who doesn't move will answer to me. Understood?"

Oh, I understand perfectly.

One of the things I learned from Finnegas and Maureen was how to deal with large groups of enemies. Every group has a leader, whether it's a commander in battle or a bullying gang lieutenant who incites his buddies to violence. Take that one out, and often the cohesion of the group will crumble.

Keeping an eye on Victor and Nadia, I warned Hemi. "Get ready, alright?"

"Always am."

Alright, fucker. Time to introduce you to Tlachtga's Inferno.

Tlachtga's Inferno was one of the many druid battle spells I'd discovered in the pages of the journals, tomes, and codices the old man had left me. I thought I'd invented the use of sunlight to fight vampires and other undead, but apparently Mogh Roith's daughter beat me to the punch. Not only that, her version of the spell was way deadlier than mine, by several degrees.

I thrust my palm out at Victor, casting the spell by concentrating stored sunlight into a tight, hot beam that I swept across his legs. This effectively created a laser beam, although practically speaking it was more like focusing the sun's rays through a magnifying glass. The concentrated light and heat, combined with Victor's natural weakness to sunlight, had a devastating effect. Three inches of the vamp's legs vaporized instantly, right beneath his knees.

Victor tumbled to the ground with a thud as a collective gasp arose from the Coven. Even those who struggled to free themselves from the ground froze, shocked and mortified at what I'd done. Meanwhile, Victor pushed himself to an upright position, pawing at his stumps in disbelief and dismay.

"My legs—you cut off my fucking legs!"

"Yup," I said as I casually scanned the Coven to gauge their reaction. So far, only Nadia looked like she might attack. I wagged a finger at her in warning. "Uh-uh, I wouldn't, girl. Not unless you want to join Lieutenant Dan there."

"Bastard," she hissed. "You've cursed him to an eternity of being crippled."

"Oh, save me the drama. He'll heal in a few hundred years—probably." I whispered conspiratorially to Hemi behind my hand. "He will heal, right?"

Hemi shrugged as he glanced about with disinterest. "Mebbe."

Oops. Well, it's too late for take-backsies.

"He'll be fine," I said in a rather unconvincing tone. "If the rest of you know what's good for you, you'll grab Victor and his legs and haul tail out of here. Or, you can stick around and experience the same. Your call."

The dude in the Darth Vader shirt spoke first. "Screw this, Vic. I'm sorry about your legs and all, but we warned you."

The other vamps muttered similar sentiments, some sticking around to help dig out their friends, while others split immediately. As a show of good faith, I softened the soil and asphalt around them so they could escape. Nadia swept Victor up in her arms, shouting over her shoulder as she strutted off into the dark.

"Luther will hear of this, druid. I swear!"

"Whatevs," I said as I sent her off with a back-handed wave.

Honestly, by that point I was too busy paying attention to the drama unfolding behind us to spare Nadia a glance. While Hemi and I were focused on the vamps, Fallyn had laid the smackdown on a couple of wolves who thought they could step to her. They were wrong.

She'd already laid one wolf out. He was bleeding and unconscious but still breathing, and she had another pinned facedown on the pavement. Fallyn ground that one's nose into the tarmac as she swept her golden gaze across the gathered group of 'thropes.

"Anyone else care to try me?" she asked.

No one answered. She briefly held the gaze of a few members in turn, until the group began to disperse, just as the vamps had. I thought the crisis was averted until I saw Fallyn tense.

"What?" I asked, but she merely shook her head.

It was then I heard the rumble of a straight-piped panhead approaching in the distance. The roar of other Harleys joined the first in a chorus, and soon a dozen headlights shot out of the dark as they headed down the side street that led to the parking lot.

"Well, piddly sticks," I muttered.

"Never mind what I said about fixing that," Hemi chortled. "Hearing you talk like Mr. Rogers is going to be fun."

I side-eyed him briefly, turning my attention back to Fallyn. "Do we stay or go?"

As soon as the vamps heard reinforcements coming, they beat feet. They'd picked up on it about ten seconds before I did, so they were long gone. That left us and the Pack—and an impending confrontation between father and daughter.

Fallyn dropped her chin to her chest. "We go."

The 'thrope pinned beneath her guffawed. "I knew you was chickenshit, bitch. I jest' knew it."

Fallyn punched him at the base of his skull, not hard enough to kill, but enough to knock him cold.

"Chickenshit that, asshole." She hopped to her feet. "Let's split, before he realizes I'm here."

"Roger that, babe."

Without hesitation, I cast a chameleon spell over the three of us. We slipped into the Druidmobile, just as the other Pack members pulled into the lot. As we drove past them, Samson howled like a madman at the night sky.

"It's my Pack, Fallyn—mine. And you won't take it from me again!"

WHEN WE ARRIVED at the State Hospital, everything seemed to be in order. Behind the gates, it was nothing but calm serenity as the sun slowly rose in the eastern sky. I'd have called it peaceful, if I didn't know any better.

"I smell blood," Fallyn warned. "And—*other* fluids."

"From inside the car?" Hemi asked.

She wore a grim frown as her hazel eyes scanned all around. "Werewolf senses. It's a mixed blessing."

The warrior hmphed. "Still kinda' cool. All I got from my mum was being able to sense death."

"What? You never told me that," I said.

"You never asked."

"Why would I ever think to ask if you could sense death?" I said.

"I dunno," he replied. "Seems like the logical thing to me."

Fallyn chuckled, although it was clear her heart wasn't in it. "Since we're on the topic, do you sense any death around here?"

He remained still for several seconds before answering. "Nah, none recent, anyway. But there's a pall hanging over this place. Like death impending, yeah?"

"Well, that's not good." I made certain Dyrnwyn was close at hand inside my Bag, then I made to exit the car. "Wait here, I'm going to scout around incognito."

"Seems like Fallyn'd be the better choice."

"True. But we're dealing with magic here. I need to see what's up." The two of them shared a look that said, *'What are you going to do?'* "Traitors," I muttered as I cloaked myself in a chameleon spell.

Taking a page from my Hellpocalypse playbook, I added a silence spell to the mix. Then, I used a little druid magic to suppress my scent. The combo wouldn't make me invisible, but it'd be the next best thing.

"Too bad the cloak is mad at me again," I said under my breath.

"Aye, it'd come in handy 'bout now," Click's voice declared from somewhere nearby. This time, he did manage to startle me.

"Gah! Why do you always have to do that?"

"Do ya' hafta' ask?" he said as he coalesced into view. "By the way, we tracked the source o' one o' the curses down ta' this location."

"Gee, thanks for the timely info," I muttered. "Tricksters, always a dollar short and a day late."

Click tsked. "As if ya' have room ta' speak. Yer' as much one o' us as Loki."

"Are you seriously comparing me to Loki?" I replied in a tone of sincere incredulity.

Click nodded. "Not in malice, but as far as the sheer amount o' trouble ya' stir up, aye."

"Um, thanks?" We'd almost reached the gate, which I was about to check to see if it was locked.

Just as I reached out, Click cleared his throat. "I wouldn't."

"Tripwire spell?"

"A subtle one, fer' sure. This way."

He headed left, hands clasped behind his back, and I followed. About a hundred yards on, he stopped in front of a section of limestone wall that was as nondescript as the next.

Click pointed at the top of the wall, a few feet above us. "Here, this'll do."

"What, no tripwire here?"

"I breached it. 'Twas weakest here. Be sure an' put yer' spectacles on afore ya' go o'er the wall. Lots ta' see."

"That does not bode well," I replied as I shifted my eyesight into the magical spectrum.

Instantly I could see the tripwire ward around the top of the wall, and where Click had diverted it. Why I hadn't thought to look for wards at the front gate, I had no idea.

"Influence o' madness," Click remarked. "Makes ya' daft, lad."

I wonder if that's why you're acting so clearheaded now.

"Aye," Click said. "Sure enough, I know what yer' thinkin'. Fer' some reason, their curse an' ma' own cancel each other out. Enjoy it while ya' can."

I felt genuinely sorry for even thinking it. Whatever the price for his immortality had been, I was certain that Click must regret his choice now.

"Sorry," I said, meaning it.

"I know, lad. Ye've a good heart, s'why I've looked

after ya' all these years. Now, don't linger up there too long, it'll make ya' dizzy."

Click disappeared with a wistfully sad expression on his face. It was the sort of look that only a deep loss could trigger. I knew it well—I'd seen the same in the mirror, many times.

After making a mental note to be kinder to my slightly mad and very maddening mentor in future days, I leapt the ten feet or so to perch atop the wall. What I saw there was disturbing, to say the least.

First the glamour came into view, a bubble-shaped illusion covering the hospital grounds so that none could see what was really happening inside. Once my magical vision pierced it, I witnessed an insane tableau that revealed the utter callousness and cruelty of the gods.

Patients ran amok everywhere, some in street clothes, others in hospital gowns and scrubs, and still others wearing nothing at all. Likely as not, many of these people had already suffered from mental illnesses. Yet, it was clear that magic had worsened their conditions.

Some rooted around in the dirt like animals, digging and sniffing for insects that they hoovered up like hors d'oeuvres. Others chased staff members with makeshift weapons, from fire extinguishers to jagged shards of pottery to a *WET FLOOR* sign wielded as a bludgeon. One lady covered her ears and screamed incessantly, so loud and hard I was certain she'd be coughing up blood soon.

The entire scene was maddening, sickening, and mind-boggling. Yet, the more I looked, the harder it was to peel my eyes away. It was almost as if the mere sight of so much insanity was calling me to become a part of it, hypnotizing me to join in. Instinctively, I knew that if I gave in, I'd never escape that madness.

With an extreme effort of will, I tore my eyes away. Just before I dismounted the wall, I noticed something that deserved one more look. Steeling myself for another go, I closed one eye and glanced over the wall and away again, so fast I barely caught a glimpse of what I sought.

Yep, I was right.

Every single patient on the other side of the wall had it—a vague, indistinct shadow figure, riding them like draft animals. Some of those shadows rode piggy-back, others on shoulders, and still others bareback as the humans they tortured roamed on all fours on the ground.

Shee-it.

Every last one of those poor souls was possessed. I was definitely going to need help to deal with this situation. Thankfully, I knew just who to call.

∾

SHOCKINGLY, Brother Carroll answered his phone on the first ring. "Colin McCool, what a pleasant surprise. I take it this isn't a social call?"

"Hi Brother Carroll. Sadly, it's not. I'm tracking down some minor deities who are up to no good, and I could use some help."

'Brother Carroll,' also known as Tuan McCarrill, was the leader of a band of demon-fighting monks. I'd run into them a while back during an investigation, and that was when I discovered Tuan was a real person. Not only that, he was alive and well, serving his faith by working incognito as a warrior monk.

It was wild, when you thought about it, and also kind of cool. Unfortunately, the other monks didn't really care for me, being a druid and all. Brother Carroll didn't seem to mind, though—heck, he tried to recruit me, even.

The monk hissed softly at the mention of deities. To the monks, all supernatural beings were demonic in some form or another, the gods most of all. "Yes, we've been monitoring the situation. You'll be pleased to know that the curse only extends a few miles outside the city."

"You mean the one that's making everyone argue and fight?" I scratched my head, wondering for the life of me why a Greek god would want to attack Maeve's demesne. Well, besides being batshit crazy. "That is good news. Any idea where it's coming from?"

I heard papers shuffling on the other end of the line.

"Let's see... no, nothing concrete yet. Whoever is behind this, they've done an excellent job of covering their tracks."

"You say you're monitoring it. Does that mean you intend to get involved?"

Brother Carroll tsked. "Not really our thing. We mostly stick to actual demon hunting, avoiding the pantheons entirely. No offense, but I prefer to leave the deific politics to more adventurous souls, like yourself."

"Well, you're in luck. I'm facing a mass possession situation. That sounds like something demonic to me."

While I awaited a response, I heard the sound of fingers drumming on a hard surface. "How do you figure it's possession?"

"Oh, I don't know. Maybe it's all the people running amok trying to kill each other. Might be the shadow demon thingies riding them like thoroughbreds. Kind of a toss-up, really."

"Hmm, yes—that sounds familiar. I suppose I can help."

"You're coming, personally?"

He sniffed. "I happen to be in the area. Give me an address and stand by until I arrive."

Fifteen minutes later, a perfectly restored, fire engine red Volkswagen Beetle pulled up. Out stepped a wiry older man with a slight paunch, leathery, sun-worn skin, hazel eyes, and an impishly playful smile.

He spotted us almost instantly, even though I hadn't lowered the look away spell on the Druidmobile. Brother Carroll wore dark slacks and black sneakers under a brown monk's cassock. He carried a leather satchel that looked a lot like an old-fashioned doctor's bag, and he had a worn shillelagh tucked into his belt.

Although he was many centuries old, I really didn't understand the extent of Tuan's powers. The gods cursed him, I knew that much, and that was the source of his unnaturally long life. It was also why he'd converted, and the impression I got was that he'd steered clear of the pantheon ever since.

I waved Tuan over, so I could introduce him to Fallyn and Hemi.

"Fallyn, Hemi, this is Brother Carroll. Brother Carroll, meet my girlfriend Fallyn and my best bud, Hemi."

Tuan extended a hand to Fallyn first, which she took with obvious reluctance. "Oh, don't worry, I'm not going to invite you to 'Vacation Bible School' or some nonsense like that. My interests are more eschatological than evangelical."

Fallyn laughed, despite her discomfort. "I'm not much for preachers, but Colin says you're alright, so you get the benefit of a doubt."

"Splendid." Tuan turned to Hemi. "Greetings, son of Hine-nui-te-pō. Well met."

Hemi shook his hand. "Same, mate."

The monk glanced around, meeting the gaze of all parties in turn. "Shall we?"

"You don't need to see the demons first?" Fallyn asked.

"Oh no," Tuan replied with a shake of his head. "I can smell them from here."

Hemi perked up at that. "What's a demon smell like, aye?"

"Like sulphur and burning tires, with the occasional bouquet of spoilt blood. It is not a pleasant scent."

Fallyn sniffed. "I can't smell a thing. Is the ward around the wall blocking it or something?"

"No, nothing like that," Tuan replied. "It's more of a spiritual odor."

The she-wolf gave the barest roll of her eyes. "If you say so."

Thankfully, Tuan ignored her attitude. He turned to address me specifically with a gleam in his eye. "Be advised, once I force them out of their hosts, these spirits will be rather angry, although the majority will be forced to return to whence they came. Some of them, the more powerful of the bunch, might be able to manifest physically on this plane. You should prepare for a fight."

"What's to prepare?" Fallyn stated. "They come, we fight. Simple."

I shrugged. "She's right, Brother Carroll. We're pretty much always ready for a scrape."

Brother Carroll looked at Hemi. "And you, James?"

"Guess I'd better light up. Give me a sec." Hemi got some space, then he did a short *haka*. By the time he finished, his ink glowed with a bright blue light, all over his body. "Ready."

Tuan acknowledged Hemi with a nod, then he rummaged around in his bag before producing a stick of white chalk. "Give me a moment, please."

As we looked on, Tuan drew a few simple symbols on the wall that surrounded the compound. When he was finished, he spoke some words in Latin before making the sign of the cross at the symbols. Finally, he stepped away with a smug grin on his face.

"That should do it," the old monk said.

"That's it?" Fallyn asked, her voice dripping with skepticism.

"More words do not a better prayer make," Tuan replied. "Faith need not be longwinded."

"I don't see anything happening," Hemi said. "Don't feel anything, either."

"Give it time," Tuan said. "As for me, I believe I'll go take a nap in my vehicle."

"You're not going to help us fight these things?" I asked.

"Oh, heavens no," he replied. "I'm too old for that nonsense. You kids have fun, though."

We watched Tuan as he shuffled away to his Bug, whistling a happy tune. Just as he shut his car door, a blood-curdling scream echoed from within the walls. Another wail followed, then another, then a chorus of screams and cries rose into the sky.

I turned to address my companions, facing away from the wall as I did so. "Okay, here's the plan—"

Before I could convey my orders, I was snatched off my feet and dragged over the wall by a brown, slimy tentacle as big around as a telephone pole.

CHAPTER THIRTEEN

H*mm... madness—tentacles. I guess this makes sense.*

When the slimy appendage lifted me over the wall, the scene that greeted me was the last thing I expected. Based on what I witnessed earlier, I expected the shadow creatures to attack us after Brother Carroll expelled them from their hosts. I even entertained the possibility of a manifestation more on the conventional side—the appearance of a few red-skinned, horned, goat-legged demons, for instance.

But nope. Instead, it was like Stephen King and Clive Barker had a bad acid trip together, then some sick deity made their nightmares real.

Undoubtedly, giant demonic *kaiju* were the last thing I expected to appear at a mental hospital in the heart of Austin, Texas. I most certainly didn't expect three such creatures to be terrorizing people, right in the middle of the facility's central courtyard. And I definitely didn't think that each would be worse than the last.

The one that had me in its grip was a writhing, twenty-foot wide mass of slick, wet, grey-green and muck brown tentacles. Several were thicker, like the one that grabbed me, while others were thinner and whip-like. Some had suckers, others had barbs, and some of its suckers had barbed teeth around them—because they were also mouths.

Disgusting.

The second creature was made of fog, at least as far as I could tell. It looked like nothing more than a giant amorphous blob of smoke and mist about thirty feet across and just as tall. Those mists swirled and changed colors in ways that made me nauseous if I looked at it for more than a few seconds.

Every so often, shadows moved inside the fog, just beyond the limits of my eyesight. I soon realized that those were people, lost within its body. Whoever fought that thing would have to make certain they didn't become enveloped by it, because there was no telling what sort of madness it induced in its victims.

The third and final creature was the worst, defying all description due to the sheer insanity it exhibited. It was all planes and cubes and tetrahedrons and every other angular shape imaginable. Structures popped up at random intervals all over its surface, folding in on the others, only to reform in a myriad of new shapes and planes elsewhere. Its size was difficult to gauge, since it had no defining shape to speak of, and gauging spatial relations was a challenge when you were staring at something so surreal.

What really blew my fuse was that the creature didn't have any color to it, per se. Instead, every single surface and plane on its body consisted of moving images, each one crazier and more horrific than the next. Here you'd catch a glimpse of a father murdering his family, there a suicide, over here a village being slaughtered by soldiers in some unnamed country, and over there someone was cutting off pieces of their own flesh.

A monster that is literally made of the stuff of nightmares. Now I've seen it all.

I caught only a glimpse of each creature, but a glimpse was enough to form a visual impression of the trio. From there, it was easy to figure out what they really were.

These damned things are madness personified. Tentacles —that's horror. Fog—confusion, for sure. And the Escher-looking thing—probably psychosis. Damn.

But were they real? What I was seeing might've been real or an illusion. Or, the forms they took could be quasi-realistic manifestations of their magic—something that wasn't entirely there that could still influence reality on a physical level. The tentacle wrapped around my waist sure felt real, though.

That was all the time I had for consideration before

the tentacle creature tossed me into the side of a two-story brick and glass building. Lucky me, I hit one of the brick walls instead of a window, although just before impact I managed to twist in time to shield my face and vitals by tucking into a ball. My Fomorian skeleton and muscle mass was dense enough to survive the impact. Unfortunately, the human skin covering my body wasn't so sturdy.

After crashing through another interior wall, I came to a stop in a bloody heap inside someone's office. I didn't need a mirror to know that my clothes were likely to be shredded. It also didn't take a supercomputer to figure out that giant madness monsters required a giant badass to fight them.

Yet, I already felt the influence of these creatures prying at the edges of my sanity, and I wondered what would happen after I fully shifted. Would their magic push me over the brink, turning me into a nine-foot-tall Fomorian killing machine?

A glimpse through the hole in the wall I'd made on my way in told me I didn't have a choice. Fallyn and Hemi were already engaged in battle, Fallyn with the tentacle thing and Hemi with the fog creature. I worried that my friends were out of their league. They were great at fighting everyday, run-of-the-mill monsters, but these things were beyond their experience, perhaps even surpassing their capabilities.

On the ground, patients ran in all directions, some avoiding the monsters, others getting swept up and "eaten," if you could call it that. I had to do something, and fast; otherwise this was going to be a slaughter.

I unslung my Craneskin Bag and took off my Kevlar-reinforced leather jacket, balling it up and tossing it inside the Bag. Then I tossed Dyrnwyn in after it, exchanging the longsword for Orna, the giant greatsword I'd taken from the corpse of Tethra the Fomorian in Mag Mell. No sooner had I pulled the greatsword from the Bag, than it began to chatter incessantly.

"Why, master, what a pleasant surprise! How long has it been since you drew me from the confines of that spatial anomaly? I only ask because it's quite difficult to gauge the passage of time in there—"

"Not now, Orna. We have killing to do."

"Oh, glorious day!" the sword replied. "More heroic feats for me to record and recite later."

In the short time I'd had it in my possession, I'd determined a few things about Tethra's sword. For one, it was nigh indestructible. Moreover, it was as loony as anyone or anything currently roaming the grounds of this mental institution.

The damned thing was intelligent, but Orna's creator had made its primary function to regale anyone and everyone who'd listen with tales of each of its owners' martial exploits. The only way to shut it up was to go into battle, threaten it with smelting, or toss it into my Bag. If I had my way, I'd leave it there, except it was damned hard to find weapons that were made for a giant's hands. Having belonged to another Fomorian, Orna fit me perfectly when I was in my fully shifted form.

Speaking of, time to shift.

I rarely bothered changing out of my clothing before I shifted. By the time things got that bad, my clothes would be trashed anyway. Instead, I'd taken to wearing the toughest, stretchiest Lycra undies I could find. It wasn't a perfect solution, but it prevented my junk from swinging free in battle. Not that I cared while I was in that form, but the shit I took from people afterward was intolerable.

As for the shifting part, that had become almost easy over the years. It was still painful as hell, but I could do it a lot faster now. Just ten seconds of the worst pain a person could experience, and I transformed into nine-and-a-half feet and 800-plus pounds of twisted steel and no sex appeal.

The downside? This was always accomplished by forcefully breaking every bone, snapping every tendon, and tearing every muscle in my body, only to regrow them bigger and better than before.

And man, was I ugly when I shifted. I looked like Quasimodo and the Thing had a baby or something. Not the Swamp Thing, or the Thing from the ice, but FF thing. My Fomorian body wasn't made of stone, but it might as well have been from an aesthetic standpoint.

Even worse, I displayed zero symmetry in this form. My right arm and hand were way thicker and more muscular than my left, my face was lopsided, my nose looked punched in and crooked, I had a badly hunched humpback—I could go on and on. The upside was that my skin was like rhinoceros hide, and I healed like a freaking mutant in this form. Naturally, that made it perfect for fighting giant, evil, lunacy-inducing monsters.

After I completed the transformation, I flexed my fingers and stretched, then I snagged Orna from where I'd propped her against the remains of a dented metal desk.

"Alright, sword," I rumbled. "Let's go kill some godlings."

"My name isn't sword, master, it is Orna, forged in the fires of—"

"I don't care," I said as I ran toward the hole in the wall where I came in, doubling it in size as I exited the building. "Now shut up and let me fight."

"Yes, master."

By the time I reached the lawn in the central courtyard of the facility, my companions were deep in the shit. Fallyn had procured a fire axe, which she used to great effect on the tentacle monster. Pieces of the thing lay everywhere, twitching and spasming as they died.

I ran up beside her, hacking and slashing off tentacles with abandon. "Having fun yet?"

"Honestly, no," she said. She paused to duck under a flailing tentacle that ended in a dozen fanged mouth suckers. "If I wasn't taking out my rage on this thing, I think I'd have already shifted and gone on a killing spree."

"Hang tough," I said as I pivoted, narrowly avoiding a two-foot thick tentacle that slammed into the grass where I'd been standing. I chopped it off and kicked it away before flashing Fallyn a wicked grin. "Once we kill these things, the feeling should fade."

Fallyn merely grimaced and kept on fighting.

As for Hemi, he danced along the edges of the fog monster's body, always staying just out of reach of any tendrils of mist that came near him. Rather than using his club as a bludgeon, he'd turned it around and wielded it two-handed, so he could stab at the center of the fog creature with the pointed end of the weapon. Whenever he did, blue light flashed, and a low wail resounded from within.

"Hemi, need a hand?" I yelled.

"Naw mate, I got it," he said as he deftly avoided a sliver of fog that drifted toward his head. "Just figuring out how to kill it, s'all."

"Alright, holler if you want company."

"Get your own, aye?" he said, a bit more testily than was typical for the normally amiable demigod.

Good idea.

With the other two creatures occupied, that left me to face the abstract nightmare of a thing that was currently chasing a trio of patients across the parking lot. In lieu of any rational form of movement, the thing sort of "blipped" forward in random spurts and jumps. With each jump, it folded in on itself before expanding outward in whichever direction it went, sucking inanimate objects inside it along the way.

What was really, truly creepy was what it did to those objects. The daemon would fold itself over a car or a minivan or a dumpster, and then it'd blip forward, leaving a jumbled, barely recognizable mass of stuff in its wake. As I watched, it turned a mid-sized sedan into a piece of modern art. The result resembled a giant origami sculpture, except that the monster had turned it inside out, upside down, and twisted besides.

My brain was just coming to grips with the prospect of what that thing might do to a living being, when I noticed something strange about the origami car. Oddly, a human eyeball stared out from a section of the hood that remained intact. I'd have missed it, if not for the fact that it blinked, right when my gaze swept past.

Holy shit, someone must've been hiding in that car when the Escher monster ate it.

I paused to take a closer look and instantly wished I hadn't, because there were more body parts fused to the twisted lump of steel, plastic, and rubber. I found a finger here, a tuft of hair there, a foot somewhere else, and tucked in the crease between an upper and lower section of a bench seat, a mouth—and it was moving. Every few seconds it'd relax and close, then it would open wide, so awfully wide, although not a single sound escaped it.

Even more disturbing was the fact that its tonsils and throat were intact. I could see that the windpipe led somewhere, back within that pile of junk and flesh. Somehow, within all those jumbled up parts and pieces of the vehicle, this person's nervous system connected all those bits together. A cursory examination soon resulted in a horrific conclusion; the victim seemed to be aware of their current state.

My Fomorian mind made note of the abomination in an almost clinical fashion. But the human half of my brain? That part of me wanted to be sick—except that my Fomorian body seemed to be incapable of displaying weakness in that manner.

At that moment, I felt pretty damned helpless, having no clue how to help this person. Hell, I couldn't even put them out of their misery, because I had no idea what it would take to kill them in that state. Then there was the question of the aftermath. Holy shit, how would one of Maeve's fixers even go about cleaning up something like that? For that matter, how was I going to fight something that could do this?

I had no idea how to stop a demon that could twist the very fabric of reality, but I had to try. It had almost overtaken the three people it was chasing, so I had to act fast. Attacking it with Orna was out of the question, as there was no telling what the sword would look like if it passed through that thing.

Lacking a better option, I queued up some druid battle magic and I snapped a lightning spell at it. While I couldn't tell if it did any damage, I at least got its attention. The creature had no eyes, so I couldn't determine where its focus lay. However, as soon as my spell hit the thing, it stopped chasing the humans, and it started blipping in my direction.

"That's right—come to papa," I growled.

I hit it with another lightning spell. In response, the damned thing sped up, blipping a bit further and with greater frequency in my direction.

If I didn't know any better, I'd say that my magic was feeding and strengthening it. Damn.

While I processed that revelation, the monster blipped forward a good thirty feet, well within range should I stand my ground. After seeing what happened to the person in the car, my general attitude about standing and fighting amounted to "fuck that," Fomorian battle lust or no. Instead, I leapt backwards a good fifty feet, denting the roof of one of those short white passenger buses as I landed atop it.

Since lightning did nothing more than feed the thing, I decided to try other spells. First, I summoned a beachball-sized fireball, imbuing it with enough explosive energy to destroy a small house. The fireball disappeared inside the Escher monster, with nary a belch of smoke to mark its passing.

Even more discouraging, the thing was jumping

faster and farther with each spell I fed it. Soon I was forced to leap greater distances to escape it.

Maybe some ice will slow it down.

I pulled all the moisture from the air that I could, cascading it in a torrent on the blacktop between me and the monster. Then I sucked the heat out of the water, turning the parking lot into an ice skating rink in front of it. Curiously, rather than slowing the thing down, it stopped at the edge of the ice.

Simultaneously, the images and scenes on the surfaces of the creature went blank, clouding over as if filled with fog. The monster flickered back and forth for several seconds, blipping forward and back so fast it almost became a blur. Then it began to edge itself around the ice sheet, oscillating as it formed itself to the borders of my makeshift ice rink.

What the hell? Is it the cold that it dislikes?

Out of curiosity, I funneled a whirlwind of air at the thing, pulling the heat out of it at the last moment, so the core temperature of the vortex was close to that of liquid nitrogen. Yet, my "cone of cold" disappeared inside the Escher monster, just as the lightning and the fireball had. Obviously, it wasn't the low temperature that it disliked.

Hmm.

On a whim, I melted water on the far side of the ice sheet, then I moved it into the monster's path and froze it again. As soon as the creature came into contact with the ice, it altered course, probing its way around the obstacle.

What the hell?

Then it hit me. Ice froze in crystalline form, and the very definition of a crystalline structure was the formation of a repeating pattern. It wasn't the cold the thing disliked, it was the *order* it represented.

Of course. This is a creature of chaos. It's only natural that it dislikes order.

With that revelation, I briefly considered shooting ice spikes at it, but that seemed underwhelming, at best. I needed to contain it, then destroy it. So, I'd seek containment first.

Before the damned thing could get past the ice, I melted the parts of the ice sheet that were farthest from it, then I formed the water into a moat that surrounded the creature. Subsequently, I froze the moat, leaving plenty of room behind and around the monster to avoid making it feel completely trapped.

Now, I need to banish it.

Using willpower and druidic magic alone, I etched the ice moat in runes to contain and ensnare the entity. Once the wards were in place, I imbued them with druidic magic, and soon they glowed with a faint green light. The Escher monster must've sensed what I was doing, because it began darting around the circle of bare pavement, oscillating rapidly as it probed for a weakness in my wards.

Before the creature could make its escape, I enclosed

the runes in two unbroken circles, one within and another without, imbuing those with druidic magic as well. Finally, I etched wards of banishment around the outside of the outer circle, and I enclosed those symbols in a final, unbroken ring that linked and locked the whole thing together.

As soon as the design was complete, I poured as much druidic magic into it as I dared, until the entire banishment spell was brimming with the order of nature. Then I triggered the spell, lighting the entire thing up like Christmas.

The only problem was, nothing happened after I triggered the spell. In other words, my banishment spell wasn't banishing anything. The demon—or daemon, to be specific—was corralled temporarily. But for some reason the spell wasn't sending it back to where it came from, and as soon as the ice melted it'd be on the loose again.

"Wait a minute—"

I facepalmed my ugly, misshapen forehead on realizing my error. Of course, this thing wasn't being banished, because to banish an entity, you had to send it back to its home plane. And duh—this *was* the thing's home plane.

As I puzzled this out, the entity continued to bounce back and forth inside the magical cage, and the sun rose higher in the sky. Still stumped, I took a moment to see how my companions were doing. Fallyn had chopped the giant tentacle creature to bits, leaving pieces of the thing everywhere across the lawn and parking lot. I searched for the main body of the monster but could find none, although I did spot a single, python-like tentacle slithering down a sewer drain.

As for Hemi's status, he was still dancing in and out of range, attacking the center of the fog creature with his club. As he did, the intricate patterns on his arms, body, and face glowed brighter and brighter. Finally, the radiance that emanated from his tattoos reached a point where I couldn't look at them directly. It was then that Hemi changed tactics, and instead of fighting defensively, he leapt right into the middle of the fog creature.

Initially, I thought he'd gone mad, that maybe the influence of these things had driven him insane. But no, his strategy was right on the money. When Hemi landed in the center of the thing, the bright blue light that shone from his ink illuminated the fog creature from within. Hemi's magic burned away all that mist, freeing the lost souls inside—and revealing the creature's true form.

That thing resembled a spindly, dog-sized spider made of shadow and smoke. As soon as Hemi spotted it, he stomped on it to pin it to the ground. Then, he stabbed it through the carapace with the sharp end of his club, twisting as he levered the stick from side to side. The monster squealed, releasing a high, pitiful shriek, then it shivered and lay still.

Two down, one to go.

I turned my gaze back to the creature that was blipping and bouncing around inside my banishment circle, and I wondered how the heck I was going to kill it. Briefly, I considered etching the same pattern into the asphalt beneath the ice. Yet, I doubted that the unordered structure of the blacktop surface would have the same ability to confine the monster.

Besides, I couldn't very well leave a madness demon in the middle of the state mental hospital's parking lot. That thing was dangerous, a hell of a lot more so than the fog monster or the tentacle beast. Finally, I admitted to myself that I was stumped. I decided to re-freeze the ice, so I'd have time to consult Tuan about what to do.

Fallyn approached as I was working on freezing the ice. The way she dripped with dark green blood, she looked like an orcish axe murderer. Her edgy, 'I might kill someone for the fun of it' expression cinched it.

"C'mon, Golden Boy—stop slacking and kill that thing already," she said through gritted teeth. "I'm about to lose it and spontaneously shift."

"Sorry, but I can't," I said as I shot an arctic blast of air at the ice. "It literally warps reality around it, and I haven't yet figured out a way to end it. The best I can do is restrain it. I'm just making sure my containment circle doesn't melt while I go ask Brother Carroll what I should do."

"Good thing there's no salt on the ground," she opined. "If we'd had freezing rain earlier in the season, there's no way your ice would've lasted."

I hung my head, realizing what an idiot I'd been. "Fallyn, you're a flippin' genius."

"What? Because I understand eighth grade science?"

"No, because—never mind. Listen, I need you and Hemi to search this place for salt. Like, a lot of salt, the kind they use for water softeners, or the stuff they throw on sidewalks in the winter."

"Oh-kay. It's a weird request, but can do."

A half an hour later, Hemi and Fallyn returned with several forty pound bags of rock salt. I directed them to set the salt down near my banishment circle, then I cut the bags open.

"You guys are going to want to give me some room," I said.

Hemi gave a one-shouldered shrug, then he headed off toward a nearby cluster of vending machines. Fallyn cocked her head and gave me a funny look, but she complied.

Once the area was clear, I cut open the bags, just enough to allow me to access the crystals. Focusing my druid magic into the rock salt, I formed it into fist-sized cubes, each one shaped to retain and reinforce the substance's natural crystalline structure. Once I had each bag divvied up into perfectly uniform hexahedrons, I slowed my breathing and triggered Cathbad's Planetary Maelstrom, using the salt cubes as the missiles for the spell.

With a hundred or more rock-hard cubes of salt orbiting me at speed, I calmly walked across the ice toward the Escher monster. As soon as the first cube of rock salt crossed the outer edge of the banishment circle, the creature stopped bouncing around. All its surfaces instantly went blank and foggy, then the thing blipped away to the far side of the circle.

"Uh-uh, you're not getting away that easily," I rumbled as I crossed inside the barrier, being careful not to scuff a single rune along the way.

I continued my approach, bringing the spinning, rotating field of missiles closer and closer to their target. The hardest part was keeping my eyes on the thing. Even in my Fomorian form, looking at it was giving me a headache.

Still, I strode forward, focusing on keeping the spell active with Orna hanging uselessly in my left hand. With no way to "corner" the entity within the circle, I extended the reach of the missiles' orbits until they almost filled the area. In response, the Escher monster flattened, spreading itself out against the boundaries of the circle in an effort to avoid being hit.

That was a losing strategy. My Fomorian bloodlust was up, and I wanted to see if this thing could bleed. I leapt forward, forcing the salt cubes' paths to intersect with the creature's body. As they connected, pieces of the thing seemed to "chip" and break off, small triangles and squares that faded away into nothingness on the wind.

The thing screamed, making a sound that was unlike any I'd heard a living thing make in the past.

Almost vibratory in nature, it started as a hum that built in volume, until it became a roar that threatened to shake the sword from my grip. My nose and ears bled, and my head pounded with every heartbeat. Still, I kept the spell going.

As a last-ditch effort, the Escher monster flattened into a sheet that extended seventy feet or more into the sky, following the boundary of the banishment circle. Then it folded over atop me, like a blanket made of nightmares that threatened to suffocate me entirely— or rather, to turn me into a cubist nightmare. Meanwhile, the salt missiles ripped into it, tearing off great chunks that diminished its structural integrity.

Yet, what remained continued to descend toward me from above. If it made contact, I knew I'd end up a jumbled, rearranged mess of flesh and bone. And I couldn't have that.

With no other option besides retreat—and Fomorians did *not* retreat—I focused on enhancing my Maelstrom spell. At the risk of taking my attention away from the creature, I split half the salt cubes away from the rest, lifting their orbit a few feet and tightening it as well. Then I took half of those and did the same thing, repeating the process until I had a dome of orbiting missiles around me.

By this time, the creature was in free fall, having spread itself so thin it couldn't withdraw itself with any speed. Since my spell was shredding it from the bottom up, it had no leverage to pull itself back to the ground again. The thing floated down atop the salt maelstrom, wailing with that weird vibrational scream that made my teeth chatter and my eardrums pound, even as my spell shredded it into ever smaller pieces.

Within seconds, little remained of the Escher monster, save for a few confetti-like bits that disintegrated into nothing as its droning scream died off into silence. I fell to my knees with blood gushing from my ears and nose, but it was done. I'd defeated a monster that defied logic and reason, simply by using reason and order against it.

Druidry, bitches. It's what's for dinner.

"Well, that was a rather lackluster battle," Orna remarked, harshing my vibe with perfect timing. "Shall I strike it from my memory?"

The sword's voice sounded like it was coming from the bottom of a very long well, but at least I could hear it. That was a testament to how quickly I healed in this form. On reflection, however, I decided I'd rather be deaf than listen to the thing's effete yammering.

"How about I melt you into slag instead?"

"Ahem. I will refrain from further comment."

"Good choice, sword. Maybe you're not as dumb as I thought."

CHAPTER

FOURTEEN

F ollowing the battle, I quickly hid, then I shifted back to my semi-human form and got dressed to avoid traumatizing the patients further. After the demons—or daemons, as it were—had been defeated and sent packing, the hospital reverted to relative normalcy. The influence of madness they'd exerted vanished, and many of the patients calmed down somewhat, despite earlier events. Thankfully, most were unharmed, but some were unaccounted for, according to the few hospital staff members who'd remained.

Those people who'd been lost inside the fog monster emerged relatively unscathed, although they remained in a semi-catatonic fugue. As for the car-person hybrid, each returned to their previous state after I killed the Escher monster. However, the poor woman who'd been inside the car remained trauma-

tized, so much that she screamed her throat bloody—
and then kept on screaming.

We tried to comfort her, but how do you comfort
someone who'd been through that? After a few minutes
of failed attempts to calm her, I was at a loss and almost
ready to dose her with some poppy seed. Thankfully, a
hospital employee came by to give her an injection that
knocked her out.

"Thanks," I said, as I stole a glance at her name tag
so I could address her properly. "Dr. Solomon."

"Thank you for saving Sharon," she said.

"Was she a patient?" I asked.

Dr. Solomon shook her head gravely, sparing the
woman a sideways glance as two orderlies lifted her
onto a stretcher. "A counselor. Although I'm afraid she
might become a patient, after what she went through."

"I'm sorry," I said. "We did our best."

"I'm aware," the psychiatrist replied. "I saw what
you three did, although I don't have any context by
which to frame what just happened. After what I
witnessed, I'm starting to question my own sanity."

"It's best if you just forget it all," Fallyn said. "Trust
me on this."

"How many of your employees saw the last bit?" I
asked.

Her gray eyes widened slightly, and she tucked a
stray bit of silver hair behind her ear. "You mean the
part with tentacles, and the fog, and the creature that

defied every law of logic and physics? Or the part where something equally monstrous and hideous destroyed it? Just me, I think. Everyone else was locked behind closed doors, trying to call for help."

I glanced at Fallyn, who raised an eyebrow as she gave me a 'don't look at me' look. Without Maeve around to provide fae "cleaners" and other resources, this was going to be hard to cover up. It made me realize that, while I rarely saw eye to eye with her, the local faery queen just might be a necessary evil after all.

Turning my attention back to Dr. Solomon, I gently touched her shoulder. "Fallyn is right. It would be best if you pretended this had never happened. People who see *events* like this sometimes run into trouble later."

"As in, they have mysterious accidents," Fallyn added, using air quotes for emphasis. "Or they disappear—permanently."

I winced at Fallyn's harsh demeanor. Raised on bloodshed, werewolves were often clueless regarding human reactions to violence and threats of same.

"Aketay ityay ownday ayay otchnay, easeplay," I whispered behind my hand, soft enough that only the werewolf could hear. Meanwhile, the doctor bristled.

"Are you two threatening me? What, are you with the government, or something?" Dr. Solomon hadn't looked especially distraught before, but now her face was drawn. She began to pale, even as she stomped her foot and squared her shoulders. "I—I won't stand for it. Not in my hospital."

I took a deep breath before continuing. "No—I mean, we're not threatening you, and we are definitely not with the government."

"Pfft. Government workers—lazy bunch of losers who can't get real jobs," Fallyn muttered. "Like we'd have anything to do with those bozos."

The doctor seethed at Fallyn's comment, while I trudged ahead, only wincing slightly at the alpha's lack of tact. "All we're saying is, there's a reason why events like this aren't common knowledge. There are people and factions who don't want the public to know that the supernatural world exists. Believe me, they'll go to great lengths to maintain that masquerade."

Fallyn snorted softly. "Bottom line? They'll kill you, lady. And they won't lose a wink of sleep about it, either."

"Fallyn," I said in a pleading tone. "*Please.*"

"What?" she replied, oblivious to the insensitivity she displayed.

Unfortunately, that was the final straw for the good doctor. Maybe it was the callous tone of Fallyn's voice, or the way her eyes turned from hazel to yellow as she spoke—I couldn't say. However, Dr. Solomon's skin tone had now gone from pale to a light shade of green.

"I think I'm going to be sick," the physician said.

My girlfriend rolled her eyes when Dr. Solomon wasn't looking, but she took her by the arm and spoke to her in a gentle, reassuring tone. "C'mon, let's find you a chair and something bubbly with high fructose corn syrup in it. Don't you worry, as long as you keep your mouth shut, you'll likely live a long, peaceful life."

At that, Dr. Solomon turned her head away and tossed her cookies, right then and there. She wiped her mouth as she glanced at Fallyn out of the corner of her eye. "You sound so calm when you say such things. It reminds me of a patient I once had."

"Oh? Was she tough and pretty?" Fallyn asked.

"She was a complete sociopath," the doctor replied. "A killer for hire."

"Yeah, I wouldn't know anything about that," Fallyn said through pursed lips, then she snapped her fingers and whistled in Hemi's general direction. One of the monsters had smashed a soda machine open during the fight, and the big guy was handing them out to patients and staff. "Yo, Hemi—toss me one, will ya'?"

I was nearly ready to rescue Dr. Solomon from my girlfriend's ministrations when Tuan appeared at my side. "Nasty trio, those three. Maniae, spirits of insanity. They're thought to be the children of Lyssa, the Greek goddess of rabies and furor."

"There's a goddess of *rabies*?"

He tsked. "It's the Greek pantheon—there's a god for every petty little thing. I imagine there's even a Greek god of toe clippings out there somewhere. Quite silly, when you think about it."

"I didn't know that you kept tabs on minor deities from the other pantheons," I said.

Tuan yawned and stretched, then he popped his

neck before answering. "If it's demonic, I know about it. All part of my calling and commission."

"I thought all Christians were given a commission to evangelize."

"Some. Most. Others get more dangerous assignments."

I side-eyed him, but he failed to offer further comment. Honestly, I didn't have the energy to pursue that line of questioning, not without getting some caffeine in me first.

"Well, thanks for the assist," I said. "I can't imagine how we'd have fared facing dozens of those things."

"Those I banished were lesser spirits, barely able to influence the physical plane," he said, clucking his tongue. "Had it not been for their stronger brethren, they'd have been limited to mere acts of infestation and oppression. That's enough to drive a person crazy, certainly, but nowhere near as dangerous as the outright possession or physical manifestations you saw here today."

I swept my gaze across the parking lot and court-yard of the facility, taking in the carnage left in the aftermath of the attack. Several staff members and many patients wandered around in a daze, while others ministered to each other as best they could. Some wept. While physical injuries had thankfully been few, the emotional and psychological scars would last for years —lifetimes, even.

"Do you perform many exorcisms like this?"

Tuan scoffed. "Like this one? No, not like this. It's rare that you see a deity exert their influence in such a nefarious manner these days."

"How do you know a deity was involved? Couldn't these daemons have just randomly chosen this place for sowing some chaos?"

Tuan sniffed, as if he'd just caught a whiff of a particularly foul odor. "The Maniae do their mother's bidding; thus Lyssa had to have done something to make this tragedy possible. Else there would have been no way the daemons could possess this many, all at once."

Now he had my full attention, and I turned to address him properly. "I didn't think you believed in other gods."

The ancient man laughed mirthlessly. "Believe in them? Of course, I believe in them. The Scriptures speak of them, and in several places, in fact. I simply do not *worship* those pretenders."

Obviously, I needed to brush up on my Bible studies, because I didn't remember hearing about other gods in Sunday school. Demons and spirits, sure, but gods? I'd have to look into that one, when I had a minute.

"Okay—you do you, then." I inclined my head at the poor, traumatized people milling about. "What about them? Think they'll get over this?"

He exhaled audibly, his mouth drawn in a taut line. "A few of them were already oppressed by spirits, thus the source of their mental illness. I imagine that being exorcised of that presence will do them some good over the long term. As for the rest, such experiences are not easily forgotten."

"Don't I know it."

Tuan clapped a hand on my shoulder. "Never you fear, I'll stick around to ensure the spirits don't return. A few holy symbols and some blessings in key places around here, and the place should be secure from such influences for a good long while."

That was a relief to hear. I smiled and extended my hand. "Thanks, Tuan. You're a good man."

"'Call no man good,'" he said as we shook hands. "But I appreciate the vote of confidence. The question is, what will you do now that you know which goddess is behind this?"

"Are you sure of their identities? The Maniae, and Lyssa?"

"Oh, I have no doubt. I've spent centuries studying such beings, after all."

I rubbed a few stray flecks of dried blood from my face as I considered the implications. "Then I have work to do. Tell me everything you know about Lyssa."

"WHAT NOW, BRO?"

"I dunno, Hemi," I said as I watched Tuan walk the

perimeter of the mental hospital. It was funny how no one questioned him, and he wasn't even glamoured. Crazy what you could get away with when you were dressed as a member of the clergy. "Brother Carroll has this place under control. But now it looks like we have a couple of gods to deal with."

"A couple?" His eyebrow nearly touched his hairline. "Bit much, aye?"

"I still have that job to do for Rube. Also, it looks like one of Eris' siblings is behind this mess, a minor deity named Lyssa."

"Alright then," he said, swigging the last of his diet Dr. Pepper. "Let's go."

"Hang on," I countered as I checked to see if Fallyn was within hearing range. She was all the way on the other side of the compound, but that didn't mean she couldn't hear us if she was paying attention. I lowered my voice while pretending like nothing was amiss. "We still have the Pack and the Coven to contend with as well. Remember, Luther and Samson are both still under the influence of Eris' curse. Until we figure out a way to squash it, that's double trouble for everyone who tags along."

"Meh."

"Dude, I know nothing scares you, but this could get messy." He gave me the brow again, so I let it go. "Alright. Let me talk to Fallyn to see where her head is at, then we'll take care of Rube's problem. Click seems to think we'll need to go through

Rube's demesne, so I guess I'd better see to that first."

"Do you even know how to find this Lyssa bird?" he asked.

"Nope. But since you and I both sent one of her kids across the Veil, I have a feeling she's going to come looking for us."

"Who's going to come looking for us?" Fallyn asked as she loped across the parking lot.

"Some rotten egg from the Greek pantheon, aye? I'll let your boy fill ya' in." Hemi gave me a knowing look, because he knew what it was like being in a serious relationship with a deity or demigod. "Gunna' find another fizzy. Be right back."

Fallyn's mouth twisted in a crooked smirk. "That was convenient. I guess we need to talk?"

"Not about us. About your dad."

"Ah." She nodded once, hanging her head. "I guess I'm going to have to deal with that eventually. I sort of hoped you'd figure this all out, lift the curse, and remove the whole evil influence thing before it came to that."

"We can try, but I can't promise anything," I said. "And the way my luck has been lately—"

She snickered. "Lately?"

"Hey, I was lucky enough to find you."

Fallyn's eyes narrowed and twinkled all at once. "Okay, you get points for that. But honestly, you have the worst luck of any Irishman I've ever known. I mean, did you piss off a leprechaun, or something?"

"Or something," I said, thinking back to the Avartagh, and how my whole crazy foray into The World Beneath started. "But we were talking about you, weren't we?"

She smiled as though her heart wasn't in it. Then she stepped in close, grabbing a handful of my shirt in the process. "I don't want to hurt my dad, Colin. That has to be my worst nightmare come to life."

"I get that. I don't even like my mom, and I couldn't imagine having to fight her. Just thinking about it is heartbreaking." I wrapped my arms around her and gave her a little squeeze. "But c'mon, your dad is tough. I gave him a pretty good beat down, and afterward he was all healed up in no time flat."

"Yeah, but that was when he was in his right mind. This curse—it pries itself into the dark recesses of your skull. I think that you, me, and Hemi are partially protected from it, because of our divine DNA. But Dad isn't, and he's acting plain nuts."

I thought about the scene in the parking lot earlier. "Okay, I can see that. What do you want me to do?"

"Nothing. You can't fix everything, Colin, no matter how bad you want to try. This is just something I'm going to have to work out on my own."

"Have you called your mom about this?"

Her lips pressed into a hard line as she growled. "I did, and you know what she said? 'This won't be the first time you have to put an alpha male in his place, and it won't be the last. Grow some ovaries and deal with it.' Then she hung up on me."

"Sheesh. And I thought my mom was a hard-ass."

"You have no idea. But like I said, I'll handle it." She leaned away to look me in the eye. "And Colin? Whatever happens, do not, under any circumstances, get involved."

"You serious? Even if the Pack turns on you?"

"Yep, even then. I have to work it out on my own, or else I'll lose them for good. And then—"

"What?" Her brow furrowed so deeply, if she wasn't a werewolf, she'd have developed wrinkles on the spot. I'd never seen her look so serious, or so worried. "Tell me, already."

"I'll be an outcast, Colin. A freaking lone wolf—an omega. It won't matter how much of a badass I am, or that Dad was under a curse, because the only thing they'll remember is that I was challenged, and I ran. To a pack of lycanthropes, that's the cardinal sin for an alpha."

"Yikes." I genuinely understood what Fallyn was saying. Other predators had weaker ties to the Pack, but not wolves.

Take a weretiger, for instance. They were solitary animals by nature, never really needing the support of a pack. That's why you never saw a weretiger or werebear vying for pack leadership. It was also why they were always welcomed into a pack when they chose to join.

But for a social creature like a werewolf, there was

nothing worse than being an outcast. To them, family and their pack were everything. If Fallyn became an outcast, it would destroy her. As a result, she'd likely leave Austin and go back to her mom's place in Switzerland.

Can't have that. Nope.

But, she'd asked me not to intervene, so I wouldn't if it came to it. I just wondered if she had it in her to put her dad in his place. *Shit.* I could never do that to my dad, and we hadn't had the relationship she'd cultivated with Samson.

"Colin…" she warned.

I sucked air through my teeth. "I don't like it, but sure."

"Thank you," she said. "Okay, so what's next?"

"Next? We track down Rube's thieving godlet, and his missing lucky churchkey."

"That sounds like either the worst quest ever, or a hell of a good time."

I chuckled. "One can hope."

ACCORDING to the bartender at Rocko's joint, all the Slavic gods, demigods, and supernatural creatures hung out at some dive on 290 east. When we pulled into the parking lot in the Druidmobile, I had a bit of déjà vu, because it reminded me a lot of another joint we frequented.

"Damn, it's like the clubhouse shat out a baby sister," Fallyn said.

Considering the gravel lot, the chipped white paint over cinder block walls, the concrete stoop, the plain metal door, and the hirsute, muscular man sitting on a barstool at the front entrance—yep, it reminded me a lot of the Pack's private hangout and headquarters. I parked the car at the edge of the small gathering of vehicles in the lot, facing the road, so we could leave quickly if we had to. After I shut the engine off, I triggered a couple of extra wards, one to let me know if anyone messed with the car, and another to shock the hell out of anyone who did.

"C'mon, let's see if we can find this guy," I said as I exited the vehicle.

When we approached the front door, the hulking brute on the barstool gave us a disinterested look. The guy was heavily muscled, but with the thick build and slight gut of a farm hand rather than a body builder. He wore carpenter's jeans and a red flannel button-down over a white thermal long-sleeved shirt, and a navy watch cap pulled down over a presumably bald head. The black, three-day beard growth on his face matched the thick shag on his forearms, and his chin looked rough enough to light a match.

He moved the toothpick he was chewing to the other side of his mouth with a grunt, scanning the distance as he spoke. "Private club," he said in a thick Slavic accent. He could've been Russian, or maybe from another former Eastern Bloc country, I couldn't tell. He pointed in a vaguely Southwestern direction. "Sixth Street that way. Tourists go there. Get lost."

"We're not tourists," I replied, summoning a small fireball that hovered above my left palm.

The doorman's gaze flicked to the fireball, then back into the distance. "Cover charge is ten U.S. dollars. Each. Not responsible for damage to personal property or friends while in club."

"They can take care of themselves," I said as I handed him two twenties. "Keep the change."

He grunted and gave us another detached sweep of his gaze. The money I'd handed him disappeared as quickly as it'd changed hands. Whether that was by legerdemain or magic, I couldn't tell.

"Have nice day," the doorman said, then he returned to scanning the horizon and chewing his toothpick.

"Right back atcha' mate," Hemi replied as he passed, pulling open the door so Fallyn could enter.

I followed close on her heels, not comfortable letting her enter unknown and possibly hostile territory first. It was a constant battle, having to remind myself that she could handle herself, and maybe better than I could in a physical scrape. Still, old instincts died hard, and I shouldered my way next to her as soon as we were inside the building.

Fallyn whistled softly. "Shit on a stick—I take back what I said about this place reminding me of the Clubhouse."

Outside, the place had looked as dive-ish as a dive can get. But on the inside? It could've been the Headliner's downtown, that swank private club where all the politicians, movers, and shakers in Austin hung out.

The ceilings were high—way higher than the building looked to be from the parking lot—and decorated with chandeliers and those fancy tassel thingies. It was red velvet, dark leather, and polished wood everywhere you looked, with gold leaf here and there as an accent. From the red carpet under our feet, to the crystal glassware I saw the bartender serving drinks in, this place had "Russian mobster's cover business and hideout" written all over it.

"Why do I have the funny feeling John Wick is going to show up shortly?" I asked.

"Why do I feel like I'm underdressed?" Fallyn added.

"Smells like Cuban cigars and fine whiskey in here," Hemi stated. "I could get to like this place."

"Enough sightseeing, you two—we have a godling to find," I said, feeling like a dick for being a killjoy. "Follow me."

"'Follow me, I'm a druid master with BDE'," Fallyn taunted in a sing-song voice behind my back.

Hemi snickered, but he thankfully remained quiet as I sidled up to the bar. The bartender, a real-life version of every young, male, big-city movie bartender I'd ever seen, was engaged in conversation with a female patron a few seats down. He ignored my presence, choosing instead to regale the young, leggy brunette with dad jokes and trashy come-on lines instead of serving another customer.

"Ahem." I laid a twenty down on the bar, resting my hand atop it. The bartender glanced at it and sneered, then he went right back to flirting with the brunette.

"Think it's hunners or nuthin' in this place, sweetie," Fallyn said. Though I faced the bar, I could hear the smirk in her voice clearly.

I laid another twenty down on the counter. "Excuse me—"

"You're excused, bub," the silk-shirted bartender said. "Now go back to Chili's where you belong."

That one got a guffaw from Fallyn and a chuckle from Hemi as well.

"Say what?" I said, snatching my forty bucks off the bar. "What's your problem?"

The bartender pulled the neatly folded, pristine bar rag off his shoulder, setting it on the serving counter behind the bar. "My problem?" he said, snapping his head around fast enough to dislodge a strand of hair from the shellac of pomade that held it in place. "I'll tell you what my 'problem' is. Look around—trash like you three don't belong here."

I was about to give him a piece of my mind, when a tall, very muscular man with curly brown hair sidled up to the bar next to me. He'd positioned himself so he stood between me and the bartender, and as he did, I noted that he smelled like body spray, booze, and anise. With his fitted designer V-neck, skin-tight black slacks, fancy Italian loafers, and masculine, yet pretty features, he could've been an extra in a *Magic Mike* sequel.

"Now, now, Oscar," the musclebound man said in an accent that was somewhere between Transatlantic and Posh. "That's no way to speak to the Justiciar of the Austin demesne, is it? Why, this young lad could shut this establishment down with a word, and then where would your employers be?"

Oscar blinked twice, obviously thrown off his game now that the Chippendale's dancer had come to my rescue. "I—I—um—"

"I'll tell you where they'd be," Chippendales said as he stabbed his index finger in the air. "Rather cross with a certain bartender. Who, as I understand it, is already on thin ice—considering how he tends to ignore paying customers in favor of flirting with attractive female patrons." The muscular man turned his thousand-watt smile on the brunette as he stage-whispered behind his hand. "I'd steer clear, m'lady. Word is he has the drips."

"Oh," was all she said, covering her mouth with one hand and grabbing her tiny purse with the other. The woman spun off the barstool, shimmying to straighten her little black dress as she stood. "Thanks for the drink, Oscar, but I just remembered I have a paper due by Monday."

Oscar sullenly watched the woman as she sauntered away, his eyes following every swing of her hips as she exited the club. His expression was almost as petulant as his voice as he turned to address my savior.

"Come on—was that really necessary? I'd been working on her all week, and just got her number."

"Ah, but you do have the drips, do you not?" the muscular man asked.

"I'm a *vodyanoy*, of course I have the drips," Oscar whined. He looked at me, waving his hands in defeat. "Look, you're obviously a friend of Porevit, so let me apologize right here and now."

"And—?" the muscular man said in his Gascon-like voice.

Oscar sighed. "And the next round's on me."

Chippendales slapped his hands on the bar, eliciting a tremor that shook the glass on the wall behind it. "That's the spirit, Oscar, that's the spirit." The man turned his gaze my direction, then to Hemi, and finally to Fallyn, doing a double-take as if noticing her for the very first time. "Tell me, fair maiden—what shall you and your companions be drinking on this fine evening?"

Fallyn rolled her eyes, but the flush in her cheeks said she wasn't entirely immune to the dude's charms. "Lone Star, in the bottle. Slim here'll probably want a bourbon, neat, and get the big man a Foster's."

"Foster's? That piss?" Hemi scowled and pointed at Chippendales as he addressed the bartender. "I'll have what he's having."

"Lone Star longneck, a Maker's neat, and two boiler-makers, coming right up," Oscar said before shuffling off to fetch our drinks.

"So, you're Porevit," I said, sizing Chippendales up.

He turned to face me, three-quarters front, leaning with his elbow on the bar and half his ass on the stool. If I tried that, it'd look awkward as shit, but he somehow managed to look rakish. "Some call me that, especially in this enclave of Slavonic mythology. But you can call me Heracles."

FIFTEEN

He smiled broadly when he said it, and I swear, his large and very white teeth twinkled.

"Heracles? As in 'Hercules'? *The* Hercules?"

Heracles nodded. "None other."

Fallyn's eyes narrowed. "Then why did the bartender call you Porevit?"

Heracles chuckled. "Because that's how they know me. I passed through some Slavic lands way back when I was searching for the Garden of Hesperides. One thing led to another, I did some favors for a few locals, then word spread. Soon they started worshipping me, and they gave me a title—'Lord of Strength.' I figured, why fight it, right?"

"Thought you were dead, mate." Hemi spoke with no malice or accusation in his voice. He was only stating facts, after all.

"I was," the man who claimed to be Hercules said. "But you know as well as I that our kind rarely cross the Veil with finality."

Hemi bobbed his head. "I s'pose."

"And speaking of *our* kind—welcome, friends," Heracles said as he gestured expansively. "Demigods maintain a privileged position in the so-called 'World Beneath,' high enough above the masses to rule over them—should we choose—but far enough below the gods to earn their favor instead of their enmity."

"Please, repeat that last part for Captain Treehugger here," Fallyn said. "Because I don't think he got the memo."

Heracles' smile broadened. "And with a wit to match her beauty! Oh, the tales I've heard of a female alpha and demititan, right here in Austin. The stories did not do you justice, dear Fallyn." He looked at Hemi and I both in turn. "And to think I'd get the opportunity to meet the famous druid, *and* the son of Hine-nui-te-pō at the same time. I must say, it is good to be among equals again."

The guy could lay it on thick, I'd give him that. If he wasn't who he claimed to be, I had no doubt he was the progeny of a god. Only a demigod could be that arrogant and self-assured.

By this time, Oscar had returned with our drinks. Just to hack him off, I laid a fiver on the counter. Indecision was writ across his face as he wavered between snubbing me and pissing off Heracles. When he snatched the bill off the bar, his ears were redder than Santa's sled.

I passed drinks to Fallyn and Hemi, smiling smugly all the while. "What brings you to Austin, Heracles?"

"I'll get to that... but first, a toast! To friends made new, maidens fair, and stories to be shared in times to come."

He raised his glass, and we clinked drink ware. Heracles slugged his down, catching the shot glass in his mouth like a champ. I knocked my glass back, using a bit of magic to evaporate the alcohol in the glass and exchange it for water before it hit my throat. Hemi and Fallyn both drained their drinks as well.

Ah, what a waste. I need to be clearheaded to take him down, though. Especially if he's who he says.

Heracles raised his empty mug high, then he slammed it down on the bar. "Barkeep, another round for my friends and I!"

"You were saying?" I said after Oscar had acknowledged the request.

Fallyn elbowed me, even as Heracles made eyes at her. "Now, now, lovely Fallyn, there's no need to browbeat the poor fellow. I promised to tell the tale, and that I shall."

He stopped talking and leaned back with his elbows on the bar. At first, I thought it was a dramatic pause, then I realized his eyes were following someone walking past. A glance over my shoulder told me he had eyes for more than just my girl this evening. It seemed Heracles was the type to hedge his bets.

"Marissa," he boomed at a waitress who passed by holding a tray of fluted glasses and champagne on ice. "We still haven't had that dance."

The waitress flashed the demigod a skeptical, lopsided smile. "That's because your idea of a dance and mine are two different things, Porevit."

She strutted off toward the VIP section, leaving Heracles chuckling. "I love it when they play hard to get, don't you, druid?"

He elbowed me in the ribs, and I was pretty sure I felt one crack. "Oof. Yup," I groaned as I began to stealth shift. "Hard to get is the best."

"Oh, bullshit," Fallyn protested. "I had to chase you for months before you responded."

"Hey! I was in a relationship," I countered.

"Ah," Heracles said as he nodded knowingly. "Relationships do get in the way at times. Why, I might be involved with dozens of suitors at any given time. Ofttimes, you must sacrifice one to please another. It is disappointing for those who lose out, but necessary. There's only so much of us to go around, after all."

Hemi laughed. "Oi, ever meet a fella' by the name of Maui?"

"Can't say I have," Heracles replied. "Is he strong?"

"Right strong. You an' him'd get along great."

"Then you shall have to introduce me one day." Our

next round of drinks arrived, and Heracles wasted no time passing them out. "Another toast!"

Oh man. This is gonna' be a long night.

Three hours and eighteen rounds later, we were sitting at a table in the VIP lounge. I'd finally gotten Heracles back on the subject of why he was here in Austin, after a lot of beating around the bush on his part. By this time, Hemi was looking even more relaxed than usual—as in, really relaxed.

As for Fallyn, she was starting to slur her words, despite her werewolf metabolism. That was probably because Heracles had talked her into doing several rounds of tequila shots with him. Tequila—ta' kill ya', as the old man used to say. And tequila in a supernatural bar? No question, she'd be feeling it in the morning.

"Heracles, you were going to tell me what brought you to Austin...?" I asked, with just the right amount of obsequiousness and curiosity to stroke the demigod's ego.

Heracles took a long slug of beer, then he wiped his mouth with his beefy forearm. "A job, nothing more. Koalemos asked me to steal some trinket for him, and I thought it a good excuse to see this city for myself."

He pulled a rusty, scratched up metal bottle opener from his pocket and tossed it on the table. The thing looked like a relic straight out of my childhood, from the patina on the metal, to the mangy rabbit's foot that hung from the beaded metal keychain on the end. I couldn't see anything special about it, not in the magical spectrum or using druid magic. Why Rube wanted it back so badly was a mystery to me.

Fae. Who can figure them out?

"Who'd you say hired you again?"

"The god of foolishness. The fellow's an idiot, but he pays well, and that's a fact."

"Koalemos, you say?" I stroked my chin. "Hmm."

Heracles attempted to slap a waitress on the behind as she walked by, but she deftly stepped out of the way. "What's the matter, druid? You doubt my version of events?"

"No, I wouldn't accuse you of misrepresenting yourself." *Openly.* "It's just that we've had more than our fair share of visitors from the Greek pantheon lately. That, combined with the timing of this job you got from Koalemos, seems a little too coincidental."

Heracles perked up at that. If the legends were true, when it came to being screwed over by the gods, he made me look like an amateur.

"Oh? Do tell."

"We just killed these—what were they called, guys?"

"Maniacs," Fallyn said with finality, sloshing her drink as she gestured in the big guy's direction.

"Maniae, aye?" Hemi countered.

"Right, Manatees," Fallyn agreed.

Heracles' ever-present grin became taut as he momentarily glanced in my direction. "You fought the Maniae?"

Aha, gotcha.

I leaned in with my elbows on the table, as if sharing a juicy secret. "We did. I killed one, Hemi killed another, and Fallyn almost did the last one in as well."

"Bull-sheet," the alpha slurred. "I chopped that thing into pisses. No way it surf-fived."

"Not many could say they faced that trio and lived," Heracles said. Despite the emotionless tone of his voice, his face was an inscrutable mask.

"Admittedly, we had an exorcist with us," I said. "He banished their flunkies, so that just left the three daemons to deal with."

Heracles chuckled dismissively, relaxing a bit at the mention of clergy. "Priests. Show them a real monster, and they wet their robes."

"Maybe so, but not this one. He was a fighter before he entered his order."

"Interesting," the muscular demigod said, his biceps bulging as he stroked his perfectly groomed beard. "I should like to meet a warrior monk someday."

Time to reel this fish in.

"Oh, I'd be happy to introduce you," I said. "He's also an expert in mythology. According to him, that mass possession we stopped had some insanity goddess' fingerprints all over it."

Heracles' gaze swung in my direction as he squeezed his beer mug, shattering it into shards. Beer splashed everywhere as broken glass hit the table in a wet, tinkling cascade. For the first time this night, I'd truly garnered the Greek hero's attention.

"I should like for you to repeat that last part, if you don't mind," he said in a low, dangerous tone.

"The part about the guy being an expert?"

By now, veins were popping out on the demigod's forehead. "Nay, the other part."

Hook, line, and sinker.

Earlier, Tuan had refreshed my memory when it came to the Trials of Heracles. As it so happened, Hera had tasked Lyssa to drive Heracles insane, and the lesser goddess did her job a bit too well. She drove him crazy, alright—so crazy that he went into an incoherent rage that resulted in the deaths of his wife and child.

"Oh, you mean about that goddess being involved. What was her name?" I snapped my fingers quickly. "Lisa? Liza? Alyssa?"

By this time, Heracles had blood dripping from his fist, which rested in a sticky red pool on the table. He'd also grabbed the edge of the heavy wooden tabletop with his other hand. The demigod squeezed, causing the table to creak under the strain. Finally, he snapped off a chunk like it was made of papier-mâché instead of thick plywood.

"Lyssa," he hissed.

"Lyssa! That's the one." I snapped one last time and pointed at him, then I affected a concerned expression as I leaned in and lowered my voice. "Wait a minute— you know that broad?"

Heracles' expression grew somber, his tone defeated. "We have... *history* between us."

Yeah, I felt bad for manipulating him. But I was starting to like the guy, and I wanted to avoid a fight. Besides, I was tired of making enemies. I'd much rather have the legendary hero on our side when go time came around, than have him wanting to kick my ass.

"Well, whatever it is, I'm sorry," I said with all sincerity. "It sounds as if it was a really bad deal."

"You have no idea, druid," he replied, staring off into the distance as he laid the broken chunk of wood on the table. "None. I'd end her if I dared, but she remains protected by the powers that be. Thus, I have been forbidden from seeking revenge."

"Tough break, mate," Hemi said. "Nuthin' like the politics of the gods, aye?"

"Indeed, friend warrior, indeed." Heracles shook himself, as if shaking off a chill, then he painted a smile across his face. "But look at me, getting maudlin when we four came together to revel and delight in festivities. Another round!"

I felt awful for reminding him of his dark past, so I held my hand up. "I got this one, my friend. You're a guest in my town, after all." I dropped two hundreds on a waitress' tray as she passed by. It was a good thing the Grove supplied me with gold—the Greek demigod could put them away. "Just keep them coming, please."

The girl nodded before flashing a smile at Heracles, but he hardly noticed now that his mood had shifted.

"Ah, the good old days. You know, I sometimes wish I could retire to the Elysian fields, and give this immortal life up for good."

"Like Rush-eel Crowe in Galadriel," Fallyn stated. Hunched over her beer as she was, she'd barely lifted her head to speak. "That scene wash epic."

"Believe me when I say, the film did not do the Fields justice." Heracles sighed as he absently picked shards of glass from his hand. I watched in silence as his skin reknit before my eyes. "But that place is not for me, not yet. Oh, what I would give for a taste of revenge."

Time to reel him in. Damn, but this makes me feel like a turd.

"You know what? That gives me an idea." I leaned in closer, running a hand down the stubble on my chin. "I'm just spitballing here, but what if I could arrange for that to happen?"

"Oh?" Heracles said, perking up considerably. "What precisely do you have in mind?"

It took a few more rounds to work out the details. We'd track down Lyssa and serve up a little druid justice, with me acting in my official capacity as the justiciar of the area. In return, Heracles would be eternally grateful.

"And you know what? You won't even have to pay my expenses. I'll just put it on the queen's bill."

"Nay, I'll not hear of it," Heracles protested. He pursed his lips, wavering for a bit before he continued. "It's just that—well, I'm a bit tapped out at the moment. I have money at home, mind, but gold is difficult to transport, and I don't trust modern currency."

"Bankers—pure evil," Hemi said.

"Indeed," Heracles agreed. "But I could pay you at a later date."

"Nope, I wouldn't hear of it," I said.

"No, I insist!" Heracles slapped a hand on the already damaged table, causing it to tilt precariously as the churchkey nearly fell off the edge.

I caught it, twirling it on my finger before setting it back down. "Hmm, maybe there's a way we can compromise. Didn't you say this thing was worth a lot to someone?"

"I did. Koalemos offered me a hefty sum for it." His deep brown eyes widened with realization. "Earlier, you said you thought it too convenient by far that he hired me whilst the Maniae and Lyssa were in town. Do you think they're working together?"

"Naw. If he's as dumb as you say, it's more likely this Koalemos dude is being duped." I looked at the churchkey. "But if it's worth that much to Koalemos— or whoever hired him—then the owner'd probably pay a hefty sum to get it back. Don'cha think?"

Heracles slapped me on the back. "Hah! I see where you're going with this, druid. You return the thing and collect a fine reward, while thwarting foul Lyssa's plans —whatever they might be. I like it." He paused dramatically, glancing at me, then Fallyn with a gleam in his eye. "However—"

Ew, boy. Here it comes.

"I cannot give it to you. The thing is magicked to stay with its owner. In fact, to acquire it, I had to win it from the previous owner."

"Wait a minute. You won this from—"

"The King Under the Mountain."

"Get out."

John hadn't told me that. He'd implied that someone had stolen it. No wonder he didn't want to go into details about how he lost the damned thing.

Heracles smiled broadly, his charm and ebullient nature having returned, now that he had a chance of screwing Lyssa royally. "It is true. The Mountain King challenged me to a contest of strength. We wagered, his trinket against my Nemean lion pelt—there was more than one, you see—and I won."

Which meant that John knew I'd have to fight Heracles for it. Rube, you rat bastard.

"Alright, so we have to compete for it. What do you suggest?"

Heracles flexed both his arms in front of his chest, glancing down at how his bulging biceps stretched his tight, blue t-shirt. "A feat of strength—what else?"

THIS BEING a private club for supernatural beings, they had a game room full of supernaturally enhanced devices. Three-dimensional pinball with levitating balls, a disappearing dartboard, a possessed billiard table with pockets that that would bite your hand off if you weren't careful, that sort of thing. But of course, Heracles had to pick something that'd allow him to show off how strong he was—and that gave him an excuse to take off his shirt.

He'd settled on one of those punching bag machines, the kind that say how hard you hit. You know, the type that causes some fool to end up in a viral fail video almost every week. Except, this one was huge. It stood twelve feet tall, putting the punching bag at ten feet off the ground, about the height of a regulation basketball hoop.

Not only that, they'd made the bag from minotaur hide and filled it with sand from the shores of the River Styx. The designer also engineered it to be super-heavy and durable. Finally, cyclopes in Hephaestus' forge designed the internals to provide resistance while gauging various levels of supernatural prowess.

Similar to the mundane versions, there was a meter on the face of the machine that was marked at different levels of strength:

Hero
Centaur
Minotaur
Half-giant
Gorgon
Hill giant
Cyclops

Hundred-Hander
War god
Titan
Kraken

Naturally, the highest setting was *Hercules*. Last but not least, the lit sign on the front of the machine said, "Hercules' Hammer" in big, bold letters. I shittest thee not.

Of course, it's his machine. Honestly, how do I get myself into these messes?

After agreeing on the contest and venue, I had to put something up against the churchkey. A bet wasn't a bet unless each side risked something, after all. It had to be something that was proportionately valuable, so I pulled Orna out of my Bag and laid it on a nearby table. Immediately, the sword began to speak.

"Why hello, master! What a pleasant surprise—and with all these people around. Are we about to slaughter the lot of them? That shall make a grand addition to my annals—"

"Shut up, sword."

"Yes, master," the sword muttered.

"A talking sword? Bah. Such as these are a dime a dozen." Heracles gave Orna the once over, stroking his thick, neatly trimmed beard as his eyes fawned over the giant black blade's exquisite craftsmanship. "Although, it is rather large—my muscles would definitely bulge whilst swinging it."

"Cuts through just about anything, and never needs

sharpening," I said, feeling like an infomercial barker even as the words left my lips. "Tested it myself."

He met my gaze, cocking his head slightly. "What else can it do?"

"It remembers every feat its owner performs, and every battle its owner engages in, then it recites them each time it's pulled from its sheath."

Heracles' eyes lit up. "Are you serious? That's splendid!" His brow furrowed. "But, do you have the sheath?"

"Oh, come one. Surely, you can get a cyclops to whip you one up."

The Greek demigod frowned, feigning reluctance, but I could tell he was all in. The guy had an ego the size of Texas. To a bro like him, nothing could be better than a sword that bragged on you incessantly.

After several tense seconds, he nodded. "Fine. Let's do this."

Half the bar's patrons had gathered to watch, including Fallyn and Hemi. My girlfriend had draped herself across two chairs, her head lolling about as she mumbled incoherently, a longneck in each hand. Hemi stood by, nursing a brew while guarding the apparently very inebriated alpha.

"Oi, brah—you sure about this?"

"Yep," I said, flashing Hemi a smile I didn't feel. "Trust me, it's under control. I got this."

"You goth tits, babe," Fallyn slurred, barely managing to raise her head from her chest to do so.

"Keep an eye on her, will you?"

Hemi chuckled. "'Course, mate."

Suddenly, a roar arose from the gathered audience. I turned to see what was up, only to find that the Greek demigod of strength had taken off his t-shirt. Which was silly, since the damned thing had been skin tight in the first place.

"Whaz goin' on?" Fallyn asked. "Did we *hiccup* win?"

Hemi shook his head. "Yeah-nah. The peacock just took off his shirt, is all."

Fallyn opened one eye, groggily looking about until she spotted the demigod's statuesque figure as he flexed and posed for the audience. She raised a longneck in the air as a bleary smile split her face.

"Her-cuh-leez, Her-cuh-leez, Her-cuh-leez!" she shouted. "Take it off, baby!"

"Hey!" I said, the hurt in my voice plain for all to hear.

"Slurry, babe," she mumbled before passing out.

I leaned over her, planting a kiss on her cheek as I wiped a bit of drool from her lower lip with my shirt. "Of course you'd turn out to be a funny drunk." I whispered. Shaking my head, I addressed Hemi as I stood. "Definitely keep an eye on her."

"On it," Hemi replied.

Unsurprisingly, Heracles went first. The guy made a huge show of it, taking a stance in front of the machine, flexing his muscles, the whole bit. He was ripped, by the way, and like one-percent body fat to boot—it was sickening, the guy was so good-looking and built. I think a couple of females and at least one male in the audience swooned before he was done.

After all that strutting about, the demigod leapt into the air, twisting his hips one way and his shoulders opposite to plant an earth-shattering punch square in the center of the bag. The floor shook as the machine absorbed the force of the blow, and the bag folded at the hinge, slamming into the top of the machine with a *whoomp* like a sonic boom.

Air displacement caused the entire front row of onlookers to stagger, one dude's toupee flew off, and more than a few skirts had to be held in place to prevent inadvertent acts of public indecency. Even as we all struggled to stay on our feet, all eyes were glued to the machine as its meter activated.

Ding-ding-ding-ding-ding-ding-ding! it went, as the lights lit up in iridescent shades of green, then yellow, then orange, and finally red, all the way up the front of the machine. When the lights reached the top, *Hercules* lit up and shone brightly, illuminating the room in golden rays of light as several buzzers, bells, and sirens went off all at once. The demigod turned to address me with a smug smile on his face.

"I'd wish you luck, but no amount of luck will allow you to beat that score," he said, patting me on the back hard enough to stagger me as he passed.

I unslung my Bag, setting it on the table in front of Fallyn. Hemi leaned close, whispering in my ear.

"Mate—can ya' beat that?"

"Only one way to find out."

I stripped down to my skivvies then and there, eliciting a few catcalls, but nowhere near the response Heracles had gotten. A few onlookers chuckled at my spare, lean, athletic build, seeing that I was made more for speed and agility than sheer strength. Then, I began to shift, and the crowd grew still.

Those catcalls and jeers were soon replaced by gasps of surprise, and more than a few angry words.

"He's a titan," someone said.

"Thought they were all dead," said another.

"*Chudovishche*," a woman said before spitting on the floor. "Porevit should slay him where he stands."

I ignored them, having become used to that sort of thing over the years. Fomorians had always been the worst of all the titanic tribes, a warmongering, murderous race that elicited a visceral, negative gut reaction from most of the other races on sight. We'd been the Visigoths, the Vikings, the barbarians of the supernatural world, and it was no wonder they reacted as they did. It was in their DNA to hate us, after all, and frankly that didn't bother me a bit.

After I transformed, I happened to glance up, only to find Heracles staring at me with his jaw on the floor. "So it's true," he said in a disbelieving tone. "You *are* a son of Iapetus. If I hadn't seen it with my own eyes, I'd not have believed it."

Since coming to grips with my parentage, I'd spent

some time researching the Fomorians. Little was known about our origins, except that we'd come as conquerers from the sea. One genealogy traced us back to Noah, but that seemed sketchy to me.

Heracles had been around a long time, spending much of his life around the Greek gods. That meant he knew stuff most people didn't, things only members of the pantheons were privy to. I'd have to look into this Iapetus cat at some point, for sure—or get Heracles drunk again, so I could pick his brain.

But not today. Today, I had to beat the Greek demigod of strength at his own damned game.

Heracles was strong, I'd give him that—stronger than I was, even in this form. However, his was a raw strength. Like most bruisers, he'd never had to rely on skill to win a fight. And why would he? When you could bench press a mountain, why would you ever need skill to survive?

Like most unskilled fighters, Heracles didn't understand the difference between strength, force, and power. Strength was the ability to overcome resistance with exertion. Force was the ability to transfer energy into something, and power was the ability to exert force in the shortest period of time.

Anyone who understood basic physics knew that mass times acceleration equaled force. To create more force in a blow, you had to get more of your mass behind your punch, or you had to move your fist faster. To transfer that force into your target, you had to be in contact with the target for a very short time. This had to be done while leveraging your strength to transmit the force you generated quickly, before it dissipated due to friction, inertia, and deceleration, among other factors.

Having observed Heracles when he hit the bag, I knew he was all strength, unrefined—with little skill to apply maximal force and power.

But me, on the other hand? I'd always been lanky instead of bulky, so I learned to be quick early on. Like Bruce Lee, who hit like a heavyweight at 130 pounds sopping wet, I knew how to transfer force.

Besides that, I was a druid, and I knew how to find flaws in anything that was made of natural substances. Sure, the machine had been forged by magic, but it was made of earth-derived metals—iron, bronze, and brass. That meant it had to have weak spots.

I couldn't tamper with it, not with all these supernaturals watching. If I did, I'd be found out immediately and disqualified for sure. But I could probe the machine and figure out exactly where its weak points were. With the right application of force and power, I could exploit that weakness, and beat Heracles without defeating him at all.

"I don't know any Iapetus, but I do know crazy," I rumbled as I rolled out my shoulders and cracked my thick, deformed neck. "In my experience, that's usually enough."

The ball was ten feet off the floorboards, give or take. I was nine-and-a-half feet tall, so I could reach it with a good overhand right. That's where Heracles had screwed up. He was just over Hemi's height, about seven feet tall, so he'd had to leap to reach the bag.

Yeah, you could get some power by leaping into a punch. MMA fighters did it sometimes, when they knocked people out with "Superman" punches. As well, the immortal Joe Louis was known to lift his back foot off the canvas to get more weight behind his right cross.

But if you want to transfer force quickly, you have to use the ground for leverage. When I squared up on the bag, I adopted a classic Jeet Kune Do *bai jong* stance. Feet staggered, rear heel and forward toe in line, weight centered, calves sprung. I rocked my hips and shoulders back and forth slightly to loosen up, like a snake ready to strike.

Then, I exploded into motion, stepping out and forward slightly with my lead foot as I pivoted and pushed with the rear. Like a coiled spring, my body tensed and rotated up my feet and legs, to my hips and torso, out my shoulder and into my arm and fist. The right cross I threw was tight, unorthodox, and whip-like, flaring the elbow at the last second as I leaned to the outside, overhanding it even as I snapped my shoulders with the follow-through.

My fist hit the bag on a slightly downward angle, one designed to capitalize on one of the chief weak points in the device—the coupling between the bag and boom. My huge, misshapen fist hit the thing with a crack rather than a *whoomp*, snapping the swivel with a loud, metallic *pop* that sent the bag crashing to the floor.

The crowd gasped, momentarily frozen in silence. I held a final pose, pausing at the end of the strike's follow-through with my eyes glued to the bulbs on the front of the housing. Nothing lit up on the machine's register, then lights began to glimmer at random on the meter. Finally, a single word lit and flashed above *Hercules* at the top of the machine's face.

TILT

The crowd roared. Money passed hands between bettors and bookies, almost all in the bookies' favor. I swung my gaze toward Hemi and Fallyn. Hemi was busy collecting a fat stack of bills from the bartender, Oscar, who looked like he'd just eaten something foul.

And Fallyn? She was still sawing logs.

Heracles' expression could only be described as dumbfounded disbelief. Eyes wide, cheeks flushed, mouth opening and closing like a fish—I wasn't certain if he was going to barf, or take a swing at me. After a few seconds, he shifted his gaze from the machine to me.

The demigod smiled ruefully, shaking his head. "Twice this day I am forced to admit, if I hadn't seen it I would not have believed it."

"You want to go again? I can probably fix the machine." I offered, hoping he wouldn't take me up on it.

"Nay. None have even come close to my score on yon device, never mind breaking the damned thing." His smile faded as he lowered his voice conspiratorially. "Although, I am going to have a chat with Briarus about this."

"Sheesh, I hope I didn't get the guy in trouble."

"Nay, he likes it when I find flaws in his devices, as it gives him something to tinker with." Just as quickly as it had fled, his cheerful expression returned. "Shall we dispense with the formalities? Fair is fair, after all."

Heracles snatched the churchkey from the table, tossing it to me. I caught it in midair, twirled it once around my finger, then I slipped it and Orna into my Bag.

"Much appreciated, Heracles. And about the other thing—"

"Revenge," he said in a low, dangerous voice, his gaze shifting into the distance, well beyond the dispersing crowd.

"Yep, that. I'll keep you posted, just in case you want to be there when it happens."

"Indeed." Heracles returned my gaze, his face bearing a smile that didn't meet his eyes. At that moment, it was a comfort to know his malice wasn't directed at me. He made a lassoing motion over his head as he shouted at a passing waitress. "Barmaid—another round!"

SIXTEEN

The next place we headed was back to Rube's to return the churchkey. Click might've been a bit on the nutty side, but he spent a lot of time flipping through the Twisted Paths, and his predictions were usually on the money. If he said we'd need to go through Rube's to accomplish a future task, I believed him.

We had to drive to Luckenbach in the Druidmobile because the chaos curse over the city was still interfering with the Oak's ability to navigate. That took time —time I was unaccustomed to taking. Sure, it was nice to hop in the beast and drive again, but I couldn't help but feel that somewhere, someplace, an imaginary clock was ticking away against us.

When we arrived at Rube's, the old gnome was sitting under a huge pecan tree in front of the bar, strumming a beat up guitar with his straw hat pulled over his face. Instinct told me I should approach alone.

Old fae like Lord John were known to be fickle, and if he was in a mood, I'd rather not subject Hemi and Fallyn to his antics. You never knew when the fae would try to trick you into agreeing to something you would rather not do. An irate, hungover werewolf and the son of a death goddess were probably too much temptation for the Mountain King to resist.

"Wait here," I said as I exited the car and shut the door.

Hemi appeared to be asleep, with his head leaning against the B post and his Hawaiian shirt lain over his eyes. "Gotcha," he said without moving a muscle.

"What if I have to pee?" Fallyn grumbled from the back seat.

She was recovering quickly, but not fast enough for her liking. I should've warned her that drinking at a supernatural bar was a bad idea. Hemi was used to it, having grown up around gods and goddesses. But Fallyn? She'd probably expected it to be just like hanging with the wolves at the clubhouse.

I reached into my Bag, rummaging around until I found supplies from my forays into the Hellpocalypse. "Here— aspirin and water. If you have to pee, do it in the bottle."

"Are you serious?" she said, laying back against the seat with her forearm over her eyes. "You do realize the challenges I might have doing that, right?"

I grabbed another bottle from my Bag. After emptying it, I chopped the bottom and the very top off with my knife. "Here, now you have a funnel. Stick the skinny end in the other—"

"Yeah, yeah—I grew up wrenching on bikes and camping out at rallies. I can figure the rest out, druid boy. But you are seriously going to owe me for this indignity."

I smiled despite her sour mood. "I'll make it up to you later. Oh, and I have baby wipes in the glove box. I spelled the seal before I put the car in storage, so they should still be good."

"You are such a boy scout," she said.

"That's why you love me," I replied as I marched away.

Halfway across the lawn, John spoke without looking up. "Your friends are safe on my lands, druid. They are free to roam, so long as they show respect."

"Your hospitality is welcomed, Lord John," I said. Fallyn would've heard the exchange, but she'd still stay in the car. I had a lot more experience dealing with fae than she did, so she tended to trust my discretion. "You'll be pleased to know that I've recovered the item you lost."

"I'll be the one to decide when I'm pleased and displeased," the gnome groused, head down while his fingers still gently strummed the guitar. The chords he played were basic, yet the result was a complex melody that bordered on the mystical. "And what of the thief? Did you punish him?"

"I bested him, yes."

"Hmph. I suppose it will have to do. Show me the churchkey." I pulled it from my Bag, offering it to him. John stopped playing just long enough to raise his strumming hand in refusal. "Not yet. Now that I know someone is after it, I'd rather you keep it. It's safer in that bag of yours than anywhere else. When I want it back, I'll let you know."

This was a strange turn. Since when did a fae not want the thing they'd paid dearly to acquire? Now I was curious what the hell the thing did. Despite that, I didn't ask, choosing instead to toss it back in my Bag.

"Regardless, our deal still stands. I'll receive passage through your lands for me and my companions, to the destination of our choosing, and for the return trip back."

"Of course, I'm of my word." He was still looking down, keeping his eyes hidden under the brim of his hat as he strummed his guitar. Figuring it was foolish to continue to bother him when he was in ill humor, I simply nodded once and headed back to the car. When I was halfway there, he spoke again. "Wait."

I stopped and turned to face him, both because his tone was strained, and because it was wise to show manners around old powers like John. He stopped playing, lowering the neck of the guitar nearly to the ground as his posture slackened. If I didn't know any better, I'd say that he looked, well, *sad.*

"Yes, John?"

"I have a message for you. From Siobhán."

Ah, that's what it is. Jealousy and fear of loss. I'd best tread lightly here.

"How is she?"

He set the guitar down lightly in the grass next to him and stood without pushing himself up from where he sat. It was an odd way for him to act, levitating himself up off the ground like that, considering that he worked so hard to appear normal most days. I didn't like it.

Rübezahl took a single step toward me. Time and space shifted between us, so that one stride took him right up in my face. His chin still hung low, and his eyes remained hidden under the brim of that straw hat.

"She is well, except that all she speaks of is you. After all I've done for her," he hissed in a near whisper, as thunder rolled in the distance. "Keeping her hidden, keeping her safe."

Great. He's gone all 'pissed off emo Gandalf' on me.

Few things were more dangerous than an ancient, emotionally unstable fae. I needed to tread carefully here, calming him while also standing my ground. The slightest indication of concession could be construed as an invitation to renegotiate the initial agreement.

Yet, that agreement was based on a wager—a wager that I won. John would be a fool to break our contract, and he knew it. Doing so would create a backlash that could have unfathomable consequences for the old gnome king. In breaking his promise, he'd be cursed by his own magic, blighted by violating the bond of his own words.

"I've not come for her yet, and I won't until she's ready to leave. But I'll say again, John—when that time comes, I will hold you to your word."

John's fists clenched at his sides, and restrained magical energy crackled in the air between us. Clouds gathered above, black and ominous, blocking out the sun and casting the spot where we stood in near darkness. I called on the power of the Oak, preparing several spells in case Rübezahl had truly lost his shit.

The fact was, I'd be screwed if he had, considering we were standing in his demesne. Yet, having some magic ready meant that I could get Fallyn and Hemi out of here, at least. My plan was to use earth magic to toss the car out of the parking lot, so they could get away. It wasn't much, but still better than nothing.

"Look around you, boy," John hissed. "There's a reason why I live here. These rolling hills used to be mountains. There's power here, old power, and I command it. You'd be wise to remember that."

Typical fae. Always lording their power over humans, and always pitching fits when things don't go their way.

"I'm aware of the power you wield. Likewise, I would remind you that magic can turn on you when it's abused. One as old and wise as you should know that better than any."

The tension in the air increased, the pressure building as John's magic strained to break free. Likewise, the thunder in the distance gained in volume and frequency. I didn't need to see in the magical spectrum to know that his magic was crashing against the restraint of his will, like a tsunami slamming against a tidal wall. One crack, and all that fury would be unleashed.

Suddenly and unexpectedly, the tension subsided, the clouds parted, and the thunder ceased. John's shoulders slumped, and in the blink of an eye he was back under the tree, strumming his guitar as if nothing had happened.

Whoa. Something tells me that was not just one big bluff.

John's face was still hidden by the brim of his hat. Though he didn't look up, his words rang clearly across the lot. "She bade me tell you this: 'Chaos is a druid's bane, but madness will prove to be a blessing.'"

"Hmm. Anything else?" I asked as I committed Siobhán's words to memory. The old, irascible gnome failed to answer. "Then I'll be off. I'll let you know when I need passage through your lands."

I left John much as I'd found him, sitting under his tree and quietly strumming that old guitar. When I got back to the car, Hemi and Fallyn both appeared to be sound asleep. She was sawing logs, and Hemi's chest rose and fell with a regularity few could fake.

I got into the car as quietly as I could, shutting the door with a soft click that spoke to the power of magic to preserve physical objects. There was little I could do about the roar of the engine, but if John's tantrum hadn't awoken them, nothing would. Anyway, soon the hum of the road would sing them both a lullaby on the way back to the junkyard.

Just before I cranked the key, Hemi spoke in a soft voice. "Everythin' go alright, mate?"

"Thought you were dead asleep."

"Was," he said from under his shirt. "Still aware, though. You learn to sleep with one eye open 'round the gods."

I turned the engine over and put the car in gear, pulling a tight turn to get us off John's land as quickly as possible. "I suppose things went as well as can be expected."

"That gnome's gonna' be trouble," he stated plainly, as if commenting on the weather.

"Yep."

"You got a plan?"

"Nope."

"Cross that bridge when it comes, yeah? S'all you can do, sometimes."

"Yeah."

I sighed and rubbed my bleary eyes with one hand. Although I might not have a hangover, after the events of the last few days, partying with Heracles had worn me out. My immediate plan was to catch some sleep once we got back to the junkyard—then we'd figure out our next steps.

"Ya' want company, bro?"

Ironically, now I actually *wanted* to be in the car, if only so I could sit and think. Having the Oak to teleport me around, I'd forgotten what a balm driving was to my soul. As much as I'd enjoy the company, presently I could use a little balm.

For starters, we still had to lift Eris' chaos curse from the city before it tore itself apart. I also had to find a mad goddess and deal with her, so I could free Maeve and restore her house. While I managed all that, I had to keep Luther, Samson, and Fallyn from clashing in a battle of wills and egos that could very well end up leaving one of them dead.

Then there was everything that would come after. Eventually, I'd have to figure out a way to get Siobhán out of Rube's demesne, without sending him into a rejected suitor's tizzy. I needed to return to the Hellpocalypse and find a way for humanity to survive the events of that timeline. And finally, I had to fulfill Finn's plan by restoring the druids to their former glory.

Amidst all that worry, something about Siobhán's situation kept bringing my thoughts back to her. I couldn't quite put my finger on it, but she'd said something previously that kept nagging at me. I was just too damned tired to figure it out now. I'd let my subconscious worry at it a while, and maybe then I'd figure it out.

Yep, I definitely needed time to think—and perhaps to simply take a few deep, calming breaths. I spared a glance at my friend, who still hadn't moved that ugly Hawaiian shirt from his face.

"No sense in us both staying awake, so you may as well get some shut-eye. We still have an insanity goddess and a chaos curse to contend with, after all." Hemi's chest was already rising and falling with a slow, steady frequency by the time I finished that sentence. My voice was a near whisper as I finished my thought. "But thanks for being there, bro."

WHEN WE PULLED into the parking lot at the junkyard, I was no closer to a solution for any of the challenges we faced, but more than ready for a nice, long nap. Fallyn and Hemi were way ahead of me, having both mumbled something about seeing me in the Grove in a few. Fallyn was one of the few people the Oak would allow into my Grove, and Hemi had been there before, so together they'd get in without me.

Just to be safe, I sent a mental message to the Oak to give them both passage. Then I spent some time shoring up the wards on the Druidmobile, both to keep it hidden from prying eyes and to ensure it remained in good repair, in case we needed to drive at high speeds across the city. When I finished a few minutes later, I grabbed my Bag from the console and slung it over my shoulder as I exited the car.

In addition to being tuckered out, my stomach had been grumbling on the two-hour drive back from Rube's. While I might've stopped to eat along the way, gas station food wasn't going to cut it—I'd had my fill of that crap after spending months scrounging in the Hellpocalypse. Now that I was back in the semi-sane version of this world, I was craving healthy food, something that would stick to my ribs.

As I crossed the lot toward the front gate, all I could think about was catching some zzz's and pigging out. And not necessarily in that order.

Sleep, then coffee and breakfast. I am so glad the Grove decided to populate itself with wildlife. Mmm, fresh duck eggs. Man, I wonder if I could teach the Grove to grind wheat. If it can brew coffee, can it bake bread and make toast, too?

Distracted as I was, I failed to notice the circle of copper wire that lay on the ground in front of the foot gate that led to the yard. It wasn't until it lit up, and the ground disappeared from under my feet, that I caught a glimmer of magic shining off the damned thing in the late morning sunlight.

Fucking transporter spell. Amateurs.

Transporter spells were like portal spells, but way more crude. When a magic user cast a portal, they were creating a direct gate from one place to another. They did this by poking a hole through magically folded time and space. As long as you didn't get caught in a portal while it was closing, they were stable and safe—unlike transporter spells.

Transporter spells used naturally occurring wormholes to move people and things from one place to another. While they required less magic and infinitely less skill to create, they were incredibly dangerous. That was because you might not come out where you planned. Plus, you never knew what might be passing by in the Between Spaces as you traveled through.

About twenty percent of the time, people didn't come out the other side of a transporter spell. Where they ended up was a mystery, although the assumption was that they got eaten by an extra-dimensional entity along the way—a dimensional shambler or a star vampire, for instance. That was why serious spell casters never bothered with them.

It was also why it pissed me off to no end that someone had left a transporter spell trap at my front doorstep. Never mind that I walked right into it. The question was, who was dumb and/or incompetent enough to use a transporter spell to capture someone?

Cerberus.

While I was flying through the great nothingness of the Between Spaces, I must've caught the attention of something odd and dangerous. Cries of "Tekeli-li! Tekeli-li!" echoed within my mind, a telepathic assault that caused my head to pound and my heart to race as it gradually grew louder and louder. By the time I popped through the other end of the wormhole, a huge, red, unblinking eye approached from the distance, growing larger as it neared.

Shit. Shit, shit, and double shit. If I get eaten by this thing, I won't even get the satisfaction of haunting the dickhead who pulled this stunt on me.

The eye had almost filled half my field of vision when I transitioned back into our plane of existence. The last thing I saw as I fell was a giant, glassy nictitating membrane as it slid across the eye from left to right. Then the wormhole closed behind me, and I felt gravity take over again.

I was falling from the ceiling upside down, of course. Being in stealth-shifted mode had its benefits, however. I was able to twist slightly to avoid falling on my head, even as I landed in a seemingly helpless heap on a concrete floor covered in thin, gray industrial carpet.

"Somebody help him up." The voice was deep, male, authoritative, and it had just a touch of South Texas Latino to it that the speaker tried very hard to hide.

Mendoza.

I was oh so very tempted to clock him and clean the floor with his agents. However, we'd been playing the same game for a couple of years now, and I saw no reason to change things up. That game went something like this: Mendoza would imply that he knew things about me only someone who was clued in would know, and I would act as if I knew nothing about what he was implying.

It was tiresome, but necessary. Moreover, it appeared he was gaining some manners, at least. The last time he pulled a stunt like this, he dropped me into a concrete cell with a ghoul, just to see what I'd do. I iced it without revealing more than fast reflexes and some martial arts skills, but that was enough to further pique his interest. The good agent offered me a job on the spot, which I declined, and I hadn't heard from him since.

Two burly dudes wearing jeans, running shoes, dark blue polo shirts, and matching dark blue windbreakers that said, "F.B.I." on the breast picked me up off the ground. One was black, the other white, and both had the requisite haircut, fitness level, tactical awareness, and professional bearing that revealed them to be former military. Probably SEALs, Force RECON, or Rangers, recruited into Cerberus after surviving a supernatural encounter in the field.

Or is it C.E.R.B.E.R.U.S.? I should ask Mendoza what it stands for—after I find out what he wants.

Once they stood me up, they patted me down. Besides the hunting knife I kept in a sheath at the small of my back, they didn't find much. They took the knife, but it was only when the white guy went to look inside my Bag that Mendoza spoke up.

"Leave it. From what I've heard, you don't want to look in there."

Damn.

As the agents backed off, I remained stone-faced, despite the shock I felt. The truth was, the agent wouldn't see anything if he lifted the flap. Yet, some individual had been feeding Mendoza privileged information, that was for sure. It had to be someone who was well-placed and well-informed—a person of influence in the World Beneath.

At that moment, I resolved to find out who that person was and shut them up. *After* I lifted the chaos curse and kicked Lyssa out of my city, of course. But one thing at a time.

The room all around was dark, but I stood in the bright glow of directional spotlights. They thought I couldn't see into the shadows, but they were wrong. Including the spec ops bruisers who'd patted me down, I counted six agents scattered around the room, two females and four males. Based on their scents, all but one of them were normal, although some carried magical trinkets—likely stuff like the transporter trap I'd fallen through to get here.

As for the odd one, she was just a bit—well, *off*. At first, I couldn't place it, then I realized why her scent bothered me. The woman smelled faintly of poisoned blood and spider silk—like Mei, the *jorōgumo* assassin that The Dark Druid had once hired to kill me.

The smell wasn't strong enough to indicate she was one of them, and she was too tall to be Mei. Yet, she'd definitely been around a were-spider recently. If I was dealing with any other government agency, I'd have considered it odd, but not with this bunch.

When they brought me to their secret lair during our last encounter, I'd caught the scent of an array of supernatural creatures. 'Thropes, vamps, fae, yōkai, trolls, zombies, and species I didn't recognize. At the very least, Cerberus was capturing and studying supernatural creatures, and I wouldn't be surprised in the least if they were experimenting on them as well.

Like I care. So long as it's not anyone I know and love.

But if it came to that? Then, Cerberus would find out what I was all about.

"Why am I here, Mendoza?" I said as I crossed my arms over my chest.

He shuffled some papers, flipping through a file in silence. It was a standard tactic—grab a random stack of paperwork and take it with you into an interrogation, so the subject thought you had something on them. An amateur's trick, but it probably worked on the uninitiated.

"Good to see you too, McCool." He shuffled more papers. "Let's see—we have reports all over social media of SNEs fighting in the streets of the state capitol. A weird, mystical cult has sprung up, one that centers on the worship of an obscure Greek goddess. And, everyone within twenty-five miles of the city's center is going nuts. Violent crime has tripled, domestic disturbance calls are through the roof, and we've got demonstrations in the streets by day and riots by night." He paused and looked at the woman who smelled like were-spider. "Am I missing anything?"

"There's the giant chiropteran creature that's been killing narcoterrorists along the Columbia-Panama border." Her accent was decidedly Southwestern Latina, her manner of speech, refined and formal. I pegged her as military, but not combat arms. "It's probably unrelated, however."

"'Probably.' I've never really liked that word," he said under his breath. The senior agent grunted, then he continued. "By all accounts, you disappeared for the last six months. As in, fell off the radar completely, and that's quite a feat when you're under government surveillance in this day and age. Meanwhile, Austin has gone to hell in a hand basket. I want to know what you have to do with it."

Well, piss.

It figured Cerberus would show up now that everything was going to shit. What I didn't expect was that they'd blame it on me. I hung my head, exhaling long and slow as I decided how to handle this.

Fight, or flee? Hmm, do I really want to start a war with the government? Never mind that—do I really want to give them actual proof that I'm one of their 'SNEs'? That's a big, fat nope, so it's definitely flee.

"Normally, I'd play along with your games, Mendoza. Do a little verbal cat and mouse, maybe drop some hints to point you in the right direction." I clasped my hands in front of me, to hide the gestures I was making with my right hand. "But today? I really don't have time for all that, so I'll just be on my way."

With a flick of my fingers, I released the cantrip I'd queued up, which caused all the lights to short out at once. The two burly agents were fast, I'd give them that. They came at me without hesitation when things went dark. That took guts and discipline, and I liked that.

I wasn't about to hurt a couple of vets for no good reason, so I sidestepped their blind tackles. Before the emergency lights could come on, I cast a chameleon spell on myself. Then I shorted out the circuit breakers for the entire floor. As a precaution, I saved enough of the electricity I'd drawn to power the magnetic lock on the door as I slipped out of the interrogation room.

"Interesting," I heard the female say as the lock engaged with a *click* behind me.

Outside the room, I found myself in your typical office building. Typical, that was, except for all the cops in the halls. It wasn't long before I figured out that I was at the Austin field offices for the actual Federal Bureau of Investigation, north on Research Boulevard near Anderson Mill.

Agents were bustling around everywhere, lighting their way with tactical flashlights as they tried to find the breaker box. I waited until one of the agents figured out that the elevators were still working. When she and another agent got on, I slipped in behind them, hitching a ride to the first floor. After I snuck out of the building, it was time to find my way back to the junkyard.

Calling a taxi or a ride-share was out of the question, as Mendoza's people would be monitoring cell frequencies by now. So, I threw my phone in my Bag, then I followed my nose across the highway to a Krispy Kreme shop. There I grabbed a large coffee and a dozen doughnuts for the long bus ride back to the junkyard.

It wasn't Luther's brew, but it was hot and the fresh doughnuts sign was on—I figured, why fight fate? When I paid, the dude at the counter pointed me to the nearest bus stop, just one-half block away. Coffee and doughnuts in hand, I headed there just in time to catch the next southbound bus, and quickly found a seat in the back.

Once I'd settled in, I promptly began sharing my box of doughnuts with a disheveled elderly man sitting nearby. After I'd had my fill, I gave the man the rest, taking some comfort in the way his face lit up when I handed him the box. Sadly, before the bus had gone another five blocks, another homeless man started a fight with him over the doughnuts. Eventually, the bus driver had to pull over to kick them both off.

Then it started raining fish. *It rained. Fucking. Fish.* And no one on the bus seemed at all shocked or surprised. Based on the chatter I heard, last week it had been blood, and a few days before that, frogs.

I need a vacation.

Fighting off exhaustion and sleep, I sipped my coffee as I pondered my run-in with Cerberus. It was just the latest complication in a long list of similar complexities, all of which I could chalk up to either Lyssa's or Eris' influence. As I rode in silence, listening to passengers bicker with each other and complain to the bus driver about silly, insignificant shit, I realized something.

I am seriously starting to hate chaos magic.

SEVENTEEN

The bus had just passed Riverside heading south on Congress when I realized I could use a top-off on my coffee. Considering I was near Luther's café, I thought, 'What the hell, why not stop in and say hi?' Besides the coffee, I might even be able to talk some sense into him.

I signaled for the bus to stop and got off. After it had left me in a cloud of diesel fumes and smoke, I jogged a block back to La Crème. The place was nearly empty, except for the usual college students and camp outs who came in to nurse a single coffee while using Luther's WiFi all day.

When I'd mentioned it in the past, Austin's coven leader had always said he didn't mind. I was pretty confident that was because half of them were Renfields who were on security detail, pulling lookout duty for their master. They were at war, after all, even if it was a war that should never have happened. As if to confirm my suspicions, I felt more than one pair of eyes on me as I walked to the counter to order.

There I was greeted by one of the many vamps who played human by working on staff at Luther's. For the younger vamps, it gave them an income to report to the IRS, plus they could dress like college kids to boot. I figured that was a bonus when you were perpetually stuck at age nineteen by the vyrus.

The barista-slash-clerk's hair was dyed every color in the rainbow, and she had more piercings than my grandma's latest needlepoint project. Besides the hair and piercings, she was a dead ringer for Aubrey Plaza, that actress from Parks and Rec. Her bored, flat expression belied the tension in her shoulders as I approached the counter. Instantly I knew—for the first time in a very long time, I was not welcome in La Crème.

"Yeah?" she asked in a tone of voice that was as aloof and uninterested as her facial expression.

"I'll have a nitro, fully leaded, sweet and cold," I said with confidence.

"We're out," she replied in an emotionless voice while examining her nails.

"Then I'll take a mocha—"

"Out," she said, chomping on her chewing gum.

"Americano?"

"Machine's busted."

"Then I'll have a drip—"

"That machine's busted, too." She blew a pink

bubble, popping it without changing the dead, completely disinterested expression she wore.

"Are you being serious right now?"

She glared at me without moving a muscle in her face. I wondered how old this chick had been when she was turned, because only a teenage girl could manage that trick. It would be a mistake to lose my cool or flex, so instead I leaned in and whispered.

"Look, I know what you are. Even if the machine was broken, you could have it running again in under a minute flat."

"I know who *you* are," she said. "Even if you weren't a dick, you could leave here in the time it took to tell me that."

"You know who I am?"

"Yeah, you're that human Luther keeps around. He's pissed at you, you know."

I thought back to the previous night and the fight in the parking lot. On reflection, maybe it wasn't such a good idea to cut that suit's legs off and then show up here without calling ahead.

"I can explain..."

The girl looked unconvinced. After glaring without glaring for a few seconds more, she went back to examining her nails.

"Is Luther around?" I asked.

"If you don't quit bothering me, I will cut you," she said with zero inflection in her voice.

I felt a sudden draft. When I looked around, Luther

was standing at the other end of the counter, near the door that led to his apartment upstairs.

"That's enough, Vanessa," Luther said.

"He started it," she stated. Just then, a mundane walked in and lined up behind me to wait his turn. With a sigh, I stepped aside to allow the man to order.

"Go ahead, I'm still deciding," I said while trying to mask the exasperation in my voice.

"What it'll be, sir?" Vanessa the barista trilled in a happy, sing-song voice. While the man stared at the menu behind her, she stuck her pierced tongue out at me, almost too quick for the eye to catch.

"Why you little—"

"Come with me, McCool," Luther said.

Vanessa was already taking the man's order. I looked back and forth from her to Luther, frowning as I arched one eyebrow.

"But—"

"The coffee can wait, druid. We need to speak— alone." He exited the café proper and headed up the stairs to his apartment at a brisk walk, not bothering to look back. Obviously, that was my cue to follow.

"Damn it," I hissed under my breath. I glared at Vanessa, pointing with two fingers at my eyes and then at her.

She copied my movements precisely, mocking me while the customer browsed the pastry counter. When he glanced up, she instantly switched gears, smiling sweetly at him and battling her eyes.

"Little shit," I muttered as I headed for the door.

Something wet and warm hit me in the side of the head as I was walking into the stairwell. I recognized the substance by scent before I even managed to wipe it off. When I pulled my hand away, the smear on my palm confirmed that it was a dollop of milk and coffee froth. Undaunted, I stared Vanessa right in the eye as I licked it off my hand.

I spat in that, she mouthed silently.

Determined to have the last word, I shot her the bird as I followed Luther into his private sanctum.

"Are you quite through harassing my employee?" he asked as I caught up to him.

Luther crossed his arms over his chest and cocked his hips. The man was in full "Mr. Sassy Pants" mode, which meant this would be an unpleasant discussion. The coven leader could be a real bitch at times, but never to me. Clearly, he'd been as deeply affected by Eris' influence as everyone else.

"The place looks nice," I said, by way of ignoring his question. There were few things worse than being bested by a surly teen. No need to rehash that humiliation. "Classy, yet understated. I like it."

Luther was fond of redecorating his apartment every six months or so. The first time I'd been here it looked like a queen's dream, all white lace and white shag and white fur pillows, with prints and paintings of Marilyn and Bacall and Wood decorating the walls. Next he'd gone mid-century modern, then deco, and now it looked liked an upscale Ikea had exploded in here.

To begin with, he had about $250k worth of furniture in the place. Every piece was a work of art, most done in veneer and ply shaped in swooping, flowing, impossible lines that were simple without being simplistic. Then there were the thoughtfully placed, Swiss- and French-modern art pieces on side tables and consoles that complimented the furniture, accenting their design by providing subtle geometric counterpoints. Heck, everything in the place was art, down to the sculptured, exposed wood lamps and the wood and brass wall clock that merely suggested the time without being specific about it.

This was old-school Scandi, not that new-school crap you found on Pinterest. *That* design aesthetic had been birthed from austerity, born out of the post-college poverty all grads experience when they're transitioning into the career stage of their lives. Not that there was anything wrong with that—I loved Ikea and modern Scandi design. But what Luther had done here was upscale Scandinavian, stuff you only found in design studios and private galleries.

Unfortunately, Luther still looked pissed. Usually, I could mollify him by complimenting his design sensibilities. Today it appeared that he was dead set on speaking his mind.

"Let's stay on track, shall we?" he began, in the saltiest tone possible. "You and your mate assaulted two of my coven members—not once, but twice."

"Ah, you mean Victor and Nadia. They assaulted us first. If your dog runs into traffic and gets hit by a fast-moving car, do you blame the car or the dog?"

"I blame the driver," he replied. "You could've retreated, and easily."

The obvious and expected answer was, 'the owner.' I didn't think he was being purposely obtuse. It was the curse at work, clouding his mind and urging him into a confrontation with me.

I hung my head, rubbing my temples. There wasn't much sleep to be had on a city bus, and the Krispy Kreme coffee hadn't helped much. I was running on fumes, and trying hard not to lose my cool.

"The point, Luther, is that I shouldn't have to. We were on public city streets, minding our own business—"

"My streets," he interjected, cutting me off.

"Oh, so they're your streets now? Not Maeve's, or the Pack's, or the humans'?"

He hissed, baring his fangs. "I should've known you'd be taking the Pack's side. You are one of them, after all."

I threw my hands into the air in frustration. "I'm not taking any side! What I am trying to do is show you how ridiculous this whole war is between the Coven and the Pack. You're all being manipulated by Eris, and you don't even know it."

This is where things got very, very curious. When I said "Eris," I felt a momentary surge of magic that muted my voice. I could hear myself say it, but it was almost like that part of what I'd said got dubbed over or edited out. It was bizarre, and frightening, and evidence of the reality-warping power a goddess of even her low caliber could wield.

"Ridiculous?" Luther spat, pushing the sleeves up on his Valentino silk shirt. "I'll not have some insignificant upstart insulting me in my own home."

Ew boy, here it comes.

Every vampire had a talent, and Luther's was major league. When he fought someone, he didn't zip around like your average vampire. He didn't have to, nope. Instead, he teleported, moving between pockets of shadow that his talent created out of thin air and magic.

Those bits of shadow acted like portals that allowed him to move instantly from place to place. What was really weird, though, was that he turned insubstantial as he *bamfed* around, dissolving into shadow himself when he disappeared. When he reappeared elsewhere, he'd reincorporate into solid form, just long enough to smack the shit out of you before he *bamfed* away again.

And that's precisely what he did to me. One second, he was standing there looking all pissed off and imperious; the following moment, Luther disappeared in a puff of shadow and black mist. The next thing I knew, I was flying over his couch and into his kitchen island and breakfast bar.

Well, hell.

I collided with two veneer and metal barstools at speed, hurled into them ass over teakettle by the force of the blow he'd delivered into my back. Fortunately, he'd pulled the attack by hitting me with the flat of his palm. If he'd connected with a closed fist, or worse, with his extended fingernails, he'd have pulped my spinal column or shredded my heart and lungs.

I took that as an indication that somewhere, deep inside the guy, he must've been fighting the curse. My task was to subdue him without killing him, and then to find a way to bring him back to reality. That was a tall order when you were dealing with a master vampire of his caliber.

Honestly, how do you fight smoke?

Me, I had no idea. But I figured, there was no time like the present to develop some new tactics.

The first thing I needed to do was to contain the fight. If this tiff spilled into the streets, it could cause a panic. Or even worse, we could end up on social media.

I could see the chyron teaser now: *Fight between skinny hipster and teleporting ball of smoke goes viral! Details at 11...*

Nope, not a good idea at all. As I recalled, Luther always teleported in line of sight, which meant either he couldn't teleport through objects, or he needed to see where he was *bamfing* to.

Thankfully, I had an affinity for all things natural, especially those made from trees. Using druid magic, I fused the apartment door to the frame, then I petrified the wood. It wouldn't keep Luther from busting out if he wanted to, but it would keep his minions from opening the door and allowing him to teleport away.

That left the windows. Could he teleport through those? Would he? Probably not. It was sunny outside, if a bit overcast, and even mature vampires avoided the sun like the plague.

Just as I'd determined the first steps in my very seat of my pants plan, Luther appeared above me. Almost faster than my eyes could follow, he grabbed me by the ankle and tossed me into the kitchen wall. Unfortunately, that wall wasn't your typical plaster and lumber affair. This building was old, so the exterior walls were solid brick.

Needless to say, the impact wasn't my idea of a good time. A half-assed judo break-fall allowed me to diminish the force of my collision, but not completely. Still, I was able to bounce off and land on one knee with my back to the wall. At least now he couldn't sneak up on me.

I looked around the place, searching for Luther and lamenting the state of his finely appointed apartment. Two of his expensive bar stools were bent all to hell, the marble counter was cracked, and I'd knocked his pots and pans rack off the wall when he threw me into the bricks. Sadly, considering what the two of us could do, we were just getting started.

"Dude, look at what you're doing to your apartment," I said as my eyes darted around the room. "Can't we talk this out?"

A shadow appeared above me, and I rolled to my right in the nick of time. Luther landed where I'd been crouching, slamming home a punch that shattered the polished oak floor. He snarled and spun on me, throwing a flurry of lightning fast blows that I barely managed to block, parry, and slip.

Knowing it was a matter of time before he hit me with a solid punch, I decided to turn the tables. I parried his right and turned the movement into a trapping motion, grabbing and pulling his wrist down and to my left. At the same time, I faked a spearing attack at his eyes, and when he flinched, I used the motion to block his line of sight to my feet.

Then I pivoted and threw a damned hard lead-leg side kick, right into his midsection. That kick propelled Luther across the room, over his couches and right at the brick wall on the opposite side of the space.

Except he didn't finish the trip. Instead, he teleported elsewhere at the apex of his arc. I figured that between teleports he was staying incorporeal, using his intermediary form to hide from me until he saw an opening.

The fact was, I couldn't keep this up, and he could.

Luther definitely had the advantage in hand-to-hand combat, and unless I did something deadly, he was going to beat my ass.

I didn't want to kill him, but I didn't care to die, either. With few options available to me, I decided to limit his ability to teleport and hide.

The kitchen counter was just a few steps away, so I blitzed over and grabbed the butcher block full of knives that sat conveniently within reach. Then I began tossing them at windows, just as fast as I could. The windows were all covered in UV-blocking film, so I couldn't shatter them, but I could punch holes in them to let rays of pure daylight into the room.

Soon, beams of sunlight crisscrossed the space from west to east. I positioned myself in front of one of the windows I'd pierced, certain that the light would prevent Luther from ambushing me. I was wrong.

He teleported onto the wall to my left, above and behind me, where the light couldn't reach. By the time I'd sensed his presence, he'd already jumped on my back, latching on with his legs. He wrapped one leg over my shoulder and the other under the opposite arm, in a move that was halfway between riding piggyback and a half-assed reverse triangle choke from jiujitsu.

Once he was firmly perched on my shoulders, he proceeded to beat the hell out of my head, face, and neck. And man, could that dude hit. In the span of a few seconds, I took more hits than a bong at Burning Man.

"Ah, shit Luther!" I yelled as I frantically tried to keep him from pulping my skull.

"You should never have fucked with my get!" he roared, which sounded kind of funny since he was using semi-archaic speech.

Meanwhile, he kept hitting me, and I kept flailing my arms as I attempted to defend myself. I imagined we probably looked like the most dangerous pair of actors from the Benny Hill Show, ever. To this point I'd avoided playing dirty, but some of those attacks were getting through, and I was starting to get a little punchy. A few more, and either I'd be at curse-crazed Luther's mercy, or my alter-ego would come out—and that wouldn't be good for anyone.

To avoid either of those potential disasters, I fumbled until I managed to grab one of Luther's wrists, then I pulled. Sure, he was an older vampire—older, not elder, mind—and a master of a coven to boot. But hell if I wasn't the strongest of us both, even in my half-Fomorian form. When I yanked on his arm, he had two choices—go with it, or get his arm yanked off. Wisely, he chose the former.

That meant he got slammed on the floor onto his back, and I wasted no time in climbing on top of him to pin his arms down. Strangely, he wasn't struggling, nor did he *bamf* away. Instead, his eyes went glassy for a second, then he glanced around the room before focusing in on my face.

That was just about the time that Vanessa and a

couple of other vamps busted through the downstairs door. There was a crash, then they came zipping up the stairs, only to find me straddling Luther while pinning his wrists to the floor. All five of us just sort of froze, with no one really sure what was going to happen next.

Vanessa was the first to speak. "Well then, don't let us interrupt your fun."

She turned on heel and skipped down the steps, and the other two vamps followed, whispering to each other as they exited the apartment.

"Hey," I shouted after them. "We were just—"

"You should probably get off me now, druid," Luther said. "The damage is done, both to your reputation as a heterosexual Lothario, and to my apartment. I, however, am back to my usual, clearheaded self."

"What? Oh, right." I looked down, realizing that I still had him pinned.

That's when I noticed it—the churchkey and rabbit's foot, dangling from my right wrist. How it got there, I had no idea. Interestingly, the metal beaded keychain had grown longer—just long enough so the churchkey could brush against Luther's forearm.

I rolled off him, staring at the thing as I sat against the wall. "I'll be damned."

Luther stood, taking care this time to move at human speed. "You will at that, if you can't find a way to pay for this mess," he said as he surveyed the damage.

"Um, I can fix most of that," I said, still staring at the churchkey.

I tried examining it in the magical spectrum again, but I got absolutely zip from the effort. By all appearances, it was nothing more than a cheap kitchen utensil attached to a dime store novelty token.

"Weird." I looked up at Luther. "And you say you're back to normal now?"

He nodded slowly. "Hmm, yes. I'll be a bit stiff until I get a good feeding in me, but otherwise I'm fine."

"What's the last thing you remember?"

"Besides coming to my senses with you on top of me?" He rubbed his chin while looking up at the ceiling. "Arriving at work, I suppose."

"And when was that?"

"July 17th, at 5:00 am."

Not long after I left for the Hellpocalypse.

I scratched my nose with a knuckle. "Dude, it's January. You've been under that wench's spell for six months."

Luther's expression darkened, and his mocha skin turned ashen. "Please do not tell me we're at war."

"Oh, you're at war, alright. Maeve's been trapped in her manse, so she hasn't been able to combat or lift the curse. Samson took over alpha duties in Fallyn's absence, and apparently the Pack and Coven have been at each other's throats for months."

He frowned as he brushed drywall dust off his shoulder. "You said 'apparently'?"

"I haven't been around for a while. I, uh, took a little trip and got detained."

His head snapped around, so he could meet my gaze. "'Detained.' Does it have anything to do with what's been going on?"

I cleared my throat. "Maybe you should sit down while I catch you up. I'll fix your furniture while I give you the rundown on recent events."

"Anytime someone tells you to sit down, it's bad. Start talking, and I'll make us both a stiff drink."

THIRTY MINUTES later I was leaving the café with a mocha in hand, a half-assed apology from Vanessa, and a promise from Luther that he'd take his coven underground until things blew over.

"However, I can't say there won't be clashes here and there," he said, examining his door as I headed for the rear exit. "But I'll do my best."

Luther also said he felt as clearheaded as can be. I didn't trust that he was "cured" though, so I warded up one of his bracelets and a gold necklace. I left him with strict orders that he shouldn't take either off until I'd dealt with Lyssa.

"Yes, Dr. Howser," he replied.

Figuring I still needed to be on the lookout for Cerberus, I left out the back door. My plan was to call Maureen for a lift, and wait in the alley until she arrived.

However, I never got that far. Ten steps out the back door of the café, a thick fog rose from the ground.

Instantly, the sky grew dark, the air cold, the wind still, and the silence complete. In response, I dropped into a crouch as I queued up several potent spells. Then I waited, and waited, and waited.

When nothing happened, I tried to get my bearings, counting the estimated number of steps it'd take to get me back inside the café. When I'd walked twice that distance, I knew I was fucked.

My next step was to try to contact someone, first by phone—no dice—and then by my connection with the Druid Oak. All I got was mental static from the Oak, so I sat down cross-legged and entered a druid trance. If I couldn't think my out, I'd feel my way out of this fugue spell, or whatever it was.

No sooner had I settled into my trance than I heard something in the distance. *Squeak, rattle-rattle-rattle, squeak* over and over again, growing louder with each passing second. Of course I opened my eyes, homing in on the direction the sound came from and keeping my attention rapt. Soon, a short, stooped silhouette came shuffling out of the fog.

The slight, stumpy figure gradually came into view, emerging slowly from the trailing mists like a ghost ship adrift at sea. She had her hair pulled back to reveal her olive skin and a round, filthy face that was old, but not haggard. Her eyes were bird's eyes, darting and gray, her expression sad and lonely. The hair she hid beneath a kerchief, over which she wore a navy watch cap with a wilted daisy stuck in the weave.

Her fingerless wool gloves were threadbare and dirty, as was the long brown overcoat she wore over stained Looney Tunes pajamas that barely reached to her ankles. Three pairs of socks helped her fit into a pair of almost comically large blue sliders, and she pushed a shopping cart that was full of trash, knick-knacks, and assorted odds and ends. Some of those were mundane, others not so much.

There was a white Bakelite TV set from the 1970s, and it was playing reruns of The Lucille Ball Show, even though the cord lacked a plug, and the wires were bare and unattached. A round bronze shield stuck out of one side, of the kind Hoplites used to carry in Ancient Greece—but it had a large chunk missing from one edge, as if a large monster had bitten it like an Oreo. She had soda and beer cans, cat food, small appliances, a screwdriver with no tip, a deck of playing cards, a typewriter with just a handful of keys—I could go on and on. All of it was weird, mismatched, broken, and likely discarded for one reason or another.

I got to my feet before she came too close. Even though she looked harmless, naturally she was anything but. I had a suspicion who it was, but I was keeping my cards close on every front. When chaos reigned supreme, it was best to make no assumptions and to question everything.

The woman stopped her cart about ten feet away,

then she shuffled around the side to rummage in the basket. Seconds later she pulled a dented green Thermos from the cart, taking her time to unscrew the cup on top, then the lid. She poured a softly glowing amber liquid into the scratched plastic mug, downing it before replacing the cap and cup both. Only after she'd tossed the Thermos back into the cart did she look at me.

"You're one of those who killed my children." No emotion, barely any inflection. She said it almost in a whisper.

"Are you Lyssa?" I asked.

At the sound of my voice, her face contorted with rage. She balled her fists at her waist as she leaned forward slightly and screamed, "You killed my child!"

Definitely Lyssa.

I said nothing as I remained on my guard. Lyssa relaxed once more, patting her pockets as if searching for something. Finally, she pulled off her watch cap, managing to avoid disturbing her do-rag in the process.

She looked inside the cap, reaching within to snatch something between her forefinger and thumb. I couldn't be certain, but it looked like an old piece of gum. When she popped it in her mouth and chewed, any doubts I had were erased, both to the nature of said item, and to her sanity.

"Told them to be careful, yes I did, did, did," she muttered. "Harmless little children, only seeking to take a romp in the yard. Nothing to play with where we're from, no pick-up sticksies or Legos or magnifying glasses and bugs. Make-believe won't do, not there, oh no."

"I didn't want to hurt them, but they were harming innocents. They had to be stopped."

"Lie. Two lies," she said as her gaze wandered everywhere but at me.

"I don't understand," I said, shaking my head.

"Third lie's a charm. Wanted to hurt, and no one's innocent, not a one." She picked her nose, digging in to the second knuckle. When she managed to pry out a big green blob of something gross, she eyed her prize like a precious jewel before tucking it under the brim of her hat. "Understands me just fine."

Somehow, I managed not to gag. "Why did you bring me here, Lyssa?"

"Has it on him, he doesn't," she replied while looking in random places at intervals. "Had it, yes he did. Sensed it and came, now it's gone, gone, gone. Need it for reasons, yes she does."

Obviously, she was batshit crazy with a capital "K". Yet, she was a goddess, and I assumed I'd wandered into an extension of her demesne. I'd be stuck here until she decided to let me out, so I stood quietly and waited for her to continue.

Lyssa looked up and met my gaze. "Three fell from the nest. Two lost, one broke its wing. Little bird, little bird, won't fly for mama no more."

Her gray eyes spun, or maybe the world did, but for

a moment I felt like I was falling into her dark, wide pupils. I experienced the sensation of drifting into madness, as if everything and everyone I knew would never be right again. Shadows became people who taunted me incessantly. I heard voices speaking inside my head, telling me to hurt others, to hurt myself. I felt sad, then angry, then frustrated, but most of all, isolated and alone.

It was as though all hope had left the world, every-where at once.

Then I heard something jangling in the distance, like a bell on a cat's collar or a key on a ring. Just as quickly as it had come over me, the spell broke, and I was free. When I came to, Lyssa was screeching a string of insults at me. She was right up in my face, so close I could smell the cat food on her breath and see the hair in her nose and on her upper lip.

"Cock-sucker-mother-fucker-shit-licker-cooch-sniffer-syphilis-sucker..." and on and on, just a constant, never-ending flow of obscenities, one after another.

I stood completely still, waiting until she exhausted the known vocabulary of curse words. Just when I thought she was done, she switched to what sounded like a dialect of Greek. That diatribe took another ten minutes at least; apparently, Greeks knew how to cuss. Finally, blessedly, she ran out of steam.

I looked at her, and she at me, then she shuffled back to her cart.

"Madness and tragedy will befall you, tooth for tooth, eye for eye," she said. "The price you pay will be steep."

It occurred to me that I should kill her, then and there. I had the Red Spear in my Bag—a proven god-killer. Yet, I didn't think I should risk it while I was in her demesne. Just as I would rather not fight Rübezahl on his lands, there was no way I'd volunteer to fight Lyssa here.

Feeling no small amount of regret, I patiently watched her wheel the squeaky shopping cart back into the fog. After her silhouette faded into nothing, the mists cleared, and I was in Luther's parking lot once more. Shaking my head at the sheer peculiarity of the experience, I took a sip from the coffee cup that had been in my hand the entire time.

Coffee's gone cold. Now I really do wish I'd killed her.

CHAPTER

EIGHTEEN

Following a brisk walk down the street to the nearest hotel, I hailed a taxi for a ride back to the junkyard. When I arrived, Fallyn was frantically pacing inside the office, while Maureen quietly pecked away at her workstation keyboard. A cup of hot coffee waited for me on the counter, likely courtesy of my favorite half-kelpie.

Before I could snag it, a five-ten, two-hundred-fifty pound female werewolf in human form barreled into me, locking me in a rib cage crushing hug.

"Oh my gosh, where the hell have you been?" Fallyn asked, shoving me away from her with force as she released me. "Hemi and I hit the Grove for a nap, figuring you'd be right along. When we got back to the junkyard, only a few minutes had passed, but you'd vanished.

"I told 'em you were likely fine," Maureen said,

reaching from where she sat to nudge the coffee cup in my direction.

I raised the cup to my nose, savoring the aroma of fresh ground beans. "Luther's blend?"

"Aye, boyo. Figured ya'd need it, after the night I heard ya' had." She crossed her arms over her chest as she leaned back in her chair, brow furrowed. "Although I'd also like ta' know where the feck ye've been."

I sipped the coffee first, and I nearly groaned with pleasure to find it hot, sweet, and full of chocolate syrup. "Maureen, you are the best." I raised the cup in her direction, and she inclined her head and smiled. "I got snagged by Cerberus. Can you believe that asshole used a transporter spell on me again?"

"What I can't believe is that you fell for the same trick twice," Fallyn remarked. "And you do know, they have these things called cell phones now. Are you hurt?"

"Pfft," Maureen snickered. "It'd take more than those tossers ta' harm him. What had us concerned was that mad goddess roamin' about."

"Well, I had a run-in with her, too. And Luther."

"Yikes." Fallyn winced. "So spill."

"I'll give you the TL;DR version. Mendoza thinks I have something to do with all the chaos and craziness going on right now. Lyssa is, in actuality, absolutely one-hundred percent batshit freaking crazy, and she's seriously pissed about us killing her kids. But there is some good news."

Fallyn cocked her head. "Yeah?"

"Luther and I tussled, and we trashed his apartment. But in the process, he somehow snapped out of the spell he was under."

Maureen had started typing, but she stopped working when she heard that last bit. "Come again, lad?"

"I think it's this thing," I said, raising my arm to expose my wrist, only to find that the churchkey and rabbit's foot were nowhere to be seen. "Crap, please tell me I didn't lose it." I dug around in my Bag, finding the thing right where I'd left it. "Phew."

Fallyn came closer, eyeing the churchkey and charm suspiciously. "Looks like a cheap piece of yard sale crap to me."

"True. Yet, that's what they hired Heracles to steal, and what Rübezahl wanted me to retrieve so badly. He asked me to hang onto it for some reason. I figure it must act as some kind of charm or ward against Eris and Lyssa's curses."

Maureen looked askance at the thing in my hand. "S'odd—the thing has nary a hint o' magic to it."

"You too, huh? I couldn't find anything unusual about it, either."

"Who cares?" Fallyn remarked as she tapped her foot. "What did Luther say about the Pack and Dad?"

"Oh, he's taking the Coven underground for a while. Said he can't promise complete peace, but he'll do his best."

Fallyn's jaw relaxed, and the tightness around her

eyes diminished. "Oh man, that is good news. Now I just have to avoid Dad until this blows over."

"Still worried about that, I guess?"

Maureen snorted softly. "I'm gonna' go check and see how that great tattooed lug is gettin' along in the warehouse. He's supposed ta' be helpin' me with inventory. I've a feeling he's gotten inta' the stock fer' the snack machine again."

Maureen slipped out the back door of the office, leaving Fallyn and I alone. "You were saying?"

"I wasn't," she said, deflating as she slumped into a chrome and vinyl chair that was more duct tape than upholstery. "But yeah, I'm worried."

I sat next to her. "Hey, everything's going to be alright."

She gave me a look that was both sympathetic and disbelieving, all at once. "Parents and boyfriends, always lying to make you feel better."

"Okay, so maybe *everything* will *never* be alright. But some things will, and those that don't we'll face together."

She covered her face with her hands and groaned softly. "This is something I have to do alone. You know that."

"Sure," I said, pulling one of her hands into mine. "But I'll still be right there with you all the while."

My tough, pretty she-wolf gave me a weak smile. "Even though the very thought of facing off with Dad

DRUID'S BANE

makes me nauseous, somehow it is comforting to know you're here."

"Hey, I get it. When Finnegas was still around, I always took comfort in the fact that I could find him here most days, puttering around the yard." I looked toward the stacks, back where the old man used to hang out, drink beer, and smoke. "Whenever I needed to talk, he was always there."

"You still miss him, don't you?"

"Yep, every damned day. Especially now. I've got two crazy goddesses to deal with, Maeve's out of commission, and the city is under at least one and possibly two curses. Plus Cerberus is after me, I have to rescue an entire timeline and prevent the extinction of humankind, and the future fate of Druidry rests in my hands. Right now, I'd give my left nut to walk out in the yard and find him there, smoking his roll-your-owns and tinkering on some old beater."

Fallyn shifted in her seat, so she was facing me at an angle. Her eyes widened slightly as a look of shocked realization broke out across her features. "Wow. And here I am complaining about my troubles."

"It is a lot. I just don't like to talk about it. Honestly, I would rather not burden you."

She frowned. "That's what I'm here for—you're supposed to burden me. Like, I want you to come to me with your troubles. If you don't, how will I ever know what's bothering you?"

"Er, good point. You want to know what's bothering me now?"

She shimmied in her chair, straightening her posture slightly. "Shoot."

I clasped hands with her, freeing one hand to scratch the back of my head. "I really do wish I could speak to the old man, just one more time. There's so much I want to ask him, so many questions he could clear up for me."

"Wasted time, right? We never appreciate the time we have with the people we love until they're gone."

She'd hit the nail on the head. That was exactly how I'd been feeling, like I'd squandered all the time I had with Finnegas when he was alive. Knowing what I knew now, I wished I could get it all back and spend that time with him all over again.

"Maybe that's what life's all about though, you know?" I said as I flashed a crooked, sorrowful frown. "Not getting do-overs makes you more aware of the mistakes you've made, and more cautious about making more of them as you get older. Otherwise, we'd never learn from our mistakes."

"Too true," she said. "I just hope I don't mess things up between me and Dad. He might be a gruff, crotchety old alpha, but he was a damned good parent. And after Mom left, we looked after each other. I just don't want to hurt him, or for something to happen that would mess our relationship up."

Despite the seriousness of the moment, I gave a wry, humorless chuckle.

"What?" she asked.

"I'm not laughing at you, but at the circumstances. I guess I'm just a bit jealous that you're aware of what you might lose. And I think I'm a little pissed at myself for not realizing that sooner, where Finnegas and I were concerned."

"Then I guess you'd better make sure you don't make the same mistakes with your apprentice someday."

"How do you know I'm going to take on an apprentice?" I asked.

"Because, when faced with the opportunity to take the easy route or the hard way, Colin McCool will always take the hard way. Honestly, I can't think of anything harder than taking someone under your wing, and being responsible for their success or failure."

"Man. When you put it that way, it makes me want to retire to the Grove and never leave."

She looked at our hands as a coy smile played across her lips. "I don't know about forever, but I wouldn't mind retiring there for an hour or two. You game?"

Just as I opened my mouth to answer, a booming, electronically amplified voice echoed from the parking lot.

"Colin McCool, this is the Department of Homeland Security. Exit the building with your hands up and peacefully remit yourself into federal custody. If you do not, we will use force to subdue you."

Fuck!

I ROSE FROM THE CHAIR, intending to go outside to confront Mendoza, but Fallyn held me fast. She was surprisingly strong for her size, perhaps stronger in her human form than I was in my half-Fomorian form.

"Don't go out there," she said, half-pleading and half-commanding.

"All I want to do is speak with them. Obviously, Mendoza wants something. If I find out what it is and give it to him, they'll leave us alone."

"If you go out there and you're wrong, you'll be left with two choices—fight, or be arrested. We both know which one you'll choose."

"Yes, but—"

"Just let the wards do their job," she said with finality. "They can wait out there all week for all we care."

"Fallyn, this is the federal government we're dealing with. If I don't cooperate, they'll trump up charges on something silly, like tax evasion, or employing immigrants illegally, or EPA violations. Then they'll come in with a warrant, or they might even seize this place." I glanced around the office, thinking of what the junkyard meant to me. "It's all I have left of Uncle Ed, and I won't give it up that easily. Besides that, I have employees to think about. If we get shut down permanently, what'll happen to them and their families?"

She lowered her gaze momentarily, frowning. "You're right. Just be careful, okay?"

I gave her a peck on the lips and stood, just as a loud explosion shook the office. "That sounded like it came from the gate."

Fallyn cocked an ear for a moment, then she met my gaze with a look of disbelief. "Those assholes breached the freaking gate. How in the hell could they get through your wards?"

After casting a chameleon spell on Fallyn, I ran out the back door of the office, intent on stopping the agents in their tracks. I had a funny feeling that Cerberus wasn't here for me, but for something else entirely. It was then I realized, if Eris' influence had affected a 500-year-old vampire that deeply, what would it do to a forty-year-old human?

When I rounded the corner of the building, agents were already filing through the twisted, shattered gates. The smell of technomancy hung heavy on the air, indicating exactly what had happened. It was the scent of overwhelmingly powerful magic, mixed with slagged metal and burnt plastic.

Technomancy was the use of technology to control and direct magic. Technomagical devices were difficult and expensive to create because they typically required plenty of R&D and lots of costly raw materials like platinum, palladium, and gold. As well, most such devices were single use, which was the chief limitation of the method. Yet, the power that could be wielded by such devices could not be denied, as evidenced by my breached wards and wrecked iron gate.

The agents were dressed in tactical gear, with body armor, black BDUs, combat helmets, and goggles. I also saw they were carrying odd-looking guns that reminded me of a bubble-making pistol I had when I was a kid. Except these rifles didn't shoot bubbles, as I soon found out.

I raised my hands in the universal sign of surrender as soon as they noticed me. In response, they raised their rifles.

"Hey, there's no need for this, I give up—"

"That's the target," someone yelled over the radio. "Fire, damn it!

I only picked up the voice coming from their earpieces due to my enhanced senses. Luckily, it gave me just enough time to cast a defensive spell. A wall of earth, blacktop, and bent steel bars shot up between me and the agents, just as their rifles went off with a collective *bloop!*

Where the rifles hit my hastily erected barrier, whatever they hit disintegrated. The wall didn't explode, or melt, or fall apart—sections of it simply were not there anymore.

What manner of fuckery is this? I wondered as I stared at the Swiss cheese my barrier had become. Then I realized an agent was looking at me through one of the larger holes. His eyes went wide, as did mine, then I ducked and he fired.

Bloop!

A circular wave of *wrongness* floated past just above me, a shimmering, transparent disturbance in the air that gave me the willys when I looked at it. Oddly enough, the energy projectile moved faster than a were-wolf could run, but not nearly as fast as a bullet. After missing me, it hit the wall of the warehouse some twenty-five yards away, partially disintegrating a circle of metal siding five feet in diameter.

Well, at least now I know the effect dissipates at range.

Still, I didn't care to get hit by one of the damned things, even from far away. I decided to do something about it before that happened. I snuck a look, and noticed that the rifles were metal, which I had a poor affinity for, but the stocks were wood.

I reached out, connecting to the wood with druid magic, then I pulled the guns toward me through a hole in my barrier. Once I had them on my side of the wall, I used more magic to hastily form a hole in the ground. Finally, I buried those things about ten yards deep.

So much for that shit.

"He took our null cannons!" one of the tac team members said as she drew her sidearm and ducked behind a car.

The same voice spoke over the radio again. "Mage teams four and seven, advance. Teams 3 and eight, covering fire."

If things hadn't been chaotic enough before, they were now. Fireballs erupted from somewhere in the parking lot, on the other side of the office, where I couldn't see. One of them whooshed toward me, and I absorbed it using druid magic.

At the same time, I received a series of images from the Druid Oak. One was of an army of ants swarming a leaf and chewing it up. Another was of a sandstorm blowing over a walled city. Still another was a tsunami crashing into a wooded coastline.

Oh, shit. This is bad.

"They're attacking the Oak!" I yelled, knowing Fallyn would hear me.

I ran to the stacks where I'd left my Oak, hastily tossing up another wall of dirt and gravel behind me to slow down the wizards. By the time I got to the stacks, there were Cerberus agents everywhere. Some bore those funky rifles, others had no weapons at all.

Half of them were suspended in the air or tied to the ground by vines and overgrown patches of thick, fibrous grass. The Oak was fighting back, but it was taking a beating. It had already been hit twice by the disintegration guns. Thankfully the hits had only taken out small sections of limbs and leaves, but it'd been injured nonetheless.

"If they hit its trunk..." I said under my breath, not willing to finish the sentence.

Rather than risk seeing such a disaster happen, I

yanked all the guns from the agents' hands, disposing of them as I had the first group's weapons.

Just when I'd finished burying the "null cannons," I received a frantic warning from the Oak. All I saw was a gigantic wall of fire in my mind. I spun around, just in time to see a fireball the size of a small bus bearing down on me from only a few feet away.

With no time to move nor cast a spell, I braced for impact. Suddenly, I was pushed back into the dirt on my ass. When I looked up, the Oak stood where I had milliseconds before.

As I watched, fire washed over its trunk, branches, and leaves. In my mind, I heard a long, high-pitched screech, the sort of sound a helpless animal makes when caught in a trap. My Druid Oak was burning, and inside my head I could hear it screaming in agony.

"Noooo!" I roared, even as I reacted out of sheer paternal instinct.

Without thought or even an effort of conscious will, a burst of pure chronourgic energy burst forth from the center of my being. That pulse of time magic spread outward in a bubble that encompassed the entire yard, freezing the junkyard grounds in the largest stasis spell I'd ever cast.

With time on my side again, stunned shock gave way to panic. Instantly, I realized both the horror of what had happened to the Oak, and the mistake I'd made in casting such a large time magic spell out in the open. Realizing I had only seconds to act before a major power noticed and came calling, I leapt into action.

Moving at near-vampire speed, I blurred around the front of the tree to survey the damage. Sadly, the bark and much of the cambium beneath had been burned from the front side of the tree, along with many branches and half its leaves.

A mature oak tree could survive something like this, but a younger tree might not. Rage boiled up from within me, and I turned to seek the person who'd done it. My head swiveled this way and that, until finally, I found the wizard in question.

He was slight of build and not much to look at, just a skinny kid in fatigues that were too damned big for him. The babyfaced agent had red hair, freckles, and a bad case of acne, and he couldn't have been more than nine-teen years old, tops. Despite his youth, I was tempted to do him harm.

So much harm, indeed...

"What in the blue blazes—?" I heard Click exclaim as he appeared out of nowhere.

I swung my head to meet his gaze, even as I held Mogh's Scythe ready and waiting to cut the Cerberus tac team wizard in two.

Gwydion looked at the Oak, then at me, then at the kid. "Oh, bugger all. Don't do it, lad. Tis' not worth it, an' the child were only followin' orders—cursed orders at that. None o' these folks is in their right mind. Ye'd hate yerself fer' centuries if ya' harmed a hair on his head. Trust me on this."

I looked at my Oak—an entity that was essentially my child—and I screamed at the sky, a raw, violent shriek of rage and frustration. Shaking with anger and pain that I could not vent, I turned to Click and spoke through clenched teeth.

"Keep an eye out while I fix things. The moment you sense trouble, release the spell for me. Hopefully, this won't take long."

The first thing I did was to encase the Oak in a cocoon, a working of my own creation that I came up with on the fly. Drawing on nature's energies, the surrounding vegetation, and guidance I received from the now very frantic Grove, I surrounded the Oak in a tough, fibrous, semi-permeable membrane. The chrysalis served three purposes: to extinguish the remaining flames, to protect the Oak while it healed, and to allow sunlight to reach it while it was still in hibernation.

Can you transport it back to the Grove to heal? I asked the Oak's counterpart and sibling.

In response, I received an image of the darkest night. That would be a "no," although it wanted to, badly. In response, I sent the Grove a message that was pure consolation, then I set about the remainder of my tasks.

Zipping around the junkyard, I gathered all the Cerberus agents one at a time. Then I used their nylon cuffs to restrain them, zip-tying them together and leaving them inside the two armored vehicles they'd presumably arrived in earlier. After closing the doors, I welded them shut, using a great deal of my own magical reserves in the process.

"Time's wastin', lad!" Click shouted.

"That—it doesn't even make any sense," I muttered as I zipped back into the yard.

Next I found Mendoza. Exercising a great deal of restraint, I treated him in similar fashion. Instead of locking him in the back of one of the vehicles, I placed him and the last remaining agent in the vehicle's driver's seats. Then I zip-tied their hands to the steering wheels of each, and I used a black Sharpie to leave a note on Mendoza's forehead.

You got off lucky. Never return.

Finally, I checked on Fallyn, Hemi, and Maureen. Hemi had been about to take a bullet for Maureen when I froze time, so I moved them both to make certain that didn't happen. Fallyn had been tossing an engine block at someone—I left her as she was. Later I'd explain to them how all the agents disappeared, after I dealt with the consequences.

"Lad, somethin's comin'—somethin' powerful!" Click shouted.

"I'm right here," I said after I'd snuck up behind him. Seeing him jump would've been satisfying, had the situation not been so dire. "Go ahead and drop the spell, then get out of here."

"But I kin'—"

"Nope. Do what I say, Click. I may need your help later if this goes south."

He shook his head slowly, clapping a hand on my shoulder. "I'm so sorry, lad. Really, I am."

Then he vanished, the spell dissipated, and time rolled on once more. As soon as it did, I sensed a magical power surge about twenty feet in front of me. I didn't even bother trying to hide the Oak with magic. Whoever or whatever was coming, it wouldn't do any good anyway. If the entity had sensed my time magic spell, then they'd likely see through any illusions I cast almost immediately.

Figuring it'd be a bad idea to look like I was ready to fight, I stood with my hands clasped in front of me, just a few steps to the left of the Oak's cocoon. Seconds later, a fifteen-foot-high portal materialized in the yard. As the scenery on the other side appeared, I almost breathed a sigh of relief. A figure stepped into view on the opposite side, one I recognized instantly.

"Colin, what happened?" Jesse asked. "I heard the scream, all the way from Austin."

I often forgot that Jesse had been involved in the Oak and Grove's genesis as well. Her connection to the two was nearly as strong as mine, although I was the one who'd ended up mastering each entity. Still, I didn't doubt that she cared for them, in her own way.

"It's the Oak, Jess. It was injured, saving me."

It was then she realized that the pulsing, green

thing behind me was the Oak. She covered her mouth as an expression of sheer horror twisted her facial features. Then, she looked over her shoulder before stepping aside—apparently, someone else was approaching the portal.

Seconds later, the Dagda's massive form filled the gateway opening. He looked at the Oak, then he glared at me, then he looked back at the Oak, his brow creased with concern.

"Tell me, boy, what in Tech Duinn happened here, and what in the bloody feck did ya' do to my Oak?"

CHAPTER

NINETEEN

Rather than state the obvious or make some smart-assed remark, I simply shrugged. "See for yourself."

The Dagda came through the portal, immediately striding toward the Oak. Halfway there, he stopped and looked at the sky with a quizzical expression on his face.

"Maeve lost her demesne to the Greeks?" he asked.

"Naw, she's merely indisposed. I'm working on that. However, the attack that harmed the Oak was due to their influence."

He hmphed at me, then he approached the Oak. After spending several minutes running his hands over the skin of the chrysalis, listening to it, and grunting, he stepped back and cradled his chin in his hand.

"Well, I can't say I'm pleased ya' let this happen. However, ya' did save its life with this bit o' Druidry."

"So the Oak will live?"

"Aye, but it'll need plenty o' time ta' heal. Have ya' tried sendin' it ta' the Grove yet?"

I nodded. "I asked the Grove if it was capable of doing so, but it seemed to be unable to perform the task."

The Dagda rubbed a hand over his beard. "Too young yet, more'n likely. I provided most o' that power ta' the Oak when I infused the acorn wit' magic. It'll be awhile yet afore the Grove matures enough to extend its reach inta' other realms."

"Meanwhile, we can't leave it here," I said. "It'll be vulnerable to another attack, and I have two goddesses to deal with."

What I didn't say was that Cerberus might return as well. I'd heard the government ARVs leaving while the Dagda fussed over my Oak. Yet, it wouldn't be long before the curse would lead Mendoza back here, and likely with more agents and firepower.

Just one more reason to take care of Lyssa and Eris, and lift these curses from my city.

I had no idea whether Cerberus had intended to harm the Oak, or whether it had been a fluke. Normally, the Oak was invisible to anyone who wasn't in its circle of trust. It might've been pure chance that they breached the junkyard at multiple points while the Oak was present.

Did Cerberus come with fire wizards because they knew I had the Oak here, or was it just dumb luck on their part? I had no idea. However, the possibility remained that someone had tipped them off about it. I didn't intend to give anyone a second chance at harming it—not Cerberus, and not the gods, either.

The Dagda gave me the side-eye. "Are these goddesses the ones who're responsible fer' harmin' my Oak?"

My Oak, you mean.

"The very same."

"Hmph. I'll take the tree ta' it's Grove ta' heal. In the interim, yer' ta' make sure the wenches get their due."

"That's a load off my mind," I said, barely stopping short of thanking him. "How long do you think it'll take the Oak to heal?"

He threw his hands up, scowling. "How long does a flower take ta' bloom? As long as it needs. The Oak will heal when it heals. Ye'll hafta' do without its consider-able powers and benefits until then."

I didn't like the idea of confronting an insane goddess without the Oak's magic reserves at my beck and call. However, I was more concerned with its health and recovery than my safety.

"So be it."

His massive, hairy face swung round, and he fixed me with a searching look. "Ye've changed."

There were a million smart-aleck remarks I could've made in response, all of them related to being hunted by members of the Celtic pantheon, and his and Lugh's lack of intervention on my behalf. Yet, I held my tongue.

Clasping my hands behind my back, I inclined my head in his direction.

"Is there anything else this druid can assist with, before the Dagda returns to his realm?"

The Dagda pursed his lips, glowering at me. "Nay, I s'pose not."

He laid a hand on the Oak's chrysalis, then they both disappeared. The portal, however, remained. I approached it, calling Jesse's name along the way.

"I'm still here," she said as she stepped into view.

"Eavesdropping?"

"Of course."

I smiled. "I take it he's still mad at me over Aengus?"

"What do you think? His son died, and he's reacting as any father would."

"The messed up part is that I wasn't even the one who killed him."

Jesse rolled her eyes. "Yes, but you were there, and that's enough for him. Give him a few centuries, and he'll get over it."

"It wouldn't have been necessary to kill him, if Aengus hadn't been such a dick. Likewise, the Dagda could've stepped in on my behalf, or at least strongly suggested that his son not try to kill me." Jess gave me a blank look, which I took as a sign I should change the subject. "Speaking of, how are things between you and the hairiest god in the pantheon?"

"He's good to me, but very controlling. My only saving grace is that he forgets about me for months on end. During those times, I'm able to roam and study and do as I please."

"And other times?" I asked.

She demurred, glancing down and away. "It's not so bad. He has me running errands for him, tending his fields and livestock, cleaning his home, that sort of thing."

A thought occurred to me, one I didn't care to give voice to, but I felt compelled to ask about it just the same. "Jess, he's not—?"

She looked up at me. "What? Oh no, not that. I think he looks at me more like a daughter, or at least a niece who isn't too troublesome. I'm cared for, and that's enough."

"But isn't Underhill dangerous?"

"Yes, but he's taught me things. Being the representative of the leader of the Celtic pantheon has its perks." She glanced over her shoulder. "Oops, he's back. Gotta' go."

The portal winked out, leaving me standing there without having said goodbye. I sensed someone's eyes on me, and when I looked around, I found Fallyn watching me from the warehouse. I waved, and she returned the gesture weakly before walking inside.

"Shit. Looks like I got more 'splaining to do," I muttered softly.

Now that I knew the Oak was safe from further attacks, I spared a few minutes to repair the gate and fence where Cerberus had breached the perimeter. Then Maureen and I set about fixing the wards. I added a few surprises just in case those bastards decided to return, traps that would trigger if technomagical devices came within close proximity.

"Ya' sure ya' want ta' do that?" Maureen asked. "Might provoke 'em."

"If they come that close to the perimeter unannounced, provocation has already happened. Besides, I warned Mendoza. Curse or no, if he comes back, he's asking for trouble."

She raised an eyebrow and tucked a strand of lustrous red hair behind one of her fine, elfin ears. "So be it. But don't expect me ta' go fightin' them feckers alone, should they come back before ya' return."

"Keep the place closed until I deal with the curse, but keep paying the staff. Go into the gold reserves if you have to, but make sure the employees are taken care of. If they show up, feel free to split. Hell, take a vacation. Heaven knows, you could use one."

The half-kelpie looked at me askance as realization dawned over her features. "Ya' know what? I jest might at that."

"Please do. And while you're getting some R&R, I'm going after Lyssa and Eris."

Maureen's wistful smile soured. "Alone?"

"It'll be dangerous where I'm going, and I don't feel comfortable taking Hemi and Fallyn with me."

"Too bad," Fallyn said as she dropped a duffel next to me. The bag made a metallic *thud* as it hit the floor. "I'm coming along, like it or not."

"Goes double for me, aye?" Hemi said as he entered the office behind her. "Gods don't scare me. Crazy ones neither."

"They're all daft, if'n ya' ask me," Maureen said. She gave me a stern look, but her voice quavered a bit as she spoke. "Don't'cha go getting' yerself killed tryin' ta' save Maeve's arse. She'd not do the same in return, an' that's a fact."

I clucked my tongue. "As much as I hate to admit it, the city needs her presence. She might not be my favorite person, but at least she brings some stability to the area. Just look at what happened without her."

"Fine," Maureen replied as she crossed her arms over her chest. "But don'tcha dare ever let the old biddy ferget that ya' saved her tail. Leverage is leverage, an' a debt's a debt. If ya' pull this off, promise ye'll play this one ta' the hilt."

"I promise." I turned to face Hemi and Fallyn. "Since I know I can't talk you out of it, and I can't leave you behind now that you're here, are you two ready?"

Fallyn approached Maureen and gave her a brief, friendly hug. "Don't fret, I'll look after him."

"I know ya' will." Maureen glanced at Hemi. "Ya' be sure ta' do the same."

"Yeah-nah, she'll be alright," he replied.

As promised, I called Heracles in the car on the way to the Icehouse. "This is Colin. It's on."

"Eh? Oh, we're being all cloak and dagger, are we? The thing—right," he said in a hushed voice. "Any idea where it'll happen?"

"Nothing yet, but if I can let you know when I get there, I will."

"Hmmm. She won't face you in your reality. Expect to be drawn into a version of hers when first you confront her."

"Already happened," I said, slowing down and pulling into a bank's drive-through while a hailstorm of minnows rained from the sky. "She's not exactly what I expected."

"She takes many forms. If you escaped unscathed, you've yet to see her worst, believe me."

"Well, it sounds like I won't be able to let you know where we're confronting her—I hope that's okay."

"Heracles, come join us!" I heard a female voice shout in the background.

"I'll be right there, my dear," he said in a muffled voice. When next he spoke, he sounded subdued. "Do yourself a favor, McCool. Bring hellebore, as it'll act as a balm for the madness she spreads."

Hellebore was a popular flowering plant that grew all over Europe and Western Asia. Normally, I'd just have the Grove whip some up. Since I'd not have access to my grove for some time, I figured it couldn't hurt to ask more about it.

"Hellebore. Any idea where I might find some?"

"You're the local druid, Druid," Heracles groused. "How should I know where to find flowers around here?"

"Fair enough. Anything else I should know?"

Heracles was quiet for several seconds. "Once you think you're going mad, you're already there. At that time, run far away from anyone you might wish to keep safe."

"Ahem. I'll keep that in mind."

"You do that. I'll see you when it's done," The Greek demigod added before hanging up.

The rest of the ride to Rube's was uneventful, except for the two protests we were forced to drive around, the giant cloud of grasshoppers we drove through, the half-dozen scuffles we saw, and the dozens of minor fender-benders we passed. It was as if chaos had taken root and blossomed in the city. Everywhere I looked, I saw Eris' stupid signs, each spouting some contrarian saying that made absolutely no sense at all.

"Wonder how much that ad agency made, eh?" Hemi asked.

"Too much," Fallyn replied. "What a bullshit job. You get paid millions and your agency provides a slogan and a font on a black background in return. I'm in the wrong business."

"Oh?" I asked playfully. "And what business is that?"

"Got me curious now as well," Hemi said as he leaned over the front seats.

"Strategic workforce reallocation," she replied.

"Whazzat like?" Hemi asked, since he wasn't in on the joke.

"It requires lots of travel, but the pay is good."

Hemi laid back in the seat again. "If they have any openings, lemme know. A bloke's gotta eat."

A few minutes later, we pulled into Rube's parking lot. Rube was nowhere to be seen, but the front door sported an actual doorknob this time. I took that as a favorable omen.

When I entered, Bal let us in without a fuss. "Boss is at the bar," he said, barely taking notice of us.

The place was nearly empty, void of patrons except for one lone individual nursing a beer at the end of the bar. "Where is everyone?" I asked.

"They know when trouble's brewing," Rube replied as he polished a mug with a dishtowel. He set it on the drying rack and laid the towel beside it. "Come with me. My Hall awaits."

WE FOLLOWED Rube down the back hall of the Icehouse, through the door marked "Employees Only" into the garden vale we traversed on my previous visit. I half-expected to find Siobhán waiting for me, but she was nowhere to be seen. I found that curious, but I held my tongue. Rather than turning back around to exit into the so-called "Hall of Mirrors," instead Rube led us into the vale, down the hill and around a bend. We followed the trail for a time, until we came upon a cave entrance in the side of the valley.

"Follow, and touch nothing," John said as he entered without bothering to see if we did, indeed, follow him.

We three shared a look, then I shrugged and headed in after him. My trepidation eased when the tunnel opened up into a vast chamber, one filled with doorway after doorway and portal after portal leading to worlds and places unknown.

"That was a different route we took, compared to my last visit," I said.

John sneered. "I move it around a lot. Can't steal what you can't find."

"How could someone steal this?" Fallyn asked.

"The same way one can steal another's heart," was Rube's reply. He stood there looking at us with a mocking grin on his face, and that's when I knew I'd been had.

"Well?" I asked.

"Well, what?" he responded.

"Where's the door?"

Rube's grin spread from ear to ear. "It's around here somewhere."

"Then take us to it," I said.

"Oh no," he replied, waving his hands back and forth. "I only agreed to allow you passage—I never said anything about acting as a guide."

I hung my head and ran a hand over my face. When I looked up, Fallyn and Hemi were staring at me. "You know what, guys? Give me a minute, alright?"

"Sure thing," Fallyn replied. She and Hemi retreated a short distance, far enough away to give the illusion of privacy, but not so far that she couldn't immediately attack if needed.

"I figured you might try something sneaky, but I didn't know you'd be this low about it."

"You cut the deal, druid. And I'm delivering."

"Fine. If you won't help us get to where we need to go, then I'm taking Siobhán back to earth, right now." I waited until he was about to explode, then I continued in a whisper. "Or should I say, Cressida."

I'd thought long and hard about how John had been acting, and what might've set him off. He'd actually dropped a couple of hints on my prior visits, saying how she was not what she'd been, and that now she was more or some-such. Being a typical fae, the wily old son of a gun just couldn't help himself. That was one of the primary weaknesses of the fae—they were always tripping over their dicks in an attempt to prove they were more clever than humans.

It had taken me a while to put it together. After reviewing Maeve's theories, the little info Crowley had received from Fuamnach, and Rube's hints, I'd figured it out. Fuamnach had once said she'd been inside Maeve's manse, but there was no way she'd be able to physically enter without Maeve's permission. Since she couldn't lie, I figured she had to have been there in a manner other than physical—meaning, she'd hitched a ride inside someone else's mind.

On the other hand, Maeve was certain she'd had a spy, and suspected the real Siobhán had been abducted and switched out with a doppelgänger. She also indicated she'd been aware of the switch for a time, and used the opportunity to feed Fuamnach false info. Meaning, Fuamnach hadn't been posing as Siobhán—which verified my hitchhiker hunch.

Then, Fuamnach advised Crowley to ask me where Cressida was currently. How would I know if I hadn't been with her myself? And why else would Fuamnach send him to find me at Rube's, unless that was where I'd last seen Cressida?

But the most compelling bit of evidence was that Siobhán didn't act like a fae. That thing she said about 'a cord of three strands'? That was a quote from the Bible. No way any fae would ever know something like that.

Moreover, Fuamnach didn't treat her as such. No, she treated Siobhán like a human slave. Not even a god or goddess would treat one of the high fae like that—not in a million years.

Thus, Siobhán *was* Cressida. That was the only logical conclusion. And when I revealed that I knew what Rübezahl had already figured out, he became practically apoplectic.

Then, he began to grow. It was a magical power that some fae had, to alter their size, mass, and strength. The Mountain King was well-known for possessing this skill, and I'd witnessed him using it in the past.

Personally, I would rather not fight him, not in his realm, and not in his strongest form. However, getting him upset was part of my plan, because anger led to mistakes.

"We can do this the hard way, John," I said, raising my index finger in the air. "Or, there is another solution."

John towered over me now, and he'd greatly changed in appearance as well. Gone was the wiry old man with weather-beaten skin and a mischievous sparkle in his eye. Now he was a giant warrior, bulging with muscle yet well-formed, with smooth skin, clear eyes, and handsome, if somewhat alien, features.

He wore fine but simple clothing, a tunic and breeches made from cloth spun in a tight weave, dyed in bright purple and green. His boots had been fashioned from soft, shiny black leather, and he wore a wide, matching leather belt with a longsword scabbarded at his hip.

Essentially, he looked like a two-story tall version of one of the high fae—like a king of old, indeed. All he lacked was a crown and scepter. But one thing hadn't changed—he was still pissed at me.

He raised a foot over my head as if to stomp me flat. I heard Fallyn's intake of breath, and I sensed Hemi tensing behind me as they prepared to do battle on my behalf. Behind my back, I motioned for them to stay calm and hold position. The last thing I needed was for Fallyn to turn into a giant wolf and send John over the edge.

His voice thundered as he roared in defiance. "Or nothing, boy! I'll squash you like an ant, and then we'll see how smart you are."

"Do it, and you'll be cursed forever—by your own magic, no less. As I understand it, forever is a very long time for one such as yourself. Will it be worth it?"

Slowly, his huge, booted foot moved out of the way, allowing me to see his face above me. John still frowned deeply, but at least he wasn't tap dancing on my head. "What do you propose?"

"While I would be within the terms of our agreement to take Siobhán back to earth, ultimately that's her choice. Yet, I believe that if she were to hear her true name, Fuamnach's geas over her would be broken, and her memories would come flooding back. Am I right?"

"Y'are," John grumbled.

"And am I also correct that such an exposure to the truth might shatter her still fragile sanity?"

"Of course it would! Why do ya' think I don't want her to leave?"

"Yet, her brother deserves to know she's alive. The fae took her, as they took him, against the terms of

329

treaties that had been established between the fae and the druids, who negotiated on behalf of all humankind."

That last part I wasn't certain about, but I'd heard Finnegas suggest as much a few times. Still, I was taking a risk here—I only hoped it would pan out.

"Those agreements stopped being enforceable ages ago," John said. "When the druids died out, so did the treaties."

"Ah, but the druids didn't die out. One of them lived, and I am his heir. Therefore, the treaties still stand."

"Make your point!" John huffed as he crossed his arms over his massive chest.

"My point is that we can compromise here, and in the favor of all parties. I propose that, for her safety, we do not reveal Siobhán's true nature to her. At least, not until she's fully recovered."

"I'm listening," the gnome said as he took a knee to get closer to eye level with me.

"I also submit that she should stay here while she heals. It's apparent to me that this place is a safe haven for her, and that her condition has improved tremendously since she's been here."

"That's what I've said all along," he agreed.

"Yet, the brother longs for his twin—and who has more right to care for family, but a twin by birth? There's power in such bonds, more power than either your magic or mine can tear asunder."

John frowned, but he nodded as well. "You speak true, druid."

"Therefore, why not inform the brother of his sister's condition, and allow him to visit her here, while keeping the secret from her a bit longer? Surely, he'd agree to this, having a love for her that runs deeper than either you or I could fathom."

"Yet I do love her—as much as I am able," he whispered.

"Of this I have no doubt. Whether she will return that love over time remains to be seen. But until she fully recovers and can make such decisions, I believe this is the best compromise for all involved. What say you, Lord John of the Mountain?"

Rube was already shrinking back to his "normal" size, and his expression had gone from sheer fury to resignation and relief. Although he aged right before my eyes as he transformed, it was difficult to see the old man instead of the twenty-foot tall warrior that had nearly crushed me flat just moments before.

"Just what would you receive in exchange for my agreement on this matter?"

I smiled. "Only that you keep to the terms of our original deal, and fulfill our more recent bargain. And, of course, that you guide us through your lands to the place where I might find Lyssa of the Greek pantheon."

Rube led us to one of the thousands of gateways that dotted the interior of the cavern. While his choice appeared to have been made at random, his confident stride and lack of hesitation told me he knew exactly where he was going. When he stopped next to the plain, door-sized opening in the cavern wall, he turned to address us as one.

"You'll be goin' to Limbo, one of the made-up planes created by various of Nyx's children."

"Limbo—don't sound so bad," Hemi remarked.

Rube's mouth twitched from side to side, as if he wasn't sure how much he should tell us. "It doesn't look so bad, not at first. But looks can be deceiving. This is a place where reality's fluid, where the very ground can shift and morph beneath your feet. That'll be hazard number one when you get there."

"Okay, so what's hazard number two?" Fallyn asked.

"The Machai and their helpers, the Hismanae," Rübezahl replied.

"Daemons, I take it?"

"Hmm, yes. Nasty little bastards. The former are personifications of war, the latter, personifications of fighting."

"They sound friendly," I said. "Can they be avoided?"

"Doubtful. They guard the gates, which you'll need to pass to find Lyssa. Then there's the goddess herself, which you'll find out about in due time."

Fallyn's nose twitched—one of her nervous tics. "How do we find her when we get there?"

Rube's expression was as serious as his voice in response. "Just listen for the screams."

"Well, this looks like it's going to be a total shit-show," I said.

Hemi pointed over my head. "Hey, the bubbles are gone."

Like an idiot, I patted the top of my head as if to find something there. "Huh. I wonder how long that's been going on?"

Fallyn snickered. "Yay, you got your superpower back. Now, if only you'd use those powers for good instead of evil."

"Har, har," I replied. I turned to meet Rube's gaze. "Anything else you can tell us?"

He stroked his beard as he contemplated the question. "Trust nothing, question everything, and if all else fails, run. I'll leave the gate open and guard it until your return."

"What if we don't come back?" Fallyn asked. "You'll be waiting a long time, then."

Rube sniffed. "If you pass through my Hall, I'll know when you're due to return. It's just the way it works."

"Handy trick," Hemi said. "Always know when company is coming, in case you want to duck out."

"It is at that," Rube replied, with just a hint of a smile. He stepped aside and gestured at the door. "You'd best be off."

The swirling mists that hid the view from the other side dissipated, and before my eyes, a scene slowly coalesced within the doorframe. On the other side, a verdant field stretched away for several hundred yards. Eventually, it broke up into pieces and chunks of land that floated off into the sky. While the nearest "sky islands" seemed to be floating upright, I noted that the further away they were, the more likely they were to be oriented differently. Some were sideways, some pointed away from us, and others were upside-down.

"Shee-it," Fallyn said. "Did anyone think to bring a plane—or a parachute?"

Rübezahl frowned. "You won't need it. As long as you can break the gravity field around each piece of rock, you can glide over to the next one in line. Problem is, there's no atmosphere beyond them, and if you miss —" he twirled his finger in the air, trailing the spiral off to his left. "Well, you'd best hope another island drifts in front of you first."

"Peachy," I muttered. As I glanced at my companions in turn, I gestured toward the gateway. "Shall we?"

I entered the gateway first, since I had the best long-range attack capabilities of the three of us. Fallyn followed next, carrying a pump shotgun she'd loaded with alternating double-ought buckshot, slugs, and sabot rounds. Hemi brought up the rear, his tattoos glowing softly, club in hand.

Whenever you entered a portal or gateway, it was important to remember you were passing into another world. Even when traveling to different locations on the same planet, conditions could differ drastically from one side of a portal or gateway to the other.

The experience was always unique as well. Sometimes, you felt nothing at all as you entered, just a change in air pressure or wind speed, or variations in temperature and odors. Other times it felt like piercing an invisible membrane, especially when you traveled between dimensions.

In this case, I felt as though I was walking from rightness into wrongness—like the Limbo side of the gateway just oozed with bad juju. I expected that feeling to pass once I became acclimated to the new location, but even after I was through and on the other side, it was a feeling I couldn't shake.

"Brrrr," Fallyn said as she stepped through the gateway. "It's like getting an ice-cold wet Willy, all over your body. Blech."

Hemi exited next, his usual jovial frown disappearing as he stepped out of the gateway. "Ugly feeling, that," was all he said on the matter.

"Take a minute to orient yourselves and prep for combat," I said.

Taking my own advice, first I looked around in all directions, noting that while the portal had faded from sight, a shimmering, transparent rectangle remained to let us know its location. Above, the sky was a dark blue, fading to various colors at random intervals across the domed expanse. It reminded me of a dip paint tub, before the artist dips the canvas or whatever into it.

Those colors slowly swirled into each other, creating new patterns and shades that were completely foreign to my experience, and it made me ill to stare at it. So, I turned my attention to the surrounding landscape, such as it was.

The chunk of land we stood on was roughly one-quarter mile across, with jagged edges that broke away into smaller, satellite pieces. While I'd assumed this piece of rock and earth was solid and planet-like, now I realized we'd simply exited onto one of the many sky islands that were visible in the distance.

Turning slowly in a circle, the vastness of this place was evident. Those floating slabs of rock, soil, and other material seemed to have no end, as they drifted in the sky in all directions, except directly overhead. I wondered, was the overall formation shaped like a planet, or more like a donut? Did it even matter? No, but weird shit like this always made me think about crap like that.

Strangely enough, there was a moon but no sun. Maybe that was because it was what passed for night-time here, or perhaps it was because this place lacked a solar facsimile, just like Underhill. Light emanated from everywhere and nowhere all at once. That meant multiple shadows were cast by us and by other vertical objects, adding to Limbo's disorienting effects.

Bottom line? The place was disconcerting on a level I'd never experienced previously. If I thought there was some other way to capture Lyssa and stop her, I'd have headed back through the gateway, right then and there. Unfortunately, it seemed we had little choice, as the only thing that had brought her out of hiding had been the death of her children.

Now we were on her turf, and not just a projection of it. I had a feeling the coming fight would be rough.

I should have killed her when I had the chance.

Just as I finished that thought, an ululating cry went up in the distance. Soon it was answered by another, then another, then more joined in, forming a chorus of trilling voices.

"Sounds like the locals are awake, aye?" Hemi remarked.

Fallyn racked a round in the shotty. "Let's go out and greet the neighbors."

TWENTY

When Rube said the Machai guarded the entrances to Limbo, I pictured a walled garrison full of troops, or maybe a manned watchtower or something. What I didn't expect was to be swarmed by a bunch of crazy-ass warriors flying everything from wyverns to biplanes to an A-10 Warthog. But when I heard the roar of a jet engine in the distance and saw the distinctive silhouette in the sky, I knew we were fucked.

"Take cover, now!" I yelled as I slammed my hands into the soil and grass beneath my feet.

Direct contact allowed me to skip over the whole druid trance thing, facilitating an immediate connection with whatever natural substances existed here. Still, I received quite a bit of resistance and feedback from the chunk of rock we were on, and it took a moment to get it to obey.

"Take cover where?" Fallyn asked. "We're kind of in the open here."

Brrrrrrrrrrttttttttt! the A-10's cannon went, just as I convinced the rock and soil to do what I wanted.

A wall of stone and dirt shot up in front of us, just in time to take the brunt of the A-10's barrage. That 30 mm cannon was no flippin' joke, and it'd shred any of us in a heartbeat if it made contact. The plane whooshed by overhead on its pass, then it banked around for a second go.

"Anybody think to bring a surface-to-air missile?" I asked as Fallyn sent round after round at the thing. I pushed the barrel of her shotgun down. "Save it for the rest. We're going to need it."

Hemi was already ducking around the other side of my barrier, and I dragged Fallyn after him as I readied a spell. Simultaneously, we began to take less accurate fire from the Gatling gun on the biplane, as well as arrow fire from the riders mounted on wyverns and pterodactyls circling above.

"Hemi—" I began.

"On it," he said as he began tossing softball-sized stones at the riders and their mounts with surprising accuracy.

Fallyn took aim as well, causing at least one sky rider to slump over the neck of their mount. With the attackers above engaged, I decided to do something about the A-10 before it shredded my barrier.

Brrrrrrrrrrttttttttt! the gun went again as rounds

slammed into the wall from the other side. I waited until the plane passed overhead to counterattack. While the max speed on the Warthog was only about 500 miles per hour, it was almost too fast for me to hit on the move.

Still, lightning was faster than even the quickest supersonic fighter, and the blast I sent from my hands hit the fuselage just off center. I must've fried some crucial electronics, because the plane veered off into a spiral dive, only to be lost from sight beyond the edge of the sky island.

"Good riddance to that thing," Fallyn said as she reloaded her shotgun. "But someone remind me to get a pilot's license and a tactical fighter the next time we travel to another dimension to kill a god."

I was about to correct her on how she classified the plane, but instead I paused to watch Hemi. He'd grabbed a bowling ball sized stone, hefting it to his shoulder with one hand as he spun, shot-putter style.

After a couple of turns, he launched the thing into the sky. It sailed directly in the path of a biplane, smashing the propeller and crushing a wing flap. That plane veered off in a similar manner to the A-10, trailing smoke with the engine sputtering.

"Two down, more to go," the big guy said. "By the way, do those things breathe fire?"

I looked where he pointed. Three wyverns had landed at the edge of the island behind a rocky outcrop where Fallyn's gun couldn't reach.

I shook my head. "Not usually, but they're deadly with those claws and teeth. Watch my back while I shift, will you?"

Hemi nodded. Fallyn scanned the horizon with the shotgun at high ready while I stripped and tossed my clothes into my Bag. I traded the clothes for Orna, then I started to shift.

"Master, good to see you again," the sword said cheerfully. "What sort of mayhem will we be engaging in today? Why, you've brought me to another dimension, one with an array of hostile creatures and entities to slay. How delightful!"

I could barely grunt in response, so painful was the transformation to my full Fomorian form. Once I completed the shift, I picked up the sword and hefted it over my shoulder. "Time to shut up now, Orna. We're about to take on a trio of wyverns, and their riders are supposed to be the literal personifications of fighting and waging war. This could be a hard battle, so I'd rather keep my mind on the fight."

"Oh, of course, master."

"Good, then let's go kill some daemons and wyverns."

I WAS ROUGHLY HALFWAY across the island when the riders came running across the plain at me, screaming like banshees and bashing their shields with the flats of their blades. They were like I'd imagined, but not, dressed as they were in bronze period breastplates, leather skirts, greaves, and strapped sandals.

Yet, they were just barely human-looking, and more reminiscent of wendigos than men and women. Tall and lanky, each was equal in height to me but sinewed in the manner of a person on the edge of starvation. Even so, they didn't lack for speed, closing the distance between us with long, ground-eating strides.

As they neared, I paid careful attention to their weaponry. Two carried short infantry spears paired with round bronze shields, while the other bore a long *xiphos*. I could see little of their faces beneath their split Greek helmets, but what I did see indicated they were not wholly alive, and perhaps even undead.

Their exposed skin was drawn, pale, and leathery, stretched so tight over their wasted muscles and tendons that I half-expected them to creak like stop-motion skeletons when they ran. Instead, they moved with a precision and fluidity I'd rarely seen in humans or fae, keeping pace with each other and holding position until they neared. They spread out to surround me, taking three points of a triangle roughly twenty feet away, just out of Orna's reach.

They circled, I watched. Meanwhile, Hemi and Fallyn kept the remaining aerial attackers at bay with well-placed slugs and stones. The tall, thin, hungry-looking warriors didn't speak, and if my eyes served me, they didn't even breathe—they just kept circling, waiting for their moment to strike.

I grew tired of waiting, so I spoke. "Are we going to do this, or—"

That was all it took to trigger their assault. Unlike movie fight scenes where the protagonist faces multiple attackers, each waiting their turn, these three didn't attack one at a time. Instead, they came at me in a coordinated effort, one feinting while the other two attacked high and low from different directions.

The one with the sword danced in with precise, rapid footwork, faking a slash at my eyes. The other two waited until I was distracted, then one stabbed at my calf from my right flank, while the other thrust at my armpit from the left. Despite the danger, on witnessing the precise coordination of the attack, my Fomorian brain nearly rejoiced.

Finally, some worthy opponents.

To a warrior race, nothing is better than facing off against an equal in battle. To know that the opponent you're fighting has taken the practice of warfare as seriously as you is what every true warrior dreams of night and day. Nothing is worse than facing enemy after enemy who are nothing but cannon fodder, and nothing is better than knowing the other guy or gal just might best you in combat.

I could only assume these were the Machai, personifications of warfare, and they were damned good.

I leaned away from the feint to my eyes, slipping

sideways as I lifted my right leg to avoid being skewered, while simultaneously whipping Orna around in a tip-down parry that deflected the third attacker's spear. Staying between these fools would be suicide, as the number one rule of fighting multiple attackers was to avoid doing it. Knowing that, I let go of Orna with my left hand, grabbing the third attacker's spear shaft and yanking on it.

Without setting my right foot down, I threw a hard front thrust kick that landed solidly on the third attacker's breastplate. The kick caved in the armor and sent that one staggering away, leaving me with her spear in hand. As she did, I stepped through, following up with a series of attacks using Orna and the spear at once. She drew her sword on the fly while backpedaling, and immediately the other two warriors were on my flanks.

I'd figured this would happen, so I kicked off my left foot and leapt at attacker number three, stabbing high and low at her face and groin both. Nobody would ever expect that maneuver, first because it was incredibly hard to pull off, and second because it was something I made up on the fly. Against all odds, the female daemon deflected the spear thrust and leaned out of the way of the sword thrust, contorting her body in ways I would consider impossible.

Then she cartwheeled away and did a backflip to get more distance. Seeing an opportunity, I threw the spear at the spot where I expected her to land. Just as she was completing her arc in the air and about to get trussed, she twisted and plucked the spear from the air mid-flight. Finally, she landed in a three-point stance, spear in hand.

It was cool and creepy and disconcerting all at once. Usually when I was in my fully Fomorian form and I tried to kill something, it died. But this warrior had brushed off my sneaky attack like it was nothing. I'd have applauded if she wasn't trying to kill me.

I still had two more of them at my back, and this fight was not looking good at the moment. Sure, I was hardcore in this form, but I could still die, especially if they bore enchanted weapons. To survive, I needed to even the odds and come up with a better strategy for winning the battle.

One thing I'd learned over the last few years about gods, was that they really didn't have the power to create anything. Sure, they could alter existing objects, plants, and creatures with magic. Yet, when it came to creating stuff out of thin air, they were absolutely incapable of doing so.

If Nyx's kids had created Limbo, they'd probably taken the same route that the Celtic pantheon had to create Underhill. Meaning, they took all the raw ingredients from elsewhere in the cosmos, then they used that as the building blocks for their new little pocket dimension. If that was the case, then everything in Limbo that had form and substance was subject to the laws of nature—and druid magic.

The beginnings of a plan formed within my devious

Fomorian brain. But before I could put it into motion, I had to be certain it would work. That meant not getting skewered like a shish kabob before I could do so.

Step one was getting them off my back. Problem was, without an active connection to the Oak and Grove, I only had so much magic at my disposal. I could still communicate with the Grove, but the Oak was my conduit to all that druidic power and magical energy. With the Oak in hibernation, I had to make do with my internal magical stores.

Not only that, but I had to save something for Lyssa. If I blew my wad now, I'd be SOL when it came time to fight the bag lady. Of course, that wouldn't matter if I got killed before then.

Guess I'd better shit or get off the pot.

While I was figuring out my next move, I was doing the dance of death with the Machai. Dodging and twisting, bobbing and weaving, hacking and slashing, blocking and parrying in a ballet of violence that made a Zack Snyder film look like an episode of Daniel Tiger. So far, it seemed we were evenly matched. I was stronger than they were and just as quick, and we seemed to be equal skill-wise.

Honestly, it'd be a damned shame to kill them, but they were in the way. Besides, these Greek gods were some evil motherfuckers. Even though my Fomorian side was having a hell of a good time fighting them, I had no use for them beyond that.

Time for you three to go.

With a thought, I triggered one of the spells I'd prepared, that major working known as Cathbad's Planetary Maelstrom. Instantly, dozens of large rocks that ranged in size from softballs to cantaloupes levitated off the ground all around me, and they began to orbit my position. The Machai were no fools—they sensed the spell when it fired up, and as soon as they saw the rocks float, they skipped out of the way like the world's deadliest acrobats.

At that moment, I could've tried to use the spell to kill them, but I knew they were too fast and wily for that. When I had the Escher monster trapped, it was easy to use the maelstrom spell to kill it. Unfortunately, if I tried to do the same to these jokers, they'd simply hop on their wyverns, fly away, and wait for my magic to run out.

No bueno.

Thus, the spell was just a distraction, and a means to catch a breather. Currently, the Machai circled at a safe distance, stalking me and waiting for the spell to end. While I had the Machai at bay, I checked in on Hemi and Fallyn, who were still picking off the Hismanae. Satisfied that they weren't going to jump into my fight, I reached out to the land mass on which we stood, harmonizing with the sky island's energy flows to see how it operated.

As far as I could tell, each sky island had its own gravity field. Limbo's magic enhanced each of those fields to approximate Earth's gravity, and it contained them to prevent all the sky islands from colliding into one another.

So, they wanted chaos, but just enough to front—not so much that the place would be unlivable. Silly gods.

From a practical perspective, I could see why they set the place up like this. You put a bunch of territorial, conniving, vicious deities all on the same continent, and you're going to have constant war. As a practical example, just look at what happened in Underhill in the alt-timeline. But give each their own mini-planet, and you might achieve a relative amount of peace.

In other words, the form followed function here. I could use that to my advantage, if I could get these fuckers bunched up where I wanted them. But, could I pull it off?

Fuck it. If RDJ could do it, so can I.

After looking around, I found a low valley that I could use to funnel them into a single spot. That was the first step. The second step was convincing them I was vulnerable. One by one, I began to release the missiles I was levitating, allowing them to spin off in random directions as I backed away from the Machai and toward the valley. As soon as the daemons sensed that my spell was ending, they took the bait by following after me.

By the time I'd reached the floor of the valley, I only had a few stones orbiting me at close range. Now, the Machai were pacing and circling my position like cats stalking a bird in a cage. They sensed blood, and they were going to have their fill of mine—or so they thought.

Time to put the second part of my plan into action.

Using the druidic connection I'd established with the sky island, I tapped into the magic that contained its gravity field. Then, I located another, smaller island in the sky nearby that cast its shadow in another direction. Finally, I poked a hole in this sky island's gravity containment field just above us, one that allowed me to direct those forces at the smaller island nearby.

Let's hope this works.

At first, nothing happened. Then the smaller island began to float toward us, ever so slowly. As it moved, it picked up steam, but by no means was it moving as fast as I needed. Running two spells at once was tiring me out, and to keep the "real" spell going, I had to release the maelstrom spell to conserve energy.

As soon as I did, the Machai sprang into action. Two of them came at me head on, while the third danced around to my flanks. Then, they attacked at once, coming at me high and low as they did before. However, this time they used a broken rhythm to throw my timing off.

Machai number one with the sword came in fast, dropping at the last second and sliding on his greaves to slash at my leg. The second one leapt over the first, stabbing at my face with its spear while in midair. I picked my foot off the ground to avoid the first attack, leaning back and parrying to avoid the second.

Yet, neither intended their attacks to land. It was the third, female Machai flanking me who delivered the critical blow. That one waited until I was on one foot and slightly off balance, then she darted in and skewered my calf.

The first two Machai continued their momentum, sliding and flying past to recover and pivot, so they could witness how I reacted. The third pulled her spear from my leg, dancing away just as I swung Orna overhead in an attempt to face her. When I tried to pivot, my leg gave out, causing me to stumble to one knee.

Well, shit. Ned Stark, eat your heart out.

The Machai began to cackle, and I could see their leering smiles through the gaps in their helmets. Using Orna as a crutch, I pushed myself to my feet. The Machai circled, stalking me as they took time to savor the coming victory.

Then, three things happened at once. First, a shadow fell over us, cloaking the valley in darkness. Second, I used druidic magic to open a hole beneath me. Third, I shot the Machai the finger as I fell into that hole, just as the smaller sky island crashed into the earth above me.

The land mass I'd pulled toward us was only about the size of a football field, maybe one-hundred yards in diameter. Yet, it was much too big to allow the Machai to dodge it at that late juncture. Instantly, they were crushed between the two islands like grapes in a wine press.

The shock wave that went through the larger sky island was considerable. In my rush to defeat the Machai, I'd failed to account for the amount of debris that would fall on top of me. Within seconds of the impact, I was buried inside my escape hole, fifty feet underground and unable to even speak or cry for help.

CHAPTER

TWENTY-ONE

There I was, buried under a few hundred tons of earth and rubble, my mouth full of rock and dirt and unable to breathe. Even worse, I was nearly out of magic, and it'd be hours before I'd regenerate enough to cast any significant spells. Back on Earth, I might be able to coax the soil and rock to part for me by using Druidry, but here in this foreign place I wasn't as in tune with everything around me.

In short, I was stuck.

If I'd been in my human or half-Fomorian form I might've panicked, but in this form I almost completely lacked the ability. Instead, I began to get angry, then I started clawing my way to the surface. Scratching and fighting like a thing possessed, I practically swam upwards through the loose dirt and debris. Finally, with my lungs and muscles burning from the exertion and lack of oxygen, I broke through the surface with one hand.

"There he is!" Hemi shouted.

I felt smaller, human-sized hands grabbing my over-sized Fomorian fingers and wrist, then they began to pull. At the same time, I wriggled and pushed rocks and dirt out of the way with my free hand. Finally, my head and shoulders cleared the surface.

Immediately, I began spitting and coughing and snorting out dirt from my nostrils. Then I thrust my other arm out of the ground. I shook Fallyn and Hemi off me, so I could leverage myself out of the hole.

After a bit more struggling, I was free. I collapsed with exhaustion, sucking air while coughing and snotting up mud from my nose.

"Ugh, that's something I'll never forget," Fallyn said. "You gonna' make it?"

"Give me a sec," I managed to croak between coughs.

"Right smart strategy, bro," Hemi said. "Bury yourself alive, so they can't find ya. Brilliant."

"Har *cough* har," I countered as I hacked up more dirt. "Those things were deadly. Had to act."

"If you say so," Fallyn remarked. "And while you were playing in the dirt, we took out the rest of the fliers that were harassing us from above."

"Trying to kill us, you mean," Hemi added.

"Whatever," she said. "Anyway, looks like its clear

sailing from here. Except we have no way to get from island to island, and no idea where Lyssa might be."

I pushed myself to my knees, then I pinched a nostril off and blew the last bit of mud out the other side.

"Again, gross," my girlfriend remarked.

I repeated the trick, if only to elicit another groan of disgust from her, then I stood and cracked my neck. "You guys didn't kill the wyverns, did you?"

"What, those dragon-looking things? Naw, mate. Why?"

"Patience, padawan." I closed my eyes and tuned into the life on the floating rock until I located them. Once I had a bearing, I opened my eyes and motioned for Fallyn and Hemi to follow. "This way, please."

Another thing I'd learned recently was that draconic species communicated telepathically. I'd discovered this after befriending a female dragon in alt-timeline Underhill. She was now living in that timeline's version of the Grove, and we'd become good friends.

Smokedancer and I had long discussions on her species, and she shared what she could about their habits, life cycles, and nature. Some things were secrets and taboo to speak of, such as dragon politics, and how they managed to remain hidden from mankind. But what she could talk about at length were the differences between dragons, wyverns, oilliphéists, and other similar species.

According to Smokedancer, wyverns were basically

primitive dragons. They hadn't evolved to develop arms with opposing thumbs, nor were they very bright. Yet, she claimed they were intelligent to a degree, and also capable of telepathic communication.

As a druid, I could create mental links with animals, which was how Smokedancer and I spoke. I was betting I could do the same with the wyverns, and possibly get them to take us to Lyssa. At least, that was what I hoped.

On nearing the place where the Machai had left their mounts, I motioned for Fallyn and Hemi to stop. "You'll want to hang back. I'd like to avoid spooking them and causing them to fly off."

Fallyn crossed her arms over her chest. "Okay. But if they try to eat you, and we're not close enough to come to the rescue, don't come crying to me."

Hemi chuckled, but I thought it best to let her have her fun. Even so, I pinched off a nostril and snorted a last bit of muddy snot on the ground before leaving. It was petty, but all in good fun.

The wyverns were just over the other side of a rise, near the edge of the sky island. I began walking in their direction while opening a channel between us. At first, I said nothing, just sort of mentally hanging back until they noticed my presence. Soon one of them got tired of waiting to see what I'd do, and it spoke.

KILLED THEM?

The sheer intensity of its voice inside my head was staggering. Apparently wyverns lacked indoor voices, like children who hadn't yet learned the meaning of "conversational volume."

Yes. But I mean you no harm.

IS GOOD. LEAVE NOW.

Wait. I can help you.

HELP? HOW?

Are you happy here?

Silence followed. I waited for roughly a minute until it responded.

NO. NOT HOME.

Where is your home?

GONE. LOST.

What if I could take you to a new home? One that would be like your old home?

OLD HOME. WARM. PREY. SUN ABOVE. GROUND BELOW. GOOD.

I know of a place like that. I could take you there.

YES. GO NOW.

I'd like to, but I have to do something here first. If you'll help me and my friends, I'll take you to a new home.

Again, the wyvern was silent. He or she must've been their group alpha, because I didn't hear the others at all. If they were communicating, they either blocked me from hearing or they did it nonverbally. At any rate, roughly a minute later, the wyvern spoke.

WILL HELP.

Good. Do you know where the mad goddess lives?

SCREAMS. DANGER. STAY AWAY.

I can't. She harmed my child. She has to be punished.

THREAT. KILL. UNDERSTAND.

Can you take us to her?

NOT TO. TRAVEL. NEAR.

I sighed with relief. If I read it's meaning, it could take us close, but no further.

That will do. Thank you.

WHY THANK? GODDESS KILLS.

FALLYN WAS a bit nervous about riding something that could—theoretically—snap her in half with one bite. Yet, when Crookedfang crouched down on his tummy and lowered his head so she could get on, she warmed up to him. Hemi, on the other hand, just hopped right on his mount.

"You look like an old hat at this," I said.

The Maori warrior shrugged. "Plenty of giant lizards in parts of our underworld. I've had practice."

Hemi's wyvern turned its head around and snarled. "Strongjaw takes offense at being called a giant lizard, it seems."

Hemi patted her neck and nodded. "Sorry, love. Won't happen again."

His wyvern half-snarled, half-mewled, then she turned her attention to the cliff we were about to jump off—both figuratively and literally, on reflection. I rode the alpha, Brightclaw, and he was waiting for my signal. All wyverns were named for something to do with their own personal quirks and their predatory nature, it seemed.

We're ready when you are.

GRAB NOW.

I took that to mean "hang on," and I did so, even though each of these creatures was outfitted with a saddle and tack. I'd asked Brightclaw how they ended up here, and he said they were littermates, stolen when they were just hatchlings. When we got back, I intended to take them to Mag Mell at the earliest opportunity, and leave them guarding Tethra's fortress. It'd be a great place for them to hunt—no people—and they'd be the perfect deterrent to keep it that way.

But first we had to deal with Lyssa. Heracles had warned that I hadn't seen her at her worst. I kept thinking of her as the goddess of insanity, but based on what Brightclaw had said, that wasn't quite right. Tuan had said she was the goddess of rabies and something else. Was it "mad rage"? Rabies or mad rage, it was basically the same thing. I only wondered how that would play out in deific form.

How far to where we find the Mad Goddess?

Brightclaw banked and soared around a large boulder that floated into our path. I noted that many of the biggest sky islands had smaller land masses and large rock formations orbiting them. It didn't take a genius to realize that leaping from island to island would've been suicide, what with all the flying debris. Some of these boulders were really moving, and getting hit by a twenty-ton rock flying at eighty miles an hour would put a cramp in any demigod's day.

After we'd cleared the unexpected flying hazard, the wyvern turned his head to make partial eye contact.

CLOSE. READY MAKE.

Using hand signals, I let the others know we were coming up on Lyssa's island. We entered a thick cloud bank, and when we pierced it and came out the other side, it was clear where we were headed. Below us, perhaps ten miles away, a giant land mass easily eight miles across floated apart from the rest, separated by an even larger margin of empty sky.

In the center of that land mass sat a building that was unrecognizable as such, at least at first. The reason I didn't peg it for a deliberately created structure was the randomness of it all. There were towers and walls and buttresses and gates, all in odd places that made zero sense. As well, those components were constantly shifting, move around at random intervals in all directions.

But strangest of all, the fortress was screaming. Initially, I thought it was the sound of stone scraping on stone, but I was wrong. The place itself emitted a never-ending shriek that was like a thousand enraged, insane people releasing a primal roar, all at once. It was disconcerting, to say the least.

Taking a tip from Greek mythology, I'd supplied everyone with ear plugs before we left. Each of us had put them in before we mounted the wyverns, but even through the ear plugs the screams could be heard. I realized that after a time it could have an effect on our sanity, and I only hoped we could take Lyssa out and leave before that happened.

LAND. HIDE.

Brightclaw banked around, swooping back into the cloud bank, and the other wyverns followed. I felt that we were descending in a corkscrew, and soon we emerged from the clouds again, but below the horizon level of the land mass. The alpha wyvern flew up until we were just below the edge, and we landed in a large cavern in the side of the island, about fifty feet beneath the surface.

OFF.

Will you wait for us here?

NO. DANGER.

I understand. Should we meet back here?

YES. NIGHT-CYCLE END. His gaze swung upwards. *TRAPS. DANGER.*

I will be careful. Thank you, Brightclaw.

I hopped off and my companions followed suit. Within seconds, the wyverns were gone, flapping their wings like crazy as they headed to who knew where. Certainly, someplace out of earshot.

After motioning for Fallyn and Hemi to come closer, I cast a silence cantrip.

"So long as you're inside, we'll be able to communicate. But anything inside the bubble can hear us, too. We won't be able to hear anything outside the bubble, so everybody take a thirty-three-degree sector and keep your eyes peeled."

Fallyn and Hemi nodded. I spotted a side tunnel leading up, then I pointed to it and signaled we should move out.

WE EXITED the cavern via a lava tube that led to the surface, about fifty feet from the edge of the island. Immediately after emerging from the tube, it was clear this island was very different from the others. For starters, the place looked like it had been through multiple natural disasters recently.

Trees had been ripped from their roots, grass and smaller trees were flattened, entire swathes of vegetation had been burned to the ground, and great fissures split the landscape further inland. Oddly enough, the damage was completely random. There might be acres of ruined forest and land, then many acres more of undefiled landscape, pristine and almost Edenic in nature. The overall effect was unsettling and haunting.

"It looks like a giant kid's playground—and he's prone to tantrums or something," Fallyn remarked.

"Or she," I said.

"If this is the work of our mad goddess, sure," she replied.

"Oi, something's coming," Hemi said as he pointed at an area of undamaged forest further inland.

The tree line was about a mile away, and I couldn't quite make out what I was seeing. From this distance, it appeared like ants were pouring out of the forest. "Fallyn, do you have eyes on that?"

"Yep, and it's not good."

I cast a cantrip to enhance my vision further, then I focused in on the leading edge of the mass of creatures moving toward us. And creatures they were—every type, shape, and species imaginable, including mundane animals and supernatural ones. There were larger members of the animal kingdom such as lions, baboons, wolves, dogs, cats, hyenas, and the like, and plenty of smaller ones such as squirrels, rabbits, mice, and rats.

Mixed in among them were a few representatives of the supernatural species—griffins, basilisks, manticores, pegasi, and the like. There were thousands of them, all bounding toward us, and as they ran they slavered and snapped and fought amongst themselves, attacking each other even as they rushed to meet us.

"Magical rabies," I said. "She's the goddess of rabies."

"You mean to tell me all those creatures have a freaking magical version of rabies?" Fallyn asked with just the slightest quaver in her voice.

I'd never known her to be afraid of anything, but it made sense in this case. For a member of the animal kingdom, contracting rabies always meant a prolonged, horrible death. For a werewolf—who were normally immune to almost all diseases—the idea of catching rabies must have been terrifying.

"All of them," I replied. "And I have a feeling it's even more contagious than the normal kind. Whatever you do, don't let them break your skin, don't get blood or saliva in your eyes, nose or mouth, and don't take a bite out of them."

"Quick question," Hemi said as he raised his hand. "How're we supposed to fight them?"

"We aren't, not all of them," I replied. "Go back and hide in the lava tube. If any end up down there with you, do as I said. I'm going to handle the rest."

Fallyn grabbed my arm as I strode out to meet the rabid horde. "Are you sure about this?"

"No. But I'm just about out of magic, and neither of you guys are as thick-skinned as I am. Trust me, though, I have a plan." I glanced at the rushing onslaught of disease-crazed creatures. "Now go!"

Hemi and Fallyn ran back to the cave. Once they were inside, I cast a weak illusion over the entrance to hide it from the coming herd of slavering wildlife. Then, I dropped my silence spell and I began bellowing at the top of my lungs.

"Hey, fuck faces! Yeah, I'm talking to you, dipshits— over here!"

That was all it took to get the entire horde coming after me. Once I had their attention, I ran at an oblique angle to the edge of the island, away from where Fallyn and Hemi hid. After I gained enough distance to keep them safe, I stopped and faced the rabid stampede.

Now, what would you call this sort of thing? A rampede? A stampebid? A horbid? Nope, it's a hordepede. Damn, I'm good.

Honestly, facing the hordepede wasn't that much different from being in the Hellpocalypse and getting chased by a mass of zombies. I once got caught in the path of a mega-horde that I estimated at over 500,000 lost souls. Evading those bastards for days on end—now that was a good time.

Compared to that experience, this would be a piece of cake. That was, if my plan worked. I waited until the hordepede was within a few hundred feet of me, then I started running for the cliff.

Brightclaw, I'm going to need your help.

WHEN HOW?

Now. I'm about to jump off the side of the island, and I'll need you to catch me.

WHERE?

Close to the cave where you left us.

TOO HEAVY. NO.

I won't be. I'll be smaller. Trust me.

The wyvern remained silent for way too long before answering. Finally, I heard his sibilant voice in my mind.

I TRUST.

I breathed a sigh of relief as I skidded to the edge of the cliff, pulling up short at the precipice. On looking over the side, I realized there was nothing below but air and emptiness. No sky islands, no orbiting rocks, nothing. When I scanned the horizon, I didn't see Brightclaw, either.

A glance over my shoulder revealed the horde was almost on me. It was time to fish or cut bait, and I had two choices—jump or fight. Climbing down wasn't an option, because I'd just lead the smaller, climbing creatures to Fallyn and Hemi.

If I jumped, I might fall forever. If I stood and fought, I'd be overwhelmed, although the mundane animals couldn't readily pierce my Fomorian skin. It was the supernatural creatures I was concerned with, and frankly, I would rather not find out what magical rabies would do to me in my Fomorian form.

Whelp, that leaves just one choice.

"Cannonball!" I yelled as I took a bounding step and jumped off the cliff.

As I LEAPT off the cliff, I twisted in midair to see if my plan had worked. It did, and like a charm, as wave after wave of rabid animals and supernatural creatures followed me over. Considering that I might only have seconds before Brightclaw flew in to save me, I began shifting back into my half-Fomorian form immediately.

Ten seconds later I was half-naked, human-looking, and still falling. The good news was that the animals kept running off the cliff, even after I was hundreds of feet below them. The bad news was that I'd forgotten—some of them could fly.

A manticore was the first to catch up to me, swooping out of the sky as it sent a hail of poisonous spines my direction with a snap of its tail. Knowing my skin was susceptible to cuts and stab wounds in this form, I twisted in an attempt to avoid being stuck. The spread on the barrage widened the further out the spines flew, and for a moment, it seemed I'd lucked out.

Then a searing pain shot through my forearm, alerting me to the fact that I hadn't any luck at all. One of the spines had embedded itself in the dense muscle of my left arm, and my hand was already beginning to go numb. My Fomorian healing factor would take care of the venom—eventually—but for the moment it seemed I'd temporarily lose the use of my left arm.

Great—just fucking great.

That left me falling past the massive, iceberg-like underside of the sky island at terminal velocity. I was rapidly heading for empty space, half-naked with only the use of one arm, and with a rabid manticore diving after me.

Could be worse, I suppose. The spines could transmit magical rabies.

That was when it occurred to me that the spines might transmit magical rabies.

Fuck!

But, one thing at a time. I needed to both stop my fall and deal with the manticore, at least until Brightclaw arrived. Moreover, I had to ensure that the wyvern would not be in danger when he came to rescue me.

The first thing I did was to brace for impact, because the rabid lion, bat, scorpion, and porcupine hybrid was closing in for the attack. I could've drawn a weapon from my Craneskin Bag and killed it, but I needed its powers of flight to survive. I slung the Bag behind me, turning and twisting as I fell to place my feet toward the creature.

When it came at me, it attacked with claws and fangs both. Lacking the use of my left arm made defense difficult, so I did the only thing I could do. When it slashed with its left forepaw, I parried it with my right, grabbing and pulling myself around to its flank.

Then, I tucked my head and wrapped my legs around it, grabbing a handful of the creature's mane as I held on for dear life. The manticore went ballistic, snapping at me as it twisted and turned in an attempt to kill me, but it simply couldn't reach, as I was too damned close.

The downside of the beast's reaction was that we ended up in a death spiral, and in a few hundred more feet we'd be past the island and out of its atmosphere.

Yet, I didn't need this thing to fly—I only needed it to crash. To achieve that end, I shimmied and scooted around, pulling with my non-envenomated arm until I could reach the manticore's opposite shoulder. Then, I grabbed its upper wing and I began to steer, yanking with all my might as I attempted to glide us toward the sky island.

Wider and wider we flew, until finally, we crashed into the wall. Just before we collided with the rocky base of the island, I twisted and pulled the manticore in front of me, using its body to take the brunt of the impact.

CRUNCH! went the manticore's wings and neck. The thing went limp, and I kicked it away, grabbing and clutching at the cliff face simultaneously. I managed to snag an outcropping, hooking into a small cleft with my sturdy Fomorian-enhanced fingers.

My body slammed into the wall as the human skin covering my hand split and ripped. Blood began dripping down from the cleft, but I was alive and no longer falling. I scrambled with both feet, scraping my toes against the rocky surface until each foot found purchase enough to maintain my position.

A hail of rabid animals fell past some fifty feet away. If the sky island's underside had been a uniform cylinder, I'd have been in the midst of it. Fortunately, it was indeed iceberg shaped, and I was near the bottom tip. Not only was I safely out of reach of the falling horde-pede, I was out of the line of sight of the remaining flying creatures.

Oh, shit—I need to do something about them before Brightclaw arrives.

It might take me hours, but if Brightclaw fell to the disease, I could still climb back up and continue my hunt for Lyssa. However, there was no way I'd leave that poor creature to such a horrible fate. I had no choice but to use the last of my magical reserves to carve an alcove in the cliff face using druid magic.

Once I had a perch on which to lie down, I rummaged around in my Bag until I found a Barrett .50 caliber sniper rifle I had brought back from the Hellpocalypse. It took some time to set up the tripod and load a round one-handed. Eventually, I got in position, prone and holding the gun as firmly against my shoulder with one hand as possible.

Then I started picking off the remaining handful of manticores, pegasi, and griffins, one by one. They began to fly toward me as soon as they heard the gunfire, so I had a few close calls. However, I worked the bolt as quickly as possible, reacquiring a sight picture and finding my next target until the last flying creature spun away into empty space.

With that task complete, I reached out to Brightclaw.

Are you there?

HERE. SAFE?

It's safe. And we need to have a discussion about indoor voices.

TWENTY-TWO

On the way back up the cliff face, Brightclaw expressed concern over my well-being.

DROOT. HUNT READY?

At first, I thought he meant to ask if I was ready to kill Lyssa. Then I realized he could smell or sense that something was wrong with me. The truth was, I felt it as well.

Druid is well. No cause for concern, Brightclaw.

The wyvern left it at that, but I sensed that he worried, both for my safety and for his own. The puncture wound the manticore's spine made had already healed and the poison had worn off. Yet, gangrenous lines radiated from the scar outward, similar to the way zombie vyrus wounds looked when the infection began to spread. I was running a fever and my stomach was cramping. It was rabies, and I realized that I couldn't risk going back to Fallyn and Hemi.

Brightclaw, take me to the surface and drop me off there. All the sick animals are gone, so it should be safe to land.

YES.

I directed the wyvern to leave me about a mile downwind from where I'd left Hemi and Fallyn. She'd come looking and pick up my scent eventually, but I intended to be long gone by then. If I could kill Lyssa before I lost my mind, then I'd likely simply be stuck here while they returned to Rube's.

I hope. But knowing them, they'll come looking for me.

Figuring I needed to keep them from coming after me, when the wyvern had departed, I squatted and scratched a message in the soil.

-Infected. Don't follow. Send Click.-

Click wouldn't be able to help, but it would keep them from trying to assist me directly. Gwydion's healing skills were sorely lacking, but he'd know what to do—even if it was locking me away in a stasis spell, forever.

Better that than to loose a rabid Fomorian on the realms at large. If I got back to Rube's Hall, there's no telling what sort of damage I might cause—or where.

After the message was complete, I shifted into my fully Fomorian form and headed for the fortress at a jog. While the effects of Lyssa's rabies curse might be worse in this form, my healing factor was greater. I figured it might give me extra time before I lost my shit completely—time enough to kill Lyssa.

One more dead god. Or one last dead druid.

What sucked was that I'd used up all my magical reserves, and it would be hours before I had enough juice to put myself in stasis. The lines on my arm were spreading quickly, and when they reached my brain I'd be toast. With that happy thought to keep me cozy, I increased my pace.

Minutes later I reached the moat around Lyssa's fortress, and what an odd sight. The first thing I noticed was that it twisted and undulated to match the ever-shifting walls of the fortress it guarded. Very odd, indeed.

Even stranger was that the moat contained a variety of liquids, and while it seemed to have a current, those liquids did not mix. Among them, I counted boiling water, acid, lava, and predator-infested waters, to name a few. Even in my current form, I wasn't eager to test my healing powers against the contents of the moat—especially not while I was fighting off this infection. I decided I needed to find a way to cross, and continued on.

As for the fortress itself, it looked like what you'd expect of a fortification designed in an age when battles were decided by spear and shield. The walls were lower than the typical medieval castle's and made of uniform square blocks, with little in the way of crenellations or battlements. I walked the perimeter of the place as I sought an alternative to swimming the hazardous chasm that surrounded it.

Roughly one-third of the way around, I came to a

raised drawbridge. Before I could even begin to devise a means of lowering it from outside the walls, it began to drop. I stopped in response, expecting another horde of rabid creatures to come running out. As soon as I halted, the bridge did as well. When I took a step forward, it lowered a hair. Realizing it was opening for me, I continued my approach.

I reached the drawbridge just as it touched down on my side of the moat. That seemed to stabilize the walls and chasm around the bridge, allowing me to walk across sans movement on the part of the fortress. Even more peculiar, the effect followed me after I entered the walls. As I advanced, I could see walls and rooms shifting and changing ahead, but when I neared them, they stopped.

Was this Lyssa's doing? I doubted it, and instead came to a different conclusion.

As I made my way further inside, I soon realized that the entire fortress was a death trap. There were trigger plates, tripwires, and switches everywhere. When the walls and floors shifted they revealed trapdoors and pits, arrow holes and spiked walls on hinges, acid showers and burning pitch pots, all primed and ready to kill. It was like something Jigsaw would dream up during a bad acid trip.

Yet, none of the fortress' traps triggered when I passed. And of course, they didn't. If Lyssa's demesne was anything like Maeve's, it possessed a sort of intelligence—in this case, a mad, malevolent one.

The fortress' purpose seemed to be to kill indiscriminately. Now that I was infected, I was as much one of these hazards as the traps themselves, so I served its purpose. What reason would it have to harm me?

Thus, I was able to move quickly to the heart of the fortress, jogging along with Orna drawn. Eventually, I came to a large arched doorway that led into a grand receiving hall. On peeking inside, I found it empty, save for a stone dais at the far end that held a low, platform bed.

While the dais and bed appeared to have once been luxuriously decorated, the silken sheets and bedding were desecrated in numerous ways. Stained and torn, worn and unkempt, it looked more like an animal's bed than a human's—or that of a goddess.

Yet, a goddess' bed it was. As I entered the room, a figure arose from where she reclined on the bed. This was not the haggard bag lady who'd harassed me outside Luther's—no, not at all.

In her demesne, Lyssa was a tall, lithe, regal woman, classically Greek with a strong jaw, spare lips, chiseled cheekbones, and an aquiline nose. Youthful yet mature in the manner only deities and the high fae could pull off, she looked on the near side of thirty, save for the worry lines and creases around her eyes and mouth. She had smooth, olive skin, dark hair that fell in lustrous curls, and eyes so brown they were almost black.

The goddess rose with a grace that lacked sensuality, as the act was all function with no wasted movement. Her figure lacked sensuality as well, being lean and athletic in the way of elite athletes at the peak of training. She was almost, but not quite emaciated, as if a sculptor had chiseled away all but the barest essentials of what her body needed to perform.

Could I say she was beautiful? No, but she was formed with impeccable economy, and there was definitely a sort of beauty to be found in that.

For all her anatomical spartanism, Lyssa moved with a languidness that didn't jibe with her previous aggressive demeanor and unhinged mental state. Combined with the sad frown she wore and her sympathetic gaze, I'd almost think she regretted seeing me here—not for her sake, but for mine.

"Druid, why have you come here? Do you seek your end?"

"No Lyssa, I seek yours," I said, my deep Fomorian voice a low rumble in the vast, empty hall.

She sighed and hung her head at a slight angle. "Again, why?"

"You came after people who are dear to me. One of them was seriously injured."

"'Eye for an eye,' druid. Is that not what I said?"

"When I killed that... *thing* you call your child, I acted in self-defense and in the defense of others. You acted out of a desire for vengeance that was undeserved. Now, I want justice."

She barked a short, bitter laugh. "I'm the wrong goddess for that, I'm afraid. You should seek my cousin

Themis if righteous retribution is what you desire. Here, you'll find only madness and death. Although, it appears you're already halfway there. A pity."

This conversation was not going at all as I'd expected. She'd been such a mental case before, ranting and raving about the violence she wanted to visit on me personally. Now, however, she was subdued, indifferent even. I couldn't figure it out.

"Obviously, I don't have much time, so tell me—is this an act?"

"An act?" Lyssa said as she sat side-saddle on her bed, tracing the wrinkled length of her bedsheets with her fingertips. "No, this is no act. You see, dear druid, I am no more eager to deliver the fate you're about to suffer than you are to receive it."

I rubbed a hand across my forehead, noting how hot and fevered I was. "You're telling me you don't enjoy spreading disease, driving people insane, and causing chaos? I find that hard to believe."

She smiled sadly. "Believe it. When Hera ordered me to afflict Heracles, do you think I enjoyed acting on her decree? I did not, nor did I take pleasure in the results of my work."

I coughed, leaning on Orna for support. "Then what about the curse you placed on Maeve's house, and the mental hospital? And sending the Maniae there to possess all those people? Why did you do it if you didn't enjoy it?"

She lowered her head, shaking it slowly in denial.

"Orders, and nothing more. We daemons may be powerful in our way, but we exist to act in the service of the gods. Eris ranks above me, and she ordered me to sow discord and chaos—so, I did exactly that. Likewise, Eris receives direction from someone else, one who holds particular sway on Mount Olympus." She glanced up, considering me for a moment beneath hooded eyes. "And that one fears your rise, just as much as Badb, Aengus, and Fuamnach."

Wow. Talk about a revelation. Finnegas thought it might happen someday, but damn.

"You know what? For all the evil you've done, you seem as much a victim of circumstance as I am. Whether you're telling the truth or not, though, I'm still going to kill you, because you had a choice in your actions. You could've defied the gods and refused to fulfill your role, but instead you chose to torture others and save your hide. So, you gotta' go. But before I kill you, I have one question."

Again, she shook her head slowly. "You will not kill me, not with my curse in your veins. Ask, nonetheless."

"Who is giving Eris her orders?"

"I couldn't say. Eris might, if persuaded correctly."

I cleared my throat, because it was getting stuffy in her throne room. "Typical, as gods and goddesses go. Well, you've been exactly no help at all. Any last words before I kill you?"

She met my gaze with a look that bordered on pity. "Yes. *Arróstaine.*"

I HAD no idea what that word meant, but as soon as she said it, spasms wracked my body from head to toe. Being in my Fomorian form, I expected to have some immunity to the curse of Lyssa's disease. However, it seemed that she was able to exert some control over it, accelerating the progression with her magic.

I fell to the floor, cracking the cobblestones as I hit the surface. My skin burned with pins and needles that pricked me all over, and I was sweating buckets. I began hearing voices, but whether they were inside my head or real was a toss up. One of those voices rose as the others faded, and I soon recognized it as belonging to someone I hadn't seen in a while.

"Ed, is that you?"

The cramps and burning subsided, allowing me to open my eyes. The empty throne room had disappeared, replaced by my junkyard back home. I stood at the front gate, facing the interior, where we processed new arrivals from auctions and donations.

Across the yard, Ed worked under the hood of an old Buick with his back to me. Although I couldn't see his face, I'd recognize him anywhere. The way he wiped his brow with his shirt sleeve, the set of his shoulders, and a body built by manual labor plus a steady diet of fast food... that was my uncle Ed, for sure.

The sight of him filled me with elation. Had it really been that long? I called out to him and waved.

"Ed, I'm back. I came to help out for the summer like we agreed."

Was that right? I remembered working at the junkyard one summer during high school—but that had been years ago, hadn't it? It didn't matter. Ed was here, and I'd missed him, so much.

Wait—that didn't make sense either. If he was here, hadn't I seen him yesterday? It was all very confusing, and I felt feverish. The sun was so very hot overhead, and my mouth was as dry as the Sahara. I'd go say hi to Ed, and then maybe find some shade.

Yeah, that makes sense. Tell Ed I'm here, then take a break.

I approached my uncle from behind, clapping a hand on his shoulder. "Ed, Mom just dropped me off for the sum—"

Ed slowly turned around, revealing a nightmare come to life. His chest dripped blood, and it was riddled with bullet wounds. He was missing an eyeball, and the socket was just a hole full of pulped flesh and brain. As I watched, maggots chewed their way out of his face, and his skin went from pink to pale to gray as it rotted and sloughed off his skull.

Suddenly, I was back in the Hellpocalypse, surrounded by burned out and boarded up buildings, dust devils, and tumbleweed. Although we stood in the middle of Main Street in downtown Farmersville, the weeds that grew through the cracks in the pavement came to my waist. Ed lunged for me, using his greater bulk to tackle me to the ground. My uncle was a zombie, and I was fighting for my life.

"Ed, stop! It's me, Colin..."

His stiff, leathery hands found my throat, crushing my windpipe and cutting off my circulation. I struggled to breathe, finding that I could barely get enough air into my lungs to stay conscious. Ed leaned over me, one eye glowing red, the other a deep, black hole that seemed to have no end.

"You want me to stop?" he croaked in a voice that was snakeskin on sandstone. "After you left me to die?"

"No," I wheezed. "Tried... to... save you. So... sorry."

"You're sorry? Sorry?" He shook me, throttling my neck and causing my head to bounce off the ground. "'Sorry' won't bring me back!"

I groped at his skeletal hands and forearms in an attempt to loosen his grip, only to find his undead strength much greater than mine. Pushing and bucking, clawing and scratching, I fought like an animal to escape, even as I began to black out. As consciousness began to fade to black, my hand dropped to my side and I felt something at my hip.

I recognized it immediately—the stippled grip of my Glock 17. Gripping and drawing it was instinctive, yet it seemed to take a Herculean effort. For some reason, I found that to be funny, and I chuckled as I drew the gun from its holster.

Fighting gravity, fatigue, thirst, and asphyxiation, I lifted the pistol and placed the muzzle against my uncle's temple. I'd never fought a zombie before, but this scene felt familiar in a way I could not explain.

"Ed," I gasped. "Please stop."

His single, glowing red eye darted to the gun and back again. "Do it, kid. You killed me once—what's one more time, right? Do it for old times sake."

"No..."

"Do it!" he screamed.

I closed my eyes and pulled the trigger.

WHEN I OPENED MY EYES, I was lying in the grass, staring up at a bright blue sky. A few wispy clouds dotted the expanse here and there, and a jetliner flew high overhead, too far away even for me to hear its engines roar. It was spring break, and Dad was home on leave. He'd promised to take me fishing, and we'd come to Lake Farmersville to camp and do exactly that.

"Colin, you got a bite. Quick, grab your pole before he pulls it in the water!"

I pushed myself off the ground, slowly and awkwardly, the extra bulk around my midsection getting in my way as I did so. Dad sat in a folding lawn chair a few yards down the bank, fishing pole in one hand with a cold brew in the other. He wore a gray t-shirt with an American flag on one shoulder, and a logo that said, "Foxtrot Uniform Bravo Alpha Romeo" on the other. His Gulf War-era, desert camo boonie hat had fishing flies stuck in the band, and on his scarred, muscular forearms he wore a G-Shock watch and the paracord bracelet I'd made him for Christmas.

"C'mon, son—grab that pole. My hands are full, so it's up to you. If you don't bag it, we'll miss out on bragging rights and the twenty bucks I paid for the pole to boot."

I blinked, shaking off the brain fog that remained from my nap. Wait—where was Uncle Ed? Hadn't he come along with us?

Probably went to get more bait. Or beer. Ed loved a cold one.

I waddled down the bank, where my Zebco rod and reel perched in a red metal pole holder, the kind with the spiral base that you screwed into the ground. As I watched, the tip curled and twitched, the line straightened, and the bobber dipped under the surface of the lake.

"Looks like a big one," Dad remarked as he flashed me a smile. "Why don't you snag him and bring him in?"

I snatched the pole out of the holder and yanked it hard, gripping it above the reel with my left hand like Dad taught me. Then I shoved the butt of the pole into my gut and started cranking the reel with gusto.

"Whoa, partner—not too fast. You'll snap the line before you get it to shore." My heart was pounding and my hands were sweaty, but Dad's voice remained low and calm, a balm to soothe my nerves. "Just give it a few cranks as you drop the end of the pole and take up slack. Pull him in a little at a time, and let him wear himself out as you do."

Taking his advice, I got into a rhythm. Crank and dip, pull and fight, rest, repeat. The battle seemed to go on forever, but I was gaining ground. Beneath the surface of the lake, a shadow danced in the depths, one that grew larger with every turn of the reel.

"Nice and easy, son. That's perfect—keep that up."

I only had eyes for the water, but in my mind I focused on Dad's voice to guide me. Now the shadow had increased in size. Could I have hooked a record bass?

The darkness surged close to the surface, slackening the line unexpectedly. I stumbled backward, falling on my behind and nearly losing my grip on the rod and reel. Then the line went taut again, the force over-coming the tensioner inside the mechanism. Gears began to whir as the line played out, faster and faster, until the cheap Wally World reel began to smoke.

"Dad, something's wrong."

"Just keep it steady, sport. He's a fighter, that's for sure, but you've got this."

I tried cranking the reel, but it was an exercise in futility. Suddenly, the line played out to the end—would it slip, causing me to lose the catch of a lifetime? Nope, the knot held, practically yanking me off my feet.

I stumbled forward, falling to one knee. Then the line straightened with an almost metallic *twang*, and I was yanked flat on my face. I looked up and saw that the shadow had grown larger where it lurked in the deep.

It's gotta be the size of a car now, even bigger.

Fear gripped me, because I realized the fish was pulling me across the slippery grass and down the bank toward the water. I tried letting go of the rod and reel, but my hands stuck to the handle. Frantic now, I managed to swing my fat legs around in an attempt to plant my feet in the dirt. However, my trainers had become slick with mud and torn grass, and I could find no purchase in the soil.

"Dad, help!"

"Just take your time, son," he replied in that calm, soothing voice. "Aughiskys are tough sum' bitches. They won't give up without a fight."

All-whatsis? What was he talking about?

"Dad, it has me—it's pulling me into the water!"

The prospect of going under was terrifying, and not just because the shadow that lurked there was bigger than anything I'd ever seen at this lake. I'd also suddenly developed a keen dread of the water itself. I was so thirsty, yet all I wanted was to get away from the water's edge, to sit somewhere hot and warm and dry, where not even a single drop of the wet stuff could touch me.

As I slid toward the water, screaming and kicking, Dad's voice never changed from his calm, soothing tone.

"That's it, my boy—that's it. Just ease it up onto the shore."

"Dad! Help me please!" I cried.

"Nice and easy. Slow and steady wins the race when it comes to killing those bastards." Dad's voice practically dripped with pride. "Gotta' pass on the family tradition, after all."

"Please Dad—I can't!"

I was almost in the water now, where the aughisky's dripping, elongated head had broken the surface. Red, glowing eyes stared at me, weeping muck and blood. It screeched a mocking whinny, baring a mouth filled with row after row of decidedly sharp, non-equine teeth.

In desperation, I looked over my shoulder, finding Dad still sitting in his chair, sipping his beer as he gave the occasional gentle tug on his line. He kept his gaze focused beyond me, fixed not on his son, but on the monster that threatened to pull me into the water. He smiled as if all were right in the world as he took another sip of brew.

"Yep, just ease him in. If he eats you, it'll be a damned shame. But you won't be the first McCool to end up in the belly of a water horse."

My feet hit the water then, and I screamed, and screamed, and screamed.

SOMEONE SLAPPED me hard across the face. I opened my eyes to find the old man hunched over in front of me, hands on his knees and frowning so hard his whiskers twitched. He scowled and took a puff off his roll-your-own, blowing the smoke in my face as he exhaled and spat a fleck of tobacco out the side of his mouth.

"You gonna' fight this, or are you gonna' let this dime store deity kick your skinny Irish-American ass all over Limbo?"

"Finnegas?"

"Get angry, boy, and stop being afraid. You're Fomo-rian, for Lugh's sake—it's practically your gods-damned superpower."

He slammed his palm into the center of my chest, pushing me backwards off my perch. I tumbled off the stack of tires, and kept falling, and falling, and falling...

I OPENED my eyes to find I was lying supine next to Sabine, on a blanket spread out in the grass at Zilker Park. We'd come here to enjoy a picnic, on a date that I didn't think was a date, although it occurred to me that I definitely should have. We were looking up at the clouds in the sky and calling out shapes we saw as they drifted past.

"Puppy dog," I said, pointing at a cloud that had basset hound ears and a long, sad face.

"Tree," Sabine countered as she gestured at a triangular cloud near the one I picked. "Or, an upside-down ice cream cone."

I squinted, blocking my eyes from the sun with one hand. "Definitely an ice cream cone. Nice."

She rolled on her side facing me, propping her head on her hand. "Colin, do you ever think about us?"

I shifted and propped myself on my elbow, so I could gauge her expression. Oddly, she wasn't glamoured at all today. Normally, she hid her figure and supernaturally fine features behind an illusion that made her look frumpy and completely unremarkable.

Today, however, she'd forgone the magical disguise, choosing instead to let her golden locks tumble around her kite-shaped face and high cheek bones. Sabine didn't need make-up or any other adornment to look beautiful; she simply was, due to the fae half of her bloodline.

She wore a bright summer dress in white cotton with a sunflower pattern. It was a strapless, off the shoulder number that barely came to her knees. I avoided glancing down at her voluptuous figure as I answered, both out of respect and because I knew she was self-conscious about it.

"Sure I do, all the time. I don't have many friends like you, ya' know?"

"Friends? Is that what we are, friends?" She demurred, looking down as she wrapped a loose thread from the blanket around her finger. "Or do you secretly want something more?"

The truth was, I didn't know how to answer that question. I'd suppressed any romantic feelings I had for Sabine out of fear I'd screw up our relationship if I acted on them. I also found it strange for her to be so forward, as she was the most shy and introverted person I knew.

"I—can we change the subject? Because this discussion is making me uncomfortable, and I'd rather just enjoy the afternoon."

Her expression darkened, as did the skies. "Why do you always avoid this topic? You know how I feel about you, don't you?"

"I don't know how to answer that. We're friends, right? I consider you one of my best friends, Sabine, and I think it'd be a shame to mess that up by—you know—complicating things."

She glowered at me, and her voice was a low whisper as she replied. "Am I just a complication, Colin? Is that why you let me die?"

Sabine leapt atop me, grabbing my wrists and pinning me down. As she did, her skin began to pale and shrivel. Within seconds, her flesh dried up and flaked away until all that was left was a blonde-haired skeleton in a sun dress, with glowing red eyes and a leering grin.

I tried to move, but somehow she held me fast. No matter how hard I bucked or how much I struggled, her skeletal hands and hips kept me stationary beneath her. She leaned over me, grinding those bony hips into me as her grave-cold breath caressed my cheek.

"Kiss me, druid—and stay with me here, forever."

My stomach roiled as repulsion and fear gripped me. I turned my head away from her, but I could feel her breath on my cheek. Likewise, I smelled the grave as she exhaled, and sensed the chilling cold that emanated from her bones, a cold that sank deep into my flesh.

This is wrong, all wrong. Have I been drugged? Is this an illusion? Finnegas told me to do something—what was it?

Then I remembered. He ordered me to get angry. But I'd been trying to avoid becoming enraged. Why was that? Was it because I wanted to avoid letting *him* out?

No, that wasn't it. I'd merged with my Fomorian side, made peace with it. No, there was another reason why I didn't want to become angry.

Lyssa.

That name triggered a rush of memories, some recent, some distant, all of them revealing the truth of what was happening. I'd been poisoned and infected, struck by Lyssa's curse. Then she'd triggered some sort of illusion, a mental prison where my worst fears were realized, over and over again.

That was how rabies worked—I'd learned that in 4H back in high school. That was the sort of stuff you did when you lived in a town called Farmersville. In 4H club, we were taught how to recognize different diseases that livestock might contract.

Most people thought that rabies made you insanely angry, but it didn't. Actually, it made you so afraid that you attacked anything you saw as a threat. Yet, the entire time you were scared shitless, and that's how I felt now.

My fear was keeping me cowed, subdued, and harmless. That was the only way Lyssa could possibly be controlling me physically, because there was no way she was strong enough to throw me around or pin me down. I hated being afraid, and frankly, fear made me mad.

That's not Sabine atop me, it's Lyssa. She was responsible for sending Cerberus to the junkyard, and because of her, my Oak nearly died. She's tapping into my innermost fears and failures, and using them against me. No one should have that power—no one.

I didn't like having anyone else in my mind. Now I really was pissed. No, I was furious, and I stoked that fury, allowing it to build deep within me.

Then, I heard it—a jangling sound, like a key on a ring.

"What's that noise?" the skeletal woman said.

Despite my rage, I was still under Lyssa's curse. Nothing had changed in my environment, and I was still on the blanket at Zilker, looking up at a now cloudy daytime sky. Sabine was still on top of me in her lich form, and I was still struggling to free myself.

Yet, I felt something new dangling from my right wrist. I looked over, and there it was—that stupid churchkey and rabbit's foot, hanging from the metal beaded keyring and bouncing off my arm.

On seeing that I'd changed something in this

complex illusory construct Lyssa had created, I felt a surge of power course through me. It wasn't much, but it was enough to twist my arm free. When I did, I flipped the churchkey into my hand, point down, and I stabbed Lyssa in the side with it, over and over again.

Now it was her turn to scream. She let go in an attempt to roll off me. I looped my left arm over hers, hooking it and hugging her into me. Then I kept stabbing.

The more I stuck her with that stupid, piddly ass churchkey, the more the illusion faded away. Chip by chip, bit by bit, Zilker Park disappeared until we were back in Lyssa's large, nearly empty throne room, lying atop her bed, the both of us covered in blood.

Her blood, of course. I was back in my half-human form, and she was on top of me. I'd ruined her side with the utensil, stabbing through skin and muscle and shattering ribs, until I'd gotten into the organs underneath. Her lung was a yellow, pulpy mess, and I was just one stab away from piercing her beating heart.

My bloodlust was up, and frankly I was still loopy from the manticore venom and my rabid fever. Lyssa lay slumped atop me, so I rolled us both over until I straddled her instead. Her heart beat inside her open, shattered rib cage—damn, but it was crazy what one of these gods could endure and live. Yet, I doubted she'd survive being stabbed in the heart with a rusty-ass old churchkey.

I drew my arm back, readying for the final blow. Just as I started to deliver it, someone grabbed my wrist.

"Hold, druid." I recognized that voice.

Heracles.

"Let me go," I snarled. "She has to pay for what she did."

He held fast to my arm, even as I struggled. While I might have been nearly his match in my Fomorian form, half-shifted, I wasn't even close. He inclined his head at the goddess beneath me, sweeping his gaze across her bloody, shattered mess of a torso.

"She already has. I want her dead as much as anyone, but killing a god of the Greek pantheon has consequences.

"Right now, you and the rest of Austin's supernatural community are in the right. You were attacked and cursed by two of Nyx's children, unprovoked no less. No one would hold any defense of your territory against you.

"But here, you've invaded their realm—or one of them, at least. You've slain several daemons over the course of your trespass, and you've assaulted a minor goddess."

"She started it."

"So she did, but not without orders, and not without help." He arched an eyebrow at me. "Do you think Zeus would care who started what, if you begin picking off members of his pantheon? I, for one, will attest that my father is many things, but I would not count forgiveness and mercy among the traits he is known for."

I looked down at the goddess beneath me, then I took a long, shuddering breath. Heracles let go of my wrist, so I stood and stepped away from Lyssa's near-lifeless body. Whether due to the churchkey, or because I'd nearly killed the goddess, I no longer felt the effects of her curse. The black lines that had emanated from the site of the manticore sting were gone.

"What will happen to her?"

He stroked his chin as he considered my question. "I believe I'll take her to Harmonia. She'll be able to keep Lyssa hidden until she heals, and safely under control thereafter. Harmonia's always had a thing for me, so it shouldn't be too terribly difficult to achieve her cooperation in the matter."

I gave a reluctant nod. It wasn't a perfect solution, but it beat making an enemy of Zeus. "What about you?"

"Me? I'm heading back to Greece. My work here is done. While I haven't received justice, for the first time in several millennia I at least feel as though I've achieved a satisfying revenge."

He extended his hand. I looked down at my own, only to find the churchkey gone. Shaking my head, I wiped my hand off on my lycra shorts, then I clasped forearms with the legend.

"Until next time, Heracles."

He winked. "Next time we party on Olympus. Come

alone, and I'll introduce you to some nymphs that will knock your sandals off."

"I'll, um, give it some thought."

"Monogamy is for mortals, druid. You'll learn that eventually." He cocked an ear to the sky, furrowing his brow. "You'd best go before she gets here. I'd rather not let anyone else know you were involved. Be well, Colin McCool."

"Right back at ya', Heracles."

With the goddess subdued, the screaming had stopped and her fortress lay still. Now, it was time to see the effect Lyssa's defeat had on my city. I adjusted the strap on my Craneskin Bag, then I sprinted out of the mad goddess' hall.

CHAPTER
TWENTY-THREE

When I exited Lyssa's fortress, Hemi and Fallyn were seated atop the wyverns, patrolling the skies in their search for me. I spotted them immediately, and met them at the cavern where we'd entered the mad goddess' sky island in the first place. After a brief ass-chewing from Fallyn regarding sticking together and running off half-cocked, we mounted the wyverns and headed for the gateway home.

Rube awaited us on the other side. After a prolonged conversation regarding the disposition of the three draconids, he agreed they were part of my party and thus covered by our agreement. Further, he allowed me to escort them through another gateway to Tethra's fortress in Mag Mell. Once there, Brightclaw took one look around, then he tilted his head back and roared.

SKY ABOVE. LAND BELOW. DROOT TRUE.

Druid true, I replied. *This is your home now, Bright-claw. Guard it well until I return.*

YES.

He flew off with the others in tow to survey his new territory. As I watched them go, I noted the changes in the landscape since my last visit. Lush greenery had replaced much of the desert, but it still wasn't completely reclaimed. When I returned from the Hellpocalypse, I'd have work to do—especially if I was going to establish a druid academy here.

After I was done in Mag Mell, Fallyn, Hemi, and I returned through Rube's Hall, exiting the cavern into his garden vale. There I found Siobhán waiting for us, surrounded by forest animals that slowly dispersed as we approached. She rose from the soft, green grass, carrying circlets of fresh flowers she'd braided for each of us.

Siobhán first gave one to Fallyn, stringing it around her neck, then Hemi, and finally, she gave one to me. "I wanted to give these to you before you left, but you were gone before I had the chance."

Although there were a variety of flowers braided into each chain, I detected a familiar scent in the mix. I lifted it to my nose, and there it was—a deliciously fragrant bouquet, similar to gardenias.

Hellebore—now ain't that rich.

Unlike stinking hellebore, which smelled like a well digger's ass crack, this was the variety native to the

Balkans. That made sense, considering the gardener who'd planted them in the first place.

"Do you like them?" Siobhán asked.

"They're lovely, thank you," I replied.

When Hemi and Fallyn chimed in similarly, Siobhán's face lit up. She really was lovely, in a waifish sort of way, and it was nice to see her doing so well. The girl was safe and happy, and that was what mattered.

"Siobhán, I really can't stay, but I promise I'll return soon. When I do, I'd like to bring a friend along. Would that be alright?"

Her eyes were downcast as she busied herself with the daisy chain around her neck. "What's he like?"

"How do you know it's a he?"

Siobhán giggled. "Because she's your girlfriend," she said, pointing at Fallyn, "and I can tell she's very jealous. So, there's no way you'd bring a girl along."

"You're correct, and I'll attest that he's a decent man. I think you'd like him very much."

"Then of course, please bring him. Just make sure he doesn't tell anyone I'm here."

It was my turn to smile. "I think your secret is safe with him."

Rube had vanished while I spoke with Siobhán, and we departed his demesne without seeing him again. I thought it was odd, but not terribly so. Now that we'd concluded our business, he likely had other, more pressing matters to attend.

Besides that, I believed that my presence around

Siobhán made John jealous. Perhaps he thought it was best to find someplace else to be during my visit with her. I only hoped he'd be as cordial during future sojourns to his garden vale.

The drive back to Austin was uneventful, if a bit tense. On entering the city limits, I noticed that a certain oppressiveness had dissipated, but the overall wackiness still reigned there. The billboards were still up, the protestors still active, and the odd meteorological events, still popping up here and there.

I wanted to see for myself that Maeve was free, so we drove by her house first thing. When I pulled up in front of her home, I examined it in the magical spectrum—everything seemed to have returned to normal. I was just about to get out of the car to make certain when my phone rang.

"Colin McCool?"

"The one and only."

"Hold please."

The person who'd called handed the phone off, and the next voice I heard was Maeve's. "You know how I hate these things, so I'll be brief. Your service to Our court has been noted. No need to get out of your car— the manse is still a bit touchy after what it suffered, and if you entered right now you might not emerge for a few centuries."

"Good to know. I take it Eris' influence still hangs over Austin."

"It does. You need to track her down and take care of her, for good."

"Whoa, hang on a second. Didn't you say you were going to do that? I mean, you are better suited to the task than I am, right?"

Maeve tsked. "Dear boy, at the moment I am in no condition to battle that chaos magic wielding trollop. We are fortunate to have survived Our recent adventure, and now it is time to regroup and recuperate."

I hung my head and massaged my temples. Even with Fomorian blood running through my veins, I couldn't maintain this pace forever. "Fine, I'll do it—but I expect to be compensated by the crown."

"Yes, yes. I'll see to it that you're paid your normal rates, plus expenses. But do be quick about it. Luther won't be able to keep his coven underground forever, and I don't know how long I'll be able to prevent Samson from tearing the city apart in a quest to destroy them."

"You really think it'd go that way?"

Her tone was serious as she answered. "They may not have numbers, but they have daylight. Few species make better vampire hunters than werewolves. Why do you think they're always at each other's throats?"

"Eh, makes sense. Fallyn's not exactly looking forward to facing him, you know."

"She needs to see to that task before her father does something they'll both regret."

Maeve knew Fallyn was in the car with me, and she meant that comment for the she-wolf's ears as well as mine. My girl was staring out the window, so it was difficult to gauge her response. If she wanted to put off the inevitable, it wasn't my place to convince her otherwise.

"Anything else I should know?"

Maeve remained silent. "There is a rumor that a major time magic spell was cast near your junkyard less than twenty-four hours ago. You wouldn't happen to know anything about that, would you?"

"I haven't a clue."

"Of course, but you should be prepared for others to ask the same. And Colin?"

"Yes?"

"Bring some friends along when you take Eris down. She's not as simple, nor as singleminded as Lyssa, and you'll find her to be a much more difficult opponent by far."

Maeve hung up with nary a tootle-loo. The woman might have driven me nuts, but I had to admit it was good to have her back. You just couldn't underestimate the value of her stabilizing presence on the city.

Fallyn nudged me with her foot as I set my phone in the console. "Everything alright?"

"Yeah, everything's fine."

Just peachy.

~

AFTER I'D CHECKED on Maeve, we dropped Hemi off at his place. The poor guy looked a little down when we pulled in his drive, and no wonder—he'd just had his first real spat with Maki. To make things worse, he left without apologizing.

No bueno.

"You gonna' be alright, bro?" I asked.

He pursed his lips as he glanced at his front door. "Yeah-nah. Gotta' face the music, aye?"

"A little advice," Fallyn said as she turned around in her seat. "Admit you screwed up, say you're sorry, and leave it at that. She'll get over it eventually, and hearing your apology will speed that process up."

"Yeah?" he asked. Unlike me, Hemi had little experience in apologizing for screwing up his relationships.

"Yeah," Fallyn said, holding up her right hand in the shape of a paw. "Werewolf's honor."

Hemi smiled and held up his fist. "Thanks, mate."

Fallyn bumped his fist, then she exited the car so Hemi could get out without squishing her. Classic coupes were a pain when your best friend was close to seven feet tall and your girlfriend had permanent shotgun dibs.

As Fallyn was getting back in the car, I yelled out the window. "And remember to tell her about the curse!"

Hemi waved an acknowledgment, then he entered the apartment.

"Think he heard me?" I asked.

"He heard you. Let's just hope he remembers. Don't

worry, I'll call Maki later to tell her, just in case. And to put in a good word for the big guy."

I leaned across the seat to kiss her, and she returned the gesture. "Thanks, babe. But werewolf's honor? Is that really a thing?"

"Yup. We're like the Webelos and Brownies, but instead of selling cookies and popcorn, we eat people."

"You are so full of shit," I said, laughing.

"You love it," she replied with a wink.

I couldn't argue with that.

When we returned to the junkyard, Maureen was nowhere to be found. What I did find was a postcard that said, "Grand Cayman—wish you were here!" across a picture of the nicest beach I'd ever seen. The card was sitting face-up on her chair at her workstation, and when I flipped it over, it said, "See you in two weeks."

I was glad she took my advice.

Out in the yard where the Oak usually sat, we found a sapling no more than three feet tall. I freaked out, assuming maybe the Oak had died, and the Dagda had started over. Then I knelt down and touched it, and was instantly transported to the Grove.

Fallyn figured it out and followed, joining me inside the Grove at my Oak's chrysalis as I examined and fawned over it. While she stood by, I knelt beside the tree. I closed my eyes and laid a hand on an exposed root, in an attempt to commune with the Oak directly.

"How's it looking? Think it'll be alright?"

I remained silent, concentrating on the tight

magical weaves and new flow lines that ran through the Oak's trunk, roots, and branches. Clearly, the Dagda had done something to the tree, but whether he'd altered it or merely cast a spell to help it heal, I wasn't certain.

The tree itself was still and uncommunicative, remaining dormant while it recovered. That meant I wouldn't know what the usually jovial but also vindictive god had done until the Oak emerged from its cocoon. Yet, I sensed life there, and energy, as well as a strong will to live.

Plus, from what I could tell, its sister was pumping magic through its roots like crazy. "Yeah, he's going to be fine. He just needs time to rest and recuperate."

"Um, hasn't it already been weeks inside here?"

"Sure, but think about it. How long would it take a tree to heal from being partially burned in the real world? A season? A year of seasons? More? I think we just need to be patient, and give the poor guy time to do his thing."

At least he's safe here. There's no better place he could be.

"Is there anything we can do to help it along?" Fallyn asked.

She was clearly concerned, as she knew how much the Oak meant to me. Just as I was learning the importance of letting people in and asking for help, I was also learning that the risk of loss was the price of entry for loving others. It was a lesson I'd already experienced, time and again. Until now, I hadn't fully understood what it meant.

As for Fallyn, I couldn't honestly say if werewolves experienced loss in the same way. When you enjoyed such a huge extended family, and when blood-letting and violence were part and parcel of life, I think you kind of just accepted that people die. 'Thropes were just closer to nature, and all that circle of life stuff came easy to them.

But the thought of losing a child—that was different. Until she had children of her own, she'd never truly understand the amount of guilt and worry I felt at the moment. Someday, she'd get it, and I wondered if I'd be the one to give her those children.

If I live that long. Two self-sufficient, magically protected children with god-like powers are all I have time for at the moment.

"I'll try a few things," I said as I opened my eyes and stood. "Maybe there's some info in the books that Finnegas left me."

She had a mischievous twinkle in her eye as she spoke next. "Plan to do lots of studying, then, now that you have some time off?"

"Among other things," I said, stone-faced. "I have some gardening to do, sunbathing, writing the first few chapters of my memoirs—"

The she-wolf tackled me, laughing as she took me to the ground and tickled my ribs. She was strong, but it was nothing I couldn't handle. Most importantly, she made me laugh, and laughter was something I really needed right then.

Soon, playful wrestling turned to nuzzling and kissing, and that led to other activities. After we finished, we went hand in hand by silent accord to my favorite swimming hole, and there we enjoyed a lazy swim together. After we were clean and refreshed, I gathered a variety of fruit, and we dined. Then we napped out in the sun, entwined in each other's arms.

It was a good way to end a terrible day. I'd miss afternoons like this when I returned to the Hellpocalypse. I'd miss my friends as well, and I reflected there was no way I'd have triumphed against Lyssa and her goon squad without their help.

A cord of three strands. Guess Siobhán was right.

I'd take care of my business in the Hellpocalypse and return to them soon enough. But first, I had one more goddess to deal with—Eris. If Click was right, she was the one behind all my recent troubles, including the river goddess who tried to assassinate me in the alternate timeline.

I'd done nothing to harm Eris, nothing except being who I was, heir to Fionn's legacy, Finn Eces the Seer's last disciple, and one of the few remaining Fomorians. I supposed that made me dangerous enough. Furthermore, I could only assume she was one of the gods who'd united due to their hatred of me—and their fear that I'd bring back the druid order in force.

Little did they know, I had a plan brewing to make all that happen and then some. The time for being on the defensive was over. Now, it was time to plan, scheme, and trick my way into a position of power that would keep the opposition at bay.

But first, Eris—and I knew exactly who I'd approach for help.

~

"HEAR YE, hear ye! Let the two-millionth, seven-hundred-and-thirty-seven thousandth, six-hundred and forty-third session of the Trickster's local number one-thirteen come to order."

Loki smacked the gavel on the podium, then he winked at a rather attractive blonde goddess in the stands. Whether she returned the gesture, I wasn't sure —I was too busy whispering to Click beside me to check.

"Has there really been that many meetings?" I asked.

"Nay. Who'd have the time fer' it? They change the number every meetin' fer' sport."

"Ah. What happens when they run out of numbers?"

Click tapped his chin. "Huh. Guess I never thought o' that. Good thing I'm not the one with the gavel."

"I—never mind."

Loki had been speaking in the background, and suddenly, I felt all eyes on me. Click whispered behind his hand to me. "Looks like yer' up. Go get 'em!"

"Ahem," I said as I stood, exiting the front row of the stands to address the audience. The place looked like a basketball court right now, although it could change at a moment's notice. I stepped out onto the planks and faced the crowd.

"As many of you are aware, one of our number has gone rogue."

"So what?" Sun Wukong said. He was lounging on the floor in front of the stands, eating pizza from the box. "We've all done it at some point. It's part of the gig."

A murmur of agreement went up from the audience. It was hardly an enthusiastic show of no support, but it did demonstrate how indifferent this crowd could be to trouble-makers. Click had made it my job to convince them all that we needed to act. To accomplish that, I had to present them with a deal they couldn't refuse.

I raised my hands in the air, gesturing for quiet. "You're right, Sun Wukong. It is in a trickster's nature to cause trouble. But generally speaking, that trouble has always been directed at individuals who deserved it—royalty, the haughty, and gods. Eris, on the other hand, tends to go after nations. And she has become ambitious recently."

"How so?" an old man in a hooded robe asked.

"She's started a cult for one, to seek widespread worship."

That elicited some grumbling, as the majority of tricksters despised being worshipped. For the most part, the members of Local #113 thought it was hubris in the extreme, and while individual motivations varied, it was why they chose to oppose the machinations of the other gods.

".rogue not, mainstream gone she's like Sounds," Heyókȟa said. ".stuff pantheon high That's"

I snapped my fingers and pointed in his direction. "Exactly! Some of you may know about my ongoing issues with members of the Celtic pantheon. While dealing with them—"

"Giving them a good drubbing, you mean!" a short, thin man wearing a shoulder quiver over a Pink Floyd concert t-shirt said. This sparked a round of light applause, and one or two loud belches from members of the audience as well.

"I appreciate that, Robin—really, I do. At any rate, I learned of a faction among the Celtic pantheon who want to return to their former glory. They strive to be worshipped once more, to make their presence known, and to rule mortals as they did ages ago."

"Every god wants that," a hook-nosed man with burnished skin said. He wore a cloak made from black feathers over a modern, stylish three-piece suit, and he leaned on a black cane with a raven's head pommel. "Secretly, in most cases. Almost all of them will deny it, but they long for the old days, every last one."

I nodded. "No doubt, you're correct, Raven. Yet, some gods realize that the world has moved on, and they understand the dangers of trying to relive the past."

"You hear that, Gwydion?" a dark-haired woman

with olive skin wearing jeans, a motorcycle jacket, and riding boots jeered.

Laverna's remark received a chorus of laughter from the tricksters. Loki slapped my mentor on the back good-naturedly. In response, Click flipped the Roman goddess the bird as I continued.

"Yet, while most of us break the rules because we believe them to be unfair or arbitrary, Eris is stirring up trouble for personal gain."

"And because it's in her nature," Loki said. "She is the goddess of strife, after all."

"True again," I replied. "But it doesn't give her the right to harm mortals on a massive scale, which is what she's doing now. My city is burning, people are dying, and if she takes things further it'll only get worse. This sets a dangerous precedent, and we need to stop her before more gods get the same idea."

I received a few nods from the crowd, but there was also a lot of grumbling.

"We don't really have to do anything," Sun Wukong punctuated his statement by stabbing the air with a half-eaten slice of pizza. "That's the whole point of being a trickster, isn't it? That we're free to do what we please, and that the rules don't apply to us?"

Many in the crowd spoke up in agreement with what Sun Wukong said. Honestly, I mostly agreed with him as well, except for the fact that someone had to stand up to Eris. Besides, protecting the defenseless was the entire purpose of the Tricksters Local—it was in the charter, after all.

"Look, I get it," I said, speaking over the crowd to quiet them down. "We're tricksters, so fuck this, fuck that, and fuck that thing over there as well."

"That's right!" Loki shouted as he raised a bottle of champagne in salute. He'd worked his way around to the cute girl he winked at earlier, and it looked like he was already tying one on. Some things never changed.

I put a bit of magic into my voice as I continued. "But what if I told you we could get one over on Eris, put her in her place, and have one hell of a time doing it as well?"

"Oh? Just what do you propose?" Raven asked.

I smiled broadly while rubbing my hands together like a cartoon villain. "Two words: Vegas. Heist."

"!out me Count" Heyókȟa shouted, just as the room erupted and hands went up all over the stands.

This ends *Druid's Bane*, Book 3 in *The Trickster Cycle*. Colin's adventures will continue in the exciting conclusion to the quartet, *Druid's Gamble*!

Be sure to visit my website at MDMassey.com to download two free Colin McCool eBooks. Simply enter your email address in the form on the home page to tell me where to send them.

Made in United States
Troutdale, OR
12/21/2023

16296613R00236